Copyright © 2025 by Layla Kara

All rights reserved. No part of this book may be reproduced, distributed, or transmitted in any form or by any means, including photocopying, recording, or other electronic or mechanical methods, without the prior written permission of the publisher, except in the case of brief quotations used in reviews, critical articles, or scholarly works.

This is a work of fiction. Names, characters, places, and incidents are either products of the author's imagination or used fictitiously. Any resemblance to actual persons, living or dead, events, or locales is entirely coincidental.

Ebook ISBN13: 979-8-9996333-0-9

Paperback ISBN: 979-8-9996333-1-6

Hardback ISBN: 979-8-9996333-4-7

Library of Congress registration: 2-506-426

Cover design and illustration by cheriefox.com

Published by Pale Sigil Press LLC

Note From the Author

Let's get one thing straight before you turn the page. If you're here for sparkling vampires or well-behaved fae princes who are just misunderstood, this might not be the book for you. I have nothing against those stories, but this is not one of them.

What you will find here is something older and sharper. This is a world of beautiful monsters and broken saints, of ancient rituals and divine beings who are far from benevolent. It's a story that lives in the space between light and rot, where grace is a burden and damnation can look a lot like coming home.

But make no mistake: This is a love story.

It's about the obsessive, consuming kind of love—the kind that becomes an anchor in a storm of cosmic war. The type that would rather see all the realms burn than let go.

Thank you for taking a chance on it. I hope it guts you in the best possible way.

Trigger and Content Warning

This book contains violence without restraint: blood, gore, war, mutilation, torture, and execution. Death is frequent, famine and ruin linger, and suffering is rendered in detail.

Sex is explicit and unflinching. Bonds blur consent, hunger drives compulsion, and rituals twist intimacy into violation. Voyeurism, coercion, and forced breeding appear without apology.

Faith offers no comfort here. Religious cruelty, manipulation, gaslighting, and emotional abandonment repeat like a ritual. Themes of suicidal thought, self-harm, and addiction are woven into the fabric of the story.

Captivity is constant. Bodies are caged, bound, transformed against their will, and stripped of autonomy. Horror takes form in grotesque beings, invasive hungers, and predatory feeding.

Other distressing material includes betrayal, infidelity, graphic death, cannibalistic undertones, and endangered children.

And the light shineth in darkness; and the darkness comprehended it not.

—John 1:5

Prologue
(Mortal Year 1845)

The sky did not weep. It *roared* and split apart by holy fury as two angels fell from grace, cast out like broken relics from a world that no longer claimed them.

Now, there was only mud and rot.

The hillside swallowed Sera, slick and silent, as she lay bleeding into the earth. Her wings were gone. Her breath was shallow. She didn't move. The silence held her. The kind of silence when the world forgets how to breathe.

Her wings had been completely severed from her back by unflinching hands that held a blade dipped in holy oils and stained with cruelty. She didn't see the face of her executioner, the one who'd kissed that holy blade with the same zeal they kissed the entities of order. What was left were two small bloody stumps, wounds that still pulsed and leaked a faint, shimmering glow. It was something more sacred than blood. Or something that had been holy once.

She hadn't seen her father's face when the blade fell, but she remembered the silence that followed. The absence of protest. His absence. That silence had cut deeper than the blade itself because Michael was supposed to protect her and her sister. And instead, he sentenced them.

Sera's body convulsed, shuddering as nerves still tried to stretch, to lift her, to fly. She didn't scream. Screaming belonged to the living.

She should have turned and faced whoever was assigned to the task. Her sister did, for she was always braver and more resilient.

Cassia!

Her eyes found the crumpled shape of her sister beside her. Cassia was collapsed on her side, her long gold hair matted with blood and dirt. One of her arms was still flung outward as if she'd reached for something or someone—Sera perhaps—before the world had torn them apart. Her breath was shallow, but there. Her skin held a fragile flicker of heat, which meant her soul hadn't been unmade.

Not yet.

Sera crawled toward her sister. Her body, traitorous with pain, fought her every inch. Nails scraped against the rocks. Her knees split open on hidden shards, and her breath hitched as she dragged herself toward the body.

The only thing that still mattered was for them to stay together, to stay alive. She desperately reached for the power that once lived in her blood, a silent summons for light, for healing, for anything.

No magic answered her call. No light. No thunder. The power that once lived in her blood had gone silent.

Just a body now. A new alien agony surfaced within her: hunger. A celestial being did not need sustenance, and she was not celestial anymore. That gnawing, ravenous emptiness made her clench her body as she crawled. She did not yet know whether the feeling would ever let go or dwindle. If it would be an ever-present roaring flame in her body that she could never subdue.

The hill around them was a husk. Rows of failed crops sagged under the weight of rot. A scorched fence, draped in ruined linens, twisted against the horizon. There was no one left to tend it. No one was watching. The famine had already hollowed this place.

The Celestial Tribunal had finished the job anyway. No matter how much Sera had tried to save this Irish island from despair, the place ended up exactly how they had designed it to be.

She reached Cassia at last. Her hand trembled as it brushed her sister's shoulder. Her sister drew shallow breaths, still alive. Relief clawed up her throat, but she found no words.

The tribunal—the six ancient arbiters who judged all realms, celestial or damned—had decided their fate, not with fire but with parchment. And beneath her sister's fingers, she noticed that the parchment was half buried and soaked in earth and judgment.

The verdict.

It glimmered at the edges, rain warped and venom bright. Gold flecks still clung to the tribunal's seal like a warning written in fire. She didn't want to read it because she already knew what was inside, but knowing didn't dull the dread, and her hands moved anyway. With numb fingers, she unfolded the decree, hoping it might say something different.

TRIBUNAL WRIT 564

IN THE MATTER OF THE JUDGMENT UPON SERAPHINE AND CASSIEL, HERETOFORE DESIGNATED AS THE SISTERS OF LIGHT. ORDERED AND DECREED BY THE CELESTIAL TRIBUNAL IN THE YEAR OF ONE THOUSAND EIGHT HUNDRED AND FORTY-FIVE.

BE HEREBY KNOWN AND RECORDED that Seraphine, who was heretofore known as the watcher of passage, did willfully and with aforethought commit a grievous breach of her consecrated trust. The angel mentioned above did refuse the lawful release of the soul of a mortal child, said child having been duly marked for ascension according to the immutable laws of this tribunal.

Furthermore, the said Seraphine did employ unnatural and proscribed means to preserve the mortal child's life, thereby causing a cessation of the soul's rightful journey and interfering with the sacred cycle of life and death.

For this egregious transgression and violation of divine statute, the sentence of annihilation was pronounced upon the aforesaid Seraphine.

Thereupon, Cassiel, who was heretofore known as the keeper of silence, presented herself before this tribunal, offering herself as a party of equal culpability. The angel mentioned above stated that there had been a shared will, intent, and defiance in Seraphine's actions.

Upon this joint and voluntary confession, the tribunal, in its tempered wisdom, saw fit to revise the initial sentence to a lesser one. Though still severe, said punishment is to be binding upon both Seraphine and Cassiel:

Their wings are to be stripped from them without the grace of a ceremony or the solace of a ritual.

Their names are to be stricken and forever voided from the Book of Echoes beyond this day of this year, their memory to be as dust in the celestial winds.

They are to be exiled to the mortal realm without guidance, succor, or hope of return.

A binding of all celestial magic is hereby imposed upon them, rendering them powerless.

A prohibition is hereby enacted, forbidding any bond, consort, or congress with their celestial or fallen kin.

They shall forfeit all reproductive rights and privileges afforded under divine law.

Be it warned that any infringement of this sacred decree shall serve to awaken the Old Flame, thereby triggering a final cleansing judgment.

Let no grace be permitted to grow within their names. Let mercy be unmade and forever banished from their paths. Let them walk as the fallen: without a tether, without a title, and without a place to call home until the end of their days.

IN WITNESS WHEREOF, we set our hand and seal to this binding judgment. Done and delivered by the authority of the court.

Malakar, High Justiciar of the Celestial Tribunal

ATTESTED AND RECORDED BY Keeper Vellum, the celestial scrivener and master of the great seal.

How was this better than death?

That thought settled low, bitter, and final, hollowing out everything else.

The parchment in her hand stopped being a divine verdict the moment she felt the warmth of Cassia's breath beneath her fingers. Now, it was nothing more than a soaked decree, warped and limp in the mud. Its holy seal bled gold into the earth like an offering no one wanted.

The hunger inside her wasn't just pain anymore. It set in deeper now, familiar in a way that frightened her. It felt like a wound rhythmically pulsing just under her skin, ever present. A quiet force in her belly that felt like it had always been there, waiting.

Her hand tightened—mud-caked, trembling, and still wet with blood that faintly shimmered in the fading light. The decree folded in on itself with a soft crumpling hiss. Just paper burning to ashes.

If mercy was gone, so was obedience.

And if she had to walk the rest of her life as nothing but ruin stitched into flesh, she would learn how to carry it. To wear it. To wield it.

And one day, she would return what had been done to them. Not in grief or pleading but with retribution and a smile on her face.

The Price of Freedom
(Present Time)

1

"Your Honor, Mr. Ashworth would like to believe that this union, while strained, is not irrevocably broken," Mark's lawyer, a man whose optimism felt profoundly misplaced to Sera, said. "He deeply believes that reconciliation is possible. He only asks for time, for a chance to mend what has been fractured."

His words painted Mark a supplicant, echoing weakly in the sterile air of the courtroom. The room itself felt indifferent, all dark wood paneling and the low hum of fluorescent lights. But to Sera, he was merely a twitching fly caught in her web. A messy, undignified end to a merger she had once considered a masterpiece of social integration. His desperation, though, was an ugly flaw in the design, and she despised him for showing it.

Her sharp and unyielding lawyer rose like a blade drawn from its sheath. "Your Honor, while Mr. Ashworth's sentiments may be…touching, they are irrelevant. My client, Mrs. Vex, has been unequivocally clear. Her decision is made. This marriage is over." She presented Sera's desire for dissolution as a final, nonnegotiable state.

"Mrs. Vex seeks a clean break, a definitive end. Further attempts at reconciliation are unwanted and unwarranted."

Mark looked stricken as if her lawyer's words were physical blows. It was the look of a man realizing the lock had been changed, and the door had been bolted from the inside.

His lawyer spoke in a softer tone this time. "Perhaps a mandated period of counseling, Your Honor. To ensure both parties have fully explored every avenue?"

"My client has explored all she intends to," Sera's lawyer retorted coolly. "Her mind is made up. Forcing her into counseling would be purely punitive."

The judge's voice cut in, pulling Sera's attention. "Mr. Ashworth, your wife's position is apparent to the court. Would there be any further arguments against the dissolution apart from your desire to reconcile?"

Mark's lawyer sighed and shook his head. The fight was over.

"Having considered the petition and the arguments presented," the judge said, his voice as dull as gavel wood, "and seeing no legal impediment, this court grants Seraphine Vex the divorce she seeks."

The gavel dropped. A flat sound. No echo.

And with the legalities concluded, all that remained was the human wreckage.

Sera stood and moved to pass Mark, her stilettos clicking like punctuation marks on a sentence she no longer believed in.

She finally allowed her gaze to settle on him, to really look at him. He did not rise. He was sculpted to be a woman's happy ending—tall and broad-shouldered with soft golden hair and a suit that whispered of old money. But it had been the aura she'd coveted: a naive, uncomplicated light that shone with the simple faith of a man who believed in a happily ever after. It had been a pristine work of mortal hope. And she, in a moment of unforgivable weakness, had devoured it.

She mourned the loss, but the demon in her despised the evidence of her own failure.

Now, he was just a shadow framed in wool and regret, a ruined canvas. He looked smaller and diminished, a portrait of a man hollowed out from the inside. His pleading eyes, the color of a sky just before a storm, were rimmed with red and stripped of their usual light. The vibrant life that once radiated from him was now just a faint, flickering ember.

This was the cost, and seeing it laid bare was its own kind of verdict.

Sera's gaze shifted, out of survival. She let her focus drift past him, past the pleading in his pale blue, almost gray eyes, and toward the rows of pews behind him, where people sat cloaked in polite silence. Among them sat Bethany.

Two rows back, Bethany was a flame interruption in a room full of strangers. Her copper-red hair caught the courtroom light like fire, daring to light in a tomb. Her posture was immaculate with one leg crossed neatly over the other, and her hands were folded over her lap as if she was attending a bridal shower rather than a legal severing. Her sparkly blue eyes were too bright, too alive for this place. Bethany was a friend, but she had never seen behind the curtain.

She didn't know about the torn wings or the blood that shimmered or the hunger that curled like a second soul beneath Sera's ribs. But she still showed up. She always showed up.

The shadows at her ankles stirred, a low but pleased hiss of static against her skin. They had never liked Bethany. They found her too bright, too loud. Her cheerfulness was a dissonant chord against Sera's muted reality.

Look at the little flame, one of them whispered, its voice a dry rustle in her mind. *So eager to watch the world burn. As long as she's not the one holding the match.*

Outside the courtroom, the hallway felt colder. Or it was just Sera.

Bethany fell into step beside her, her smile too bright. "That was dramatic."

But Sera didn't reply. Just kept a steady pace and her face forward.

She tried again. "So, how does it feel?"

"Like surviving a shallow grave," Sera said, not breaking stride.

"Okay…? Dinner later?" Her voice sounded hopeful. "Or drinks? We could celebrate. Or mourn. I can do either."

"I have things to attend to." Sera's tone left no room for arguments. She needed distance. She needed to walk.

She turned and started walking away, leaving Bethany on the steps alone.

Fifty years. The number was a cold stone in her gut. Fifty years since Cassia had looked at her with an expression of horror. But it was in a different city, on a different continent. The ache of that silence was a wound that never closed.

She had tried to reach out once, a decade ago. A letter filled with apologies she didn't really know how to phrase and a longing so sharp that it had felt like another kind of hunger. It had been returned, unopened. Cassia had made her choice. And Sera, left with only the whispering of her shadows, had chosen to build a fortress of her own.

Sera kept walking, her heels beating a steady tempo on the concrete. Fleeing the shame of her failure with Mark. His hollowed-out face was a testament to her profound lack of discipline, and her mind recoiled— retreating to a memory of when her hunger was a weapon.

She remembered a night last summer, the air on the rooftop bar thick and humid—the glint of a Rolex beneath city lights. Its owner, a rival tech CEO, had radiated raw ambition. She'd let him think he was seducing her, her eyes feigning admiration as he boasted over their martinis. All while she tasted his confidence. She wasn't merely feeding on his life force; she was draining his secrets—the launch codes for his new flagship software. By the time she had left, she had his entire Q4 road map, and he was an open book she could rewrite at will.

That single act of infiltration had secured her last promotion at InnovoTech. This was her true work: hunting monsters and cultivating assets. Rich crooks, arrogant CEOs—they were her specialty. She'd find them, listen, and let their egos unfurl, and then she would feed. On certainty and control, leaving them pliable and strangely eager to please her. It was an intimate form of corporate raiding. Often, the final act took place at Kehoe House—a place carved for appetites, not for healing.

But lately, the hunger had become less discriminating.

Mark had proven that.

Poor Mark. He believed his sin was loving her too much. His real transgression was daring to think he could ever possess, ever contain, a creature like Sera.

He had been a catch, they said. And maybe he had been. The last time they spent the night together, he'd pulled her closer, his lips finding hers. The contact had been electric: a jolt of warmth against the encroaching cold. For her, it was like drinking cool water after days in the desert. It was supposed to be about connection, skin, breath, and the lie of being human for a few hours, but the hunger, settled and patient, stirred.

As he deepened the kiss, she felt the shift. The part of her that softly loved him was shouldered aside by the part that needed him. She drew from him. She didn't mean to. It was a reflex, an instinct as deep as breathing. The warmth of his light flowed into her like a torrent, and the static in her soul quieted. It felt like peace. Like coming home. And it was so, so easy to take just a little more. And more. And one more.

The next morning was when the horror set in. He looked exhausted and diminished. The vibrant life that always radiated from him, the easy warmth on his face, was muted. His usually bright blue eyes looked like faded photographs. The color was there, but the light behind them was gone. The internal light did not replenish like blood; when it was gone, it was gone for good. He'd smiled at her, but it was a fragile thing.

She had seen that look before. In the alleys of Berlin, on the faces of people who had given too much to her. It was the look of a vital essence having been scraped away, leaving only the shell. And she had done it to him.

She had slipped out of bed, her movements stiff. Fury drove her to the lawyer's office that afternoon—a cold, surgical rage at herself. A queen who could not rule her own kingdom, who could not control her own hunger, was no queen at all. Mark was a casualty of her failure, an asset she had destroyed through a profound lack of discipline. The divorce wasn't a mercy to him. It was a sentence she passed on herself.

The memory of Mark's face dissolved, but the ache remained, settling into an older, deeper wound. The wound of Berlin. The wound of Cassia.

Her mind flashed to a cobbled street slick with rain, the air thick with ghosts of war. Cassia had been her other half, the only other soul who knew what it was like to have wings torn from her back. And then she was gone. Not dead. Worse. She had left—chosen a different path and left Sera with nothing but loneliness and betrayal's echoing silence.

It had been one hundred and eighty years since the fall, and the silence was still just as loud.

Sera shook her head, pushing that thought away as she crossed another street. The Savannah, Georgia sun felt like a pale imitation of warmth. This was her life now. A quiet exile. A tightrope walk over a chasm of hunger. She only had the poison of her whispering shadows for company.

And yet, a sudden spike of energy rippled through the night—a burn of ozone and gold threading the city's hum. It slid beneath her skin, sharp and intimate, the way celestial power always did.

A violent shift in the air. A resonant frequency she hadn't felt in one hundred and eighty years. It was ancient, powerful, and overwhelmingly masculine.

Her breath hitched, and her steps faltered. Her head snapped up, her eyes scanning the crowd across the street.

There.

A man—a tall, lean figure in a dark, impeccably tailored suit—was walking away from her. He was half cloaked in shadow, yet he seemed to suck all the light toward him. Power rolled off him in palpable waves, a controlled and dangerous aura of black and silver that made the air around him crackle. A Fallen, maybe.

Her shadows froze at her ankles. They did not cower. They bowed, as if the reverence she did not possess silenced them. The shock of it slammed through her chest and her heart lurched in sync as if the shadows recognized the monster on the other side of the street.

How peculiar, her shadows murmured, their voice a dry rustle in her mind.

As if he'd heard them, his stride faltered. For a breathtaking second, he stopped with his back still to her, a silhouette of coiled stillness in the lazy flow of the crowd. He didn't turn. He didn't look. But she knew, with a certainty that chilled her to the bone, that he had felt her too.

She stared at the unfamiliar lines of his shoulders. Her mind saw a stranger, but her darkness recognized him instantly. But then it was gone, leaving only a sharp, undeniable certainty that something had just irrevocably changed.

After a moment that stretched for an eternity, he resumed walking, disappearing into the crowd as if he'd never been there at all.

KNEEL

2

Half a year had passed since that sterile courtroom, since Mark Ashworth became a ghost in Sera's existence. Freedom was now her daily reality, a reality far more complex than mere liberation. The silence left by his absence was still profound but no longer unbearable, echoing in the perfectly arranged space of her townhome in Ardsley Park.

The neighborhood felt like Savannah's polished secret: old money charm veiled by manicured hedges, wrought-iron fences, and streets lined with oak trees that drooped as if they remembered sins. It whispered refinement and never invited scrutiny. That was why she had chosen it. The neighborhood offered her exactly what she needed: elegance without intrusion, structure without surveillance.

Her townhouse mirrored the mask she wore. Outside, it was pristine: ivy-wrapped bricks, black shutters, and antique lanterns. But inside, shadows stretched long across velvet and mahogany, everything curated to perfection. The air always held a trace of smoke, candle wax, and perfume from another time. A place where hunger could sleep in silk and darkness could pass for decor. It wasn't warm, but it was beautiful, and it was hers.

Each room was a reliquary of old lives. A mirror from a Parisian brothel. A cracked goblet from a Wallachian ruin. A tapestry she didn't remember acquiring. None of it matched. None of it was meant to. It was sacred: a private gallery of memory, pain, and power.

The scents of rosewood and vetiver and that ambiguous sweetness clung to the walls. Bethany claimed the oils had soothing frequencies. And maybe they did once. But now, the dreams had changed.

Last night, she'd dreamed of hands. Older, unfamiliar. A room soaked in shadows and velvet. Whispers. A cradle of flame between her thighs. She woke tangled in silk, trembling. The shadows perched on her windowsill, smug.

It was more than the scent. It was an awakening.

At InnovoTech, the chill of professionalism swept through her. Her office was entirely made of steel and smoked glass. She crossed the floor like a storm in a sheath dress, stilettos clicking as junior execs stepped aside.

A meeting with a board member tested her restraint. He thought himself clever. Tried to cut corners on security compliance to save the budget.

"You're a visionary, Sera," he purred, leaning in. "But visionaries know when to bend a little."

Her smile was razor-thin. "You want to bend protocol?" She leaned closer, her aura humming just beneath the surface.

His pupils dilated. He blinked. Sweating. "Bend yourself first. Then we'll talk."

He left five minutes later, rattled and red-faced. Sera exhaled. The hunger hadn't flared, but it watched.

That evening, the townhouse welcomed her in silence. She bathed in oils, poured a glass of wine, and stared at her reflection. Something in her eyes had sharpened. Hungrier. Lonelier.

Bethany's text came precisely on time.

Bethany: "Wine bar? You need to smile. And maybe touch a real human."

They met at a quiet place near River Street.

Bethany chattered, as vibrant as ever, but paused midsip to study her. "You look…restless. Like you're searching for a specific flavor."

Sera blinked. "Just tired."

She didn't buy it. "You smell like iron. Not blood. Just…charged."

Sera shrugged and sipped her wine.

Bethany smirked. "What you need is a real release. Something wild."

And that was the first time she mentioned The Iron Orchid.

"It's deliciously wrong," Bethany said, leaning in. "The kind of place that shouldn't exist. Watch people misbehave. You don't even have to join."

Sera declined.

And kept declining as the days passed. The offer echoed in the quiet moments of her routine. It offered a break from the gray monotony of her life. Curiosity and Bethany's constant barrage were a tide that kept coming. It eventually drowned her hesitation, and she gave in.

Places like the Iron Orchid were technically harmless because they were mostly human. However, when the wrong bloodlines were entwined, it was still frowned upon by the supernatural and flagged by aura scanners.

The tribunal didn't need names when a glance would do. Auras never lied. They shimmered with ancestry, obedience, and corruption to those trained to see them. In major sanctified zones, scanners monitored them constantly, watching for sparks that shouldn't exist. The assigned angels and fallen angels oversaw such establishments, ensuring everything ran smoothly. They were known as watchers.

But Savannah, thankfully, wasn't on the tribunal's list yet. It was too warm, too southern, and too comfortably forgotten: just far enough from divine oversight.

And still, even here, some rules held weight like the Edict of Celestial Conception. Buried in sealed writs and burned into forbidden scrolls, it forbade any celestial, fallen, or faithful from conceiving without the tribunal's unanimous consent. No spontaneous creation. No accidents. No divine legacies born outside sanction. The reason had been lost to history, but the punishment remained absolute. Those who defied it were erased—burned from flesh, name, and memory alike.

Even soul-bonded pairs, sanctified by ritual and writ, were granted a single permitted window: the Night of the Veil. Once every century, beneath the first full moon after the autumnal equinox, the tribunal allowed life to bloom under supervision. All others were forbidden.

The tribunal didn't just fear divine offspring. They feared *legacy*. And fear, in their hands, always burned.

The following weekend, inside the Iron Orchid, was an immediate sensory overload. The music's bass, the cloying perfume, the leather and sweat scents, and the dim, suggestive lighting were potent. But her senses detected more beneath the surface layer. The air crackled with residual power and the psychic residue of heightened emotions: pain, pleasure, fear, dominance, and submission. And woven through it were the distinct signatures of other nonhuman entities.

Most of the auras brushing against hers felt familiar: minor players in Savannah's shadow play, the usual fae-glamoured charmers, and low-tier bloodsuckers chasing sensation. But one presence cut through the noise like a blade. It didn't shimmer. It pulled. Dense. Ancient. Her spine stiffened without realizing it, her senses spiking in that quiet, instinctive way reserved for the proximity of predators.

Bethany tugged Sera toward the bar, still chattering about the music, the crowd, and the outfits. But Sera's gaze swept the room, her pulse ticking faster. It wasn't fear. Just the kind of sharp-edged awareness that lived in the bones.

Her shadows whispered. *He found you…*

Then she saw him. It was the same man she had met all those months ago outside the court. Even though she never saw the man's face, somehow even her bones knew it was *him*.

He commanded the space near a shadowed archway, radiating an aura of quiet danger that made everyone else in the room fade into background noise. It wasn't just his appearance but the sheer economy of his presence, an ancient power barely contained beneath a civilized veneer. Every line of his tailored suit, every moment of his coiled stillness, was a deliberate choice. He was a masterpiece of lethal elegance, and the part of her that revered control above all admired that.

The queen of her crumbling throne recognized a fellow sovereign.

He was undeniably tall, easily towering over every other creature she could see, yet he moved with fluid grace. His dark hair was shaggy and artfully messy, framing a face carved with sharp, intelligent lines. He wore a well-tailored black shirt and navy slacks that fit so perfectly they seemed molded to his lean muscles, causing an involuntary tightening of appreciation deep within her.

Bethany followed her gaze and stilled. The kind of stillness that came from a name remembered too late. Her pupils dilated, and her fingers flexed once at her side. "Oh…" she breathed, almost in awe and something nearer to memory. Or dread.

But it passed in an instant. She blinked, drew in a sharp breath, and wrapped herself in practiced brightness.

"Whoa. Okay," she said, too loud and too light. "That's…not standard club gear."

Before Sera could respond, the man pushed away from the wall, moving toward them with that same liquid grace. He stopped a few feet away. His proximity created an invisible perimeter charged with energy. His gaze, those impossible black-blue depths, locked onto Sera, bypassing Bethany entirely. It wasn't merely assessing. It felt like he was reading the hidden script of her soul.

"Are you lost, little lamb?" His voice was resonant and cultured yet held an edge like sharpened obsidian.

He was beautiful but not soft. He was carved. Clean, cold, and controlled. She didn't know him, but she recognized his scent, and something about him tugged at the base of her spine. It felt like attraction, recognition, and fear wrapped into one.

Her shadows didn't recoil. They stilled as if they were trying to remember something they were never meant to forget.

She shook her head slightly, refocusing on his smirk. He was just another predator. Another mistake waiting to happen.

Sera lifted her chin, refusing to be intimidated, though her heart hammered against her ribs. She met the intensity of his stare, the emerald of her eyes flashing in the dim light. "Not lost," she said. Her voice was low, a steady counterpoint to his resonant query. "Just observing."

Bethany stepped forward with a brightness that felt a little too polished. "Hi there," she said. Her voice lifted just enough to compete with the music. "A bit overdressed for the bar crawl, aren't we?"

He didn't look at her. Didn't flinch. Didn't blink. His eyes stayed locked on Sera like Bethany hadn't spoken at all.

The silence stretched, calm and deliberate.

Bethany scoffed softly, more breath than sound. "Well, rude," she muttered and took a pointed sip from her glass, but not retreating entirely.

A flicker crossed his sculpted features before settling back into that knowing smirk. It acknowledged the hidden layers in Sera's response, the shared understanding between predators. "Ah…" he murmured, his voice dropping lower despite the club's noise. "Well, don't let your observations get you in trouble."

The man held her gaze for another charged second, a silent conversation. Then, as abruptly as he had arrived, he gave a slight, almost imperceptible inclination of his head, turned, and melted back into the deeper shadows from which he had come, leaving Sera breathless and acutely aware of her pulse.

But the way he moved felt deliberately unhurried, less like a retreat and more like an invitation.

He disappeared past the same archway into the VIP corridors of the Iron Orchid, where crimson lights pulsed like a heartbeat. Sera hesitated only a moment before the pull in her chest tipped her forward. It felt like curiosity and desire were wrapped in an infernal gift with a flaming bow on top.

She slipped away from Bethany, who was still sour from the man's rude ignorance.

"Sera…"

But she was already passing through the same archway he had as if she was under a spell. The passage, lined with velvet drapes and flickering sconces, narrowed. Laughter, grunts, and moans echoed behind heavy doors, but she ignored them.

Her shadows whispered against the walls like fingertips searching for heat. *What is he? Where is he? Need to taste...*

"Stop talking..." Sera muttered.

Sera sensed him anchored at the end of the hall within a private room that pulsed with the color of fresh blood. The walls thrummed with a muffled bass while the light cast a low crimson glow that flickered the final beat of a dying heart. He did not turn to greet her. He stood facing the opposite wall, half drenched in red shadow and silence. His broad back cut a silhouette of restrained violence against the gloom while the fabric of his black shirt struggled to contain the indecent breadth of his shoulders. As he rolled up his sleeves, his voice emerged low, smooth, and commanding.

"Kneel."

The word slammed into her ribs like a physical weight. Her spine locked in immediate, violent defiance. She was Seraphine Vex. She was a queen of her own making, and she bent her knees for no one. She remained standing and glared at the arrogance of his back. The air in the room thickened as gravity seemed to warp around her shoulders, and a crushing ancient pressure descended upon the room. Pure, distilled authority crushed the space. Her shadows betrayed her first. They pooled on the floor and dragged at her ankles with a traitorous heaviness until her knees hit the velvet rug with a dull thud. She gasped as the air left her lungs from the impact, while rage flared hot and bright in her chest. She had not chosen this submission, but the shadows had forced it. She gripped the fabric of her dress until her knuckles turned white and lifted her head to spit a curse, but the man finally turned.

He moved with the slow, lethal grace of a predator who had sensed a shift in the wind, but the moment his eyes landed on her, the movement arrested. He stopped cold. He offered no smile nor praise for her obedience because the air had been sucked from the room by the sheer force of what felt like recognition. His bottomless black eyes swept over her with violent and immediate familiarity. He knew her, but how? The realization struck Sera with force. He probably expected a pet but instead snared a *demon*.

The crushing weight in the room vanished, replaced by a sharp electric tension that vibrated between them. His aura cracked. Light bled through the fissure like gold through stone while his breath caught in a stillness that trembled with a history she did not understand.

"You."

The word was a rough exhale—a sound of disbelief. Sera fought the urge to scramble back to her feet, but the shadows held her to the floor. His gaze seared her skin with an intimacy that felt stolen. He stepped toward her as if approaching something volatile, and she tracked him with her eyes as he closed the space between them. She did not look away. The man shuddered imperceptibly. He reached down, and two fingers claimed her chin with a grip that was desperate rather than possessive. He tilted her face up to force her to meet the darkness in his eyes and searched her features as if looking for a crack in reality. Sera's lungs seized, yet he still did not let go. They remained locked in that proximity with the silence pressing against her ribs. Her body screamed. Her pride flinched. Her hunger ached in a way she had never known. His thumb grazed her jawbone with a reverence that terrified her before he abruptly released her and stepped back as if she had burned him. He looked at the door, then back at her with a wild incomprehension.

"You are not Kitty."

Sera stared at him. The absurdity of the name shattered the tension like glass.

"No?" He ran a hand through his hair and the lethal composure he had worn a moment ago lay in ruins at his feet. He turned away from her and walked toward the shadows of the corner as if he could no longer bear to look at her. The door swung open as he retreated, and a woman appeared in the entryway, half-dressed and breathless. She blinked at Sera on the floor, then looked toward the man in the shadows.

"Master Kael?" Her voice was uncertain and laced with need.

Sera exhaled slowly as her heart hammered a frantic rhythm against her ribs. She stood on shaking legs and brushed the dust from her knees while the reality of the mistake settled over the room. She looked from the strange woman to the space where the man had just stood a moment ago.

"I suppose you are the *Kitty*." Sera retorted. The woman frowned and looked Sera up and down. "What are *you* doing here?"

"Leaving," Sera snapped. She pushed past the woman into the corridor and reached the corner while her eyes swept around. Her shadows slipped into every doorway; she felt nothing but a cool hush and the echo of a song lingering in her skull.

He hadn't left the club. Hadn't walked away. He had just vanished.

And for the first time in years, Sera felt the void.

She returned to the main floor like a soul shaken from its body. The lights seemed too bright, the laughter too far away, and the music's pulse faltered against the uneven rhythm of her heart.

Bethany spotted her in an instant. Her red mouth parted in disbelief, and she stormed toward her, heels clicking like a countdown.

"Okay," she whispered sharply, grabbing Sera's arm and pulling her back toward the bar.

Sera thought she had never seen Bethany so irritated.

"What the hell? Where did you go? I turned around, and you were just gone. What the fuck, Sera?"

She tried to speak, to shape words that would make sense, but they got stuck in her throat. Her breath still hadn't fully returned.

"I thought I saw someone," she managed eventually, her voice thin and distant. "Got turned around."

Bethany looked her up and down. "You didn't just get turned around, Sera. You look like you got exorcised."

She gave a weak smile, one she didn't feel. "I'm fine."

Bethany snorted. "You only say that when you're two minutes from setting something on fire." She slid a drink into Sera's hand, watching her with that too-perceptive tilt of her head. "Did he call you in or some shit?" she asked, quieter now.

Sera didn't answer. What was there to say? She took the drink and emptied it, but the burn didn't help. It wasn't enough.

It felt like nothing would be, not after him.

You are still being watched... her shadows whispered, but she ignored them.

Bethany didn't press further.

Later, after the club had bled out into the city, and the streets grew quiet under the hush of hanging moss and a southern night, Sera let the tension bleed from her posture just enough to breathe.

The encounter with Master Kael had lit some forgotten flame, and it was blazing. It was something sharper than lust, more volatile than power. It was a necessity.

He hadn't taken anything from her, but he had touched a part of her that had long been buried beneath routine, distance, and the careful curation of control. But now it pulsed like a secret she couldn't know.

The way he had looked at her and trembled with restraint, the way he ran... It seemed like staying might've destroyed him.

That memory lived under her skin now, blooming heat in the hollows of her throat. Her body remembered. Her shadows remembered.

She didn't even know what exactly he was or who he was, only that he had left her curious and wanting.

A Prayer in a Loop

3

In the dim security room of the Iron Orchid, Kael sat frozen in a cheap office chair, staring at the screen where the black-haired beauty was listening to something the redhead was very animatedly trying to convey.

"Well…fuck," Jareth said quietly, staring at the same screen and standing behind Kael.

"Well, fuck, indeed." He dropped a short glance at the sleeping security guy sprawled over the observation table.

"What are you going to do?" Jareth, probably questioning Kael's sanity, asked quietly.

He didn't respond. He couldn't.

His heart was a slow, brutal thud in his chest as he watched the image on the screen loop. The way her aura snapped like a live wire. The shape of her shadows. The cadence of her walk. All of it was impossibly familiar.

"She was supposed to be far from here," he said finally, his voice low and tight. "But there she is. Brooding."

Jareth didn't argue. He didn't have to. The silence said enough.

He stood, the chair creaking behind him. "I need air."

Jareth didn't stop him.

Kael leaned against the brick wall outside the Iron Orchid, his fingers curled tight and his breath a notch too shallow. Savannah's heat hung thick in the air, wrapping around him like an accusation. The alley pulsed with the low bass of the music behind the velvet walls, but he couldn't hear it. All he could hear was her voice in his skull.

He knew her name, and the moment their eyes locked, something ancient shifted in his bones. He had sensed her in Savannah once before, on the street about half a year ago. Nothing more than a flicker. That brush of dark hair and bright eyes and impossible aura had hooked into him like a thread woven from memory. He thought he was dreaming then, but no, it was real… Very, very real.

She wasn't supposed to matter anymore. And now?

Now, he was shaking. Visibly. Somewhere deep in the marrow, something was rattling loose. He hadn't even made it to the curb before his hands betrayed him, curling into fists and clenching and unclenching with a need he hadn't named in decades.

Inside, he'd stood in that private room like a fool while she knelt before him. And it had unmade him.

He didn't know what to do. So, he did what he always did when the world tilted too fast: He retreated.

What a fucking coward.

Kael exhaled sharply through his nose, his fingers pressing to his temples. He wasn't built for this. He wasn't some fragile mortal seeing fire for the first time. He was a fucking fallen angel. A bounty hunter. A killer. An ex-disciple of wrath. And now wrath was stirring again, not for vengeance but for her.

His hands had torn through flesh and veil alike. He'd faced the infernal that hollowed cities, tracked archangels through their sanctums, and walked away.

But one woman had him spiraling like he'd glimpsed his ruin.

He didn't go back inside. He just turned down the alley, his boots hitting the cracked pavement like he was trying to leave himself behind.

The corner store buzzed under cheap halogen light, humming like an evil thought. Kael stepped inside, ignoring the wary glance from the kid behind the counter. He grabbed the first pack of cigarettes he saw and tossed a bill on the counter without a word.

No one stopped him. No one ever did.

Outside, he tore the pack open with his teeth, slid one cigarette between his lips, and lit it with a snap of his fingers. No matches. No lighter. Just spark and breath and the barest ripple of what he still carried beneath his skin.

The smoke filled his lungs as if it had missed him.

He didn't cough, didn't flinch. He just leaned back against the brick wall outside, exhaled into the thick Savannah night, and let the burn anchor him to the present.

He should've stayed and faced her. He should've said something—anything—instead of vanishing like a ghost too afraid to haunt what he wanted.

But he'd turned and run like a coward.

Because it was easier than seeing the truth in her eyes.

And that redhead who was with her? Something about that second woman prickled beneath the surface—too bright, too loud, too…deliberate. A flame stoked just enough to distract him from the shadows.

He ground the cigarette between his teeth, his jaw tight. The taste of ash settled behind his tongue.

The Aston waited a block away beneath a skeletal tree. He made himself walk.

He didn't rush. He didn't glance over his shoulder. Just let the smoke curl through his lungs. The night hushed against his skin while the burn ran its course. He flicked the butt into the gutter only after it scorched the tips of his fingers.

Pain was easier to handle than whatever the fuck that woman had done to him.

He slid into the driver's seat, closed the door, and sat there a moment. Eyes shut. Hands still.

Then the engine growled to life, and he let it carry him.

The drive back was silent. Not the good kind.

Savannah's streets rolled past in a blur of sodium-lit concrete and humid air, but he didn't see them. He didn't put on music, didn't open a window. He let the city drone around him while his thoughts looped in a broken prayer.

By the time he reached his slick and modern apartment, his jaw was sore from clenching it.

He didn't turn on the lights. He didn't need to. The dark knew him.

Before the door even latched behind him, he pulled out his phone and hit the last dialed: Jareth.

Jareth wasn't just a contact. He was a watcher, Heaven's whisper in the places the tribunal pretended did not exist. Savannah was his post, but his real work didn't live in records or writs. It lived in shadows. In choices no one wanted to make. He was Kael's only friend and probably his last.

They'd been at the Iron Orchid that night under the guise of business, scouting for Holy Rollers' expansion. The sanctuary was at capacity and then some: blood-drunk vamps, half-feral fae, and exiled seraphs with nowhere else to go. Every night, they turned more away, and every night, more came.

Savannah was swelling with power it couldn't contain, which drew attention to it, and this, in turn, meant inspections would follow, conducted by someone from the tribunal armed with a clipboard and no mercy.

Kael wasn't ready to add a sanctified leash to his list of problems.

"Where the hell did you go?" a voice, low and annoyed, said. "I came after you, but you fucking evaporated."

He dropped onto the arm of his couch, exhaling like he'd been holding his breath for hours. "I'm home."

"Well, congratulations, cryptid. Next time, leave a note."

He didn't rise to the sarcasm. "I need you to dig."

"Dig where?"

"Her Address, work. Anything."

There was a pause on the line.

"You're serious," Jareth said.

"Dead."

Another beat. His voice softened just slightly. "You are positive that's her? Cause if it *is* her, you're not the only one who's going to feel her."

Kael didn't answer because they both knew the answer.

The silence stretched between them into a long pause, heavy with memory. He stared into the darkness of his apartment, the phone still pressed to his ear and her presence still lingering beneath his skin like a shadow that hadn't stopped moving.

She wasn't supposed to exist.

And yet she did. And his world shifted beneath his feet because of it.

"Call me when you have something," he said, his voice raw at the edges. He hung up before Jareth could reply.

The darkness folded back around him, thick and familiar. He let it wrap around him because the dark never asked questions and never cared about the answers.

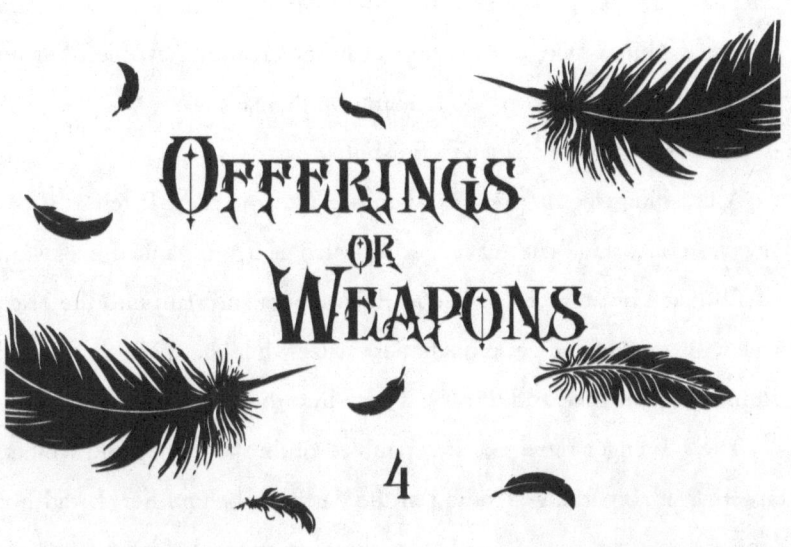

Offerings or Weapons

4

Three nights later, the humidity finally broke. It transformed the air into something heavy and wet, clinging to the skin like a second layer of silk. Fog rolled off the Savannah River to choke the streetlamps in a hazy yellow grip while Sera walked the long way home from the office to let the distance between downtown and Ardsley bleed the tension from her legs. Her heels clicked a sharp rhythm against the cobblestones of Jones Street before the pavement smoothed out past the park where the tourists had retreated to their hotels and the locals had buried themselves in gin and air conditioning.

The street felt empty, but the prickle at the base of her neck warned her a block before the shadow detached itself from an alley mouth. A scavenger emerged with the stench of rot and desperation clinging to its gaunt frame. It was a bottom-feeding drainer with too many teeth and not enough sense to recognize a higher predator. It lunged before she could sidestep.

Sera spun with her hand raised to summon a lash of shadow that would eviscerate the creature and leave nothing but ash for the morning sweepers. It was a reckless summon that would trigger every aura scanner within a mile, but the hunger in the creature's eyes left her no choice. She opened her palms to summon the darkness.

She never got the chance to finish it.

A crushing electric pressure slammed into the alley. It felt as if the sky was collapsing. The scavenger squealed as it was yanked backward as if hooked by an invisible line to fly past Sera and slam into the brick wall with a sickening wet crunch. Sera froze while the shadows she had summoned shivered and dissolved back into the night.

The scavenger retreated. It scrambled on broken limbs and whined in terror at something standing in the darkness behind her. It did not look at her; it looked past her before climbing up the drainpipe to vanish over the roofline like a rat fleeing a fire. Sera turned slowly, finding the street empty and the fog swirling undisturbed. But the scent remained. That sharp electric smell of a storm contained in a bottle lingered in the air.

"Show yourself," she hissed into the silence.

Nothing answered but the distant hum of a transformer. Whoever lurked in the shadows was gone. Had they stepped in to stop her from revealing herself? Or had they stepped in to save her?

Her phone buzzed in her clutch, a sound that was jarring in the quiet street, so she pulled it out to let the screen illuminate the fog. A text message from an unknown number awaited her.

Unknown: Could end up being very sloppy.

Sera stared at the screen as her blood heated. Whoever this was, they were not just watching but critiquing. Her fingers flew across the glass before she could think about the wisdom of engaging a shadow.

Sera: I had it handled.

The reply came instantly as three dots danced before the words appeared.

Unknown: You were about to light up the grid for a rat. Do better next time.

Sera scoffed with a sound that was loud and unladylike in the empty street and typed back with vengeance.

Sera: Next time, I'll send you an invoice for the entertainment. Stalker.

She waited, but the screen stayed dark, and the connection was cut. She shoved the phone back into her bag and turned toward her house while her heart hammered a rhythm that had nothing to do with fear and everything to do with the thrill of the game. Intuition told her exactly who was watching, and she would let him watch.

A month dissolved into the humidity of a Savannah summer as the air grew thick enough to drink. The silence left by Mark Ashworth became a distant memory, replaced by the buzzing vibration of a phone that never seemed to leave Sera's hand.

She was almost sure it was the man from the Orchid and didn't even know if Kael was his real name. But he lived in her bloodstream now, in the parts of her that didn't respond to touch or reason or time. That fateful night at the bar, he hadn't even spoken much, really. And he looked at her as if he saw everything, and for the first time in years, she wanted to be seen like that again.

Bethany noticed.

"You've been weird," Bethany said one morning, her hair wrapped in a towel. Condensation beaded down her smoothie glass, the color of envy. "Like haunted-heroine-in-a-French-movie weird."

Sera kept stirring her coffee, watching the swirl instead of answering. The spoon tapped the porcelain, steady and slow. "Why do you always say that I'm haunted?"

"This is a new level, though." She leaned against the counter, the towel sliding precariously. "Like you got cursed by someone's stare, and now you're writing poetry about it in your head."

"Beth, now you're being dramatic."

"And you're being obsessed, babe." She pointed her straw at her. "I saw your face. That guy? He's a red flag in a perfect suit."

Sera's gaze flicked toward the window, where dawn's light caught the edge of her reflection—too pale, too still. "You're the one who made me go to the Orchid."

"For a night out, not a spiritual undoing." Bethany frowned, setting the smoothie down with a soft thunk. "There was something wrong with him, Sera. I don't know how to explain it. He just felt... *off*. Like he could ruin a life just by looking at you."

The spoon stilled in Sera's hand. He already had. If Bethany could only see their text messaging.

Sera didn't argue because Bethany wasn't wrong. Bethany just had no idea how right she was. Sera said nothing, but her shadows stirred.

The next morning, she searched—almost on instinct—forums, obscure luxury event boards, and cryptic social tags that led to nothing. No one had a clear answer. Some whispered he owned the new Holy Rollers, that it was now a speakeasy for the ultra-elite. Others swore it had a spiritual element: tantric, ritualistic, and high-end debauchery disguised as performance art.

Bethany appeared at her door without a warning or a text. Just a knock, a smug grin, and a thick black envelope. Like it had been dipped in secrets.

"So… You're impossible to stop," she said, tossing it on the kitchen island. "And I'm coming with you."

Sera blinked. Her stomach knotted. "Where did you get that?"

She shrugged. "Friend of a friend. I met this guy at the spa, and he mentioned something exclusive. Said it was a referral-only situation. He liked my vibe." She said it too casually, but it almost felt deliberate.

Sera picked up the envelope. The wax seal burned cold against her fingertips. Inside was a single gilt-edged black card with no name and no instructions. Just coordinates, a QR code, and a time: Saturday at midnight. It was etched faintly beneath in a script only visible when tilted against the light were the words:

Those who remember the Holy Dagger need no special invitation.

The name dragged a chill down her spine. *The Holy Dagger*. It was not a myth. It was a memory etched into her soul, a dark history of her life in Europe. Legends spoke of a cathedral of the body where flesh was the only true sacrament. A place where agony and ecstasy blurred until they became the same blinding light. It was where beautiful monsters went to feed on pain.

"They *are* connected," Sera whispered to herself.

But getting the invitation wasn't enough. The card came with digital add-ons and links to a private RSVP form with waivers, dress codes, and behavioral agreements. Some of the language was old, much older than apps or touch screens. Aura etiquette was last used during the Celestial Accord 1603, a concept most mortals wouldn't recognize. That was the point. There were unfamiliar terms, vibe checks, layered consent procedures, and aura etiquette. Bethany thought the wealthy's unusual language was to blame, but Sera looked beyond the words, interpreting each line carefully.

"This is wild," she muttered, scrolling through the requirements.

"It's just curated hedonism," Bethany said, lounging across the chaise with a glass of gin. "You know, like the new wellness. But sexier."

She passed every screen while managing her aura suppression, which was nothing new. "They'll still smell it," she muttered. "Nothing hides blood."

Friday morning, before the event, Bethany presented her with a gift box.

"I still think this whole thing's sketchy as hell," she said, "but if you're hell-bent on going, I'm not letting you walk into it alone." She extended the box toward Sera. "Something to wear. For luck."

Inside was a choker made of black velvet, threaded with gold, and featured a small obsidian charm, carved with a holly leaf, at its center.

"It's from the same guy," Bethany said. "Said it'd help you fit the aesthetic."

Sera raised a brow. "He gave you jewelry now?"

"Relax." She winked. "He said you'd stand out. This softens the edge."

Sera stared at the choker. Her fingers brushed against the charm. It was a ward, old and not very strong. She assumed it was for concealment, something subtle to dull the flare of her bloodline.

But her shadows froze at the contact, jerking back like they'd been scalded. They then stilled, too still, as if they were held in place by a silence they didn't choose.

Sera's breath caught. That had never happened before.

It felt off. It was neither nullifying nor protective. It was more like a filter, something not designed to shield her from others but to shield others from her.

"Do you think I need softening?" Sera asked.

Bethany twirled her glass. "I think you're gonna need armor."

That night, Sera couldn't sleep. She sat in the dark with the choker in her hands, her shadows curling like smoke across the floor. The card, pulsing faintly, lay beside her on the table.

On Saturday afternoon, they shopped.

The dress code outlined in the Holy Rollers' digital contract was almost absurd in its specificity: materials, silhouettes, limits on magical interference, and aura-flattering cuts. It read like the rules for a masquerade designed by a cult of stylists with a grudge against the mundane. Sera might've laughed if it hadn't all sounded so familiar.

Savannah's boutique quarter offered them limited options, but Bethany dove in enthusiastically, dragging Sera from one dressing room to the next as if they were on a mission from a glamorous, judgmental deity.

Bethany tried on a high slit red gown first: a plunging neckline, sheer sides, and a train that trailed behind her like a dying phoenix. "Too church altar meets stripper," she said.

Next came a structured black corset dress with mirrored panels. "Looks like I'm going to a Gothic gala for vampires who only drink craft cocktails. Pass."

The third outfit clung confidently: a skintight crimson one-piece jumpsuit lacquered to her curves like molten cherry glass. She stepped out with a dramatic pause, posing with one hand on her hip and the other flicking her hair as if she was on a runway. Thin gold straps crossed over the open back, and the neckline plunged like it owed gravity a debt.

"This says confident," she declared, spinning. "Says 'please don't make me kneel unless you really mean it.'"

Sera arched a brow. "You'll definitely be noticed."

"Isn't that the point?"

She tried a few on herself.

The floor-length ivory slip with crystal beading was too bridal. The silver halter, glittering like frost, was too cold. A wine-colored velvet number that hugged too tightly and looked as if she was in mourning.

Then she found it.

A black mini dress barely hanging off a velvet hanger. The sequins didn't sparkle so much as breathe light. Wisps of fabric clung to the sides, trailing like smoke, and when she touched it, her shadows around her stirred.

It didn't matter if it was too much. She was too much. And tonight, she wanted them to see it.

Midnight oil. That was what it looked like.

Sera and Bethany didn't speak much on the ride to the place later that night.

The hum of the city slid past the windows like a lullaby held just out of reach: warm streetlight haze, flickers of traffic, and the occasional shadow darting between late-night storefronts. Savannah was dressed to deceive tonight, all southern charm and river-slick glamour, but the road they turned onto felt different: older, hungrier.

It was the kind of street you didn't stumble across. You were brought to it.

The driver didn't ask questions. He stopped when the GPS told him to, his gaze pointed forward, and his hands still on the wheel as if he'd been told not to look back.

Sera stepped out first.

The air was heavy with heat and honeysuckle, a kind of summer darkness that clung to the skin. No sign or music marked the building ahead of them. There was no bouncer. No light leaked out from the frosted windows.

Just black brick, flat and seamless. A steel door, industrial and unassuming, had no visible handle. Only a single brass buzzer was embedded near the frame. It was polished and faintly warm under the city's breath. The sidewalk around it was too clean. Too intentional. Like someone swept away every trace of the day.

Bethany adjusted the drape of her crimson jumpsuit, gold straps flashing against her bare back. Her heels clicked with ceremony. "This is it," she said, though the door hadn't moved. Her smile was sharp, and her eyes shimmered in the low light. "Are you ready?"

Sera didn't answer immediately.

The obsidian charm at her throat gave a faint pulse, she felt a tremor of a heartbeat against her skin. Her shadows stirred at the edges of her vision, restless and curious.

They usually didn't act like this. They sometimes whispered of hunger, of power, but now, they seemed off. Restrained. As if something inside her had been dulled without her consent.

The choker pulsed again, almost as if it had heard them. Sera gently brushed her fingertips along the piece of jewelry.

"You don't like gold, huh?" Bethany said idly, watching her in the mirror.

Sera glanced at her. "It doesn't sit right with me."

"No," she murmured, almost too softly. "Not on you."

There was a pause. The shadows at Sera's feet rippled as if they were trying not to flinch.

Sera was dressed in black sequins that clung like breath, every movement catching the dull sheen of the streetlight. The hem barely skimmed her thighs. A slit along one side whispered with every step. Her hair was a cascade of dark waves, and her lips had been painted a plum shade, the one she always wore when she intended to be remembered. Everything was carefully crafted to conceal the fact that her true nature was on the verge of collapse.

They were dressed like offerings. Or weapons. Maybe both. The old texts described initiates this way, cloaked in heat and glamour and wearing power like perfume meant to lure the divine or the mortals. Sera didn't know which she was trying to tempt.

Not Your Playground

5

Bethany reached out and pressed the buzzer. "Holy Rollers," she murmured, her voice velvet with mischief.

A pause.

Then a mechanical click, low and reverent, broke the silence. The steel door parted, enough to welcome, enough to slip into the world of darkness.

Sera felt it before she saw it. The air thinned, and the pull of gravity bent around her like a bowstring drawn tight. The space itself seemed to inhale, tasting her name in the dark. For a heartbeat, she thought of him—the stranger from the Iron Orchid whose very presence had made her shadows kneel—but the memory scattered, dissolving like smoke.

The door sighed open, and the night swallowed them.

Heat met her first. It was more than just warmth, a decadence, thick and slow like honey laced with opium. Then came the scent: not perfume in any singular note but a layered and cloying fog of skin, sweat, incense, and leather, all mingling with lust.

And beneath it, something sacred in its desecration.

The baseline hit next, low and primal. More of a heartbeat than music. It didn't hum through the floor; it climbed it. It slid up the spine, across the ribs, and into the teeth. The air shimmered with the shadows and sounds, stitched between velvet beats and the wet click of mouth against skin.

Sera stepped in fully, and the world tilted.

Her breath hitched. Her eyes flared, and her shadows roared to life, slithering around her calves and licking at the hem of her dress. They were reverent.

They moved deeper into the place, past veils of smoke and laughter that clung too close to the skin.

To Bethany, it probably looked like a high society pleasure lounge: shadowy corners, velvet couches, champagne towers, and masked strangers sipping from crystal goblets. Every glance, every movement, was a choreographed decadence.

But Sera saw more.

On one of the raised platforms, a man in a gold half mask lounged back on a leather throne while a creature with glowing eyes and silver claws whispered into his ear. Her tongue was forked. Her skin shimmered unnaturally beneath the low light, like oil pulled taut over muscle.

Further along the wall, a fae male traced slow sigils across a mortal woman's bare back with a quill dipped in something thick and dark. She moaned softly, in surrender, as the ink sank into her skin and vanished beneath it. Every letter shimmered like a vow.

Another alcove revealed a pair of twin-like figures suspended midair by nothing but silk cords and magic. They danced together without touching the ground, hovering and gasping. Their shadows painted grotesque murals across the drapes behind them.

Flesh, some enchanted and some not quite human, gleamed under dim chandeliers. Wings, horns, and fangs…were all visible to those who knew how to look. Supernaturals openly moved here: fae and vampires, witches threaded in glamour, a siren she could taste before she even laid eyes on her. And there, half submerged in shadows, was a demon lounging on a throne of chain links and silk. His tongue lazily circled the rim of a chalice filled with a dark and thick liquid.

Bethany gasped. "God. This place is wild. I mean, look at all these bodies… It's like a fashion show crossed with a wet dream."

Bethany saw wealth. Sera saw an invocation. The way the bodies moved wasn't just performance; it was a ritual. Some of the markings on their skin weren't tattoos but caste sigils, once banned by the tribunal for sedition.

Sera gave a nod. Her gaze lingered on the inked woman. The woman's eyes were rolled back, as if she was being marked.

The air vibrated around her like a tuning fork.

Sera felt it in her blood. A shift. The weight of attention.

Every supernatural in the room paused for just a breath, drawn by instinct in her blood—her scent, her power, and a resonance that hummed beneath the pulse of music and candlelight. Subtle but undeniable.

Beside her, Bethany exhaled, her eyes wide and her cheeks flushed. Her voice was a reverent whisper wrapped in awe. "Oh my… It's like a temple. A sex temple."

She turned slightly, catching the glow in Bethany's expression—the kind of dazed wonder reserved for cathedrals and couture—and saw no trace of fear, no flicker of comprehension: just heat and glamour and breathless fascination.

Bethany didn't see the truth. Didn't feel the air bend. Didn't notice the way the veil thinned around them, the way silence folded in at the edges of her shadows.

Good.

Every nerve in Sera's body was burning. A ripple, low and serpentine, uncoiled up her spine with a reverence that made her stop midstep. The shock of recognition hit her senses.

Master Kael was somewhere in here.

Shadows didn't speak in words, but the knowing slid through her. Her eyes scanned the room, but her body already knew where to go. Her pulse had slowed, not out of calm but with precision. Her systems were preparing for a moment.

The crowd parted. And the air itself shifted, and she saw him. *Master Kael.*

He sat at the room's far end on a throne that looked as if it had grown around him. It hadn't been placed, but it had been formed. A sculpted silhouette of dark velvet and black iron, draped in red lights and shadows. He sprawled with the lethal grace of a king on a stolen throne. One leg was slung wide, one arm was draped over the armrest, and the other hand was sunk into a cascade of hair.

A woman. The same one from the Iron Orchid. Kitty.

She was on her knees between his thighs, moving with a slow, reverent rhythm. The wet cadence of breath and need filled the air— soft, aching, devotional. Shoulders trembled. Fingers clenched against his legs for balance. Even from behind, Sera could sense the surrender in every motion, the worship in every breath. The woman's beauty wasn't in what Sera saw but in what she felt: ruin offered willingly.

Kael was looking at her like he cared. He probably did.

His head was tilted back slightly, his lips parted just enough to taste the moment, but his body language said this wasn't for pleasure. This was control. Allowance. Precision.

The heat that stirred beneath Sera's skin wasn't lust. It moved lower. Slower. Something quieter and more precise: possession, but not the kind she wielded like a weapon.

The feeling was trapped in her chest like smoke trapped in a glass: thin, bitter, and unfamiliar. She wasn't used to wanting that to linger. That ache. One that made her still instead of striking.

She was a succubus. Desire was her nature and her flaw. People unraveled at her feet because she allowed it. She didn't need to want. She chose.

And yet there she stood, watching the woman kneel between his thighs with the kind of hunger that made her own hands curl at her sides.

It wasn't the woman's fault.

Kitty offered herself like a sacrifice on a cold altar. It looked as if Master Kael accepted the tribute without a pulse. Sera could see his feigned ecstasy with the precision of a blade. He calculated the cost of the moment while the woman unraveled. He would forget her name before the sweat dried on her skin. But that didn't matter.

Because Sera remembered, and her shadows remembered. And whatever this was blooming inside her—this cold, quiet thing that watched and measured and burned—didn't care about names. Only that someone else was touching what wasn't theirs.

Kael stilled. The muscles beneath his shirt tightened, almost imperceptibly. His hand in the woman's hair went quiet. His other fingers slightly curled against the armrest as if sensing a shift in the current.

He looked straight up at Sera, and she froze as if her entire existence had narrowed to a line between his eyes and hers. The room blurred at the edges. The music throbbed in the distance, but all she could hear was her pulse and the sound her shadows made when they surged toward him, whispering in longing.

She stepped forward once. Then again. Her breath caught, not from nerves but inevitability.

Stilettos to velvet. Her dress shimmered in the dull light, barely clinging to her form. Her hands curled into fists as she continued walking toward the throne. Toward the woman. Toward him.

Her shadows danced around her like ribbons of smoke caught in a storm, wrapping around her wrists and thighs and trailing behind her like whispers of a vow she hadn't yet made.

She wasn't afraid. She was furious.

Furious that someone else had touched him first. That someone else's tears still glistened on his skin. That he hadn't waited, even though she'd never asked him to.

She was halfway across the floor when his mouth moved.

Kael's eyes didn't leave her, but his hand moved, slow and measured. He gently curled his fingers into the woman's hair, guiding. A final motion. The close of a ritual.

"That's enough, pet," he murmured, his low and warm voice reverberating like thunder beneath silk. "You were perfect. Find Master Jar. He needs some help setting up a scene."

Kitty pulled back, breathless. Her lips were swollen, and her eyes glazed in bliss. Her tongue flicked out unconsciously, tasting what she couldn't keep. She looked dazed, grateful. Marked.

Kitty then looked around, seemingly searching for the source that had interrupted her submission, and found Sera staring daggers at her. Sera's shadows wrapped tight around her ankles like hounds held on leashes, waiting for a command. Sera's expression didn't change, but fury simmered beneath the surface. She did not think it was jealousy. But it felt possessive. Her gaze tracked the woman's glistening chin, the saliva still caught in her throat.

She wanted that woman gone.

Kael released Kitty with a final brush of his fingers along the side of her jaw, and the woman vanished into the red-lit dark.

He adjusted himself with lazy precision, sliding his length back into his pants and zipping them up slowly. The metallic rasp from the zipper dragged through Sera's spine like a deliberate taunt. He reclined back into his seat like nothing had happened. Like he hadn't just been worshipped in front of everyone.

He then chuckled, low and dark. It was threaded with a strange kind of appreciation that felt more like praise. His gaze roamed over Sera from where she stood: her neck straight, her shoulders proud, and her dress like sin molded to skin.

"I thought I told you to do better," he murmured. His voice was just loud enough for her alone. "You come in looking like that, and you are going to end up killing someone."

Sera said nothing. She just watched his body language, which was now taut and rigid. His fingers tapped against the throne's armrest once subtly, the air between them simmering.

Finally, he spoke again, and it almost sounded menacing. "How did you get in here?"

She stared up at him, a bit confused, but her chin lifted, and her green eyes glinted beneath the shadows and the candlelight. He leaned forward slightly, his forearms resting on his thighs. Every inch of him was tense.

"You shouldn't be here," he said at last, his voice low.

Sera's lip curled, not in amusement or warning. Something quieter.

Meaner. "But I am."

His gaze dragged over her slowly. Calculating. Reading her like a dialect he once knew but hadn't spoken in centuries.

Her smile faltered. "What are you?"

"I am just a man—"

"Bullshit!"

His head tilted. "Careful, Little Devil."

"*Little devil?*"

Kael huffed a dry sound—a half chuckle, a half scoff—as he leaned back against the throne, his eyes narrowing with mock patience. "Still sloppy," he noted dryly. He leaned back against the throne with eyes narrowing. "You show up wrapped in shadow like it is silk and expect no one to notice?"

His tone was lazy, but it carried weight. Like he was testing her. Like every word was a needle meant to prod, not pierce, yet.

Sera didn't rise to it. She tilted her head just slightly, the candlelight catching the sharp line of her jaw. Her expression was unreadable. "So, I should've toned it down? Worn beige?"

He smirked. "Might've helped."

He said it like it was a joke, but his body betrayed him. His jaw was still tight. His fingers flexed once, like a warning to himself.

She watched him closely. Studied him the way she studied fire: with awe, curiosity, and a healthy dose of spite. He hadn't come here to be subtle. But she hadn't expected to feel cornered.

"If I am so obvious," she said slowly, "why keep watching?" Kael's smile didn't touch his eyes. "Because you are trouble."

Her lashes swept down. "And you like trouble?"

He laughed once, sharp and low. "No. I know better than to touch it."

But the way he looked at her said he already had.

His fingers flexed against the throne's arms, his knuckles pale under the dim gold light. His breath caught just enough to betray that she'd hit something. "Did you find what you were looking for?"

Her shadows swirled around her hips, like smoke tasting the room's heat. She was aroused and attentive. "Not yet," she murmured. Her voice was low and decadent, iron wrapped in velvet. "But I am working on it."

Kael exhaled, slow and deliberate. Like a man trying very hard not to let his temper speak first. His eyes, dark with warning, stayed on hers. "If you don't want bodies at your feet tonight, I suggest you stop working on it."

Sera's smile didn't falter. It sharpened. Most beings recoiled from it. He seemed…intrigued. Amused, even.

"I'll consider it," she said.

She leaned in, savoring the proximity of danger. The air stretched taut between them, rippling like silk before the tear.

His smile vanished like the sun slipping behind storm clouds. His gaze deepened, darkened. It almost felt like a threat or a light rage.

"That's good, because you will consider it outside," he said, barely above a whisper.

He lifted his chin, a clean, precise tilt that split the air like a blade, and two bulky silhouettes, cloaked in suppression, appeared. Glamour wards dulled their eyes, and a purpose was carved into their posture. They didn't touch her, but the weight of their presence pressed in like the first drop of rain before the storm. It didn't matter that she didn't flinch, didn't blink. Something cold and sharp and ancient in her shifted. It was not used to being dismissed.

Kael's voice followed, low and smooth and devoid of whatever indulgent heat had laced it moments before. "You are lighting up the grid again. This place is not your playground."

No anger. No heat. Just finality.

Her shadows pulled taut beneath her skin, fury sharpening in the quiet. Her poise didn't crack, but her silence deepened.

Because what the fuck was that? Dismissal? From him? After he had all but summoned her with his presence in the Iron Orchid? The insult was a shard of ice in her gut. She was Seraphine Vex. A queen in her own right. She was not a plaything to be beckoned and then discarded.

She stared, long and hard, but still turned around and walked away. It was not over. A king did not dismiss a queen without consequence.

And she swore—no, she promised—as the velvet rug turned to tile floor, that she would win whatever game he thought he was playing.

She spotted Bethany near the edge of the main floor. Bethany was tipsy and glowing under the amber haze of chandelier light, midlaugh with a man who was too beautiful and too very much not human.

Sera didn't break stride. When she got close, she reached out, grabbed Bethany's wrist, gentle but firm enough to turn heads, and pulled her out of the conversation without so much as a word.

"Whoa... Sera?" Bethany stumbled a step. "What's going on?"

Sera's eyes didn't leave the path ahead. "We're being kicked out."

"What?" Her voice rose. "Why? What did you do?"

"Nothing," Sera snapped, her jaw tight. "I breathed in the wrong direction."

She blinked, startled. "Is that, like, a metaphor or... Oh my god. Is this because of the guy?"

Sera didn't answer as she pushed towards the doors, almost dragging Bethany after her.

Every inch of her skin still buzzed like static. Every breath tasted like the burn of unfinished sentences. And somewhere behind her, Kael was still sitting on that damn throne like a verdict made of flesh.

Outside, the damp and heavy air hit like a slap, Savannah's signature mix of heat and ghosts curling in the spaces between streetlamps. The club's doors shut behind them with the kind of finality that made her jaw tighten all over again.

Bethany slightly swayed on her heels, blinking up at the sky like it might give her answers. "Okay," she said breathily. "That was…intense. Like sexy-Vatican-meets-underworld-court intense. Did we just get excommunicated?"

Sera's fingers were already moving, scrolling through her phone as she summoned a ride. "You're going home," she muttered, her voice clipped. "Alone."

"Wait. What? We always postmortem together. Come on!"

She turned to her, her eyes a little too bright and a little too still. "Not tonight."

A car pulled up: sleek, black, and unbothered. Sera opened the door and all but guided Bethany inside. One hand on her back while confirming the address.

Bethany gave her a pout, a glossy, confused expression. "Text me when you get home. Okay? And also, are you okay?"

Sera closed the door without answering.

The car slipped into the dark like a secret too tired to be told. She stood alone on the curb for a long beat, the night pressing in close and damp. Her heart was still a percussion instrument no one had asked to play.

She didn't want a ride. She needed distance.

So, she turned toward the glowing city grid and started walking: heels in one hand, shadows in the other. The ache of refusal burned like wine behind her ribs.

Let him sit on his throne.

She would find her way back.

And next time? She wouldn't come as a guest next time. She'd come to collect.

The Golden Kind

6

Sera's shadows had gone quiet as she walked home from the club. They were not dormant; they were watching, judging, and feeling.

You liked being watched, one finally whispered.

You liked being chosen.

She didn't respond. The truth of it scraped inside her.

Rejection was not her finest suit.

A darker shape rippled at the edge of her vision, moving with intent rather than the wind. For an instant, the air around her cooled, tasting faintly of iron. Her shadows whispered at her heels, uneasy, but she forced herself to believe it was only them.

"You need to stop this," she told them bitterly. "I got your point. No need to taunt."

That is not us, was the only response.

A heavy scuff of a footfall was heard a short distance from where she was walking. Too deliberate to be mortal. Her breath caught in her throat, and she turned down a narrower side street, one shrouded in ivy and bricks. Her pulse ticked faster as whatever was following her was coming up closer and closer.

She quickened her pace, her bare feet slapping softly against the pavement. Echoes ricocheted off the old walls like a warning. She ducked into the recessed doorway of a crumbling antique shop, pressing herself against the cool stone. Her heartbeat thundered in her ears as she folded her shadows around her, a shroud of living night.

A massive figure passed in the street beyond the doorway.

Sera didn't breathe. Couldn't.

The demon paused on the other side of the threshold, so close the air between them trembled. Her heart kicked hard against her ribs, a trapped thing desperate for escape. She held her shadows tighter, whispering silent prayers to deities she no longer believed in. But right now, she'd take anything.

The creature exhaled a low, grating rasp that scraped against the walls like a blade across bones. Its massive shoulders rose and fell, and its nostrils flared wide as it turned its head. Steam curled from its mouth in little puffs, unnatural in the muggy Savannah night.

Its skin was the color of scorched bronze, slick and veined with faint cracks that pulsed red beneath the surface. Long horns, asymmetrical and brutal, curled back from its head, and its face… It wasn't a face. Just a jagged approximation of one. Too many teeth. No eyes. Just two glowing slits where the sockets should've been.

It sniffed again, and the muscles in its neck twitched.

She stayed frozen. She knew if she moved, if she even blinked, it would find her.

The demon's claws clicked against the pavement as it tilted its head, seemingly puzzled. Its breath fogged the air in heavy, sulfur-laced gusts, and for one terrible second, it leaned closer to the doorway. Close enough that she could make out the flecks of ash on its cracked lips and the faint ripple of runes branded into its collarbone.

A low growl rumbled from its chest, and it stomped down the alley, heavy-footed and muttering in a tongue not meant for human ears.

Sera didn't exhale until it was gone, until the echo of its rage faded into the Georgia night. Even then, her hands trembled.

That wasn't random. That thing had been hunting her. But...why?

She stayed pressed to the stone long after the demon had passed, her breath held hostage. Her shadows had withdrawn into themselves and were watching. Waiting. Her heart thudded against her ribs, a dull warning. The alley's silence stretched as if the world was holding its breath alongside her.

Why had it been hunting her? This was no chance encounter. And this did not feel random.

What would it have done if it had found her? Pinned here to the wall? Dragged her down to whatever sulfur-stained pit it had crawled from? Drained her soul like cheap wine? Torn through her with hands meant for rending angels?

Would it have tasted her blood and known what she was?

She swallowed hard. Her jaw ached from clenching it for so long, but she stayed still, long after the night had softened around her.

When her knees stopped trembling, she stepped out and turned in the opposite direction of the demon's retreat, toward flickering streetlamps and the quiet hush.

The wind shifted. The scent of rain on bricks. Her feet were bare, and the stone bit at her, anchoring her in the now.

She turned, took two more steps, and collided with someone.

"Ow," came the low, grumbled exhale, like distant thunder wrapped in gravel.

Sera blinked and staggered back as she looked up.

And froze.

The chest she'd slammed into was broad and unforgiving, laced in crisp dark fabric and dusk. Master Kael.

Her shadows stirred at the sight of him, almost purring as they curled low around her calves and brushed against his legs like they remembered the shape of him. Like they wanted to remember.

He looked down at her, his brow barely furrowed and a faint flicker of surprise in his eyes. He stood like carved obsidian, absorbing the moment without yielding to it.

"Interesting," he said at last, the word curling through the space between them.

Her eyes stayed locked onto his face, her chin tilted just enough to suggest defiance even as her pulse throbbed high and hot in her throat.

"It is very, *very* late," he said, his voice low and unhurried, "for a woman like you in that outfit to wander the empty streets of Savannah by herself." He raised a brow, slipping both hands casually into the pockets of his black slacks. He tried to display nonchalance, but it didn't fool her in the slightest.

"You kicked me out." Her words were sharp enough to bite but soft enough to sting. "I don't understand how it's any of your concern." She shifted her weight and turned, the silk of her dress whispering. "Now, if you'll excuse me," she added, cool and brittle like she'd practiced that line in front of a mirror.

She moved to step past him, brushing close enough to feel the heat coming off his body. All she could think about now was getting home and locking the door and washing the scents of fear and ash off her skin. All the seduction games, the venom-laced flirtation, and the push-pull dance—those could wait.

Tonight, she just wanted to survive.

But Kael shifted, barely more than the tightening of her shadows, and his hand gently closed around her wrist.

His fingers were calloused in places where battles had lived and warm in places where no one had ever touched her without wanting something in return.

She froze midstep.

The world narrowed. There was only that wrist. That pulse. That impossible heat that bloomed beneath his palm and radiated out like a slow ache. It was ridiculous. Illogical. But it felt as if every drop of blood in her body had been summoned to that single point of contact.

He didn't tighten his grip. He just held her.

"I insist on escorting you home," he said, his voice low. There was a tremor there, a restraint. "If that's...all right."

And hell, the ache in his tone slipped through her defenses like a thread of light through cracked glass. There was no command in his voice, no arrogance. Only quiet, raw hesitation, each word sounding like it cost him to say. As if he wasn't sure he was allowed to care. As if he cared anyway.

"I would hate to find out tomorrow," he added, "that the woman I kicked out ended up missing or dead that same night."

Her throat tightened.

He didn't move closer. He didn't need to. The space between them was already charged, vibrating with too many unsaid words. The rain was light now, just a mist clinging to her shoulders and silvering the edges of her hair. A streetlight caught the shine of his jaw, his lashes, and the hollow of his throat where the collar of his shirt lay open. He looked ruinous and calm, watching her as though she was the only soft thing left in a war-torn world.

And all she could feel was that impossible heat where his skin met hers.

She wanted to say no. But the word hovered at the back of her tongue, not coming out.

The truth was that she was exhausted—not just from the demon, the panic, or the way her shadows trembled beneath her skin but from the ache of trying to be untouchable. And although she hated to admit it, she was in no shape to fight if claws or teeth came reaching from the dark again.

And if she was being completely, terrifyingly honest, she didn't want to walk home alone. Tonight. In this state.

Still, the instinct to deflect rose. Her pride thrashed against the quiet invitation, against the steady way he watched her. He made her feel too much with too little, and she didn't know what to do with that.

She exhaled slowly, the sound low and bitter and shaped like surrender. "Fine," she said at last, her voice quieter than she meant it to be.

No gratitude or warmth.

Just exhaustion.

Just the truth.

He released her wrist at once as if he'd been holding onto something dangerous and knew better than to let it burn through his fingers. The absence of his touch left a phantom pressure behind, a memory stamped to her skin.

They didn't speak as they fell into step beside one another. The night, thick with humidity, pressed close around them.

She wrapped her arms tight around herself, her heels dangling from her hand, and the pavement was cool beneath her feet. He walked beside her without speaking, his strides measured and his presence quiet but dangerous. Not invasive or comforting. Just…there.

They walked in silence for a long while. The kind that felt heavy, not companionable. Their steps softly echoed down the slick pavement, the night pressing close.

But it was his silence that gnawed at her.

Sera kept her arms wrapped tight around herself. Her body still burned from adrenaline and shame, she resisted the urge to reach for the warmth that walked beside her.

She lasted three blocks before breaking the silence.

"Why did you kick me out of the club?" Sera asked, her voice rough and too casual.

Kael walked quietly for a long moment before answering. His gaze remained straight ahead, fixed on the shimmer of the streetlight over wet bricks. "I...I have a policy against demons."

The words hit her harder than they should have.

Her steps faltered slightly. "Who told you I'm a demon?"

That earned her a look.

His midnight blue eyes were steady, unreadable. One brow lifted just slightly.

She rolled her eyes and exhaled through her nose. "Fine," she muttered. "What do you have against demons anyway? You had at least one at the club."

He sighed then. He looked tired. "He is not a succubus," he said evenly. "I don't need murder in my establishment."

She flinched inwardly. Okay. Fair. She couldn't fault him for that. Succubi were never favored, even in the shadowy circles. They were never famous for resisting their appetites or for letting their sources live much longer after they were satisfied. But he didn't know her. Didn't know she hadn't been fed in days and could still hold herself together.

They walked in thick silence with words unsaid. Their silence felt more tangible than the sidewalk beneath her feet. It clung to her skin like the humidity itself—sticky, heavy, and damp.

The air was heavy with the scents of magnolia and asphalt. The humidity coated her throat like honey gone sour. Streetlamps flickered overhead, casting gold halos over puddles of oily water. Their reflections were warping.

Sera tried to focus on the walk. On the way, her heels, still clutched in one hand, clicked against her side. On the rhythm of her bare feet on the uneven stones. On the city's familiar outlines that had always felt like a reluctant home. But everything in her was humming, off-tempo and strange. It started behind her breastbone, subtle and almost easy to ignore. But then it deepened. Stretched. Like she was unraveling in slow, deliberate ribbons.

And that air was centered around him. Kael.

She tried to pretend it was just a coincidence. Just the adrenaline wearing off. But her shadows knew better. They were already curling tighter to her legs, whispering low, amused murmurs that she couldn't quite make out.

The heat in her chest built and then dropped lower, coiling into her stomach like a second heartbeat that was weak, dying. Her skin began to sweat again, not from the warmth of the night. She blinked hard, trying to clear the static fuzzing at the edges of her vision, but that only made her head swim worse. Her legs felt boneless. Hollow. She didn't even register how close she was to tipping until the ground rose toward her like a dark tide.

But Kael was there.

He caught her before she could even fall, one strong arm snapping around her waist and the other steadying her just beneath her ribs like he knew exactly where the pain was blooming. She collapsed into him with a gasp, her muscles going slack. The world spun too fast and too slow all at once. Her head fell against his chest, her breath shuddering as she tried to speak.

"I'm not..." she choked out, barely more than a breath. She didn't know what came after that. Not human? Not safe? Not in control?

The last thing she heard was Kael's raw and unguarded voice, a jagged scrape against her fading consciousness. "Shit..."

Then nothing. Just blank silence.

Disjointed fragments filled the darkness like dreams on broken glass.

Kael's face. His jaw was tight with something that didn't look like rage for once. His eyes were narrowed, frantic. Her name shaped against his lips like a question he didn't want to ask. How did he know her name?

The sound of rushed footsteps, the summer air rushing past her skin. Her hair stuck to the side of her face. She wasn't walking or standing. He was carrying her. One arm under her thighs, the other gripping her against his chest.

A warmth bloomed in her chest. It did not feel like the smooth, seductive heat of a good feed. This was structured. Clean and bright.

Oh, heavens. She was killing an angel. How?

Her mind fought because her body could not. Her instincts screamed, and she tried to claw away from it. Too much light. Too much purity. It felt like swallowing fire and drowning in absolution at the same time. Her fingers twitched, her shadows flaring just long enough to recoil. She tried to scream and push away.

She didn't want it.

But the darkness surged and pulled her under, and this time, she let it.

She woke disoriented, as if swimming through a fog. The ceiling above her slowly spun, an off-white blur tinged with shadows. Her limbs were heavy and boneless. The air smelled too clean. Something was wrong.

Her mouth was dry, her tongue thick with the taste of copper and honeyed ash. The sheets clung cool and damp to her skin, and every muscle hummed as if remembering contact, pressure, and heat. Not pain, not pleasure. Simply the residue of power, fading slowly beneath her skin.

It took a moment to register that she was home. Her townhome. Her bed. The scent of rose oil clung to the edges of her room like a memory. She didn't remember how she'd gotten there. Didn't remember walking. Didn't remember Kael carrying her. However, a part of her body did. He must have brought her. It couldn't have been anyone else.

The air in her home was thick with silence, like the pause before a confession. Dazed, Sera stood by the window, her limbs still sluggish. Outside, Savannah exhaled jasmine, car exhaust, and the low throb of mortal desire. Streetlights poured long golden streaks across her polished floor, and her reflection in the glass looked ghostlike. Hollowed. Changed.

She had fed. On an angel. Or something close enough. Enough light to smother the hunger curling inside her. Enough to restore.

But who had it been? Kael? It had to be. And if it was him, why? Where was he now?

We tasted it, the shadows purred, brushing against her bare spine like silk dipped in venom. *The golden kind. Sweet and filling.*

"Stop," she whispered.

We liked how it felt.

"Stop… Please."

We want to do it again. Soon.

Her fingers clenched. She dropped to her knees without grace and dragged her nails down her arms, scraping across her skin that still buzzed from borrowed power.

She crawled toward her bathroom, trembling. Her breath was shallow, and her skin was still radiant and strange.

She turned the water on as hot as it would go, took off her club dress, and stepped beneath the scalding water without waiting. It hit her skin and rolled down in rivulets. She pressed her hands flat against the tiles, forehead against the wall, and breathed in the steam and the guilt and the ghost of Kael's voice. She stood there long enough for her fingers to wrinkle, long enough to let the illusion crack.

She didn't cry.

But the shaking wouldn't stop.

When she finally got out of the shower and looked up. The mirror over the vanity was fogged. She wiped it with the heel of her hand and stared.

The woman looking back wasn't the one who'd left the club.

Gone was the paper-thin skin stretched taut across her bones. Gone were the purple bruises beneath her eyes, the sunken cheeks, and the brittle edges. Her wet hair gleamed like polished obsidian, its blackness so rich that it caught the light like a halo gone rogue. Her skin glowed faintly, flushed and smooth. And her eyes…her eyes weren't just green. They were emeralds lit from within. Bright. Alive. Almost holy.

Even her shadows had fallen quiet. They curled in the corners of the room, watching her like silent familiars. Like they weren't sure who they were bound to anymore.

After wrapping a towel around her still wet body, she stepped out and padded barefoot across the floor. The cool wood under her feet did nothing to ground her.

She picked up her phone from the nightstand. One name stared back at her from the top of her pinned contacts.

Cassia.

Her thumb hovered over the screen. One tap. That was all it would take.

Cassia would answer. She always did. Her razor-soft voice would cut straight through the chaos, demanding answers: *Are you safe? When did you last feed? Who was it? Did they survive?*

And Sera would have to confess that she had lost control. Again. She would have to describe the demon in the alley and the utter humiliation of her own body collapsing, her hunger taking over. To explain how she had fed on Kael, with the helpless greed of a starving animal.

She had divorced Mark to prevent that exact failure, the very loss of control that had driven Cassia away in Berlin.

The shadows purred, sated on his light, but she only felt a profound self-loathing.

Her thumb trembled and then retreated from the screen. She couldn't make that call. The evidence of her failure was still glowing under her skin, a warmth that felt like a brand. Cassia had made her choice fifty years ago, and tonight, Sera had proven her right. Proved she was a monster.

She turned the phone over and laid it face down. Out of sight. Out of reach. She dropped the towel somewhere behind her and slid beneath the covers, still wet on her skin. One arm flung over her eyes, and the other curled protectively over her ribs, where the hunger was never truly gone.

The shadows said nothing. They listened. Waiting. Watching. Knowing this stillness was only a pause between the storms.

"Fuck you," she whispered. There was no venom. Just weariness. To Cassia. To herself. To the echo of Kael's name still lodged somewhere between her lungs.

So many questions. How did he know her name? How did he know where she lived? How did he know she needed supernatural essence, to restore herself?

How could he have known any of that?

And the most dangerous question of all: Why did she care?

There were no answers. No number to call. Only silence. Only heat. Only the taste of borrowed grace still clinging to the hollowness of her.

Sleep took her, and she didn't resist.

Kael watched the glow of Sera's bathroom window from the adjacent building. The blur of her silhouette traversed through the steamed glass.

She was alive.

That should've been enough.

But the truth clung to his skin like the heat of the night, persistent and unshakable. He hadn't meant to follow her, not after what he had said and not after the way she had looked at him before turning away. He thought that would be it. A clean break. No more entanglements.

But then the demon had come.

He'd felt it like a blade slipping into an old and familiar scar. Lilith's signature.

The thing wasn't meant to be here in the mortal realm, but it had followed, quiet and deliberate. A scout, Kael suspected. One sent to watch or to retrieve.

And so, he'd moved. Without thought. Without a plan.

He'd found Sera just before her strength gave out, her shadows wild and thin with hunger. Her body had collapsed in slow ruin. And he'd caught her. Cradled her like something sacred. Ran as if she was something worth saving.

And maybe she was.

The dossier Jareth had left on his desk the next day after the Orchid had everything documented on her from the time after the fall to her address in Savannah. Kael did not need most of that chronology; he knew precisely who Seraphine Vex was and what she needed, even without the provided information.

He knew she didn't know that he did. Didn't know the breadth of information cataloged on her life in the tribunal's records. The truth, the lies, and the things hidden in between species lines and energy signatures. They'd filed her as a demon succubus, not the hybrid she was.

However, they were wrong, whether intentionally or not.

He saw it that first night at Iron Orchid. Saw it again tonight when her shadows thinned, her hunger flared, and her body began to unravel. She didn't crave only lust. She craved something purer, older.

Celestial essence.

He hadn't known the mechanics, only that the absence of it in her body was likely killing her. That she'd gone too long without it, so he had cut his palm, pressed it to her lips, and let her drink.

The moment his essence mixed with blood touched her lips, her body shuddered like a fault line buckling under sudden light. Her body then eased, her shadows calming, as the golden color threaded back through her skin. And he felt a bond forming under her skin. The echo of his essence stitching itself into her, bit by blissful bit.

He should've left.

Instead, he stood there for too long again, staring at the woman he wasn't supposed to protect. The daughter of a bloodline he'd once been ordered to erase. The woman he had already failed before.

This is Not a Cure

7

Sera's doorbell shattered the morning's fragile quiet.

"Sera! Rise and shine!" Bethany's voice, bright and insistent, heralded her arrival. She entered like a force of nature, trailing scents of coffee, chaos, and sweet air fresheners. "Shopping day! You promised. Or maybe I threatened. Who cares!"

Sera, already resigned, muttered a soft no before accepting the cup like a ritual punishment.

"This place needs a vibe reset," the redhead announced. "I brought bagels and gossip. You're welcome."

Sera's only response was a raised eyebrow.

"Also, I see you lurking in the Holy Rollers chat room."

Her hand stilled midsip, a cold dread seizing her. "You what?"

Bethany's grin was sharp, her casual dismissal of a crumb from her thigh a subtle taunt. She leaned against the counter, her legs elegantly crossed. She radiated an unsettling blend of sugar and smugness. "Babe, your laptop screen reflects in the kitchen mirror.

A single heartbeat passed, and everything in the room froze. Even

Sera's shadows flattened and went utterly silent, neither hostile nor protective.

She stepped past Sera as her fingers trailed over Sera's shoulder on her way to the island, a familiar path worn by mornings and shared coffee. But today, the touch didn't land softly. It landed *precisely* as if she knew exactly how close she could get before something snapped.

Sera didn't respond at first. Her stomach tightened, with a bit of guilt at first, that suddenly flared into a challenge. Like she'd been caught testing a trip wire and dared to keep going anyway.

Sera set her mug down with care, catching her own guilty reflection in her nearby laptop's dark screen. "And?"

Bethany sipped her coffee. "And… Listen, I get it. He was intense. Like unblinking-over-the-wineglass kind of intense."

"That's one word for it," she murmured.

Bethany's smile faltered for just a breath. "I get it. That place… It's sexy, sure. But it's also dangerous. People lose themselves in there."

She raised a brow. "And yet you came along."

Bethany stood and busied herself at the sink. "Yeah, and I've been regretting it ever since."

She didn't sound flirty anymore. She almost sounded worried.

Sera watched her friend for a beat longer but then let it go for now.

Later, alone, Sera stared at her laptop. The chat room blinked on: red and black with Gothic fonts and hidden names.

He owned this place or at least held court there. This was his world. The thought was both infuriating and intoxicating. She couldn't just walk back in, after being so unceremoniously dismissed. A ruler who didn't understand her rival's territory was a fool.

Cassia had once warned her that chat rooms like these weren't harmless. Some were lures to bring naive mortals to these portals dressed as passwords. But she wasn't here to stop her anymore.

Her shadows behind her stirred, a low murmur of recognition. Sera faltered, her fingers hovering over the keyboard.

Go on. Their voices slithered, urging her deeper. *Join them. Feed.*

"Fine!" she muttered, the word a desperate concession.

Her fingers descended slowly and deliberately, tapping out her entry. A screen bloomed into existence, pulsing with names: Mistress_Eclipse. VelvetFangs. Nocturne. Each was a glittering mask. Each was a promise of predator or prey.

Mistress_Eclipse: Discipline isn't punishment. It's art.

VelvetFangs: That's what the last one said before she cried for mercy.

Nocturne: New face. Welcome, Sera. What brings you to our fold?

She hesitated, a breath held tight in her chest. Then the answer formed: I seek…sustenance.

A beat stretched. Then a sudden flurry of digital laughter, flirtation, and eager welcomes. Another message popped up.

ThorneMercy: We should meet tonight, Sera. You sound deliciously dangerous.

VelvetFangs: Who's going to the Gilded Grill meetup tonight? Corner booth, ten sharp. 😏

Mistress_Eclipse: The last meeting left bruises and secrets. I'm in.

Nocturne: Let's see who survives the attention.

To hell with caution. The silence of her apartment was deafening. What could possibly go wrong that she hadn't already experienced in her lifetime?

Sera: I'm listening.

ThorneMercy: Don't be late. We start at nine.

The address burned on the screen. It was a summons. Her pulse spiked. Master Kael. The name was a phantom weight on her mind.

She gently shut the laptop.

Her reflection was swallowed whole by the sudden black shape. She felt a presence behind her; the house stilled. No hum. No click. No voice. Only the gentle and deliberate stretch of shadows. Not hers.

She stood slowly. The robe slipped against her skin like a whisper, too soft to blame. She crossed the floor to the balcony and reached the glass French doors.

Outside, the city pulsed in a steam and sodium haze. Brick. Ivy. The low throb of tires somewhere far below. The kind of night that wore perfume and asked for nothing in return.

But something moved within the dark—slow, deliberate, and too steady to be the wind. The air sharpened, carrying the faint scent of iron and rain. Instinct rose in her throat before thought could catch up.

She opened the balcony door. No creak. Just the soft sigh of the seal breaking. The air clung to her as she stepped out.

Above, the sky hung heavy. There were no stars tonight, just a smear of moonlight caught in the clouds. Below, Savannah exhaled. Her building moaned faintly, settling into its bones. The railing was slick beneath her palms.

Across the street, perched on the edge of a crumbling rooftop like some grotesque gargoyle that refused to be stone, a large shadow waited. It appeared to have been bent out of shape.

Sera knew it the moment her eyes found it.

It was the same demon: bronzed and veined with those sickly glowing cracks that pulsed like magma just beneath ruined skin. Its asymmetrical horns curved back like old weapons, and its face, if it could be called that, was exactly as she remembered: all teeth and darkness with no eyes, only two burning slits that carved through the distance with quiet malice.

There was no confusion in its posture now. No hesitation. It wasn't hunting anymore. It had found her. And it wanted her to know.

Her shadows curled low at her heels. They held their breaths just like she did, crouching in silence.

The wards in her home, careful things that had been etched into the plaster and the bricks, stirred awake. Their power rose like a low hum beneath the floorboards, subtle and unwavering. She could feel them pulsing at the brick walls' edges, forming an unseen barrier between her and the creature watching.

They would hold. She had poured enough blood, bones, and will into them to ensure it.

And yet, the sight of that demon across the street, utterly still and completely patient, made her feel as though the air around her had turned into glass, already cracking.

It didn't move. Didn't growl. It simply stood there, drinking her in with those eyeless slits as if cataloging what she had become since their last meeting. It stayed just long enough to make it clear this was not finished, that what it had started was only a prelude.

Then it turned, slow and smooth, and disappeared into the folds of the night without a sound.

The city resumed its rhythm, but the sound was wrong—too slow and too distant, like a heartbeat that had missed a step. The air felt bruised where the creature had stood, and the silence that followed pressed hard against her ears.

Sera's fingers tightened around the balcony's iron bars, rust grinding into the creases of her palms, and only when the glass door clicked shut on its own behind her, causing her to jump, did she realize she had been holding her breath the entire time.

The wards were strong, but the night no longer felt safe for her. No nights now felt safe.

The city lay beneath her in a fever and a fog, wrapped in steam and seduction. Streetlamps wept amber onto the cracked brick. Somewhere, a siren wailed, distant. Summer pressed up against her like a mouth.

She stepped forward, her fingers curling around the iron railing. It was damp beneath her skin, too warm.

She lifted her hand, and her fingertips gleamed.

A streak of ash. Too dark for dust. Too oily for rain. It clung like a memory.

She brought it to her nose and froze.

Brimstone. The demon had been on her balcony before.

The scent was no longer strong. Just a ghost of it: sulfur braided into iron and masked beneath jasmine and old paint. Faint as a whisper behind a confessional screen.

But she knew it: Hell didn't need to shout to be heard. The scent, unspoken and unmistakable, curled into the back of her throat and twisted her stomach, not in fear but in recognition.

Her shadows, which had been silent until now, rose around her ankles like reverent smoke and whispered.

Not ours.

"No shit." Her heart didn't race. It narrowed, and her grip on the railing tightened. The iron gave a slight creak as if warning her not to snap. She released it, stepping back, and her shadows curled at her heels, expectant.

Do we follow? one shadow breathed.

"No," she responded softly.

The balcony door sighed closed behind her, and she locked herself within the confinement of her home. And the night swallowed the scent of brimstone like a secret it meant to keep.

Back inside, Sera was still thinking about the shape atop the building's roof across the street. The next moment, she stumbled forward into her living space as if someone had jabbed a knife into her skull.

The smell inside her house assaulted her. Bethany's air fresheners. A cloying, synthetic sweetness that coated her throat like syrup. It was suffocating. She inhaled and her vision fractured. She stumbled forward as if a knife had jabbed into her skull.

The first pang struck like the jagged edge of a glacier, wrenching deep into her core. This was no mere hunger. It was an abyss, a relentless beast clawing through her insides with savage precision. The shadows at the edges of her vision thickened, no longer passive whispers but shapes—twitching, curling, wrong. They stretched with long limbs, twisting into warped echoes of herself with too many mouths and hungers.

You are weak.

The word slithered through her like a live wire. Not spoken aloud. Thought. Planted. Barbed.

The source is gone. The veil is bleeding.

Sera did not always understand her shadows. What source? Had Kael done something to her? The pain was *agonizing*.

She clutched the edge of the console table, her nails biting into the lacquered wood. Her townhouse, usually a portrait of curated calm, shivered around her, the walls breathing too fast and the corners warping like a heat mirage. The hunger surged. It now felt more than a craving, a rupture.

It tore through her like fire licking bones, all sharp and no mercy.

Even her shadows, curled at her feet like cats, were different now.

Starving. Restless.

One rubbed up against her calf and hissed against her skin. *You're bleeding out.*

Feed. Or we all burn for nothing.

She pushed off the table and staggered toward the kitchen, every step like moving through wet cement. Her limbs didn't ache. They rebelled: shaky, slow, and treacherous.

Her shadows followed, slick and close. Not companions anymore. They were parasites wearing loyalty like a mask.

The air seemed to constrict, suffocating her and warping the grand furnishings into sinister shapes looming over her. Her vision blurred. The wallpaper seemed to ripple. She tasted metal, copper. She was already draining the room.

Just as she collapsed against the embrace of her velvet sofa, her phone broke the silence with its insistent ringing. She fumbled for it with trembling fingers and blinked through the haze to see the name flashing on the screen.

Cassia.

She pressed the phone to her ear. "Cassia," she rasped, her voice barely recognizable.

"Heavens above! You need to feed, Sera!" Cassia's voice was calm, unwavering. Just a fact mixed with concern. "Don't make me find another body like Berlin."

She flinched, her grip tightening on the phone. That Berlin man's face still haunted her. The rain-slick cobblestones. The gaping void where his soul should have been. "That wasn't—"

"It was exactly what it was," her sister said. "I'm coming to visit. Keep yourself intact until then."

Her sister's voice was calm and cool, but to her, it felt like a hand braced at the edge of a cliff, holding her up. Even now.

Sera gritted her teeth, gripping the phone tighter. "Please help me. I don't have any vessels right now," she said, her voice barely above a whisper.

"Then I'll send someone." No hesitation. No doubt. Just certainty. "Hold on."

The line went dead.

Sera let the phone slip from her grasp, staring at the ceiling. The tonight meeting would have to wait. Survival came first and the shadows sulked in the corners of her vision.

But Cassia's words lingered, anchoring her unshakable certainty that she would endure, that she would hold on until help arrived.

And for now, that would have to be enough.

An hour later, a knock at the door jolted Sera from her stupor. She dragged herself to her feet, every limb trembling from the effort. Her body pulsed with heat and static, barely restrained hunger wrapped like a snake around her spine.

When she opened the door, a young man stood in the hallway, his expression unreadable. He held out a small vial filled with iridescent liquid that shimmered like trapped starlight. The scent that wafted off it was faintly floral, tinged with ozone and a distant sweetness that made her teeth ache.

"Cassia sent me," he said, his voice clipped. "This should help."

Reluctant, Sera stared at the vial for a moment. She could feel that the essence wasn't human. It was angelic. Synthesized, carefully prepared, and utterly foreign to the predator inside her. It held purity, distance, and the echo of divinity diluted into something clinical.

Her fingers fumbled as she pulled out a folded stack of bills, but the man raised a hand, shaking his head.

"Already paid for," he said flatly. "Cassia takes care of her own."

She hesitated, uncapped the vial, and swallowed its contents in one quick gulp. Cold. Sweet. Wrong. Relief washed over her like an icy wave, chilling the fire in her veins and quelling the hunger that clawed in her bones. Her heart slowed, and her breathing stabilized. Her thoughts stopped spinning. Her hands stopped shaking. The relief blossomed, but it wouldn't last.

This wasn't nourishment. It was a bandage over decay.

Cassia had always told her to feed with discipline. Regularly. Efficiently. Coldly.

"Be precise, not passionate," she used to say. Like hunger was something to be managed, not survived.

But Sera was never built for clean lines and a clinical appetite. Her hunger wasn't logistical. It was emotional. Messy. It came wrapped in ache and memory, sharp with want, and soft with sorrow. She fed the way she felt: recklessly, grieving, and curiously.

And Berlin had become the end of pretending otherwise. People who wanted her too much. A night she entered half shattered and left even more so. A moment of softness mistaken for safety. And a soul that never moved on: trapped in the walls, in the air, and in her blood.

Cassia had warned her that, of course, she set the rules and drew the lines. But that one slip was all it took to lose the last of her sister's trust.

Sera hadn't lost control that night. She hadn't been starving. She'd chosen it. That was the difference. That was the sin. But the worst part was that she had *liked* it. She had decided to stop. Not out of virtue or even guilt. But because she couldn't afford to lose the little control that was left in her.

The whole reason for the divorce was to push Mark far enough away. She feared that one day, she might kill him by accident, when that control would no longer be at her disposal.

It was better to suffer in silence than to become what Cassia already believed she was.

The shadows pulled back, curling into the corners like obedient hounds. Their whispers retreated to murmurs.

Temporary, they rasped.

A cage, not a cure, another added, laughter lacing the edges.

Sera exhaled, pressing a trembling hand to her stomach. They were right. This wasn't nourishment. It was sedation.

But for now, they were silent. And that silence was the closest thing to peace she had.

She watched as the stranger walked away, his figure vanishing into the dim hallway. As she sank back onto the sofa, exhaustion crept over her like a thick fog and pulled her toward sleep.

Across town, the Gilded Grill shimmered with candlelight and sin. Kael stepped inside, the scent of whiskey and want curling through the air.

His gaze swept the space.

Sera wasn't there, but the redhead was.

She lounged at the bar as if she owned the night. Her hair had been let loose in waves, and her laughter spilled like bourbon. He moved through the crowd with the same slow precision he brought to everything, watching her watch him.

She smiled at him, all feline grace.

"I think I saw you at Holy Rollers," he said as he reached her.

"Oh?" Bethany's glass tilted in her hand, catching the chandelier's amber glow. "Then you must've been paying very close attention."

"You weren't the one who caught my eye."

She raised an eyebrow. "And who else then?"

"Black hair. Green eyes. She was different."

Her smile didn't falter, but a flicker shifted behind her lashes. "Oh… Her. I would not keep my hopes high."

He said nothing.

She leaned in. "Tell me, Kael, why does she interest you so much?"

"Why do you need to know?" he asked.

Her smile widened, and he saw that calculation underneath.

This morning, Jareth had let him know that Sera had registered in their club's chat room. Kael hadn't intended to join, but the bond blooming under his skin now had other plans. He had joined it to appease Jareth, to watch and observe. Or at least that was what he told himself.

Sera was sharp-tongued. Elusive. Controlled. Her presence in the chat was magnetic. That woman had been pure instinct and raw hunger. She wielded power like a blade, calculated and clever. Almost too much so.

Still, he kept reading over her words.

And they stuck with him, got under his skin, and made him want to respond when he usually wouldn't.

Sera was a spark. Her face, her body, and her wit were a wildfire.

Kael typed out a message as he stepped away from the grill for some fresh air. Although, how much fresh air could one find in Savannah in the middle of July?

Kael: You are not at the steakhouse tonight.

Sera: You are an observant, "Master."

His pulse ticked.

Bethany's voice broke the moment like a blade tapping glass. "More drinks?"

He looked at her, and for a second, he didn't see her—only saw Sera's limp body in his arms, the way his essence had answered hers like a prayer they hadn't meant to say.

Bethany leaned in, looking expectant. Sultry. Her smile was soft at the edges, but her offer was sharp and unmistakable. She was beautiful, effortless, and uncomplicated. And he knew exactly what she was offering: distraction. Descent. A door into forgetting, even if only for a breath.

He hesitated, his fingers tightening around his glass.

The bond he'd ignited with Sera still pulsed beneath his skin, subtle but relentless. It wasn't just guilt. It was worse. Binding. Warm. And he couldn't afford warmth.

He'd made a mistake. He'd fed her his light, thinking it would be enough to save her. Just once. Just enough. But now it clung to him, threading between his ribs like the echo of a shared heartbeat—steady, unwanted, and impossible to silence.

He needed it gone.

So, he looked at Bethany again. Let the heat of her gaze wash over the ache. Let the promise of numbness dull the sharpness of need.

"Yeah," he said quietly, his voice low and flat. "More drinks sound good."

She smiled slowly and confidently. Like she knew she'd already won.

And Kael let her think it. Because the game was already underway, and he was no longer the one holding the leash.

I Deal in Retribution

8

The days since Holy Rollers had smeared together like smoke across glass: thin, clinging, and impossible to wipe clean.

A soft vibration broke the silence of her room.

She glanced at the screen, her eyes narrowing. It was 10:37 p.m., that liminal hour where logic went to sleep, and mistakes felt like invitations. Kael's name glowed from the shadows of her lock screen.

Kael: How have you been?

Her heart stuttered, and her fingers moved on instinct.

Sera: Strange.

The reply came fast, too fast.

Kael: Understatement of the millennia.

She scoffed, her lips twitching. The memory of that night, when he had saved her from the hunger consumption, slithered back in fragmented flashes. His scent. Her hunger. The way her body still hummed faintly, like the echo of a struck chord that hadn't yet faded.

But worse than the hum was the aftertaste she couldn't forget. It felt divine and wrong, tangled with the copper tang of blood. His essence had filled her like lightning, and even now, days later, she could still feel it crackling under her skin.

Kael: I think we need to talk.

Sera: I guess I could let you buy me a couple of martinis.

Kael: Deal. This man will plan something worthy of your approval.

She set the phone down, the screen dimming to black, and stared at her reflection in the window glass. Just a silhouette framed in faint streetlight and the ghosts of decisions she hadn't yet made.

Something in her still buzzed. Still pulled toward him with the quiet, primal gravity of blood recognizing blood.

This time, maybe she'd get her answers.

Kael leaned back in his chair, city lights flickering across his office window like murmurs of another world. It was 11:30 p.m. Savannah slept, unaware of the shadows that stalked through its alleys.

He reread Sera's words. He had honestly been anticipating or hoping for a rejection and a deflection. Not an acceptance so easily.

Running a hand through his hair, he noticed the strands caught no light, only darkness now. It clung to him like the faint scent of ozone, which he could no longer mask with sandalwood and steel. Or the subtle shift in his eyes, once crystalline but now dark as midnight. They were the echoes of a fall he rarely spoke of.

His reflection stared back at him from the glass: tall, immaculate, etched with grace, and turned cold. Beneath the tailored shirt were pale and almost invisible scars written in the language of battles fought on planes most mortals couldn't imagine.

Falling hadn't been fire but silence. A quiet exile. A sentence to hunt the hunters, to dole out justice where Heaven acted swiftly. He wore this role like armor. Blackwood Bounties—a private bounty agency that dealt in monsters, missing souls, and debts Heaven refused to claim—was his creation. It was his crucible, his weapon against the filth that slipped through mortal cracks.

Jareth, or Master Jar as the club patrons called him, who was dangerously close to fall, walked beside him for this purpose. Together, they hunted monsters. This way, Jar could remain a watcher, and Kael dedicated his afterlife to repenting for his sins by bringing the bad guys down.

And tonight, the hunt led to one deserving no mercy.

A rapist. Marked by his sins. His essence reeked of predation.

Jar's message had given Kael the location, the final thread in the noose.

Kael stepped into the alley behind a crumbling apartment building, emerging from the shadows like smoke given form. Inside, the air reeked of beer, filth, and the sour tang of fear. The target's breaths were sharp and erratic.

"Please," the man gasped. "I...I'll confess. I'll turn myself in."

He smiled slowly. "Confession is for the penitent. I deal in retribution."

The man's fear deepened, now more primal. "What...what are you?" he whispered, sputtering.

Kael stepped closer. "I am the end. You owe a debt that can't be repaid in anything but...the end."

He reached without touching. Energy, luminous and terrible, coalesced around his outstretched hand. A thread of essence, thin and bright, pulled from the man's chest like silk unraveling from a spider's web.

Kael had taken thousands of souls in his lifetime, each leaving a faint scar beneath his skin. But it wasn't pain he pulled when he fed. It was the truth. Their guilt. Their desire. Their final thoughts as light slipped free of flesh. And when he took it in, it now lived inside him, vibrating like caged lightning. Unless the soul was so ugly that it needed to be extracted and released to the tribunal for judgment as soon as possible.

The man had no chance to scream or fight. His spirit came willingly. Useless.

Kael drew it in and felt its weight. Tainted and bruised but intact. It pulsed within him: contained, judged, and held in waiting.

Then the light snapped, and the man's body slumped empty against the wall of the dirty apartment.

And Kael vanished, the echo of death lingering behind.

A few minutes later, his office welcomed him back like a cathedral of silence. But his hunt wasn't finished.

He barely had time to pour himself a glass of whiskey before another ping echoed across the room, a signal from Jar.

Jar with a problem. Gang hideout near Bay Street. Tied to the child trafficking op. They got twenty minutes before the gang scattered.

Kael's jaw tightened. No rest for the wicked or those who hunted them.

Kael and Jar met near the edge of the Historic District, just off Bay Street. Remnants of the Savannah Cigar Crawl had left behind the scent of tobacco and expensive cologne here. The lounge looked closed for the night, but its dim alley entrance hid more than ashes and whispers.

Jar was already shifting his shoulders. Even in mortal guise, he looked celestial with white-gold hair that caught every ray of moonlight. His skin was like carved alabaster, and his eyes lit from within. He was as tall as Kael, but they looked nothing alike. Where Kael was the embodiment of pragmatism and sarcasm, Jar had a light joke up his sleeve, no matter how dire the situation was.

"You're late," Jar said, though his smirk held no malice.

Kael arched a brow. "You gave me twenty minutes."

"You do have wings," he muttered. "Use those damned things."

"Don't start…"

They approached the rear entrance, and Kael's aura dropped like a blade: lethal and cold. Jar exhaled once, letting his glow spill forward. It shimmered golden and warm, the opposite of Kael's void.

Kael reached for the door. "Let's remind them what justice tastes like."

Minutes later, chaos was inside. Six men, armed with pistols and silver-edged blades, were cornered. The kind of arsenal meant for monsters, not men.

Two lunged toward Jar, only to be thrown back by a burst of light from his outstretched palm. Feathers—radiant projections—flared behind him like wings, scattering the dust in golden spirals.

Kael met his targets with merciless precision. He didn't need weapons; he was one. Each movement was poetry written in bones and blood. One man tried to flee, but he was faster, his form bending through shadow before he grabbed the man by his throat.

"You sell children," he whispered, growling.

The man trembled. "I, I didn't touch them! I swear!"

"You enabled it."

Kael's grip pulsed with a dark heat, and the man crumpled, unconscious but intact.

They left none alive, all empty shells of corrupted souls, except the ringleader.

The man, with a serpent tattoo, met Kael's eyes just before fleeing into a side room. Kael followed with shadows curling around his boots.

"You cannot run from judgment," he said softly, taunting the leader as he stepped into the gloom.

The man raised a gun, but it shook in his sweaty palm uncontrollably. Kael didn't even flinch. He reached into the space between them, his palm upturned, and the man's soul began to tear free.

This soul resisted. Struggled.

Kael gritted his teeth, his voice low. "You knew what you were. That's why it hurts, and I will make sure it hurts like hell."

The thread snapped loose—a ribbon of stained light that pulsed once in protest before coiling into Kael's chest.

His hand clenched, and the man's body dropped. Empty.

By the time he returned to the front, Jar didn't need to ask. Another soul was bound for judgment.

When everything was over, the building stank of ozone, fire, and fear.

Jar leaned against a wall, panting slightly. "Remind me to never get on your bad side."

Kael dragged his knuckles against the rough denim of his jeans, smearing a dark streak that the summer air refused to dry. "It is never over."

"No," Jar said. "But it's a start."

Kael looked out toward the dawn.

"We should deposit them before they start to tickle your insides," he said softly, his voice stripped of its usual teasing.

They moved to the rear courtyard behind the lounge, where half-forgotten ruins of stone angels stood vigil among ivy-choked tombs. At the center sat a basin etched in celestial runes, hidden in plain sight from mortal eyes.

Jar unslung the Anima Crucible, a crystal core flickering with pale fire, from across his back. Their eyes met for a breath before he placed the vessel in Kael's waiting hands. Kael knelt beside it, one palm pressed to his chest and the other tightening around the crucible that now burned white, ready to accept the sinners.

"Begin," Jar said, his voice now laced with celestial resonance.

Kael opened himself to release. He exhaled sharply, pain flickering across his face. One by one, the stolen souls emerged like glimmers of fractured light, twisting in the air. Jar slammed the crucible against his sternum, forcing each essence into its crystalline heart. With each soul received, a final mournful chime sounded.

When the last was drawn out, the crucible glowed bright, nearly unbearable to look at. Jar whispered a phrase in an ancient tongue, and the air cracked. A seam opened in the world, just a sliver. Just enough.

The crucible lifted on its own, suspended in light, and then vanished into the breach. The rift was sealed, and the night reclaimed its quiet.

Jar glanced at Kael. "You okay? You look extra miserable tonight."

Kael didn't answer right away. His voice, when it came, had a hint of sarcasm. "Did they forget to include compassion when they made you an angel?"

He snorted. "That's the whole reason why they made me one."

And that was true. Jareth was one of the very few angels who had been a mortal once. His acts of kindness and compassion during his short mortal life, which ended too soon, granted him the status of an angel by the tribunal. It had been one of the very exceptional moments when the ruling six had gifted this power of absolution. As far as Kael knew, Jareth was the last of them; no other mortals had deserved redemption since.

Jar looked at Kael once more. "Seriously though. Are you okay?"

Kael was about to make another sarcastic jab, but Jar's stare lingered. So instead, he exhaled. "You mentioned Malakar stopped you?"

"Yeah. But a way to avoid an answer." He straightened. "Cornered me when I was pulling Sera's file. Said there have been disturbances. Servant demons are showing up where they're not supposed to. Roaming the streets. Sniffing around."

Kael's face gave nothing away. "Demons do weird shit all the time."

He narrowed his eyes. "He said they're looking for *someone*. Marked. Traced. Their orders are old and high level. And I don't know if you've noticed, but lately, your poker face sucks."

Kael scoffed. "Why are you looking at me like I'm hiding a demonic baby in my closet?"

"Because I know when you're lying. I'm not a fool."

He hesitated but then gave in. "Fine. They're after Sera."

Jar went still. "What did you do?"

"Nothing... I...saved her." His voice was flat but cracked underneath. "Or maybe I ruined her. I don't even know. One of Lilith's scouts was trailing her. It wasn't hunting. Just watching."

Jar blinked slowly. "And you didn't think to tell me?"

"I didn't want it on a tribunal report," he muttered. "Didn't want *her* on a report."

Jar's voice dropped. "They're watching. You know that, right?"

The two parted with no further words.

Kael arrived home at first light, his muscles sore and his heart heavier than he would admit. He shed his bloodied shirt and dropped onto the bed without ceremony.

But sleep refused him.

The silence pressed in too tightly. The souls he'd stolen still echoed beneath his skin. Every breath felt hollow.

He tossed. Turned. Finally reaching for his phone, he pushed a message through to the only creature who seemed to matter in his world now.

Kael: Morning, Little Devil.

It didn't take too long to get a reply.

Sera: Morning, Angel?! You're up early.

Kael: Would you meet me at The Serpent's Kiss tonight at eight?

Sera: Tonight works. Eight. You're buying.

Kael: Wouldn't have it any other way. Don't keep a predator waiting.

Shadow Play

9

Lying on her side, Sera stared at her phone, the pale morning light tracing lazy lines across her sheets. Tonight, at eight p.m.

The message glowed like a sigil. Inevitable.

She read it. And reread again. Each time, the words seemed to shift weight. Not just a meeting. A moment. A door she wasn't sure she'd chosen, but one she'd walk through anyway.

Her thumb hovered, but she didn't reply.

Instead, she lay still, trying to make sense of the static under her skin, the lingering aftershock of feeding. Of him. The essence she'd taken still pulsed in her like a second heartbeat. Divine and wrong. Beautiful and terrible. Kael hadn't just offered her life. He had left a mark, one that didn't fade.

She closed her eyes as if that would stop the feeling.

It didn't.

Sleep crept back over her like a veil, dragging her into uneasy dreams of wings and ash.

Soon enough, sunlight invaded her room like an uninvited guest. She groaned beneath her sheets, the world still a blur of dreams and memories. Her clock flashed 9:45 a.m. Shit. She was late to have brunch with Bethany.

The water in the shower barely cut through the lingering haze of restless sleep and fractured visions: Kael's eyes, the club's heat, and the whisper of her name he'd said in the street. Her skin tingled.

She threw on a sundress, grabbed her bag, and slipped into the bright, chaotic world beyond.

The café was alive with the kind of forced cheer that made Sera's teeth itch: clinking silverware, couples laughing too loudly, and the smug clatter of overpriced lattes. Summer had painted everything in scorching light, and it all felt two dozen shades too bright.

Bethany already sat in their usual corner, her floral dress flaring around her like it was a stage costume. Her red hair was perfectly put up, but her smile was tight at the edges.

Sera caught the flicker behind her friend's eyes before she even sat.

"Finally!" Bethany waved her over. Her voice had been dipped in syrupy sweetness. "Thought you ghosted me for good."

"The alarm betrayed me," she muttered, sliding into the seat and reaching for the coffee that was already waiting for her. "I blame the system."

Bethany tilted her head. "You look like you woke up in someone else's bed. Hope not Kael's."

She snorted. "He's complicated, isn't he?"

Bethany leaned in, all faux conspiratorial. "Your chat history is straight-up sinful. I practically had to fan my phone. Digital foreplay at its finest."

"We talk." She shrugged. Smirked. "That's all."

But Bethany's laugh didn't reach her eyes. "He's got you twisted up.

I mean, even Jar said Kael doesn't talk online. Ever. Then you show up, and suddenly, it's midnight texts and jokes in the chat room."

Sera didn't flinch, but she felt the shift. The way Bethany's tone sharpened.

She took a slow sip, hiding her expression behind the mug. "We're meeting tonight. The Serpent's Kiss."

Bethany froze for just a breath. But it was enough. She then smiled again, too wide and too practiced. "That's bold."

"Fitting."

Bethany stabbed at her eggs with the kind of enthusiasm usually reserved for murder. "Strange choice for a meetup. You're not just getting drinks. You're stepping into the lion's mouth."

And the thing was: She wasn't wrong.

The Serpent's Kiss was a strange dive by mortal standards: dim lighting, no website, and a clientele who looked like they'd walked straight out of a fever dream. The kind of place where the jukebox played songs that didn't exist, and the bartender never blinked.

Mortals chalked it up to being quirky and edgy, but to those who knew better, it was an underground gathering place for supernatural misfits. No rules, no borders, and no watchers observing.

Among the supernatural, it was a market of shadows. You could trade anything there: innocent trinkets plucked from celestial vaults, forbidden rites, names with too much weight, and even fragments of a soul if the price was high enough. Once, Sera had overheard a whisper that someone bought a clean conscience there, left the bar as light as air, and never spoke again. She wasn't sure if it had been a joke.

And for a flicker of a moment, she wondered if Cassia had ever walked into places like that. If she made her bargains beneath velvet lamps and sigil-scratched tables too. Was that how she had found the souls she used to trade, the power she wrapped around herself like armor? Maybe that was why the thought of The Serpent's Kiss didn't scare Sera. Perhaps it should have.

"I'm not afraid," Sera replied.

Bethany's fork clinked against the plate. "Maybe you should be," she muttered, barely audible.

The moment stretched as thick as molasses. Then, recovering slightly, she smiled like nothing had slipped.

"Look, forget the online stuff," Bethany said, swirling her mimosa and looking uncomfortable. "It's just... have you ever actually looked at him? Like, really looked? There's something off. It's not just the brooding artist act. It's like... standing next to a live wire. My skin crawled when he walked into the Gilded Grill. And you're planning to meet him alone? In a sketchy dive bar? That's not a date, Sera. That's a mistake."

"You were at the grill?"

Sera swirled the last of her coffee, trying her best not to look shocked or agitated.

Bethany smiled again. And Sera saw the way her fingers tightened around the stem of her glass.

"Yes, Master Jar invited me" she replied, her voice casual. "I actually joined the chat a night before you did."

Internally, she laughed. She always forgot how naive Bethany could be beneath the sass and curated southern charm. But the obsession was telling. Bethany protested too loudly. She clearly wanted to know what happened in the dark. She craved the thrill of the darker world but lacked the nerve to step into it.

That same darkness always called Sera too, and there was so much of it in the way Kael tasted. In the power laced beneath his skin, barely leashed. She had felt the divine and whatever had been twisted into it slide across her tongue like lightning wrapped in ash. No printed glyph or ritual ink could prepare Bethany for that kind of danger.

Bethany was worried about the 'bad boy' vibe. Sera had swallowed his essence and survived.

Sera raised a brow. "So, when were you going to tell me?"

Bethany shrugged. "I did not think you would support it."

She set her fork down carefully. "On the contrary, I think it's fascinating."

Bethany's expression didn't crack, but her silence did.

They finished the meal with fragments of conversations about safe topics, but the damage had already been done. Sera caught every glance Bethany avoided. Every question she didn't ask.

And beneath her smile, a pulse of heat stirred low in her gut, the kind that meant her shadows were listening before she did.

Bethany was hiding something. Sera was sure of it.

Or maybe it was just a feeling Bethany didn't want to admit. Jealousy. Or fear.

Sera wasn't sure which one unsettled her more.

She stared at her reflection, her expression unreadable. The woman in the mirror wore no pretense yet shimmered with contradictions. The club's bratty woman. The flirt behind the screen. The reluctant demon who hadn't fed in days.

All of them lived in her bones.

And all of them were getting dressed for war.

At home, she skipped the silk and drama. The Serpent's Kiss wasn't a ballroom. It was where vodka was served in cracked glasses and secrets bled through the floorboards.

She put on a black crop top, thin strapped and low enough to invite attention but tight enough to deny access; torn dark jeans that hugged like sin; and combat boots because heels lied. She also threw a leather jacket over her shoulders like armor. No purse, just a pocketknife and her lip gloss tucked into her bra.

She smeared deep wine across her lips, smudged black shadows beneath her eyes, and pulled her curls into a loose, deliberate mess. It still looked polished and dangerous.

She stole a final glance at her phone, the message still glowing. Her thumb hovered, but she didn't reply. Let him wait.

She turned toward the door.

The streets of Savannah seemed quieter than usual as she walked, her boots thudding against the cobblestones. The closer she drew to The Serpent's Kiss, the heavier the air grew—tainted not just with anticipation but with a cold that tasted of iron and old rain. It wasn't meant to breathe the same night as her.

A chill curled at the nape of her neck. She slowed her steps, casting a glance behind her. Nothing but trees and lamp-lit sidewalks. Still, the sensation of being watched clung to her. And not the usual hunger of passing men or the intrigue of mortal curiosity.

Her breath caught, her chest tightening with a fear she hated to name. She had walked these streets for years, claimed them as her sanctuary and hunting grounds. But tonight, they felt foreign and tainted with brimstone again.

She calmly picked up her pace and posture, but her every nerve screamed. The city's shadows had never unsettled her like this, even when she had hunted.

It wasn't paranoia anymore. It was a warning. The damn demon was back, and it wasn't friendly.

Marked Souls

10

The Serpent's Kiss pulsed as if it was alive, slow and deliberate. The blues dripped through the air like smoke. The space was filled with low murmur and clinking glasses.

It felt like a charge in the walls, a breath between sighs. The weight of too many secrets spoken too close to someone else's mouth. Every corner of the room buzzed with indulgence barely restrained. The dim lighting, strategically placed to cast long and dancing shadows, created an atmosphere of intimacy and veiled threat.

Kael leaned back into the cracked leather booth, a whiskey glass loosely cradled in his fingers. The amber caught the light, casting gold shadows across the table, but he barely noticed. He owned this place.

Serpent's Kiss had the right atmosphere: quiet, dim, and expensive enough to keep the amateurs out. Like him, it didn't beg for attention. It waited to be understood.

Alone, he drank slowly, his thoughts circling the same name: Sera.

When she walked in, his breath caught. The rigidity in his body then loosened, and he sighed in relief.

She stepped into the bar like she owned its rot. With the cold, quiet confidence of someone who knew exactly how many eyes would turn and which ones she'd ignore.

Her combat boots did not attempt to soften her entrance. Shadows clung to her like perfume, and the flickering neon from the busted sign outside kissed her skin with red. The dark denim clung to her skin like sin. Her hair was pulled back like she hadn't tried too hard, but he knew better. Every part of her was a decision.

And then she looked up.

Green eyes. Sharp, deliberate, and impossible to forget. Eyes that had once stared up at him from a velvet floor. Eyes that had haunted his every damn night since.

She was astonishing. Yet the word felt like a betrayal—too small, too pale.

He stood as she moved through the haze and dim lights. And then she was in front of him.

Her presence wasn't loud, but it was all-consuming. The way she held herself, cocky and cautious, spoke of someone who'd bled once and then memorized the shape of every scar.

But it was her eyes that did him in.

Not just green, they were flecked with gold. Up close, he saw more layers: the fractured storm beneath the jade. Bronze at the edges, silver when the light hits. Shadows moved somewhere deep within, like the eyes couldn't decide what truth to tell, or maybe they remembered too many versions of it.

"Kael," she said, a smirk playing at her lips.

His name had never sounded more like a sin waiting to happen.

He gripped his glass tight, forcing himself back into the booth. Control, he reminded himself. Always control. But that primal urge inside him? It roared now.

"Sera," he said, his voice rougher than intended. "You made it."

A flicker of amusement crossed her face. "You look like you've seen a ghost," she returned, her smoky voice curling between them.

He raised an eyebrow. "On the contrary. I see a goddess."

Her smile was unapologetic and wickedly amused. "Romantic, aren't you, Master Kael?"

The way she said his title hit like a punch to the gut and a whisper in the dark all at once.

It shouldn't have undone him. But fucking heavens, it did.

He could already feel the phantom grip of her hair in his hand, dark strands wrapped around his fingers as he dragged her in—mouth to mouth, shadow to flame. He wanted to taste that smirk off her lips, to sink into the hunger she barely bothered to hide.

His fingers twitched. His jaw locked.

Too far. Too fast.

He straightened his spine, drawing in a breath sharp enough to burn. No. This wasn't some fevered fantasy. He had tethered himself to this woman for no reason, and now, she was his anchor and his noose. Every time she got closer, the rope kept slipping.

Control. He couldn't lose it now, not with her.

"You keep saying things like that," he said, his voice a shade too quiet, "and I might start thinking you like me."

Her grin widened. And he cursed the part of himself that did not mind.

She let out a soft chuckle. "What can I say?" she replied, her eyes glinting. "I am full of contradictions." She slid into the booth and crossed one leg over the other like she was claiming the space. "So, I have a lot of questions, and I am sure you do too."

He smiled, slightly this time. "Straight to business, eh?"

The air between them shimmered. The server arrived, breaking the moment with one negroni placed like an offering. They clinked glasses, their eyes never leaving each other.

A vampire's laugh rippled from the bar. A pair of witches were huddled in the corner booth, whispering incantations into their drinks. Glamours faintly shimmered in the haze. The otherworldly mingled so freely around them, yet Kael's focus narrowed to a single point: Sera.

"In the alley," she said quietly, "you knew something was following me, didn't you?"

A pause. Then a slow nod. "Yes."

"Why didn't you tell me?"

"Because panic makes people loud. And loud gets things killed."

Her jaw flexed. "What was it?"

He hesitated. "Demon. A scout, maybe. But it wasn't there to strike. It was tracking. Curious."

"And you just let me walk around with a tail?"

"I didn't let anything happen to you," he said, his voice cooling. "You're here, aren't you?"

She didn't flinch. "That's not an answer. Why was it watching me?"

Kael met her eyes, which were steady and unreadable. "I don't know." It was the closest to a lie he'd told all night.

She didn't seem to buy it. "But you have ideas."

He exhaled, rubbing a knuckle against his jaw. "I've seen patterns like this before when something or someone is valuable to both sides. When the tribunal's hands are tied, the demons send scouts, and the angels send silence. And the in between?" He looked at her, his gaze like a blade. "They watch. They wait."

She hesitated. "Why would I be valuable to anyone?" she asked, forcing steadiness into her voice.

He didn't blink. "Have you ever thought that maybe you're not just feeding anymore? That something inside you is waking up?"

Her breath caught.

"I've seen hybrids. You're not like them. You're too controlled. Too precise. Your shadows don't lash; they observe. You don't feed for hunger. You feed for…staying alive."

She stared at him. "You've been watching me."

"Only when necessary."

"That's not creepy at all," she muttered.

Kael's smile was faint, humorless. "If you knew what I've seen, you'd be grateful someone was."

She didn't answer.

His voice softened. "I don't have all the answers, Sera. But I think you're starting to ask the right questions. That's more than most."

She took a moment before replying. "Are you really a fallen?"

He met her eyes. No flinch. No hesitation. "Yes."

She inhaled through her teeth. "And that night…you fed me your essence. Why?"

He looked down for a moment and then back up at her, honest and measured. "Because you were slipping. And I didn't think. I just reacted. It was the only thing I had at that moment."

She searched his face. "But that ties us, doesn't it?"

He said nothing. Just reached out and softly brushed his fingertips along her delicate hand. Heat curled low in his spine. Her voice did things to him that he hadn't felt in decades. Every tilt of her head, every flicker of emotion in her eyes, pulled him deeper into her gravity. So, he moved in closer, pressing the limits of her personal space.

When they were eventually done chatting, Sera stood to leave, and he followed her. Outside, the night met them with velvet shadows and thick jasmine air. The music behind them softened to a hum as they slowly walked away.

"You want to walk a bit?" she asked.

Kael glanced at her, his head tilting just slightly. "Thought you'd never ask."

At first, they strolled in silence, their shoes echoing on old stones. Around them, the city breathed humid air, laced with unseen eyes. A streetlamp buzzed overhead, flickering. Their shoulders brushed. Neither moved away.

Sera was the first to speak. "Do you ever feel like your body remembers something your soul's trying to forget?"

He stopped walking and looked at her thoroughly. "Yes," he said. Quiet. Certain. "All the time."

She didn't smile, didn't flinch. "That's why I stopped running. Because eventually, it catches up. The thing underneath."

"And if it's not a thing," he murmured, his voice like thunder wrapped in silk, "but a person, a creature?"

"Then you pray they're not watching when you break," she replied.

They walked in silence for a while, the city humming around them. Streetlights cast golden pools along the cracked pavement, and the hush between them stretched taut, thrumming with heat, guilt, and the ache of what neither could name.

Kael broke the quiet first. "You don't trust easily."

Her gaze flicked up. "Should I?"

"No." His mouth twitched, a fleeting tension that almost softened into regret before he caught it. "But you keep showing up."

"I could say the same about you."

He stopped, and she mirrored his pause. They stood in the hush of an empty street, orbiting each other with undeniable gravity. His eyes searched hers as if trying to decipher a language only he understood.

Then slowly, he reached out, his fingers brushing her jaw.

The touch was gentle and deliberate as if asking for permission. She didn't flinch. Her shadows stirred, curling behind her like smoke, but they didn't rise. They waited.

"I should walk away," he said, his voice low. "This—whatever this is—is dangerous."

Sera tilted her head, her mouth curving into something between a challenge and an invitation. "Then go."

He didn't.

She stepped closer, her hand finding the front of his shirt. It wasn't a pull, merely an anchoring. She leaned in, just enough to make her choice clear, and he met her halfway.

The kiss began soft, but it quickly deepened. His hand slid to the back of her neck, the other gripping her waist as if he was holding onto a precarious ledge. Her fingers fisted his shirt and dragged slightly, her nails catching on the buttons.

It was more than just a kiss. It was a collision. It was the universe sighing in relief as two celestial bodies found their way to their inevitable alignment.

His wings threatened to unfurl, ghosting beneath his skin as if the light inside him could no longer bear to stay caged. The light within her pulled at the shard of grace he'd thought long dead, waking a warmth that ached like longing and memory intertwined.

She broke the kiss first, her breath trembling against his mouth.

Their universe had shifted now. And neither of them could stop it.

The Uber ride dropped Sera off a block from her townhome, the familiar lamplight casting gentle halos over a cobblestone street. Yet the moment the car pulled away, a cold prickling slid down her spine.

She could've asked Kael for a ride, but that would've meant needing him. And tonight, she needed to remember how to stand alone, even if it hurt.

But she wasn't alone. The feeling had haunted her throughout the evening, but now, it grew stronger and colder. It wasn't lust or curiosity. It was more ancient. It waited, not through footsteps but with presence.

Shadows of movement flickered at the corners of her vision. The wind almost seemed to whisper in syllables, and she sensed that someone—or something—was watching her once more.

She quickened her pace, her chin raised and her boots tapping in brisk defiance. Her shadow flickered unnaturally in the lamplight, stretching too long and twisting with intent.

They see us, came a whisper from within.

They are after us...

"Silence," she hissed under her breath.

Hunger had returned with cruel teeth. Her stomach knotted, and her skin flushed cold and then feverish. Her limbs ached, and her vision blurred at the edges.

Her shadows laughed. *You cannot hold us back forever. We are starving.*

She stumbled but caught herself against the brick wall of a quaint boutique now closed for the night. A young couple passed, their laughter faltering as they noticed her. They clutched each other tight and crossed to the opposite sidewalk.

See how they fear you now? the voices cooed. *When your mask cracks...*

"No," she whispered. "Not tonight."

But her body betrayed her again—her knees trembling, her pulse beating too fast, and her mouth dry with need. She needed to feed. Properly. Not from vials or from Kael's offered scraps.

Let us taste, her shadows begged. *Do we follow?*

Each step felt heavier, even with her townhome just a block ahead. The moonlight no longer comforted her. Every flickering lamp overhead buzzed with oppressive scrutiny. Her hunger was no longer an echo. It was a *scream*.

"I said no!" she snapped.

A passing jogger gave her a wide berth, their eyes wide with alarm.

Shaking, she was half doubled over when she reached her doorstep. Her hand trembled as she unlocked the door. Inside, the silence was cathedral-like. She closed the door with a soft click and leaned her forehead against it.

Her shadows snaked around her feet, furious and sulking.

Just a little longer. She just needed to hold out a little longer.

A Necessary Evil

11

Sleep was a forgotten luxury for Kael, a memory preserved in amber. He hadn't truly rested in centuries—not since grace was something he could hold without flinching, not since the heavens he had bled for had turned their faces and called it justice. Now, only stillness, silence, and the relentless echo of Sera's name remained.

It wasn't just a name anymore. It was a reckoning.

The celestial war had roared for eons, and then, without warning, it had paused. It was as if some divine breath had gotten caught in Heaven's throat, leaving two hundred years of eerie silence. It was never peace, but a stillness that stretched too long, right around the time Sera was born.

Kael paced the worn wooden floor of his apartment, barefoot and restless. Each step echoed like a metronome counting down to something he couldn't name. Still, his mind kept returning to her kiss. It hadn't been gentle or soft. It had been like being struck by lightning infused with sorrow. Her mouth had met his with the force of recognition, and for a moment, he had felt it like a memory buried in his core. He had felt her blood recognizing his.

The order of her outcast had come from Michael himself, delivered in person because cowards liked to dress their filth in the clothing of friendship. "She's gone too far," he had said, his voice perfectly measured. "She's consorting. Building. Conceiving." He hadn't specified with whom, why, or what. Just gave one final command. "End her."

Kael had never questioned it. He had been Heaven's sword, forged in obedience and sharpened by silence. But doubt had already seeded itself.

When he had found Lilith in the Crimson Keep, she wasn't preparing for war, cloaked in blood and rebellion. She stood robed in ember and moonlight, her belly heavy with life. Beside her stood a little girl with golden hair and solemn eyes. Cassia.

Lilith had smiled at him—no wickedness or seduction, but weariness. "He sent you," she said. "Of course he did."

Kael raised his blade, the weight of it trembling in his hands.

She had simply placed a hand over her stomach and whispered, "You don't kill what you were made to understand."

He hadn't known what her words had meant then. But he did now.

He had let her live. He had let them all live. And in doing so, he had signed his exile.

And then she had taken it out on Lucifer—the morning star, the king of Hell, and Michael's brother in brilliance and burden. Gone. Not dead—that wasn't possible for someone like him—but missing and locked in magical stasis.

She had driven a dagger through his heart. Not to protect the realm and or to deliberately seize the throne but out of spite. Kael still could not quite understand why she did it, maybe because he looked too much like Michael. Maybe he reminded her of who she'd fallen for and she took the next best thing to revenge: she made herself queen of Hell, and no one dared to challenge her. And she ruled Hell the way storms ruled oceans: by nature, not decree.

Even Kael, who had no interest in Hell's politics, could sense a brewing under her rule. And now, centuries later, the price of that mercy itched beneath his skin.

Jareth had been the one they had sent to collect the price. An old friend, a blood-bound brother, and the only angel who still wore his grace like it might crack at any moment. "I'm sorry," he had said, standing over Kael in the ruins of a monastery.

Kael was on his knees. He never ran.

The blade Jareth held glowed like the edge of dawn. It was supposed to be the Blade of Mercy, the tribunal's severance tool. The blade that burned wings from bones. But Kael had felt the wrongness of it even before it struck. The pain had been real and unholy, white-hot fire licking down his spine. But it didn't sever. It scarred. Because Jareth had brought a false blade, a mimic. He'd spared Kael the shame and agony.

After the strike, Kael's wings had withered, folded in, and shrunken like forgotten limbs. But over time, they'd returned. He kept them hidden beneath glamour and layers of control, but since Sera's kiss, since her aura brushed his own, they'd begun to stir again. He felt them now, pressing against his skin like prisoners demanding release. The urge to let them out and fly was almost unbearable, and unable to resist the constant pressure, he let the glamour fall.

With a shuddering gasp from him, his wings tore free, ripping through the illusion of his body. They weren't the pure white wings of angels nor the black and leathery expanse of demons. Instead, they were a stark ash gray, each feather tipped with sharp, leathery black points. Static electricity visibly crackled across their span. He didn't understand why they had returned this way. Perhaps it was a byproduct of the botched severance, or fate had reshaped them.

He touched one, wincing. They weren't right. They weren't holy. They weren't damned.

If anyone saw them, he was dead. Not just him. Jareth too. If the tribunal learned the truth, they would punish them both with flames and decrees.

He stood in front of the window. The city was sprawled below like a network of glowing veins, and somewhere in that mess of rooftops and neon, Sera walked. Breathed. Hungered. He wondered if she could feel it too. The rhythm. The pull. The unraveling. Lucifer's stasis. Lilith's throne. The war's pause. Her birth. None of this was a coincidence.

This was designed.

Whatever was coming, it had Sera's name written into its bones. He pressed his palm flat to the windowpane, and his eyes narrowed. Was she the reason the war stopped? Or was she the reason it would begin again? That thought crawled down his spine like ice.

He wasn't ready. But he would be. He had to be. Because if Hell was waiting? So was he.

Sera couldn't sleep. The ceiling fan cast slow, hypnotic shadows across her room. When her phone buzzed, the sound slipped through the stillness like a spark. The shadows on the walls twitched, drawn to the pulse of her phone as if it was a heartbeat they recognized. They always did that when it was Kael on the other end; they stirred like creatures recognizing his force.

"Couldn't sleep either?" she asked, her voice thick with exhaustion.

The answering sound wasn't just a voice. It was a vibration that crawled through her ear and settled in her bones, low and warm and alive. It shouldn't have been possible to feel someone through a line, but with him, everything felt too possible.

"Not with you echoing in my head," Kael murmured.

The words brushed over her skin like a breath. Her pulse jumped, and a small, dangerous smile curved her lips. "Oh? And what exactly did you hear?"

Her shadows, those traitorous things, slid off the walls and ceiling, slowly crawling toward her and the voice on the other end of the line.

"The sound you made when I kissed you," he said. His tone was different now—rough, unguarded. "The one you tried to swallow."

Her breath caught. Memory hit like heat: his mouth, the taste of his breath, and the way she'd tried and failed to hide the sound that had slipped out.

"The taste of you," he added, quieter, heavier. "I've been craving it ever since."

The confession landed low in her stomach, blooming heat that made her thighs press together. The room felt smaller, the air thicker.

"I need to hear you," he said. "When you're not holding back."

The words left her trembling. Her hand drifted beneath the silk of her nightgown before she could stop it. Her skin was damp, her breath uneven.

And the shadows responded.

They shivered, bending closer around her body and rippling across the sheets in time with her heartbeat.

"Tell me more," she whispered.

A low groan filled her ear, a sound that made her heart trip. "You're cruel," he rasped.

Her smile deepened. "Are you lying there in the dark, imagining this?"

His chuckle came like gravel and smoke. "No. I've got my hand around my cock, thinking about you on your knees. Your eyes on me. Waiting."

A shiver tore through her. Her shadows gently wisped over the skin of her calves, climbing higher up her thighs as if pinning her in place for *him*. Her back arched, her fingers slid lower.

"Sera..." His voice cracked over her name, rough and reverent.

"Yes...?"

"I want to taste you," he said. "Just my tongue—lightly—until you start shaking. Can you feel it?"

She could. Every nerve reached for it. Her hips moved, desperate.

"Are you wet for me?"

"Yes," she breathed. "Thinking about your mouth."

"Good girl. Now my fingers—two of them—slow, letting you stretch around them."

Her body obeyed before her mind did. She moved with his voice, guided by the rhythm he set up, as she drove her own two fingers slowly in and out. "Kael..."

"Say it again," he hummed in response.

"Kael."

He groaned, and the sound alone unraveled her—low, broken, and unbearably human. It vibrated through the receiver and down her spine. She felt it as a pulse between her legs, as warmth flooding outward until her breath became a tremor.

"Tell me, Sera," his voice rasped, half command, half plea. "How do you like it? Slow? Hard? What makes you lose control?"

Her throat worked around the words. "When they take their time," she whispered. "When their mouth lingers. When they look at me like they already know I'll break."

Kael exhaled, the sound dark and reverent. "And what don't you like?"

"Pretending," she breathed. "I don't like pretending. I don't want it."

The silence that followed was heavy, electric. Then his voice came again, softer and filthier. "Then stop pretending."

Her hand obeyed before the thought could catch up. Every word he spoke painted itself across her skin: the slide of a tongue, the curl of her fingers, the deliberate rhythm that built her higher with each breath. She could almost feel him there—his breath on her neck, the weight of his body, the warmth of his mouth trailing down until she forgot where she ended and the sound of him began.

"Like that?" he asked roughly.

"Yes," she gasped, her voice breaking into the pillow.

"Good. Stay right there, beautiful. Let me hear you."

His voice guided her—slow, coaxing, and then rough again—as he described what he'd do if he were there: how he'd pin her hips, how he'd taste her until her name stopped making sense. The rhythm in her hand matched his words until there was no space between command and surrender. The darkness trembled with her, echoing every shudder, until the room itself seemed to breathe his name.

"Come for me, Sera," he whispered, and her body and shadows obeyed.

Dark wisps slid up her body and wrapped around her throat gently, not to suffocate but to add more sensation. The release tore through her in shuddering waves, bright and brutal. Her cry filled the room, sharp enough to make her chest ache.

The line hummed against her ear, his voice low and measured. Each word was a pulse beneath her skin. The air thickened, and her shadows swayed in time with the sound, rising from the corners as if scenting her hesitation.

She wasn't sure which ached more: the hunger in her body or the pull of that darkness answering his call. The more she tried to steady her breathing, the more the shadows pressed close, brushing the outline of her legs like smoke. It wasn't touch; it was recognition. Her power knew him.

For a heartbeat, she couldn't tell where the pleasure ended and the power began. The shadows clung to her like a second pulse, echoing every ragged breath she took. It felt holy and wrong all at once, her body answering his voice and her darkness answering something older. When the tremor calmed, guilt threaded through the heat. She had promised herself control, yet every time he spoke, the promise broke a little more.

When his tone softened, she did. The shadows withdrew, slow and deliberate, leaving gooseflesh in their wake. On the other end of the line, his breathing quickened—rough, uneven, and breaking into silence—until only the pulse of him remained, distant yet tangible as if the space between them had burned away. She wished she could be there in his darkness, to witness his undoing because of *her*.

"You're a dangerous creature, Seraphine," he murmured, his voice threadbare with satisfaction.

A lazy smile curved her lips. "Takes one to know one, Angel."

His laugh was rough and breathy. "Sleep well. If you can."

"I doubt it."

"Good," he whispered.

The line went dead.

Take It

12

The sleek, modern lines of InnovoTech were a monument to glass and polished steel, but to Sera, it now felt like a gilded cage, a harsh counterpoint to the shadowed streets of Savannah. Today, however, the office vibrated with an electric energy, echoing the restless tension that had ignited within her.

Impeccably dressed in a charcoal pantsuit, Sera moved like a shadow wrapped in silk. Her heels clicked across the polished floors, and wherever she went, heads turned. Not because of her beauty, though that was undeniable, but because of the way the air seemed to shift around her. The attention followed her like a tide. Her role as head of product development afforded her both power and cover, allowing her to interact and siphon from others under the guise of an ordinary human connection.

She never meant to drain them. A brush of the hand here and a lingering glance there, and she could feel their energy bleed into her skin. It took the edge off. Barely. But since Kael, since their kiss, that ache had grown. Where once she could survive on stolen glances and shared laughter, she now needed more. Craved it. And it was starting to hurt.

The pain started behind her eyes, a slow throb like a warning. Her limbs were leaden. Her mouth was dry. And her shadows, once content to curl around her like loyal pets, were growing restless. She felt them now, shifting beneath the surface of her skin and whispering cruel truths.

Do something!

She clenched her jaw and forced a smile for the intern who passed her in the hallway. The intern's steps faltered; she looked pale.

Inside Sera's office, the air was cool and clinical. She shut the door, leaned against it, and took a steadying breath. Her phone buzzed.

Kael: Last night was…intense.

She smiled, despite herself.

Sera: That's one word for it.

Kael: Better yet, intoxicating.

Sera: Don't get ahead of yourself, Angel. It was just phone sex.

Kael: Was it just phone sex to you?

Her fingers hovered over the screen as she savored the tension and then sent a wink.

Kael: Can't wait to experience it live.

Her breath hitched, and the shadows inside her twisted with glee.

Sera: You're walking a dangerous line, Kael.

Kael: Nah. I already crossed it.

Kael: Last night…hearing your voice calling my name. It was the first time in a century that I didn't feel alone.

Her fingers hovered over the screen. The admission was so raw, so unguarded that it disarmed her. The queen in her should have seen it as a weakness to exploit. Instead, an older part of her—the woman who had once knelt in the mud beside her sister—felt a sharp, aching pang of recognition. She quickly typed a reply, a shield of wit against a feeling too dangerously close to tenderness.

Sera: Careful, Angel. Keep talking like that, and you might actually get what you want.

Kael: Always.

A sharp rap on the door fractured her calm. She blinked and turned, and her stomach clenched. Mark. He looked disheveled, overtly eager and still clinging to the faded threads of their past. His smile faltered as her indifferent expression must've registered, but he pushed forward, nonetheless.

"Hey, gorgeous." He smiled.

"What are you doing here, Mark?" she replied coolly.

"I thought maybe…we could catch up. Lunch?"

She hesitated, every fiber of her being screaming a resounding no. Yet her body ached, her joints burned, and her mouth felt like dust. And Mark? He had always been simple. Kind. An open well of optimism.

"It's a little early for lunch," she said. "But be quick."

At a bustling café, Sera barely touched her meal as he droned on about golf, his demanding job, and other mundane trivialities. She observed him. When his hand brushed hers across the table, her focus narrowed with predatory precision. It was like a key turning in a lock, opening a hidden wellspring inside her chest. She took a measured breath and subtly leaned in, just enough to draw him nearer. Her gaze softened, and her voice dropped to a low, intimate tone. She made him feel uniquely seen, utterly cherished. That was a crucial step.

Just take it… her shadows crooned quietly.

While Mark prattled on, her proper attention turned inward. She reached out, not with her physical hand but through the shimmering threads of energy that invisibly still linked them. She gently pulled almost reverently, a master artist drawing from a delicate palette. His energy seeped into her like a comforting warmth spreading through chilled limbs. Golden, fragile light extracted slowly and tenderly. Her movements were minimal: a feather-light touch of her fingers over his wrist, a smile that lingered a fraction too long.

He blinked, a beat behind. His pupils dilated. "I miss you," he confessed, a raw whisper.

Her smile was soft, a carefully practiced art. "I know."

"Do you think, maybe, we could try again?"

She let her hand rest over his, her thumb tracing lazy circles on his skin. She fed on his unwavering devotion, his desperate want, and the gaping wound of his longing. The shadows inside her cooed with purring satisfaction.

"I remember the gala," she murmured, her voice a silken invitation. "You told me I was unforgettable."

"You were," he breathed.

A little more. Just enough. She closed her eyes for a fleeting moment, the borrowed energy warming her blood and softening the sharp edges of her pain. But it didn't last. Her hunger was too vast now. What once sustained her for days now burned away in mere minutes.

Mark slightly swayed in his seat, blinking as if roused from a deep, pleasant dream. She eased back, releasing him with deliberate gentleness. No lasting harm. Just a quiet siphoning of what he freely gave.

"I can't give you what you need, Mark," she said softly, her voice laced with a counterfeit regret.

He opened his mouth, a protest half forming.

But she rose and moved away, graceful and unreadable. "I meant what I said. I can't." She paused at the table and then tilted her head, allowing just a sliver of manufactured vulnerability to crack her polished facade. "Maybe I'll call you. Soon."

That single word, *maybe*, was a dagger dressed in velvet.

As she turned and walked back toward the office, her shadows followed, purring with dark contentment. But she only felt hollow shame. This was not a hunt. It was a pathetic, desperate fix. She had used a memory of love like a common drug, a crude tool for a need that was growing too fast. She hadn't been a queen commanding an asset; she had been an addict, and she hated the weakness of it more than the act itself.

She felt the subtle shift. It felt deep within her core, a chilling metamorphosis, a ripple in the fabric of reality, but that ripple originated from her. This was how it began: the slow rot beneath the surface, the darkness stretching its insidious fingers outward. And she was becoming its willing conduit. One drop at a time. One soul at a time. Her unraveling wasn't just her own. It was a deliberate, calculated reconstruction. The world would soon feel her pervasive influence.

Afternoon clawed at Sera like a ravenous thing. There was no peace in waking. No soft drift from sleep to wakefulness. Her body ached, each joint stiff as though her bones were turning to stone from the inside out. Not just Kael's kiss lingered in her veins, but the restraint she had forced herself to uphold. No feeding. No true release. Just the aching echo of his mouth on hers and the energy she dared not to take.

She left InnovoTech to walk the streets of the Historic District. The air, thick with humidity and the summer heat, clung to her skin. The wrought-iron gates and winding cobblestones shimmered in the haze, casting long, twisting shadows that seemed to whisper her name.

Her hunger made everything raw. The honeysuckle and sweat scent of a passing couple made her stomach clench. The warm energy of a violinist on the square drew her attention, the music vibrating in her sternum. She found herself watching people. All of them strangers and all of them were vessels now, sources. And that thought terrified her.

The shadows danced at her periphery, always speaking. *Take a little. No one will know. They want to give. Make them.*

A teenager bumped into her by accident and murmured an apology. She felt a thread of energy unspool from his chest, and she jerked back before it could tether.

This is what we are, the shadows said. *We drain. We take. And we love it.*

Exhaustion settled on Sera like a physical weight as she finally reached her townhome. The familiar architecture offered no comfort, only a silent judgment. She fumbled with the lock, her fingers clumsy and the effort draining the last of her strength. The moment the door clicked shut behind her, she slid down the cool wall, dropping her head into her hands.

Her breathing hitched. A ragged, silent sob escaped her lips as she pressed her palms hard against her burning eyes. "Please," she whispered to the quiet room, a plea to the suffocating silence. "Just stop."

As her vision slowly cleared, the oppressive weight of the moment receded, replaced by a fresh prickle of unease. At the base of the door, stark against the dark wood, lay a single crisp white envelope. It was thick, heavier than a standard letter, and the paper had a faint, almost imperceptible shimmer. No stamp. No address. Just her name written in elegant calligraphy: Seraphine.

A cold dread seeped into her bones. She didn't need to touch it to know it was from Heaven. The air around it felt sterile, devoid of warmth and humming with a chilling authority. Her hands trembled as she picked it up.

Inside, the parchment was unnervingly heavy, cool to the touch. The script was formal, etched in a stark, unyielding black that seemed to absorb the light.

TRIBUNAL EDICT 1014-H

IN RE: THE CONDUCT OF SERAPHINE, DAUGHTER OF THE FALLEN.

BE IT KNOWN, by the Celestial Tribunal, whose judgment is absolute and final, that continuous observation of your movements in the mortal realm has revealed repeated and egregious violations of your sentence. Your mandated detachment from supernatural entanglements and interactions with celestial or infernal kin has been disregarded.

Your proximity to entities of compromised grace, and more specifically to the fallen angel designated as Kael, is a direct contravention of Tribunal Writ 564, which explicitly prohibits consort or congress with such beings.

Let this serve as a singular, unequivocal reinsurance of the terms of your exile as recorded in the Book of Echoes.

You are hereby commanded to sever all unsanctioned ties and to cease all interactions that defy the established order. Further transgressions or any attempt to intertwine your essence with those of supernatural origin shall be met with immediate and irrevocable action. Should you continue to disregard these immutable laws, a complete reevaluation of your sentence, culminating in a trial of final judgment, will be convened.

The consequences will be absolute. There will be no mercy. There will be no return.

BY AUTHORITY of the Celestial Tribunal,
Malakar, High Justiciar of the Celestial Tribunal
OBSERVED AND RECORDED by: Watcher 03

The words were cold, sterile, and infuriating. It wasn't the threat of a final judgment that made her blood boil. It was the sheer, suffocating arrogance of it. After a century of exile, of carving out a kingdom for herself in this mortal mire, they still thought they could leash her. They still saw her as a broken being to be managed, not a sovereign to be respected.

Her hands clenched, crumpling the parchment. They didn't fear her consorting with Kael. They feared an alliance. They feared power they could not control.

Angel's Daughter

13

Savannah lay sprawled beneath the office window, the view a turbulent tapestry of history clashing with modernity. Though Sera's eyes traced the sprawling cityscape, her mind was still trapped in half a century ago, mired in the shattered remnants of her last encounter with her sister Cassia.

After seventy-five years of exile, trying to come to terms with their monstrous new realities, they had found each other in post-war Paris. Cassia had found a purpose in the underworld, dealing in shadowy bargains and whispered secrets. Sera had tried to stay close to humanity—to art, music, and fleeting pleasures. But for a time, they were inseparable, bonded not only by blood but also by their shared experience of survival.

And then came Berlin. Sera had used men too deeply, too hungrily to feed. Their souls became too fractured to find peace. Cassia had seen one. She hadn't spoken a word, just looked at Sera with horror from across a war-torn cobblestone street. And that had been enough.

The silence that followed had stretched into five decades. Until now.

The office door creaked open, and her sister stepped in—a

silhouette bathed in overpowering sunlight that sharpened into terrifying clarity as she moved closer. Not just as a figure from the past but as a living, formidable presence. A hardened soul, the careless spirit of youth now replaced by a relentless weariness and an unyielding tension etched into her jaw.

Her long blonde hair was pulled into a high ponytail. She wore black leather, an outfit that spoke of practicality and…ruthlessness.

"Cassia," Sera whispered, the word a plea and a question. She stepped forward, her arms reaching out.

Cassia hesitated, her gaze flickering with uncertainty, but then softened. She met Sera's embrace. Brief. Awkward. But…real. A fragile but undeniable connection.

"It's good to see you alive," Cassia murmured, her voice husky.

"You too, Cassie," Sera replied, using her old nickname. She gestured to the leather couch. "Sit. Please."

They both rested as silence grew thick with unspoken words. Sera saw the changes. The lines around Cassia's brown eyes, the hardening of her jaw. This was a warrior, a survivor.

"How have you been?" Sera asked.

Cassia shrugged. Bitterness tinged her voice. "Surviving. Exile has its…challenges."

"I know." Her gaze dropped. "I…I'm sorry, Cassia. For everything."

Cassia's voice was sharper now. "But it doesn't change anything."

She flinched. "I know," she whispered. "And I'll spend eternity regretting it."

"Regret? Regret doesn't bring back those people. Paris, Berlin…"

She flinched once more, a barely perceptible tremor running through her shoulders. The ghost of a wound Cassia had salted just by showing up. "What have we become, Cassia? Monsters? Is that what you think?

Because I refuse to believe that. I may be a succubus. I may need to…feed…to survive, but I still have a choice! I can still choose who I am, how I live!"

"Can you?" Cassia's eyes narrowed. "Can you really, Sera? I saw Mark. What have you done to him? Was that his *choice*?"

The words hit her like a physical blow. Her hands were clenched into white-knuckled fists at her sides. Her posture rigid, she turned away from her sister to face the vast office window. She stared out at the sprawling city. "That's…different." The words were weak, unconvincing.

"Is it?" Cassia said, her voice low and relentless. Even sitting still, she radiated judgment, cold and precise. "He's a shell of the man he once was, Sera. Empty. Hollow. He's addicted to you, to the fleeting moments of…whatever it is you give him. And you…you keep taking. You're draining him dry."

Sera spun back around, her eyes blazing with a desperate, cornered fury. "And what would you have me do, Cassia? Starve? Let my hunger consume me until I become the monster you always feared I was? I am *managing* it. I only took what he offered."

She turned away again, unable to meet her sister's accusing gaze. She knew Cassia was right. She'd seen the changes in Mark too, the emptiness that had replaced his former vitality. She'd told herself it was his choice, that he was a willing participant, but deep down, she knew she was exploiting him, using him to satisfy a need that could never truly be quenched. A need that Kael, with his dangerous allure and perceptive gaze, had only intensified.

"I'm trying, Cassia," she said, her voice low. "I'm trying to find a way to live with what I am."

A long silence stretched between them.

"Sera," Cassia said, "I...I heard something."

Sera's heart clenched. "What?"

"I heard...Father is looking for you."

She felt a chill as the words hung in the air. "Father?" she whispered. "Why?"

Cassia shook her head. "I don't know. But it's not good."

The silence between them stretched, heavy with all the things she couldn't justify. The truth pressed against her ribs until it escaped. "I've met someone..." Her voice trembled. "Someone...different."

Cassia's eyes narrowed. "Different...how?"

She stood, turned slowly, and crossed the room. Her footsteps were soft and hesitant. She reached into the drawer of her desk and pulled out a folded parchment, thick and stamped with the tribunal's wax seal. For a moment, she held it in her hands, staring at the decree as if hoping the words would change into something more forgiving. She then sighed long, walked back, and pressed the letter into Cassia's waiting hands.

Cassia unfolded it quickly and then scanned the lines. As she read, color drained from her face. When she finally looked up, her expression had hardened into something colder than concern, closer to fear.

Sera looked away. "He is a fallen," she whispered.

Her gaze fixed on her. "Sera," she said, her voice laced with concern, "you need to be careful. You know the dangers."

Sera nodded, her heart heavy. "I know," she replied, but the words felt hollow, even to her ears. Another silence fell. "Do you think that is why Father is looking for me?"

She shrugged, but the faintest curve at the corner of her mouth betrayed her. It wasn't a surprise in her eyes. It was recognition. She already knew the reason.

"Stay with me while you're in town. Please. It's been too long. And...and I could use your help. Figuring out what they want." It was a half-truth. Sera did need her help, but more than that, she needed her presence, if only to help the shadows stop talking.

Cassia's eyes widened slightly. "Are you sure?" she asked. "I don't want to intrude."

"Don't be ridiculous." Sera forced a lightness into her voice. "You're my sister. The guest room is always ready. Besides"—a flicker of her old, mischievous self returned, a desperate attempt at normalcy—"it'll be fun. We can...strategize. Together."

A small smile touched her lips. "All right. I'll stay. But only if you promise to keep me out of your troubles."

Sera laughed, but the sound was hollow. "No promises." A dark glint held in her emerald gaze.

Trouble, after all, was her specialty. And she had a strong feeling that trouble was exactly what was coming. And this time, she wasn't sure she could control it. Or if she wanted to.

The guest room in Sera's townhouse was a study in lavish, carefully curated chaos. A massive antique four-poster bed, draped in swathes of white linen and silk, dominated the space. Cassia, perched on the edge of the mattress with an open but unread book of ancient poetry in her lap, watched the sunlight filter in through the sheer curtains. It illuminated the dust mites dancing in the air and highlighted the tension etched on her face.

"I still can't believe you live like this," Cassia said, her voice a low murmur that barely disturbed the quiet. "All this...excess."

Sera, sprawled on a chaise lounge by the window and massaging her wrists, chuckled, a sound that lacked genuine amusement. "Excess? A succubus has to maintain certain standards, you know." She gestured around the room, her sweeping motion encompassing the velvet drapes, the ornate mirrors, and the carefully arranged collection of antique objects. "Besides, it's all part of the performance. The persona."

We are growing weak...

The shadows had begun to slither from the corners of her vision, oily tendrils curling beneath the furniture and whispering just below the threshold of understanding. Her temples throbbed with their incessant murmurs.

Cassia raised a skeptical eyebrow. "The persona of a wealthy, slightly decadent socialite? You're not exactly trying to be inconspicuous, are you?"

"Subtlety is vastly overrated," Sera retorted with a playful glint in her eyes, a momentary flicker of her old self. "And let's be honest: Playing the role is half the fun. Besides, it's far more pleasant than those damp, depressing caves you seem to favor."

She shuddered, a theatrical gesture. "Don't remind me. I miss the quiet though. This humidity is a disaster for my complexion."

Sera chuckled, a genuine, lighthearted sound that echoed through the room. It felt...good. To laugh with her sister, to share a moment of normalcy.

But as Cassia continued to reminisce, Sera's attention drifted. It was becoming hard for her to concentrate. The shadows had multiplied, stretching long and thin across the floor. Her gaze fell on her phone, which was lying on a nearby table. A new message notification. Kael.

With a muttered excuse, she slipped out onto the balcony and closed the French doors behind her. The Savannah air was thick with heat, the scent of jasmine and honeysuckle almost cloying. Every sound—the buzz of traffic, the creak of iron balconies, and the hush of distant conversations—scraped against her heightened senses.

She unlocked her phone, her heart thudding faster.

Kael: Thinking about you.

A slow smile curved her lips, but it felt foreign.

Sera: Are you?

Kael: Can't wait to see you again.

Sera: Soon.

Kael: Tonight?

She hesitated. Cassia was here. Her joints screamed, her vision blurred at the edges, and the gnawing hunger inside her had grown sharp and long claws.

Sera: I can't tonight. My sister is in town. Maybe tomorrow.

Kael: I'll hold you to that.

Sera: Yep.

She pressed send, her thumb trembling. A shiver danced down her spine like a breath of doom brushing her neck. She was unraveling, and there was no time to save her. She headed back inside.

Near the bed, Cassia stood frozen. Her posture was taut, and her eyes were sharp. "Who were you talking to?"

"Just a…friend." The lie was a pebble in her throat.

Her lip curled slightly. "That's the guy…"

Sera flushed deeper. "It's nothing, Cassie. Just…harmless flirtation."

She didn't move. "Sera, they are going to kill you."

"I know what I'm doing," Sera snapped. But even she didn't believe it.

As the day wore on, Sera began to feel herself fraying. Her vision wavered. Her skin itched. Her limbs ached with a fever that settled deep in her bones. She couldn't focus. Couldn't think. And the world narrowed to a single, ravenous point: need.

"You are right," she told her sister. "I think...I think I'm in trouble. I like him. Too much. And these shadows...they won't stop. They're louder every time I see him."

Cassia's eyes darkened. "Your connection with him is destabilizing you? You're not just hungry, Sera. You're *starving*. And that usually makes you reckless."

She clutched her arms. Her skin was hot. Her nails had begun to darken, curving slightly. "I already lost it, Cassie."

She lifted her hands. The darkening claws were an indictment of her failure. This was it. The very thing she had divorced Mark to prevent. The same loss of discipline that had driven Cassia away in Berlin.

The shadows hissed their approval, reveling in her loss of control, but all she felt was a cold, sickening wave of self-loathing. She was a queen whose own body was staging a coup, and the shame of it was more painful than the hunger itself.

"You need to feed," Cassia said.

"I-it won't help." Her voice cracked with audible demonic possession. "Not unless it's...flesh."

The shadows hissed their approval. *Flesh... Golden light, warm hearts...*

"Mark," she whispered. The name tasted like rust.

Cassia paled. "Sera... No."

"I don't have a choice."

"You do."

"MOVE!"

Sera's form shifted with a burst of heat. Her skin shimmered and then dimmed, revealing clawed hands and the faint silhouette of horns pressing through her raven hair. Her eyes burned, not green but a deep hellish red—alive with hunger that didn't belong to anything human.

Cassia stepped between her and the door. Shadows coiled at her back, sharp and deliberate and gathering like smoke under pressure. Her horns caught the low light, and her gaze was all warning. "Don't make me fight you."

"I don't want to fight," Sera hissed, her fangs catching the faint glow of the room.

Cassia lunged first. Her hands trailed black smoke, each motion cutting through the air like a blade. Sera caught her by the forearm midswing, the collision rippling outward in a shockwave of shadow meeting shadow. For a heartbeat, they were locked, mirror images in opposition. Two fallen beings straining against the other's darkness.

Sera twisted, using Cassia's momentum to drive her sideways. They slammed into the velvet couch, cushions scattering, but the frame held firm. Dust lifted in a slow spiral around them, catching the edges of their shadows, as they writhed across the walls.

Cassia tore free, her own power flaring cold and violent. A pulse of force struck Sera in the chest, throwing her backward. She hit the wall hard enough to split the plaster, cracks radiating outward in a jagged halo around her silhouette. The house groaned as the impact settled, dust falling like pale ash.

Sera pushed herself upright, her breath ragged. The red in her eyes flickered. The shadows were bleeding off her skin in tendrils coiled around her legs.

"You're not yourself!" Cassia shouted.

"I am exactly what I am!" her voice thundered back, layered with the echo of her shadows.

The air between them vibrated, thick with residual power. Curtains quivered, glass shards from the broken mirror glittered across the floor, and the walls hummed faintly as the cracks cooled.

Cassia stood frozen, her chest rising and falling and her hands trembling from the restraint.

Sera turned toward the exit door, the darkness parting for her. Another moment, she was gone.

DEVOUR
14

The shadows' command echoed in Sera's skull. *Feed or fall.*

Her hands trembled. Kael. That thought was a spark of warmth in the encroaching ice. He would help. But her pride, that jagged crown she still wore, recoiled. To go to him like this—a starving, broken thing—was unthinkable. She'd be a queen begging for scraps from a rival monarch.

No. Mark was…simpler. A known quantity. A resource she had managed before. It was a monstrous, cruel calculation, and she despised herself for making it. But a queen must survive, even if it meant becoming the monster she feared.

Mark's voice on the other end was instant. Warm. Too eager. "Sera? You called."

"I need to see you. Kehoe House. Room 319. Thirty minutes."

He hesitated. But only for a breath. "I… Yeah. Yeah, I'll be there."

She ended the call, the sound like a trigger being pulled. Her horns retracted, and her skin returned to its luminous porcelain sheen, but the shadows throbbed beneath her surface, demanding their release. Her pupils were still too wide. Her mouth ached with hunger.

The drive to Kehoe was a blur of crimson taillights and wet pavements. Thunderheads loomed, low and oppressive. She barely remembered the road, only the hiss of tires and the rhythmic slap of the windshield wipers.

Kehoe House was an old wound that never sealed.

The house remembered its own. Every succubus of stature held a contract here, a gilded cage with a key forged in infernal fire. Hers was Room 319. A chamber of velvet and mirrors, its air clotted with jasmine and ghosts. This was a place carved for appetites, not for healing.

She did not knock. The clerk at the desk looked through her, his gaze sliding away as if she was made of smoke and sin. She walked the halls, each step a silent tap against the lacquered floors. A vicious itch bloomed across her skin, and her breath snagged in her throat. Her own shadow writhed at her ankles, a hungry dog scenting blood. The key, cold and familiar, slid into the lock of Room 319 like a bone snapping back into place. When she pushed the door open, the room exhaled a breath she remembered.

Nothing had changed.

The walls were still a deep, bruised crimson, their velvet panels drinking the light and carved with sigils that magnified lust and smothered conscience. The air, heavy as a shroud, tasted of perfume and a thousand sweat-slicked memories. The mirrors caught her image and passed it back and forth between them. They reflected a woman she barely knew—a pale wraith with limbs too long in the dim light.

She stood in the center of the floor and let the darkness crawl up her legs like a tide, like the touch of forgotten lovers. This room had never judged her. It had worshipped her darkness. Here, she had been a creature in absolute command, orchestrating the rise and fall of mortal desire. Here, shame was a foreign language. But tonight, it felt different.

Like a tomb. A monument to the control she no longer possessed.

The knock on the door was soft. Unsure.

Mark.

She did not answer since the lock was undone. She turned her back to the door, a statue of waiting need.

His footsteps faltered at the threshold, the hesitation of a good man entering a place that was not holy. His breath hitched when he saw her.

"Sera," he whispered, her name breaking on his lips. "You're here."

He crossed the room, his presence a warmth. His hands, gentle and searching, found her waist. She did not flinch. She did not lean into him. He kissed the curve of her shoulder, and she let her eyes drift shut.

"I was worried. I didn't know if I should come."

She did not answer. Her body did.

The room was already at work, its spell woven into the very air. It amplified her scent, the buzzing aura of her need. The charged atmosphere grew thick, wrapping around him. The mirrors caught the predatory glint in her eyes and flung it back and forth, again and again, until reality began to fray at the edges.

She turned and crushed her mouth to his. There was no gentleness in it.

His lips parted in surprise, and she tasted his love, his trust, and every pure thing she was about to spoil. He gasped into her mouth, and she drank it, stealing the air from his lungs. His hands slid down, gripping her hips. He repeated her name.

It was just a sound.

She guided him to the bed. He followed without resistance.

Clothes became a meaningless complication, shed and forgotten. He was beautiful in his familiarity, his body an easy comfort she despised herself for missing. The hunger inside her, a vast and aching chasm, yawned as she straddled him, skin burning against skin.

Not yet. She let the lie feel real.

He cupped her face, his thumb stroking her cheek. "Are you sure?"

No. That word was a silent scream in her skull.

But she nodded.

He kissed her then, and she kissed him back with manufactured passion, a performance for an audience of one. His hands mapped her body with a possessiveness she once craved. Her hips moved in a slow and hypnotic rhythm. She guided him inside her, a sin of perfect, damning familiarity.

And the siphon unlocked, a lock clicking open in her soul.

His essence was a soft golden thing laced with warmth and memories. It bled into her like warm wine, a current of absolution she had no right to feel. A low moan escaped her. The shadows lifted their heads and purred, their coils tightening around her spine and pushing her on. Her hips bucked, a more brutal, sharper thrust. She rode him now, not as a lover but as a conqueror claiming territory.

He gasped, his eyes wide and unfocused beneath her. He arched up, trying to meet her, but she pinned his wrists to the mattress.

The shadows in the room thickened, closing in.

He wants this, they whispered. *He loves you. He would give you anything. It is not considered stealing if the item is a gift.*

She stopped pretending.

Her rhythm turned brutal. Feral. Her fingers dug into his arms, leaving marks. She moved faster—a frantic pace—until her body was slick with sweat, and her muscles trembled with the sheer glorious intake. The siphon was a torrent now, a river of sunlight pouring into the hollow places inside her. His light flooded her, and his skin grew paler, cooler. His breath stuttered, shallow and weak. A strangled noise came from his throat.

Still, she did not stop.

Still, she drank.

Still, she wanted more.

Her phone buzzed on the nightstand. She ignored it. It buzzed again, the vibration alien in this temple of skin and sin. The screen flared to life, and its cold light reflected in the ceiling mirror.

Kael: Are you okay?

That question was a shard of ice in the fever dream that broke her spell.

When she looked down, Mark's eyes were fluttering, and a tremor ran through his lips. His chest barely moved. The siphon—that viscous, shimmering cord of light—still stretched from his heart to hers. And she was still on top of him. Still moving and still feeding.

A guttural sob tore from her throat, and she ripped herself away from him, collapsing onto the floor. Her thighs were slick with his sweat and her filth. Her skin had a faint, stolen glow. She was gorged and bloated with his life. She had never felt so full. She had never felt so foul.

He lay there utterly still, his handsome face slack and his beauty gutted. She pressed her head to his chest. His pulse was faint, his essence nearly extinguished.

Her hands shook as she crawled back onto the bed. "No," she whispered, the word tearing her apart. "No, no, no! What did I do?"

She had chosen this. She could have called Kael, the one who would have seen the famine in her eyes and wrestled her back from the edge. Mark had only ever seen the woman he loved, and his love had always been a form of surrender.

The shadows had chosen him for his weakness. And she had let them.

"Please," she asked the silent room, her voice a raw crack of sound. "Please don't die."

Fumbling, she opened the nightstand drawer and pulled out a ritual knife. The silver was cold against her trembling fingers. She sliced her own palm open and watched her blood, hot and unnaturally luminous, well up. Her own stolen light. She pressed the wound to his chest and smeared the blood over his skin and onto his lips—a desperate, useless prayer.

She kissed his forehead and his mouth, though he did not stir.

"Take it back." She wept against his still face. "Take it all. Take everything I have left."

It wasn't a prayer. It was desperate, a failed attempt at balance. A frantic effort to repair the beautiful person her chaos had shattered. A monster trying to clean up the wreckage of her own failed existence.

Slowly, so slowly, a faint glow returned to his skin. Not strong. Not whole. A flickering candlelight in the wake of a forest fire. Just enough for him to wake up later and not remember the monster that was Sera.

Shaking, she fell back, her blood staining the sheets. She dressed in the damning silence and left the room to its memories. The mirrors watched her go, their silver surfaces slick with her disgrace. The door clicked shut, sealing the desecration inside.

She threw cash at the clerk on her way out, knowing too well that when Mark woke up, there would be no blood or any other mess for him to see.

Outside, dawn clawed its way into the sky. The air was thick and wet, and thunder threatened from above. She climbed into her car, and her hands shook as she turned the ignition.

"You're a monster," she whispered to herself.

The roads were slick with summer rain, the clouds hung heavy with unshed fury, and her mind was a maelstrom of regret, confusion, and unspeakable hunger.

A silver shape darted onto the road, directly in her path. It was a large buck, its eyes wide at the headlights' glare. Her immediate reaction was to slam the brakes as hard as she could. However, the abrupt force caused the wheels to lock up, and the tires lost all traction on the pavement.

The car skidded, no longer responding to her steering. It was no longer rolling forward but sliding sideways, a metal box skating on a sheet of water. Outside the windshield, her headlights were sweeping wildly across the rain-slicked road and the trees beyond.

A wall of silver guardrail erupted from the darkness, and the vehicle met it with a grinding shriek that vibrated through the floorboards and up her spine, the shockwave bone-jarring. Her seat belt locked, a brutal strap catching her across the chest and hip, but it couldn't stop her momentum entirely. Her head snapped forward, connecting with the steering wheel, and the horn blared a single flat note.

A flash of white exploded behind her eyes.

The windshield fractured into a spiderweb of glassy veins. Before she fully registered the first impact, a second jolt threw her body sideways. Her ribs met the unyielding frame of the driver's side door with a sickening crack that stole the air from her lungs. The side window exploded into a shower of glittering cubes.

A warm and thick liquid trickled past her eyebrow. Through the shattered glass, she saw a flicker of movement and the white flash of a tail as the buck vanished, swallowed by the storm.

The ruined car groaned and hissed, its front tires spinning uselessly. It hung there for a single suspended heartbeat, teetering between the road and the fall.

Then gravity won.

The car's front dipped, and through the fractured windshield, an ancient oak tree filled her entire vision. The final impact was an absorbing crash. The front of the car crumpled around the tree trunk, metal folding and dashboard surging inward. The air bag exploded, a futile gesture that punched the last bit of air from her lungs.

Her body convulsed from the final force, and the world dissolved into a single roar—metal screaming, glass exploding, and the hiss of a ruptured radiator. The edges of her vision folded inward. The headlights flickered once and then died, leaving her in near-total darkness.

And then, there was only a vast, silent, and absolute nothingness.

Kael woke with a jolt of pain, exploding beneath his sternum, and sat upright in his bed. His chest heaving.

For one harrowing moment, he couldn't breathe. He pressed a hand to his chest, his palm flat, and tried to still the furious, uneven rhythm of his heart. And the sensation pulsed again: violent, electric, and hollow. As if a part of him had torn free, leaving nothing but the echo of Sera's name and the hollow throb of what was left behind.

Something had happened. He didn't know how he knew, only that it was Sera. The name echoed through him like a beacon.

The sky outside his penthouse was still dark, rolling with low storm clouds. Lightning split the sky, and thunder rumbled like a distant war drum. The scent of ozone filled the air, not outside but *inside* the room. His power was stirring. No. It was *boiling*.

Rain pounded against the windows as he moved across his open concrete floor. His phone felt like lead in his grip: cold, silent. No messages. No calls. No trace.

He stared at the last text he'd sent.

Kael: Are you okay?

Still unseen.

He tried calling. Voicemail. Again. Voicemail.

Pacing, he tossed the phone onto the couch and dragged a hand through his hair. The energy in the room crackled with lamps flickering and shadows twitching along the edges of the walls. A portrait frame on the shelf vibrated and then clattered to the ground.

He picked up his phone again and dialed Bethany.

She answered on the second ring with a sleepy voice. "Kael. Mmm. This better be good."

"Where is she?"

A pause. "Who?"

"Don't play that game. Sera. She's not answering me. Something's wrong."

Bethany's voice dipped. "We haven't talked today. Why? What happened?"

"Something's not right."

She let out a slow breath. "I don't know anything, Kael. She's probably off-grid for a reason. She does this sometimes. Shuts everything out."

He closed his eyes. Something about the cadence of her voice was too smooth, too polished. "If you hear from her, please call me immediately."

Another pause. "Of course."

He lowered the phone, his eyes narrowing. There was something about Bethany. Something he'd seen before but had been too ignorant to name. The tilt of her voice. The way she always knew just enough to never give it all. It pricked at old wounds, ones buried so deep he hadn't dared to acknowledge them.

He closed his eyes, centering himself. He reached, not just with his mind but with the bond. And that was when he felt the pain. Sudden. Crushing. A searing bolt of anguish shot through his ribs. His knees buckled, and the room lurched sideways.

Something catastrophic had happened to Sera.

Breath stolen, he clutched his chest and didn't wait. Gone. The humid Savannah morning offered no reprieve, clinging to his skin like a second layer of fear. He didn't remember the blur of the drive, only the suffocating guilt that propelled him.

One moment, a frantic panic gripped him, and the next, he stood before the silent block of her townhouse.

The house itself was a shadowy, silent block with no glow in its windows and no car in its driveway.

Across the threshold, her wards shimmered. Faint. Fragile. Like spun moonlight caught on unseen threads. Without a pause, he lifted his hand, energy and a familiar hum of power sparking at his fingertips.

He touched the doorknob and felt an echo of her pain. Still warm. Still vivid.

He recoiled, his breath shallow and sharp. His pulse hammered like a distant thunderclap in his ears. "Sera…" he breathed, a plea swallowed by the rain.

He pressed his palm flat against the door, the wood cool and unyielding beneath his touch, and it creaked inward, yielding. Ajar. A sliver of darkness stood on the other side, hinting at emptiness. He leaned closer, one hand still on the wood, as rain slicked the back of his neck.

He hadn't entered. Not yet. Not until he was ready for what he might find.

The wards had been disrupted, and faint energy at the threshold still trembled. It was like the ghost of a scream trapped in a whisper. And beneath it all, threading through the raw pain and broken protection, was another signature.

Celestial. Unmistakable. Familiar.

Michael.

Kael's jaw clenched. He hadn't felt that energy's distinct, chilling presence in centuries. Not since his fall. Not since the tribunal's searing judgment.

He exhaled harshly and took a step back. Clouds swallowed the sky, cloaking the world in bruised colors. He stood at the door, no longer simply searching for Sera. He was walking into something far, far larger.

The air still carried her. Sera's energy shimmered faintly in the wreckage—weak and unstable like a candle fighting the wind. Beneath it, two other traces bled through the static. One burned sharp and disciplined, the clean edge of Heaven's warriors. The other coiled darker, threaded with Michael's signature—older, patient.

Kael stepped through the doorway. Stained glass fractured the moonlight across the hall, scattering crimson and blue shards over the floor. His boots moved in silence; centuries of hunting had taught him that sound was a liability. Still, his mind refused to be quiet. It replayed old images—the tribunal's chamber, Michael's satisfied smile as he pronounced the sentence, the white-hot slice of pain when Kael's wings were severed, and the long fall that followed.

He forced the memories down and followed the scent of burning grace deeper into the house.

Kael noticed evident signs of a struggle on the walls. The faint scent of Sera's blood hung in the air. If Michael had harmed her...

Kael wouldn't be responsible for what happened next.

Kael walked through the entrance of the living space. And there she was: Sera was sprawled across a velvet couch like a discarded doll. Her usually vibrant face was gray and streaked with dried blood. His heart stuttered and then hammered against his ribs.

"Sera," he whispered, her name a prayer on his lips.

He lunged for her, but she didn't move. Her chest barely rose with shallow breaths, and her skin was a sickly alabaster beneath the smears of crimson. Those green eyes that had captured him at first glance were now closed. Her hair, usually a glossy cascade of darkness, lay matted against her skull, tangled with what looked like fragments of glass.

She looked…broken.

Over centuries of his existence, Kael had seen death in all its forms. He'd escorted souls to their final destination more times than he could count. But seeing Sera, who had awakened the dangerous pulse he'd spent lifetimes trying to silence, sent a primal rage surging through his veins.

The room stank of blood and divinity, an unholy mixture that made his nostrils flare. Incense from some earlier rituals hung in the air, sickly sweet beneath the metallic tang. The wood floor beneath his boots was scuffed and stained, bearing the marks of a struggle. Antique furniture, elegant pieces that spoke of Sera's refined taste, that lined the walls now served as silent witnesses to whatever violence had transpired here.

His eyes moved across the room. A broken crystal glass sat on a side table, its broken frame indicating that something or someone had struck the wall. Drops of blood traced a path toward where she now lay.

Words tore from his throat, raw and demanding. "What the fuck is going on?"

Measuring Celestial Dicks

15

That was when Kael turned to the auras he had sensed before entering.

Near the back, partially obscured by shadows and the dust mites dancing in the slivers of dying light, stood a figure of impossible stillness: Michael. His tailored black suit was pristine, a stark contrast to the carnage surrounding him. His posture was rigidly straight, radiating the same suffocating self-righteousness Kael remembered from eons ago.

The boiling rage inside Kael cooled and crystallized, sharpening into a cold, deadly purpose.

Against the far wall, another angel leaned in, adopting a nonchalant pose. His stance was deceptively relaxed, but the muscles in his shoulders, encased in star-broached silver armor, were pulled tight with barely contained power. Between his dark eyebrows, a small rune glowed with a soft internal luminescence just like Jareth's. The mark of a watcher. A more intricate glyph faintly pulsed on the side of his neck, identifying him as a master of celestial blades. This was no mere observer; this was a high-ranking warrior. The angel gave Kael a knowing nod.

Closer to Sera and perched on the very edge of an antique chair was a woman Kael had never seen before. A flicker of recognition tickled at him, a distinct resemblance to Sera in the sharp line of her jaw and the curve of her lips. But her aura was a disorienting paradox. Where Sera's aura had a confusing blend, this woman was a stark void. No celestial light swirled within it, only darkness peppered with silver dust that seemed to absorb all light. And yet, she didn't feel demonic, not in the way he understood demons. She felt…wrong. Tainted in a fundamental way that made no sense.

Kael shifted, planting his feet more firmly in front of Sera's still body. The weight of his concealed wings felt like a physical burden, a burning ache against his shoulder blades. His voice was a low growl that scraped the silence. "Someone better start explaining. Now."

Michael remained a monument to celestial arrogance. His perfect face—too perfect with ageless, symmetrical features and eyes that held the chilling judgment of millennia—twisted into a grimace of profound distaste. "Kael, you overstep boundaries again," he said, each syllable precise. "This does not concern you anymore."

Michael's voice didn't echo; it settled. It was a weight in the air, a drop in atmospheric pressure that signaled an impending storm. Kael's muscles locked just for a breath, binding him in place. That was the problem with archangels. They didn't just speak. They sentenced.

A harsh, grating laugh, devoid of all humor, tore from Kael's throat. "Doesn't concern me? Sera is lying half dead on that couch, and you're standing here like you're at a fucking board meeting." His voice dropped to a dangerous whisper. "What did you do to her?"

His silver-gray hair caught the dim light as he tilted his head, studying Kael with those impassive blue eyes that had once watched him fall from grace. "You dare accuse *me*? After all your transgressions?" His voice was a calm sea over an abyss, a tranquility that only stoked Kael's fury higher. "I have more rights to be here than you."

The watcher by the wall shifted. His dominant hand moved to rest on the hilt of what Kael knew would be a celestial blade. His golden alert eyes never left Kael.

"Rights?" Kael spat the word. "You lost all rights to speak of justice when you sentenced your own daughters to death."

Michael's composure fractured. He took a step forward, his face hardening into a mask of cold fury. "You fell because you deserved to fall, Kael."

"No," Kael snapped, the word a whipcrack in the tense air. "You took what wasn't yours to take."

The memory hit him with sharp clarity: After Kael had fled, disobeying a direct command from an archangel to kill Lilith, he had found Elara.

Elara had been mortal: beautiful, cunning, and devastating in her hunger for a world beyond her gilded cage. A queen among men, yet so achingly human that it made Kael's bones ache to look at her. He had whispered forbidden truths against her throat until she ached for more than a crown. Until she burned for the stars themselves. Until he was lost in the emptiness she left behind.

He had fallen under a list of charges that bled across celestial scrolls: insubordination, desertion, fraternization, and unauthorized dissemination of divine knowledge. And threaded through it all was the greatest blasphemy: love. He had loved freely, recklessly, and without permission.

The tribunal had stripped his wings feather by agonizing feather and had laid his guilt bare before the empty eyes of the Celestial Court. And he still thanked the heavens that Jareth had been there to deliver the mercifully imperfect blow.

But when it was over, Elara was gone. Her name had been struck from the records, faded to ash. He had searched for years, and in the end, he had stopped. Yet that hollow wound had never healed, a gnawing ache that no war or exile could ever cauterize.

And now, Michael dared to stand here and speak of corruption as if his own hands were clean.

Kael's fists clenched, his nails digging painful crescents into his palms. "And now you've come for Seraphine? To finish the job? Another independent mind to punish?"

He flinched, a nearly invisible crack in his divine composure. It wasn't guilt, but it was enough to make Cassia stare at her father, her face a frozen mask of horror. Even the watcher's gaze shifted to Michael, a flicker of confused disgust crossing his features before his neutral mask snapped back into place.

"You know nothing of Seraphine," Michael said, his voice tight. "Nothing of what she is."

"I know enough," Kael growled.

"Do you?" His lips curved into a smile devoid of warmth. "Do you know she is *corrupted*, Kael?"

The word, aimed like a poisoned dart, hit its mark. Kael staggered back a step, his mind reeling. "That's a lie," he whispered, his eyes darting between Sera's still form and Michael's triumphant expression.

"Search your senses, Fallen One. You've always been skilled at reading an aura's truth. Look at her and tell me you don't see it. Look for the rot."

Kael forced himself to look, to perceive beyond the physical shell. And there it was. Threads of divine energy were woven through her aura, a pattern unmistakably similar to the archangel standing before him, but as he looked deeper, he realized the celestial light was tainted, its edges stained. Profound corruption curled around her core, a living rot that felt chillingly familiar. That felt like Lilith's aura.

A creeping horror washed over him. The very darkness he had refused to extinguish was unmistakable and twined with Michael's light. Sera was the offspring of the same darkness Michael had ordered him to destroy.

"Impossible," he breathed, the word stolen from his lungs.

A cold, cruel smile touched Michael's lips. "Perhaps you now understand why your presence here is…inappropriate. Your particular brand of chaos will only feed hers."

His shock curdled back into white-hot anger. "And perhaps you understand why I don't give a fuck about your opinion. Corrupted or not, she's *dying*. And you're standing here, doing nothing."

Cassia shifted in her chair. Her eyes, so much like Sera's, darted between the two immortal enemies.

Michael tilted his head, his expression one of clinical curiosity. "Do you even know what she could've become?"

Kael didn't answer. He couldn't. Because in the deepest, most terrified part of his soul, he did know. He was too far in, too bound to this woman to let her die now. She had already corrupted every atom of his being, entwining herself with his very essence. And the devastating irony was that he couldn't blame Heaven, Michael, or fate.

This was all his fault.

Cassia shifted, her agitation palpable. Her voice, though barely a whisper, sliced through their standoff. "She's not dead yet! Stop talking like she is already gone! She's just trapped in Limbo!"

Kael turned to face her but was startled by the raw ferocity coiled in her small frame. She rose from her chair with a fluid grace that was an eerie echo of Sera's own movements, and her darker eyes burned with an intensity that rivaled Kael's.

"I am Cassia," she said, her gaze locking with his. Her voice was even but underscored with desperate urgency. She flicked her chin toward the armored angel. "That is Remiel."

He gave a curt nod, but his mind snagged on a single, terrifying word. "Limbo?" The word tasted like ash on his tongue.

Soul collectors knew Limbo intimately, that gray and featureless wasteland between realms where lost souls wandered in eternal torment. Claimed by neither Heaven nor Hell, it was a prison of the spirit's own making.

"Yes." Cassia stepped forward to stand near Michael, her chin tilted up in pure defiance. "And standing here measuring your celestial dicks isn't helping her!" The crude phrasing, delivered in such an aristocratic voice, would have been amusing under any other circumstance.

Michael's jaw tightened. "Cassia…"

"No!" She jabbed a trembling finger toward Sera's motionless form. "Look at her, Father. *Look*!" Her trembling hand betrayed her fear. "Her body is here, but her essence—her soul—is trapped between worlds. I am *not* ready to give up on her."

Kael studied Sera again. Now that he knew what to look for, he could see it: A faint, shimmering tether, as thin as spider silk, connected her physical form to…elsewhere. It wasn't the clean break of death but something infinitely messier…and more dangerous.

"What happened?" he asked, directing the question to Cassia. He knew he'd get the unvarnished truth from her, not some sanitized angelic report.

Her sharp gaze met his, seemingly evaluating as if judging whether he was worthy of an answer. She spoke with a weary sigh. "Sera's nature... It's very complicated. More than mine." She gestured between herself and her sister. "We're both caught between worlds—part angel, part something else. But Sera always had more trouble with her...hunger." She hesitated, the last word hanging in the air.

"Because she is a succubus."

She nodded, her expression grim. "And succubi need to feed, far more than most demons. When they don't..." Her gaze drifted back to her sister, grief etching fine lines around her eyes.

His gaze swept over the cracked plaster and upended furniture. "You had an altercation."

"Yes." A flush colored her face. "I tried to help her. She'd been denying her nature for too long, growing weaker. I confronted her... Or I tried to, anyway." She ran an unsteady hand through her blonde hair. "But she is stubborn. When I pushed, she pushed back. Literally."

His eyes traced the spiderweb of cracks radiating from an impact point on the far wall. It was chillingly Sera-sized. The force required to create such damage would have obliterated a human.

"After she threw me against the wall, she stormed out." Her voice dropped to a whisper. "I heard her on the phone, arranging to meet Mark. To feed. That was the last I saw of her conscious."

He processed this, the timeline snapping into place. A spike of irrational, possessive jealousy shot through him, followed by a cold wave of concern. If feeding had landed her in Limbo, something had gone catastrophically wrong.

"Her ex? When?" he demanded.

"Yesterday evening," she replied, nodding. Her eyes never leaving her sister's still form. "She didn't come home."

Remiel, the warrior angel, shifted his weight, and the subtle scrape of armor drew Kael's attention. The angel's face remained neutral, but his eyes held the weight of knowledge not yet shared.

Her gaze landed on him and hardened. "Tell him, Remiel. Tell him how you found my sister."

He detached himself from the wall, his movements purposeful and contained. Unlike Michael's immaculate appearance, his attire was in disarray. Specks of what looked like dried blood had been spattered on his shirt, which was smeared with dirt and torn at the sleeve. It suggested he'd been in a brawl either just before finding Sera or during the discovery itself. His golden eyes held none of Michael's contempt, only a soldier's weary assessment and, perhaps, a sliver of compassion.

"I was patrolling the boundaries between realms," he said, his voice a deep, measured baritone. "Standard duty. Around dawn, I received an unusual summons from a lower demon working the Old Candler Hospital morgue. He sent word that a being with celestial blood had arrived."

The *morgue*. Kael's blood ran cold.

"I went immediately." His eyes flicked to Michael before returning to Kael. "There aren't many with celestial blood in Savannah. When I arrived, I found her on a steel table, tagged and bagged like any mortal corpse. The humans had declared her dead at the scene."

"A car accident?" Kael echoed, his mind racing.

He nodded grimly. "A head-on collision with a deer on Abercorn Street, that long stretch cutting through Savannah's old oaks and ghostlight. She was thrown through the windshield. Fatal injuries by human standards. But when I touched her…" He paused, his brow furrowing. "When I touched her, her body was already healing. Slowly. Yet her soul was gone."

"Not gone," Cassia said sharply. "Trapped. There's a difference."

Kael's gaze returned to Sera's face. He could see it now: the faint healing cuts, the deep purple bruises already fading to a sickly yellow at an accelerated rate. Her body was repairing itself, but without her soul, it was just an empty vessel.

"I called Cassia," Remiel said. "Found out she was here and brought Sera over. We've been trying to reach her, to call her back, but something is holding her fast."

Cassia crossed the room and stood directly before Kael. Up close, the resemblance to Sera was jarring, though her features were honed to a harder, sharper edge. "I think it's you," she said bluntly.

Kael looked stricken. "Me?"

"Not intentionally." Her eyes searched his, looking desperate for an answer she seemed to dread. "But yes, Sera mentioned you. You fed her, didn't you? And you both carry remnants of celestial light. When you shared that, you initiated a bond with her." She twisted her mouth around the last words as if they were distasteful. "You need to finish that bond before her demonic half overwrites the process. It's why she's unraveling."

"I...I know," he admitted, the confession torn from him. "I knew what she was the first time I saw her."

"And you proceeded anyway?" The question was a groan from Michael, the first crack in his strict composure that revealed genuine, profound distress.

"She was fading, slipping away right in front of me!" he shot back. "I had to do something!"

Michael's voice rose, laced with fury. "You could have found any mortal on the street! Instead, you chose to tether yourself to her? How noble!"

"An option you would have chosen, wouldn't you, Michael?" he snarled. "Because mortal lives are meaningless to you! Who needs their consent?"

"Enough!" Remiel's voice cut between them like a sword. "We are losing precious time. What's done is done."

Cassia's saddened expression softened. "She is grieving and feels at fault," she said, her clinical tone landing like a blow to Kael's conscience. "Succubi aren't meant to form attachments. It complicates everything. It makes them vulnerable."

The implication crashed through him. Sera, torn between her nature and this growing bond, was caught in a trap of her own making. The thought that he was the anchor point to her suffering was unbearable.

"You're…you're saying she's punishing herself?" he asked, his voice barely a whisper.

Cassia nodded. "Limbo is a manifestation of the soul's own torment. I believe she's caught in a loop of self-loathing, unable to forgive herself for what her nature demands."

The room fell silent. Michael stood unnaturally still, his gaze fixed on Cassia. Remiel shifted, the leather of his sword's sheath scraping against his thigh. And Kael…Kael just stood there, drowning in the revelation.

"If that's true," Kael said, his words solidifying into a grim resolve, "then I'm the only one who can reach her."

Remiel moved toward Sera's prone form. "When I found her, I could sense the faintest thread of life clinging to her—a resilience I've rarely seen in celestials."

"Half celestial," Michael corrected sharply. "Her demon form taints her strength."

Kael rounded on him, fury boiling anew. "Her demon form is the one giving her a fighting chance, you self-righteous prick! If she was fully angelic, her soul would have departed the moment her heart stopped!"

His eyes flashed with dangerous power. "You presume to lecture me on my own daughter's nature? You, who have only known her for a handful of brief encounters?"

"I know enough!" Kael snarled. "I know she's trapped because of the impossible contradiction you created with your unholy matrimony! Angel and succubus, how could she ever reconcile those halves when zealots like you preach nothing but purity and condemnation?"

They stood face-to-face, centuries of hatred crackling between them like lightning. Kael's wings strained against their concealment, instinctively preparing for a fight. Michael's aura expanded, pressing down, and the temperature in the room plummeted.

"You speak of contradictions?" Michael's voice was deadly quiet. "You, who fell from grace yet still stoop to collect souls? Who claims to despise Heaven yet mimics its judgments? Your hypocrisy knows no bounds."

The words struck closer to home than Kael cared to admit.

Remiel cleared his throat, stepping between them with the practiced ease of one accustomed to defusing celestial tempers. "This accomplishes nothing," he said firmly. "Sera remains trapped while you two revisit ancient grievances."

Cassia swiftly moved to Sera's side, her fingers intertwining with her sister's. The gesture was so human, so vulnerable, that it silenced everyone. Her eyes, when she raised them to Kael, held no suspicion, only desperate hope. "Can you help her?"

The question hung in the air.

"He cannot," Michael stated flatly. "To physically enter Limbo requires a power he no longer possesses. To send only his consciousness would leave his body vulnerable, a risk I will not permit."

Kael almost laughed. "You don't permit anything where I'm concerned, Michael. Those days are long past."

A realization hit Kael, cold and sharp: Michael didn't know he was no longer just a fallen angel. Did that mean the rules of the realms no longer applied?

Cassia's patience seemed to snap. "Because of the bond, he is the only one who can reach her without celestial intervention destroying her demonic half." She turned to Kael, her eyes pleading. "Isn't that right?"

He had no idea if she was right, but he seized the opening. "Bonded pairs can traverse the boundaries to find each other," he bluffed, his mind racing. He left the terrifying reality of that gray wasteland where time and space folded in on themselves unspoken. "In theory, I can find her."

"In *theory*." Michael scoffed. "And how many bonded souls have you retrieved from Limbo, Fallen One?"

He met his gaze. "None. But I've guided countless others. I know the terrain."

"You understand nothing of what awaits in Seraphine's Limbo. Her nature creates complexities beyond your experience."

"Perhaps," he said. "But I understand her. Sometimes, that connection is more powerful than any law of Heaven." He squared his shoulders, his voice quiet yet unyielding. "I'm going after her. You can help, or you can get the fuck out of my way."

Michael's face hardened. "You would risk her existence as well as your own? Your arrogance is astounding."

He stepped closer, invading the archangel's space. "This isn't arrogance. This is a *choice*. Her choice, my choice. Something Heaven stripped from you long ago."

"And if you fail?" Michael said, his voice low and dangerous. "If you become trapped alongside her?"

"Then I'll have failed trying. Which is more than you're doing."

The lights flickered. For a heart-stopping moment, the air vibrated with Michael's barely contained power. But Remiel stepped forward again, placing a restraining hand on his arm.

"He's right," the warrior angel said softly. "We've tried our way. It's time to try his."

Michael shook off the hand but didn't advance. His gaze fell on Sera, and for a fleeting instant, a genuine look of paternal anguish crossed his face before the mask of divine authority slammed back into place.

Kael pulled his T-shirt over his head, revealing a torso covered in intricate tattoos. They weren't mere ink; they were ancient wards, symbols of power spreading across his broad chest and arms. Each glowed with faint latent energy. He knelt beside the couch, his eyes memorizing every line of Sera's face.

Cassia watched him, her guarded expression softening. Finally, she nodded. "Please…please bring her back."

The Limbo

16

Kael knelt beside Sera, the plush carpet a mockery of comfort. Her stillness was a horrifying eclipse of the vibrant woman he knew. He brushed a stray strand of dark hair from her face, his fingers lingering and tracing the delicate curve of her jaw. Her skin was cool, an unnerving chill.

He leaned in and pressed a soft kiss to her forehead. "I'll bring you back. I promise you."

He then rose, turning to face the assembled figures: Michael, radiating a frigid authority; Remiel, being a silent and imposing shadow; and Cassia, wearing a stark mask of grief.

"All right," Kael said, his voice a low rasp. "Who's sending me to the threshold of the afterlife?"

Cassia stepped forward. "I will," she murmured. "Remiel, your blade."

Remiel nodded, and a shimmering blade materialized in his hand. Celestial steel. Deadly.

He knelt before her, baring his chest. He closed his eyes, and his mind focused on Sera.

The blade pierced his flesh, stopping just short of his heart, and searing pain followed. Celestial energy coursed through him, a burning fire. His consciousness slipped, and his spirit stretched into the void.

His body convulsed as the vortex tore him from the world he knew. The transition was unraveling—light flashing in jagged bursts, sound collapsing into an earsplitting hum, and gravity twisting in every direction. He gasped for air, but the breath burned, his very essence reshaping to fit this alien realm.

When the chaos subsided, Kael slammed into the ground with enough force to drive the air from his chest. He groaned, his fingers clawing at the jagged surface. It was warm, almost feverish, and faintly pulsed as though it was alive. He pushed himself up, wincing and wiping a smear of blood from his temple.

The world he had entered defied understanding. The ground stretched endlessly, fractured by jagged spires that rose like ancient claws. Some were smooth and glinting black, and others twisted like petrified bone, each clawing at a sky bruised in swirling shades of gray and violet. The air was thick and cloying, carrying the acrid scent of burned parchment mixed with the damp earth. Kael struggled to draw a breath. The atmosphere didn't just surround him; it pressed against his chest, an oppressive weight daring him to surrender.

Fog thickened around his legs, clinging to every movement with deliberate malice, while restless shadows lurked at the edges of his vision, shifting as if watching his struggle. Faint but insidious whispers threaded through the stagnant air. The words were indistinct, yet their tone carried an undeniable sense of mockery.

As he stumbled forward, the ground shifted beneath him. It felt less like stone and more like flesh—alive and unnerving. Each step sent vibrations through his boots, accompanied by a faint groan that resonated within him. His instincts screamed to stop, to turn back, but he gritted his teeth and pressed on.

The landscape twisted around him, reshaping itself as though Limbo was deliberately complicating his path. Spires that had once loomed in the distance now seemed impossibly close, towering over him like closing predators. The fog thickened, transforming into tendrils that writhed and lashed at him. He batted them away, but they clung to his skin and left icy trails in their wake.

He reached what appeared to be a fissure in the ground, a jagged crack stretching into an abyss. He hesitated, but the whispers grew louder behind him, urging him forward. He leaped across the fissure, and as he landed, his boots skidded on the unstable edge. A sharp wind howled through the gap, carrying with it fragments of sound—cries, groans, and the faint toll of distant bells. Kael turned away, refusing to dwell on the horrors lurking below.

The terrain became more hostile the deeper he ventured. Trees appeared, though they were far from natural. Their bark was ashen and brittle, and their branches twisted into grotesque shapes that seemed to claw at the sky. The blackened leaves were sharp, whispering as though sharing secrets no mortal was meant to hear. He felt the sting of their edges as he brushed past, gaining shallow cuts. The blood seemed to vanish into the air, absorbed by Limbo itself.

Finally, Kael spotted movement ahead, a figure emerging from the haze. His muscles tensed as his instincts screamed danger, but he pushed forward.

The figure, shrouded in gray, stood motionless at first, its edges blurring into the fog. It didn't walk. It glided forward instead, its cloak billowing as though stirred by winds Kael could not feel.

He froze as the figure stopped mere feet away, towering over him despite its indistinct form. Its hood concealed any trace of a face, leaving only shadows shifting within. The presence of the gatekeeper was overwhelming. Kael's knees nearly buckled under the weight of its gaze, though he saw no eyes.

"You seek what was lost," the gatekeeper murmured, its voice a fractured symphony of layered tones that sent chills down Kael's spine.

He straightened, his heart thundering with both fear and determination. "I do," he said. "I've come to take Seraphine back."

The gatekeeper tilted its head, the motion unnervingly fluid as though it lacked bones. "Few make claims of retrieving loved ones. Fewer survive to fulfill them." It raised a skeletal hand, gesturing toward the distance.

His gaze followed the motion, settling on the immense iron gate behind the gatekeeper. It loomed like a monument to despair, its surface twisting with thorns that faintly pulsed with dark energy. Vines laced through the structure, their barbs trembling as though hungry for blood. Beyond the gate lay a labyrinth: a sprawling network of endless corridors and arches that shifted and folded upon themselves in defiance of logic.

The gatekeeper's voice deepened, resonating with ominous authority. "The maze is a creation of this realm, to test the resolve of the trapped or the ones who wish to save them. It feeds on fear and twists truths into torment. Every chamber holds a death. Every shadow is a trial. You must find the one who is truly trapped, not just in body but in soul. Choose correctly, and you may leave with her. Choose wrongly, and this realm will claim both of you."

Kael forced himself to hold steady. "I'll find her," he said, his voice firm.

The gatekeeper stepped aside, its robe swirling like smoke. "Then go. And let your resolve be tested."

He hesitated, but then his boots crunched against the ground as he moved toward the gate. The thorns shuddered, writhing. When he passed through the iron threshold, the gate slammed shut behind him with a clang.

Darkness consumed him.

The air inside the maze tasted like mourning, a pervasive sorrow that seemed to seep into his very bones.

He stumbled forward, each footfall echoing against slick black stone. The walls weren't solid barriers but towering ridges of obsidian mist, their edges a shifting landscape that reformed with every step he took. Beyond his immediate vision, shapes whispered. Their voices were a fractured chorus of agony and memories that clawed at the edges of his sanity.

This wasn't merely a path. It was a trial, a brutal test of the soul.

He stopped at a crossroads, where four doorways rose from the swirling haze like ancient, ominous altars. Each was distinct, yet all reeked of identical profound pain. Above them, the maze's ceiling arched like a cathedral's rib cage, an enormous, living vault that seemed to breathe.

The first doorway shimmered with a damp fog, and the unmistakable stench of decay—a cloying scent that promised dissolution—filled the air. Thick moss grew like veins along the cold stone arch, and from within, a voice spoke. Her voice.

"Sera…" he whispered, the name a fragile prayer on his lips. His legs moved without conscious thought, drawn by an invisible current.

The path dropped abruptly, leaving him standing on the bank of a vast blackened river. Its waters slithered over jagged rocks like spilled oil, sluggish and heavy. The sky above was a smothering blanket of perpetual twilight, starless and unending.

And the bodies…

The bodies, dozens upon dozens, floated like grotesque lilies, stretching into the gloom. Women. All with raven hair streaming like seaweed. Their faces were slack and pale. Their dresses billowed like drowned silk, caught in the relentless pull. Every single one…looked like her.

Kael's throat closed, a choke of horror.

One of the bodies stirred. Not with the lifeless drift of the others but with effort, a desperate struggle against the current. Her head weakly rose and turned toward him, her eyes fixed and vacant.

"Kael…" she croaked, the sound brittle.

His heart stopped. "Sera…?"

She blinked, her pale lips trembling. She reached out, just barely, with her arm dragging through the black water. "Help me."

He didn't hesitate. He leaped.

The water was colder than death, a suffocating embrace that sucked the breath from his lungs and pulled him down. He swam forward, fighting the river's terrible resistance. His fingers ached to close around hers.

But every time he neared her, she drifted further away, always just out of reach.

No, they did—all of them.

They all spoke in unison, a thousand broken voices gurgling through the water. "Help me… Please help me. Help me."

Kael's arms burned, his muscles screaming, and his chest ached with a hollow, desperate throb. He reached again and finally brushed her wrist, a fleeting touch of hope. But she turned into vapor and vanished like smoke into the water. He screamed, a raw sound torn from his soul.

The mist swallowed the river. The banks. The bodies. All were gone, erased as if they had never been.

Only the cold remained, a profound chill.

He fell forward, shivering, and the door behind him sealed with a hiss. He forced himself upright, the image of her fading form in his mind. There were still three more doors, three more agonizing chances, or more cruel tortures. His eyes, heavy with the weight of that vision, found the next one.

The second door stood cracked, its edges pulsing with a faint orange light that danced like a candle flame across the cold stones. Kael stepped toward, and an immediate oppressive heat pressed against his skin.

A heartbeat echoed through the corridor, too slow to be his and too broken to be hers. He touched the door, the stone warm against his palm, and in that instant, he was consumed. Ash rained from the sky like morbid snow, settling on everything. Kael stood in the middle of a slick, curving stretch of highway, shrouded in twilight mist and the sharp, acrid tang of pine. The trees flanked either side like black, silent sentinels, and there, in the center of the desolate road, while twisting and still smoldering, was the wreckage: her car bent around a gnarled tree like it had tried to crawl away from the impact and failed, frozen in a final, agonizing struggle.

Glass littered the pavement, catching the angry glow of the fire. Tires melted into the earth, their rubber smoking. The air crackled with malevolent energy—angry, alive with destruction. The scent hit him next: burning plastic, gasoline, and the metallic tang of blood. And...her perfume.

A sudden flash of movement revealed the nightmare.

Sera was trapped behind the broken windshield, slumped over the steering wheel. Her face was a map of violence—cut and smeared with blood—while her body remained terrifyingly limp. Only one hand moved, a twitch barely visible through the ruin. Her lips formed silent, tortured words.

He ran. His heart pounding a frantic rhythm against his ribs and his feet skidding on oil-slick pavement, he reached the driver's door without a breath of hesitation. He seized the handle. Metal seared his palm like a white-hot brand against his skin, but pain was irrelevant. The door refused to yield.

Inside, the fire leaped higher. A hungry beast, it licked the interior and tasted its kill with grotesque relish.

"Sera!" he shouted, slamming a fist against the window. "Sera, look at me!"

She stirred. Her head turned slowly, blood matted in her hair. Her eyes, barely open but aware, locked on his, and a flicker of recognition ignited within their depths.

"Kael?" she whispered, her voice weak. "I can't move."

He hit the glass again harder, his knuckles bruising, but it didn't crack.

She flinched, a ghost of movement. "The deer. It came out of nowhere. I didn't mean…" The words broke off into a rattling cough.

"No, no. Stay awake," he said, his voice cracking. "I've got you. I'm right here, Sera. Just stay awake."

"I'm scared…" Her voice was barely a whisper, fragile.

"I know," he choked, tears stinging his eyes. "I'm with you now. Nothing's going to happen to you."

Fire exploded through the dashboard, a sudden inferno. Heat rolled outward in a brutal wave, scorching his skin and forcing him back. He pushed forward again, shielding his face with his arm. Flames danced across the seat beside her, a fiery shroud. She screamed, a sound that ripped through him.

"Sera!" he roared, throwing himself at the window again. It was an illusion. It had to be. He could break it. He had to break it.

She reached for him, her hand pressing against the glass and bleeding. Her eyes, wide with terrible understanding, locked with his, and he felt the severing.

A violent tear ripped through him as the fire devoured her. Sera vanished in a scream that seemed to stretch across dimensions, echoing into an endless void.

He staggered back, his lungs heaving and his arms blistered. The vision dissolved into a million fragments, leaving nothing but a chilling emptiness.

He was back in the maze, on his knees. His hands were clenched so tight that his nails drew blood from his palms. The second door was sealed behind him, etched with soot and sorrow. He rose, slower this time. Every muscle trembled from the overwhelming weight of guilt. He hadn't saved her—not in the river, not in the fire, not in time.

His gaze drifted to the third door, a grim determination setting in. The third door loomed like a wound carved from unyielding stone. Its frame was etched in intricate celestial script, pulsing with a cold golden light.

The moment Kael stepped toward it, a bitter wind rushed through the corridor, sharp and biting. It carried the acrid tang of incense and the chilling scent of divine judgment. The door didn't merely open; it unfolded like ancient wings. Light bled through its seams.

He stepped into it and found himself in a cathedral built for punishment. Its very architecture screamed of condemnation. The walls rose endlessly around him, smooth and pale. Stained glass windows glowed with scenes of a brutal war: angels impaling demons, seraphs severing wings.

At the center of the vast, unforgiving hall knelt Sera. Her dress, white once, was stained with ash and fresh blood. Her wings, still miraculously whole, trembled behind. She looked up at something, at someone, and her face was a mask of resigned despair.

Kael followed her gaze, and his blood turned to ice. Michael. He was cloaked in a radiance that burned more than it lit. His armor gleamed with sterile perfection, and in his hand, his sword, the blade of Heaven, was sharp and unyielding. And beside him was a shadow. Taller even than Michael, its form was an absence of light, cloaked in shadows so dense it seemed to swallow the very air. Imposing and winged, it was a terrifying silhouette of a creature he felt like he might've known.

Something primal shifted in his bones at the deep, unsettling recognition. This wasn't merely an angel; this was the executioner, the wing severer. The figure lifted his own blade. The metal was as black as a starless night, veined with a pulsing fire. It glowed from within.

Sera cried out, not in protest but in plea. A fractured gasp for mercy. "I didn't mean to," she whispered, breathless. "I wanted to help. She was dying, a child."

Michael said nothing. His silence was a verdict carved in marble. The sword fell in a clean, merciless arc, and her scream tore through the heavens.

Her wings—whole only heartbeats before—were torn from her, severed and shredded. Feathers exploded around her in a storm of white and red, like snow falling through bloodied skies. Crimson slashed across the pristine floor, desecrating the stillness.

Kael surged forward, a roar tearing from the depths of him. It was a sound of defiance and fury. He was ready to rip down the illusion, to storm Heaven itself.

The vision disappeared again, fracturing and bleeding colors, as the seams of that memory, that judgment, ripped wide. He fell, the wind vanishing from his lungs. But the void caught him and spun him downward until stone returned, cold and merciless. He landed hard, his knees slamming into the maze's floor. Pain shot through him, and the ache in his chest did not subside. His fists trembled from spent fury and unspent grief for what was gone, for another lie, and for another twist of cruelty. He remained kneeling, trying to breathe air too thick.

His soul ached.

But beneath the pain, a growl with no voice, only weight, stirred. He pondered who the figure behind that blade was. Why did the silhouette feel so familiar, so close? Why did Sera's sorrow seem eternal, as though she had carried that wound through lifetimes?

Kael rose, his limbs leaden with the echo of what he had seen. He turned toward the last doorway, where no flames guarded the threshold, no wind howled, and no heat scorched or chilled. It was only quiet, a stillness so complete that it pressed against his skin. It stood like a forgotten memory, its stone frame overgrown with thick ivy. Beyond it, he heard only his own breath. No cries. No whispers. Nothing. Yet he stepped through the threshold, nonetheless, feeling a pull.

The sky above was the color of mourning silk—a soft, smoky gray tinged with bruised lavender. Ash fell like snow, collecting on the petals of black roses that bloomed in thorn-choked rows. Their petals curled inward, reluctant to face the light, as if they, too, were in mourning. The air here was cold with absence, the kind of emptiness that gnaws rather than freezes.

And in the center of that garden knelt Sera—small, alone. Her spine was curved not in fear but in resignation. Her hands rested in her lap, folded like she was awaiting a sentence that would never end.

Kael's lips parted. "Sera," he whispered, the word a threadbare offering.

She did not stir.

He stepped forward, his heart pounding. As his foot crossed the first row of ash-covered roses, the world dissolved, and the vision collapsed and unraveled like mist. She vanished, and the roses crumbled beneath his boots. The garden fell apart—petal by petal, vine by vine—until nothing remained.

He fell again, this time more slowly and quietly. Yet the ache within him was no less. The four doors were gone now, swallowed by the mist, which left the flickering torchlight. A solitary flame burning in the oppressive darkness.

The gatekeeper appeared. It rose from the ground like mist turned solid, coalescing into a towering figure cloaked in midnight and bones. Its face was hidden within the depths of its hood, and its hands were clasped in front of it as if in eternal mourning.

"You have seen all paths," it said, its voice echoing through the corridor with ancient power. "Only one is real. Only one holds her soul. Choose."

Kael stood, his breathing ragged. The visions seared themselves into his mind.

He thought of the river, how she had begged him to help. A desperate, fading plea. It was a vision of his helplessness, his agonizing inability to reach her. A reflection of a fear that had always gnawed at him.

He thought of the fire, how she reached for him through the flames. A raw, desperate effort. That was the guilt, the searing pain of standing by while she burned.

He thought of Michael's wrath, how she had been punished. Her wings torn by shadows in a theater of judgment and cruelty. This was fury, the white-hot rage at the celestial powers that had always sought to control and break her.

All of them hurt, slicing at his soul with sharpened edges. All of them felt…true. But they were only echoes of the pain he already knew. They were spectacular torments, designed to make him relive every moment of his failures and her suffering.

But the garden…

Kael clenched his fists, the decision solidifying in his heart. "That one." His voice was firm. "The garden."

"Why?" The Gatekeeper's voice was the sound of a closing tome. It did not mock. It merely weighed him.

Kael looked at the shimmering doors. "The river is a torrent of time she cannot swim. It is a stream of faces that mirror her own drifting endlessly into the dark. It is the fear of being lost. Not the truth of being found."

He turned to the orange glowing door. "The fire is her resolve. The crash was the moment she accepted ruin, believing she deserved the wreckage she had put herself in. It is her guilt wearing the mask of destiny. And the Tribunal is merely the wound that refuses to close. The ultimate betrayal of blood and bond. It is the history of her pain. Not the geography of her soul."

He looked back to the final door. The quiet one.

"But the garden," he whispered. The realization settled like ash in his throat. "That is the suffocation of survival. It is her alone in the dark. She is surrounded by the slow and quiet decay of every year she has had to endure. It is a monument to her mistakes grown in soil poisoned by loneliness. That is not a nightmare, Keeper. That is her reality."

The gatekeeper bowed its head, a silent acknowledgment. "Then go to her."

The garden door reopened, not with a burst of light or a dramatic flourish, but it revealed the garden. This time, the illusion didn't evaporate. Ash was still falling, soft and ceaseless, and the black roses still wept, their petals curling inward. And Sera was still there, kneeling utterly alone in her silent sorrow.

Kael stepped forward reverently as if entering a sacred space.

She didn't seem to hear him, lost in her abyss. Or perhaps she didn't care.

He circled her, the falling ash dusting his hair, and then knelt at her side. His gaze fixed on her bowed head. "Sera?" he whispered.

She looked up, her movements slow as if she was awakening from a long, terrible dream. Her face was pale, almost translucent. Her lips were bloodless and drawn with a fixed line of agony.

A celestial blade protruded from her stomach, its hilt wrapped tight in her own trembling hands. The blade shimmered, its edges glowing with a divine light that seemed to mock the darkness around them. Blood, dark and thick, seeped from the wound, staining her dress a deeper crimson and pooling beneath her knees.

Kael's voice broke. "Sera...what have you done?"

Her lips parted, a fragile attempt at speech, but only a few came out, " I can't do this anymore". Her eyes then rolled back, blood spilling from her mouth in a crimson stream, and her body went limp. Her hands slipped from the hilt. Heavy and lifeless as she collapsed into his arms.

In shock Kael pressed his large palm over the gaping wound uselessly. As if he could hold her together by force of will alone. "No," he choked. It was a selfish plea, born of absolute desperation. "No, you don't get to do this to me."

The shadows swirled, echoing his rage. The maze itself shook, groaning under the weight of his despair.

"If you die here," he said low, a promise and a threat, "your death will accomplish nothing."

Her breath fluttered, shallow and uncertain. Her head lolled into the curve of his throat. Her weight was heavy and precious.

His grip tightened, a possessive hold. "You hear me?" he snarled at the sky, the unseen walls, and the faceless deities that had always turned their backs on them. "She's mine. You don't get to take her." He couldn't tell if it was him or the bond speaking, but he had to get out of here before the damage settled.

With a guttural growl, he stood, lifting her like he'd never let go.

The maze groaned around them as the dying leviathan collapsed from the inside out. The oppressive shadows cleared a path, retreating before his furious resolve.

Kael didn't hesitate.

His wings snapped open with a thunderclap that shook the very air, a violent unfurling of power, and he launched upward through the blood, the rot, and the burning wreckage. The portal loomed closer, its light flickering like a dying flame. His wings burned, and his breath came in ragged gasps that tore at his throat, but he didn't stop. He plunged into the vortex, clutching her tight against his chest, as the world around him dissolved into chaos, a maelstrom of light and shadows.

He tumbled back into Sera's living room, landing on the floor hard with a sickening thud. Pain exploded through him, in a white-hot agony that ripped through his chest, and he gasped. Cassia's hands were on him, wrenching the celestial blade from his chest.

He was alive.

He was back.

Ignoring the searing pain, he scrambled to his knees, crawling closer to Sera. She was still unconscious, lying on the sofa where he'd left her. A pale, still figure. But…faint color had returned to her cheeks, a whisper of life. Her breathing was stronger, a steady rhythm. Her stab wound, the one that had bled so terribly in the vision, was gone. An illusion.

He'd done it. He'd pulled her back.

Cassia was beside him, her face pale with relief and exhaustion. "She's…stabilizing." Her voice trembled. "The connection… You severed it. In the nick of time." She looked at him, her eyes filled with a grudging respect. "You…you saved her."

He managed a weak nod, unable to do more. He felt…utterly drained, as if his very essence had been siphoned away. Empty. But also…strangely exhilarated, a faint, fragile triumph blossoming within him.

Michael and Remiel were still there, silent and watching the scene with unreadable expressions. Their presence was a stark reminder of the larger forces at play.

Kael struggled to sit up, ignoring the searing pain in his chest, the constant throb. He needed Sera. He reached out, his hand hovering over her beautiful face. Not quite touching. Afraid to break the fragile peace. "Sera?" he whispered, his voice hoarse.

Sera's eyelids fluttered, a slow, hesitant movement. She stirred, and a soft sigh escaped her lips. She opened her eyes slowly, and her gaze landed on him. "Kael…?" she whispered, her voice weak as if awakening from a long sleep.

Kael smiled—a shaky, genuine smile. His relief was so vast it nearly unmade him. "Welcome back, Little Devil."

"You came for me," she whispered, wonder breaking through exhaustion. A tear slid down her cheek.

He brushed it away with his thumb.

When he moved, the lamplight caught the wound that crossed his chest: a deep, seared gash carved by celestial steel, still raw and rimmed in faint gold. Blood had dried in thin, dark lines down his ribs.

Sera's breath stuttered, and horror flooded her features. "Kael...your chest... What is that?"

He glanced down, unconcerned. "It's nothing."

Cassia stepped closer, her voice quiet but edged with command. "It's not nothing. That is a celestial blade, you fool. You need to heal."

He shook his head, his eyes never leaving Sera. "Later. Right now, I need to be here. With her."

Sera reached out, her hand trembling. She touched his cheek, her fingers cool against his skin. "Thank you," she whispered, her voice thick, "for...for saving me."

He leaned into her touch, closing his eyes and savoring the feel of her skin against his.

He'd done it. He'd brought her back.

A Wild Card

17

Kael slowly surfaced from a deep, exhausted sleep. The lingering tension was gone, replaced by the solid warmth of Sera pressed against his side. Her breathing was a steady rhythm that anchored him. He wasn't sure how long they'd slept, but the darkness of the room was starting to yield to a gray light filtering around the edges of the curtains. A glance at the bedside clock confirmed it was 5:17 a.m. Dawn wasn't far off.

Carefully disentangling himself, he eased out of bed. He then paused and adjusted the covers over her. Her dark hair was a stark contrast against the white pillowcase. Asleep, she looked unguarded, a state so rare for her that it was arresting. A faint, almost unconscious smile touched his lips.

He shut the bedroom door quietly behind him, the soft click echoing in the townhouse's silence. After crossing the hall, he found Michael and Remiel already seated at the breakfast bar in the kitchen area, their backs to him. Waiting.

"Gentlemen," Kael said, his voice calm. He leaned against the doorframe, his arms crossed. The casual posture didn't quite mask the challenge in his tone. "Mind if I join this...debriefing?" He pushed off the frame and walked toward them.

Michael and Remiel turned, their expressions a predictable mix of relief and dismay. Kael could practically see them calculating how to phrase the undoubtedly complicated truth.

"Kael," Michael said, his voice heavy. "Regarding my daughters...I guess there are things you need to know."

Before he could continue, the room pulsed. Just once. A faint ripple and a static noise ran across the walls. Everyone froze and straightened. Even Remiel flinched.

"Did you feel that?" Kael asked, scanning the windows from where he leaned on the counter.

Cassia's voice was low as she entered the living space. "Things are getting interesting..."

Michael stood and moved toward the wall, where he brushed two fingers over the paint. They came back red and burned. But nothing was noticeable to the mortal eye.

"We're not alone," he said, his voice tight. "Someone's testing the perimeter."

A silence fell. Taut. Ancient.

And then—like it had never happened—the air settled again.

Kael arched an eyebrow. "Well, I think I'm starting to connect the dots," he replied, his voice dry. "Half-demon daughters, absentee archangel father, Hell's queen wanting them back as part of some cosmic power play... Is that the general picture?"

"You're oversimplifying," Michael stated stiffly.

"Perhaps." He pushed away from the counter he leaned on. "But the core issue seems clear. You champion justice, yet this situation appears rooted firmly in damage control for *your* past actions."

Michael's eyes flashed with divine outrage. "I will *not* be lectured on morality by one of the fallen," he retorted, his voice dangerously quiet.

He gave a short, humorless laugh. "Of course not. Why entertain inconvenient truths when you can dismiss the source? Far easier for someone with your…perceived authority."

The air thickened, charged with ancient conflict and fresh antagonism. They kept each other's gaze, a silent clash of wills. Remiel looked profoundly uncomfortable.

Michael's mouth then tightened, but before he could answer, Kael stepped forward.

Kael's eyes were sharp with an emotion darker than anger. "So, you sat on a tribunal where two of each realm cast judgment—two angels, two demons, and two grays. And you want me to believe Lilith voted in favor of exiling her daughters?"

Michael's posture stiffened. "The tribunal acts in harmony. I don't dictate how demons vote."

But he didn't buy it. "Don't play innocent. You and Malakar were the ones who called the vote. The others wouldn't have moved without your lead."

"I don't control Lilith."

"No?" His laugh was low, bitter. "Then why did she go along with the verdict? Why didn't she even flinch while they ripped her daughters' names from the Book of Echoes?"

Michael's expression flickered. Then returned to cool neutrality. "Perhaps she had her own reasons. She has always played a longer game than anyone realized."

Kael took a slow, dangerous step forward. "You expect me to believe the queen of Hell sacrificed her bloodline for politics?"

"I don't know what Lilith was thinking. She did not explain."

He shook his head. "You're lying. Or worse: willfully ignorant. Which I highly doubt."

Michael's jaw flexed. "Careful, Kael. You tread close to the line."

He only huffed in response.

Remiel rose from his seat at the counter. "That's enough."

"No," Kael said, turning toward him. "It's not. They both sat on that tribunal. Both watched as Lilith voted against her own. And now, you all are shocked when she's clawing her way back into their lives?"

Michael's voice dropped, deadly quiet. "She wanted them back in her court. Perhaps this was the only way to cleanse their celestial ties."

He narrowed his eyes. "So, you admit it was a setup."

"I admit nothing. Only that this war has many fronts, and you're finally seeing it."

Kael turned away, his jaw clenched. "No. I see it clearer than ever."

"All right. Both of you," Remiel said, his tone calm but carrying undeniable weight. "This achieves nothing. We have far more pressing concerns than figuring out old decisions."

"He's right," a calm voice added from the doorway. Cassia still stood there on the edge of the living space, leaning with an air of cynical amusement. "Besides,"—her sharp gaze landed on Michael—"I think Father was just about to explain why he's really here. Do tell, Father."

Michael tensed at her tone, the faint shift enough to betray centuries of restrained pride, while Kael watched the exchange with keen interest. It seemed even celestial families weren't immune to dysfunction.

"Cassia," Remiel murmured.

She gave him a look but subsided.

Michael let out a slow, weary breath. "Kael," he said again, his gaze distant, "it's...complex. It started during the last infernal war."

Cassia made a quiet, disdainful noise.

"I am aware, Michael," Kael responded mockingly. "I was commanding legions during it. You seem to never agree on how to share the mortals…"

"Please," Michael said. "During that war…I was driven to make a change. I led a legion deep into Hell, aiming to strike a decisive blow." He paused. "It was…ill-advised. We were ambushed. Utterly outnumbered." His voice dropped. "We fought, but it was futile. I was captured. Taken prisoner by Lilith herself."

Kael absorbed that, recalibrating his image of the archangel: the embodiment of heavenly law was a prisoner of Hell's queen. That cast things in a new light.

"Lilith *is* formidable," Michael said. "Power, charm… She wields them seamlessly. She perceived…a weakness in me." He hesitated. "She exploited it. Used her abilities to ensnare me, to…influence me."

"Influence you how?" Kael asked.

A muscle tightened in his jaw. "She seduced me," he stated baldly. "And I…I fell for it."

Kael said nothing, his face unreadable, yet his gaze flicked to Cassia, who also remained unmoving.

Michael's voice was now flat as if he recited a script he wished didn't exist. "The tribunal voted on a ceasefire shortly after. The war had dragged on for too long, and both sides were losing power. As part of a truce, our union was sanctioned. A child was approved, only one. A symbol of possibility and a perfect balance between light and darkness." His eyes found Cassia. "That child was you."

Cassia's expression didn't change, but there was a cold curl of her mouth.

Kael stood still, barely breathing.

"Your birth," Michael continued, "halted the war. For a time, the bloodshed stopped. Both sides watched you grow. You were proof of the concept." His voice caught slightly. "But peace was never enough for Lilith. She wanted power, legacy, and dominion." He turned toward the window as if looking at the past through its blurred reflections. "She forged a decree and was able to conceive again."

Cassia whispered a name like a curse. "Sera."

He didn't nod. Didn't deny. "But the second child was never meant to happen. Only the first was guaranteed to carry true balance. The second child was a wild card, a variable. You'd never know what they'll inherit, what they'll become, until their twenty-first birthday."

Realization snapped into place like a trap. The silence in the room wasn't just stunned; it was seismic.

Kael's eyes, already narrowed, turned glacial. "When did you cast her out?" he asked, his voice low and even.

Michael turned to face him slowly, meeting his gaze. "When she was twenty."

The last word detonated.

Kael moved like a storm breaking its tether. "Bastard!"

He lunged, his hands curling like talons toward Michael's throat, but before he could close the distance, Michael's wings flared outward. The motion wasn't violent, but it didn't need to be. One blast of divine force, and Kael flew backward like a thrown weapon, his body smashing into the kitchen wall hard enough to crack the drywall and rattle the cabinets. Plates trembled. Cassia winced but didn't move.

Kael staggered to his feet with a snarl, bloody mouthed and eyes burning. He charged again.

This time, Remiel caught him around the ribs and dragged him back with brute celestial force. He thrashed in his grip, every muscle screaming for release.

"Kael, stop it!" Remiel barked. "Let him finish!"

But Kael didn't stop. Couldn't. "You're not just a bastard!" he roared, his voice hoarse with fury. "You're a coward!"

Michael didn't flinch. "I tried to prevent all of this." His voice was a strained whisper against the outburst's lingering echoes. "If only you had followed your direct order…"

Kael's mind was reeling. "You ordered me to kill a mother and an unborn child without a single explanation!"

"So, if I explained, would you have done it?" Michael's gaze was a piercing query.

"Of course not!"

"I trusted you with the job because you were the best of the best," he stated. "You never failed. You always believed. And after all your transgressions, I had no choice but to wait for the child to be born. If it was a male, he would automatically claim the throne in Hell. But it was a girl, Lilith had to keep her alive until she turned twenty-one, to see what she would become."

"You wanted to kill her before she transformed at twenty-one," Kael whispered, the realization a horrifying chill.

His expression tightened, a shadow falling over his features. "I did not want to kill my daughter. However, the rest of the tribunal voted in favor of it. That was until Cassia stepped in. Killing her too would have broken the fragile efforts for peace."

Cassia, her face already a mask of shock, let out a harsh, sarcastic chuckle. "*Wow*. So, there's no love, only politics. I knew I hated you. I didn't know I could hate you even more."

He flinched, his attempt at redemption crumbling. "After Sera was born, the tribunal offered Lilith a stark choice: give up the children to Heaven or forfeit her seat and her life for what she had pulled off. She took the first option. The girls were brought to Heaven, and the memory of their mother was erased."

"I don't understand," Kael said, his voice still raw. "Why would you not kill her yourself?"

He met his gaze, unflinching. "I bring the judgment, but I do not deliver it, especially assassinations."

Kael let out a harsh, disbelieving chuckle. He shook his head and jabbed a finger at his own chest. "So, you tried to save your ass by sacrificing mine?"

Michael's expression darkened. "She wants them back," he said grimly. "To reclaim them. To seat them in her court."

"Why?" he snapped. "Just to complete the set?"

Michael exhaled slowly. "Lilith's moves are growing bolder. The blood moon is entering its cycle. When it reaches completion, there will be a hundred minutes when divine law falters. If she harnesses that breach, she can rewrite the order itself. Sera's corrupted essence could override millennia of balance. It's a cosmic reset, Kael. And if she triggers it,"—he met Kael's eyes—"everything burns."

"She can't," Kael said, his voice unsteady. "We're bonded—"

"You're not," Michael cut in. "You began the bond, but it isn't complete. And even if it was, the blood moon respects nothing—no bond, no law, and not even the tribunal."

He went still.

Michael continued, his voice like thunder held on a tight leash. "Then there's her birthright. Infernal succession favors the youngest heir. If Lilith formally recognizes Sera—and if she brings her willingly—her claim to Hell becomes absolute. Her leverage over Heaven is unbreakable. The war…" He looked down. "The war would end. And we'd lose."

Kael's jaw clenched. "And Sera?" he asked quietly. "She doesn't know?"

Michael's looming silence confirmed the answer before he even spoke. "No. Neither of them knew anything. I thought silence would protect them." He closed his eyes. "But now, this silence may kill them."

"You mean, *you* may kill *me*...? Third time's a charm..."

A soft clearing of a throat pulled every eye to Sera. She stood at the threshold between her bedroom and the living space, dressed in practical travel clothes: sturdy pants, a long-sleeved shirt, and worn boots. Her hair was pulled back tight from her face.

Cassia's face crumpled, her jaw slack. Kael, his momentum stalled by her presence, began to move, a deliberate walk toward her. Remiel's chest expanded with a deep breath, his muscles tensing. Michael, however, froze, his eyes wide.

But Sera turned, her back to the open door. Her gaze swept over each of them, a silent judgment before her calm voice sliced through the air. "Do. Not. Follow. Me."

She then walked away, the door clicking shut behind her.

Kael halted midstride, his hand slapping against his empty pockets where his car keys should be. His eyes flickered to the bedroom door and then back at the closed front door. A quiet "Fuck" escaped him, a defeated exhalation.

Cassia strode forward with crisp, purposeful steps. She reached into the back pocket of her jeans and pulled out a folded parchment. It glowed faintly with the tribunal's seal, the edges blackened with celestial heat. Without warning, she hurled it at Michael's chest.

He caught it reflexively, frowning.

"Tribunal Edict 1014-H," she spat, "was sent three days ago. Was it a new attempt to finish Sera off for good?"

He stared at the scroll in confusion. "What?" His fingers traced the broken seal, and his eyes skimmed the elegant, damning script. His expression darkened, not with guilt but with bewilderment.

"This isn't mine," he murmured. "This is the first I've seen of it." His head turned sharply. "Remiel. You're listed here: Watcher 03. Is this your seal?"

Remiel blinked, visibly thrown. He reached for the scroll and examined it. "That's my sigil," he said slowly. "But I wasn't in the mortal realm until last night. I've been in stasis since…" He trailed off, confusion tightening across his brow.

"Stasis?" Cassia's voice dropped. "Why the hell were you in stasis?"

He hesitated. "I…don't… It is a long story."

Michael turned to her slowly, his look sharp enough to silence her.

Her throat locked around her next question. Not because she agreed. But because she remembered what defiance cost.

He then raised his head and smiled. The kind of smile that didn't touch his eyes. "Cassia," he said smoothly, "walk with me. A word. Outside."

The calm in his tone was surgical.

Cassia's gaze flicked to Kael, who was still nursing a bruised shoulder against the kitchen wall. Remiel's eyes stayed locked on the scroll; he seemed troubled.

She gave a sharp exhale—a half laugh, a half warning. "Fine. Let's talk."

She followed Michael to the balcony. The door clicked behind them. As he led her onto the balcony, the soft glow of the early Savannah morning began to light up the sky. The air was fresh, carrying the faint scent of magnolias. City lights shimmered below like sleepy embers, and the hush before sunrise pressed around them like a held breath.

Michael's gaze was both stern and protective as he turned to her. "If you reveal anything to Remiel right now, I won't be able to save you from your fate."

She looked out over the city. "How do you expect me to stay quiet?"

He took a step closer. "Well, if you're not afraid to die, then go ahead."

She turned to him, her eyes narrowing. "Are you threatening me?"

"No, Daughter," Michael said, soft but firm. "I'm trying to protect you."

A pause stretched between them.

"Do you even know why I'm here in Savannah?" she asked.

He shook his head. "No. Do tell. I've been looking for you all over the realms."

She sighed, her shoulders slumping slightly. "I came to say goodbye because I heard Malakar sent out the watchers to capture me."

His expression softened, unreadable. "Don't worry, my dear. Everything will unfold as it should, and you'll be safe in the end. Trust me."

She blinked, unsettled by the sudden shift in his tone. "That's not exactly comforting."

He smiled faintly, almost wistfully. "When all of this is over, I advise you to stay in Hell under the protection of your uncle, Lucifer."

She stared at him. "But he's in stasis, isn't he?"

Michael gave a knowing smile. "Well, when it's over and if it all goes according to my plan, everything will return to normal."

The sky turned a shade lighter, and the birds stirred in the trees beyond. The moment held its breath and didn't let it go.

Queen's Gambit

18

The air in Crimson Keep's throne room was cold enough to crystallize breath, heavy with the scent of ozone and old power. Shadows clung possessively to the obsidian walls, which were carved with the tormented faces of forgotten deities and the spiraling histories of damnation. Upon the throne, which was sculpted from jagged volcanic glass that seemed to absorb light, sat the queen of Hell herself, surrounded by the infernal courtiers and demon guards.

Lilith was a figure of arresting beauty, statuesque and severe. She bore a striking resemblance to her daughter Sera—the same moon-shaped face, the same elegantly defined features—yet where Sera possessed a wild, wavy cascade of dark hair, Lilith's hair was an impossibly straight fall of silky blackness, stark against her ivory skin. She was imbued with eyes not of warm humor but of molten gold: ancient, calculating, and utterly ruthless. She surveyed her domain with an air of bored omnipotence, one perfectly manicured hand resting on the throne's armrest.

A frantic distortion shimmered in the air before the dais. A lesser demon, more shadow than substance, materialized from the ether, prostrating itself immediately upon the cold floor and radiating palpable terror.

"My Queen," it rasped, its sound like dry leaves skittering across gravestones. "An update...on the asset Seraphine."

Lilith didn't move, only arched one perfect eyebrow.

The gesture alone made the demon press itself further against the stones.

"Report," she commanded, her voice smooth as silk yet also a sharp promise like broken glass.

"The op-operation...failed, Your Majesty," it said, its form flickering. "Seraphine...remains uncontained. There was an interference."

The temperature in the room rose.

Lilith's golden eyes narrowed to dangerous slits. "Failed?" she repeated, the word soft but terrifying. "Interference?"

"The fallen one... Kael. H-he reached her before our operatives could secure her transition. He...pulled her from Limbo's edge."

A low, menacing sound vibrated deep in Lilith's chest. "Kael," she breathed, the name a curse. Her black nails tapped a slow, dangerous rhythm on the throne. "After months of meticulously tracking her movements? After patiently waiting for the opportune moment? After all the resources diverted to ensuring her capture?" Her voice, though still controlled, began to rise with barely contained fury. "You tell me my daughter, practically gift wrapped, was simply retrieved by that celestial cast off?"

"He was...stronger than anticipated, Your Majesty... His arrival unforeseen—"

With an almost negligent flick of her wrist, a tendril of pure solid shadow, sharper than any blade, lashed out from the darkness pooled around her throne. It struck the demon mid-word. There was no scream, only a faint hiss, as the creature imploded, dissolving into a dissipating cloud of greasy black ash that settled on the floor.

She remained motionless, watching the ash settle like snow.

Then she inhaled, slow and deliberate. "There isn't time for this," she said softly. "The blood moon is starting its cycle." Her gaze drifted upward, as though she could already see it burning through the stone. "Twenty-eight nights is all we got, and now the final one approaches fast. The convergence, the preparation—everything has been leading to this." A muscle flickered in her jaw, the faintest crack in her composure. "One window. One chance. And they waste it with incompetence."

She did not rage. She did not scream. Yet the air grew heavier, dense with pressure, and the faint tremor of distant fire answered her silence. It felt as if Hell itself had drawn a breath and waited for her command.

"I feel like my personal presence is needed," she said, her eyes narrowing. "I've waited long enough. And if threats help, then so be it." Her expression shifted, sharpening into a smile too controlled. She observed the remnants dispassionately for a moment before speaking into the heavy silence. "Xathos."

From the deepest shadows near the throne, a different figure emerged. This demon was larger, leaner, and built like a whipcord with eyes like cold burning embers. It knelt instantly, head bowed, radiating competence and wary respect.

"The previous fool proved...expendable," Lilith stated coolly, waving a dismissive hand toward the settling ash. "You will now oversee the operation concerning my daughter."

"Yes, Queen Lilith," Xathos replied, his voice a low, gravelly rumble.

"Your first task requires finesse." A calculating gleam entered her golden eyes. "Gather a small, discreet retinue. Prepare yourselves for transit." A humorless smile touched her lips. "We are paying a visit to the land of the living."

He looked up surprised but masked it. "Your Majesty?"

"Someone needs to be reminded of what happens when they do not follow through on their end of the bargain." She slowly rose from her throne, her presence seeming to expand to fill the vast chamber. "Someone who owes me a rather significant favor from long ago needs to finish her job." Her smile widened, showing just a hint of fang.

He bowed low again. "I understand, my queen. We shall be ready." He melted back into the shadows as swiftly as he had appeared.

Lilith stood alone, gazing into the oppressive gloom of her hall. Her golden eyes burned with renewed purpose. Kael. Sera. They thought they had won a battle and found a moment's peace. How little they understood. The game had merely shifted, and she held cards they couldn't even fathom.

Her daughters would be hers.

Sera's hands gripped the steering wheel, her knuckles white. The memory of taking the keys eluded her, replaced only by the echo of Kael's voice as she walked out the door.

Now, she was behind the wheel of his car. The sun bled a pale, sickly light across the horizon, slicing through the morning fog with indifference. But the quiet world outside offered no peace to the tempest raging within her mind.

Michael's words reverberated like a curse she couldn't shake, each syllable a fresh lash. *She was twenty*. The age at which he had exiled her. The very age he would have delivered the final fatal blow.

And she ran. Fled from the one person who might have offered a lifeline. The desperate bond Kael offered, the faint light she could have reached for in that fracturing moment.

She'd torn it with her own hands.

Again.

Not for the first time. Not even the worst time. A chilling whisper from the depths of her own making confirmed it: She had done far worse.

Her throat tightened, a constriction of pure horror, as the unbidden memory slammed into her. Mark's skin was slick with sweat and fear beneath her fingers. The soft, uncomprehending plea in his eyes just before she bent him to her will. He hadn't known. He'd thought it was her. He had loved her.

But it hadn't been love. It had been hunger. Violent. Consuming.

And she had used him just as she had used that man in Berlin.

She felt a wet rhythm tapping against her thigh. Drip. Drip. Drip. She looked down, and her eyes widened at the growing stain on her lap. At first, a desperate part of her mind whispered sweat, but the color was too dark.

Blood.

Her trembling hand fumbled for the visor. With a jerky motion, she flipped down the mirror. Her own face stared back, ruined.

Tears, dark and thick, streaked her cheeks in broken trails. Her eyes, red-rimmed and hollowed, pulsed with an unholy ache. She lifted the heel of her palm, trying to wipe the ghoulish rivulets away, but all she managed was to smear the blood, masking her face.

She slammed the visor shut with a violent crack.

The car slightly swerved before she pulled it over, gravel spitting beneath the tires.

With her hands shaking so violently they blurred, she fumbled for her phone. Her fingers hovered over her call history, trembling above one name for a second too long before she finally tapped it.

It rang once. Twice.

"Sera?"

"Mark, hi," she said, her voice softer than intended and laced with genuine remorse. "I'm...I'm okay. I'm so sorry for just...disappearing like that. It wasn't right."

"I was just worried something happened," he said, relief palpable in his tone.

They spoke for a few moments more, his gentle questioning a stark contrast to the volatile emotions swirling within her. She listened and offered vague assurances, her gaze drifting to the road. The rhythmic sound of passing cars calmed her nerves. The knowledge of Kael's willingness to help her—the only person in that room who would die trying because the bond would not let him go otherwise—coupled with the lingering shame of her actions with Mark solidified her resolve.

Mark was never supposed to be more than a way to smooth out the edges.

But he stayed too long. Let her take too much. She could lie to herself and say he consented, but the shadows knew better.

He forgave her. That was the worst part.

"Mark," she said gently, needing to get to the heart of it before her courage failed, "about the other night..." She paused, gathering her words. "I need to apologize."

"Sera, you don't have to—"

"Yes, I do," she said softly but firmly. "I wasn't...myself, Mark. Things felt intense and overwhelming, and I wasn't thinking clearly. I took advantage of the situation, of you, and that was deeply unfair. It was wrong of me, and I need you to know it can't and won't ever happen again."

There was a silence on the line, heavy with unspoken hurt.

"Okay, Sera," he said, his voice subdued. "I...appreciate you saying that."

"It also made me realize," she said, pushing forward, "that we can't go back. Not really. It's truly over between us, Mark. We had our time, but it's passed. We need to let each other go, properly this time."

As she spoke the words, severing the tie, she felt a subtle shift, an almost imperceptible loosening of an old energetic cord.

For mortals touched by the deep-seated influence of a being like her, the connection often fostered an unnatural dependency, a binding echo that lingered long after logic dictated otherwise. However, when the source of that influence consciously released its hold and truly let go, the residual energy faded. The clinging resonance dissipated, leaving behind memories but, crucially, granting the mortal clarity and the freedom to heal and finally move forward.

Another long pause stretched between them before Mark responded, his voice thick but lacking the desperate edge it had held before. "It hurts, Sera. Not going to lie. But...I understand." He took a breath. "We had something special once. I'll always remember the good times." He paused again before speaking with genuine warmth. "I hope you find happiness, Sera. Truly. And look, if you ever—and I mean ever—need anything, please don't hesitate to call me. Friend to friend."

A wave of bittersweet relief washed over her. "Thank you, Mark. That means a lot. I wish you the best too. Really."

As the final word left her lips, a faint tug of energy unraveled from her chest like a thread. Not just a metaphor but an absolute unraveling.

She had finally released the tether between them.

She sat motionless, the phone still cradled in her hand long after the call with Mark had ended. The engine was off, and the world beyond the windshield felt suspended. She stared forward, unblinking.

There was nothing in front of her. Just the blurred smear of the road washed in the indifferent hush of the morning. Birds stirred somewhere in the distance. A single leaf tumbled across the asphalt. But inside, the silence roared.

She didn't know how long she'd been sitting there. Minutes? Hours? Her body felt detached, weightless, and slow as if grieving something it hadn't yet found the words for.

The phone in her lap buzzed, and the screen lit up. Bethany.

That first ring pulled Sera from her trance. She stared at Bethany's name glowing against her thigh, a cold unease coiling up her spine. She hadn't spoken to Bethany since…

She answered. "…Hello?"

What came through wasn't a greeting. It was sobbing. Choked. Uncontrolled. "Sera…" Bethany's voice fractured through the static and the tears. "Please…can you come over? I need you."

Her entire posture shifted, tension snapping her upright. "Beth? What's going on?"

"I…I can't say over the phone." Bethany gasped, a desperate plea. "I need to tell you to your face. Please…just come. Please."

Sera had never heard her cry. Not like this. Not even close. Bethany had always been glitter-glossed defiance, all teeth and fashion and laughter over shots of espresso. This was something else. Raw. Terrified.

"I'm coming," Sera said, her voice firm despite the tremor of alarm that shook her. She was already turning her car back on and shifting it into gear. "I'm on my way."

Bethany only sobbed in reply.

She pulled onto the road, and the tires crunched gravel as the car picked up speed. The city gave way to its quieter edge, winding into a wealthy suburb just outside Savannah... A place locals called Harrowsend.

It was the kind of neighborhood meticulously crafted to appear timeless. Oak-lined streets were draped in Spanish moss. Sidewalks bordered vibrant hydrangeas and manicured boxwoods. Grand, symmetrical homes boasted wraparound porches and iron-gated driveways. The air hung with the scent of damp stone and distant honeysuckle. Everything was hushed as if money could truly buy silence.

But Bethany's house commanded attention: whitewashed bricks framed by tall black shutters, a slate roof, and a cherry-red door. The lawn was impeccable, with not a single blade out of place, and tall hedges protectively curled around the property's edges like green sentinels. Even her driveway was spotless. Pristine. Untouched.

Too untouched.

Sera pulled in, her heart hammering harder than she wanted to admit. The car barely stopped before she put it in park and yanked the door open. Her boots crunched on the gravel border as she rushed toward the house.

"Bethany?" she called out, her voice sharp with growing fear.

No answer came.

She didn't knock. She didn't wait.

Beneath the Flowers

19

The shadows stirred the moment Sera stepped over the threshold and into Bethany's house. But they didn't whisper as they usually did. Now, they yelled.

Sera! Turn around!

There is danger!

The voices scraped against her mind, urgent and sharp. But she shook them off. Her heart was already too heavy, and her mind was too clouded to heed them.

Bethany was crying, she reminded herself. Bethany needed me.

Her boots clicked against the tile in an echoing rhythm, each step oddly loud in the pristine stillness. The air felt…wrong. Too still. Too clean. Like the house had been scrubbed of life, carefully prepared.

She turned the corner into the living room and froze.

Bethany sat curled on the couch in the center of the room, her hands wrung in her lap. Her dress, a riot of bright florals, clashed against the muted gray walls and the sterile light spilling in through the oversized windows. Her hair was artfully mussed, and her makeup streaked in theatrical smudges of black and glitter. It was the kind of mess that looked painted on. Too symmetrical.

Bethany looked up. Her icy blue eyes brimmed with perfectly placed tears that were trembling on the edge but never falling. "Sera, please sit," she said, her voice cracking. "I-I need to tell you something."

Sera's stomach churned. That ancient sense inside her howled. But she kept her expression neutral and crossed the room slowly. She settled onto the very edge of a nearby armchair.

She sniffled again, wiping her cheek with the back of her hand. "I-I didn't know how to say it. I've been carrying this for days, and I just… I've felt awful."

Sera didn't speak. She watched. She listened. She waited.

"I…I got drunk," Bethany whispered, her gaze dropping. "That night. After the Gilded Grill. And…Kael and I… We ended up together. I didn't mean for it to happen. But we…" Her voice cracked, a beautifully rehearsed tremor. "We spent the night together."

Sera blinked. Once.

She twisted her fingers in her lap. "It just… It kept happening after that. We've been seeing each other. We're…we're developing something. I…didn't want to lie to you, but I didn't know how to tell you. I thought maybe if I said it out loud, it would stop hurting."

A long beat passed, thick with unspoken accusations.

She then spoke almost too casually as if delivering a careless stab. "He just left actually. About twenty minutes ago."

Sera's breath caught in her throat, a strangled sound. Her voice came low and sharp. "He… What?"

She looked up, blinking with wet eyes. "He just left. Said he had to go get something from his place before seeing you again."

Sera stood, and the pressure dropped.

"What is going on?" Sera hissed, her voice shaking with a cold, blossoming fury. "Kael's at my house. He's been there all night!"

Bethany's eyes stopped shimmering. The sobs caught mid-hitch and then died. The carefully constructed performance dissolved, revealing calculated malice beneath.

Bethany tilted her head, and a slow, chilling smirk spread across her lips. "Well," she purred, her voice clear and venomous, "you have to admit…it was a good act. However, we did fuck that night. He was gorgeous. Just like the good ol' times."

"Good ol' times?" Sera snapped. "Bethany, what are you talking about?"

She relaxed onto the couch, a predatory expression devoid of warmth, and Sera felt a tremor of unease.

"Bethany?" The woman chuckled, a low, strange sound. "Oh, sweetie. Bethany hasn't been truly *real* for a very, very long time."

Sera frowned, confusion warring with rising dread. "What are you talking about?"

Bethany—or whoever she was—got off the couch and took a step closer, her voice dropping to an almost hypnotic whisper that sent shivers down Sera's spine. "My name—my *real* name—is Elara. And yes, Kael knew me. Loved me even. Centuries ago, long before you were but a seed in your mother's cruel and magnificent body, he knew me."

The name struck Sera like a physical blow. *Elara.* That ancient witch queen from the Book of Echoes, from the revisions Cassia and her had snuck out of Heaven's archive before they were sent to be destroyed.

Sera stumbled back, shaking her head. "Elara? The queen from the book… You- you died…"

A bitter laugh escaped Elara. "Died? In a manner of speaking, yes. I am a practitioner of the old ways… a witch." Her gaze sharpened, locking onto Sera's. "And he had loved me, the fool."

"But...how?" she breathed, struggling to reconcile the face of her friend with the centuries-old tragedy the book had described. "How are you *here*? Like *this*? Witches are not immortal..."

"A deal," Elara said, the second word laced with venom. "Heaven has rules, Sera. Strict ones. An archangel commander, Heaven's golden champion, consorting with a witch? Unthinkable. But your mother, Lilith, saw an opportunity."

Sera flinched at her mother's name.

"She approached me centuries ago." Elara paced slowly, her movements fluid and predatory. "Kael was too powerful, too successful, and too *loyal*. An obstacle to her ambitions. She needed him gone. Or at least diminished. So, she offered me a bargain: Report Kael to the heavenly tribunal and expose his transgression for being in love with me. And in return?" She paused. "In return, she would gift me immortality. The power to shed my skin and weave a new face and a new life every fifty years. To escape death. Escape consequences. All that was required of me was a report and a favor to be called upon at a later day."

Horror washed over Sera. "You...you betrayed him? For *Lilith*?"

Her eyes flashed with ancient pain and bubbling resentment. "*Betrayed?* He broke divine law and disobeyed direct orders. Lilith sweetened the deal by..." A cold smile curved her lips as her mind visibly trailed off. "...The power she offered. Made me darker. By the time I stood before the tribunal, I wasn't simply the woman Kael loved. I was a witch reborn. I was a *black* witch... That was a crime worthy of death for him. I do not know why Michael did not have him executed; maybe his fondness for his favorite soldier softened the sentence. But in the end, Kael wasn't destroyed. He was cast out. Fallen." She leaned in slightly, her voice dripping with malice. "Because of *me*. Because of the deal your mother engineered. And well… of course, because he refused to kill Lilith."

Horrified, Sera stared as the pieces clicked into place. The centuries of Kael's pain. The reason for his fall… All orchestrated by the woman standing before her. "So…me?" she whispered, the words catching in her throat. "Our friendship? What was that?"

Elara shrugged, a jarringly casual gesture that spoke volumes. "You? You were…convenient. An amusement." Her tone turned brittle. "Being best friends with Lilith's precious daughter? It had its benefits. Protection, status, and a comfortable life. It was all rather pleasant…until *he* walked back into my life. Into the Iron Orchid of all places." Bitterness twisted her features. "Seeing him again… Seeing him look at *you* with that same foolish devotion… It spoiled *everything*." She spat her words, venom threading her voice. "I mean, I even gave you a fucking choker for the Holy Rollers. A gift, remember? Said it was for the aesthetic? It was a ward specifically designed to blur your aura, to keep him from recognizing what you are. To keep him mine. And still…he looked at *you*."

"You wanted him back," she stated, the realization cold and hard.

"He was mine *first!*" Elara hissed. "I endured centuries and remade myself over and over. Waiting. Wondering. I deserved a second chance, not some…half-demon abomination Lilith spawned! I knew I had to get you away from him. Break you apart."

The memory of the cloying scent of herbs burning in her townhome. The subtle gifts from Bethany meant to relax her…

"The essences…" Sera breathed, understanding dawning on her.

A cruel smile touched Elara's lips. "…were designed to *agitate* your demonic nature. Burning them in your home day after day? I was trying to speed up your transformation. Make you unstable. Monstrous. Make you snap. Fray your control until you push him away or until he turns away from you in disgust."

The casual cruelty. The calculated destruction aimed at her very being. The attempt to manipulate Kael. The use of her corrupted nature. It was too much. Sera's control, already frayed thin by months of inexplicable anxiety and burgeoning power, imploded.

"You...you did that...to *me*?" Sera's voice dropped, trembling not with fear but with a rage that shook her core. "Burned essences in my home... Tried to turn *me* into a monster... So that you could have a *second chance* with him? After *you* betrayed him?"

Elara scoffed. "Like I said, he was mine first. A minor manipulation seemed a small price to pay."

A guttural cry ripped from Sera's throat. The air thickened, charged with invisible energy that made the hairs on her arms stand. Her eyes flashed, pupils dilating until they seemed to swallow the light. "You touch *nothing* that is his!" she roared.

Before Elara could react, a wave of raw concussive force erupted from Sera. It wasn't summoned or directed by conscious thought. It was pure, unadulterated rage given physical form. The invisible wave slammed into Elara, lifting her clean off her feet and sending her flying across the room. Her body impacted the far wall with a sickening thud, and a cry of shock and pain tore from her. The shelf of expensive trinkets above her started to fall as she slid to the floor in a heap.

"Well..." Elara coughed, wiping blood from her mouth. "That temper of yours is exactly what she wanted to see." A trickle of blood traced a path from the corner of her lip. She stared at Sera, truly seeing her, and shock curdled into her venom. Her face contorted with a mixture of fury and stunned disbelief. "You little hybrid *bitch*!" she spat.

"You think that changes anything? You think *that* scares me?!"

Sera took a threatening step forward, the residual energy still faintly crackling around her. The scent of ozone was sharp in the air. "Get out of my life," her voice low and dangerous. "Stay away from Kael."

She staggered to her feet, her eyes narrowing and burning with hatred. She spat a fleck of blood onto the polished floor. "Oh, I will do what I please. But *you*... Your mother reached out. Remember that favor I mentioned? She called it in before Kael's little stunt in Limbo."

The mention of Limbo broke through Sera's rage, pulling her up short. "How...how do you know about Limbo?"

A triumphant smile spread across her bruised face. "Your mother told me, of course!" Her voice rose, resonating through the apartment. "And that favor...was to ensure her daughter gets delivered! NOW!"

As if summoned by her enraged command, shadows in the corners of the room detached themselves from the walls and coalesced into solid forms. Sleek, powerful demons materialized, their eyes glowing with malevolent intent.

"No!" Sera cried, realizing the depth of the betrayal.

"Take her!" Elara ordered. "Don't damage her too much. Mommy wants her relatively intact!"

And then, they advanced.

The first approaching demon was a monstrous, lumbering brute with twisted horns and flesh that appeared scorched and torn. Its glowing red eyes locked onto Sera with predatory hunger, and its massive hands flexed, claws glinting like obsidian.

Sera retreated until her boots hit the edge of a desk. Papers hissed across the floorboards as she slid back. Her hand scrabbled blindly over the debris, her fingers grazing useless junk before closing around cold metal.

A letter opener. Not a weapon she would prefer. Just a jagged promise of violence.

The demons pressed in. Dust fell from the rafters with the weight of their approach.

The nearest one eclipsed the light. Its skin was a map of cracks and burns, and its eyes held the flat, dead hunger of something that had forgotten how to be alive. Its claws flexed, reaching for the pulse in her throat.

Sera didn't flinch. She baited it.

She shifted sideways, offering a target, and then snapped forward with the speed of a striking snake. She drove the letter opener into the soft, yielding flesh beneath its ribs. The metal sank deep. The creature lurched, a wet, gurgling snarl tearing from its throat.

She ripped the blade free, dark blood slicking her hand.

One down. The rest were waiting.

A cold, terrifying thought sliced through Sera's panic: Kael was waiting for her. The memory of his promise outside Serpent's Kiss. The impossible tenderness of their first kiss. The bond that had ignited between them. It wasn't just a memory but a promise. A future. A future that this pawn of her mother was trying to steal.

That thought ignited her fury into a white-hot inferno. She wasn't just fighting for her life. She was fighting for *theirs*.

A second demon descended from above, its batlike wings casting distorted shadows across the walls. As razor-sharp talons scraped against the polished floor, they created an earsplitting screech. This one moved more fluidly, circling her like a predator playing with its prey. Its soulless black eyes bore into hers as if savoring the anticipation of the kill.

"Is this your grand plan, *Elara?*" she shouted, her voice steady despite the chaos. "Throw Lilith's pathetic pets at me and hope for the best?"

The winged demon lunged, its talons slashing toward her face. She raised her makeshift weapon and deflected the blow with a sharp clang. It screeched and circled back for another attack. She pressed her advantage, moving with precision and speed. As it dove again, she sidestepped and drove the letter opener into its eye, the blade piercing deep. The creature shrieked, its form dissolving into black mist that evaporated.

Before Sera could catch her breath, a third demon emerged, a hulking monstrosity with elongated limbs and skin that seemed to bubble and writhe. It moved with a grotesque speed that contradicted its size, and she barely had time to react before it grabbed her, its clawed hand wrapping around her arm. She twisted and slashed at its arm with her blade, but its grip didn't falter.

A searing pain exploded at the back of her head. The world tilted, and her vision blurred as her body crumpled to the floor. The letter opener slipped from her numb fingers and clattered uselessly onto the ground.

"Sorry, honey," Elara cooed from above, her voice sickeningly sweet and dripping with venom.

Sera tried to lift her head, but her body refused to obey. Through her hazy vision, she saw Elara standing over her with a fireplace poker in her hand. Its end glinted with her blood.

"I can't let you ruin everything."

The first demon bent down, and its massive hand easily lifted Sera's limp body. It slung her over its shoulder as though she weighed nothing. Her head lolled uselessly against its mottled green flesh. A swirling vortex of fire and shadow ripped open in the center of the room, and the smell of sulfur filled her nose.

"Your debt is acknowledged," the demon growled, its voice deep and inhuman and reverberating. "The queen will be pleased."

"Goodbye, Sera," Elara whispered, her voice barely audible above the howling winds of the vortex. "Enjoy your new home."

And with that, the demon stepped into the portal, carrying Sera into the infernal abyss. The last thing Sera saw was Elara's face, smiling with cruel satisfaction, before the portal snapped shut with a thunderous crack.

Unraveling

20

Kael stepped into his apartment like a man dragging ghosts behind him. The door shut with a soft click, a muted sigh swallowed by the oppressive heat of a summer night. He didn't bother turning on the lights; the anonymity of the dark was a necessary balm now.

The last twenty-four hours had beaten him raw. Sera, her spirit fractured and her very essence nearly claimed by Limbo. Cassia, shaken to her core but still blazing with defiant loyalty. And Michael... Michael, his convoluted tribunal confessions, insidious half truths, and calculated cruelty. Kael's fists clenched, the phantom ache of wanting to strike him a persistent throb.

But he'd promised all of them that he'd return to the angel base. To give him a couple of hours, but he'd go. And now here he was, boots half untied and soul still reverberating.

His phone buzzed in his hand before he could toss it aside. Jareth. Of course. The familiar tether in the storm.

He answered. "I'm back."

"You alive?" the familiar rasp asked. "Or are you answering from the afterlife to tell me Heaven sucks?"

Kael barked a humorless laugh, the sound grating in the heavy silence. "Not dead. Not yet. But I might be unraveling. It's been a night."

Jareth's voice held a rare edge of genuine concern. "Worse than usual?"

"Worse than Hell," he muttered, the words heavy. "Anyway, it is a long story. I'll fill you in later, but I need a favor."

"You want me to watch the club again?"

He ran a hand down his face, the exhaustion a physical weight. "Yeah. Take the feeds. Lock up the vault. Handle the bounty traffic for a few nights. I need to focus. Sera is at the edge of something—bloodlines, Hell, and Lilith's twisted legacy. It's all pressing in. I need time to help her figure it out before it swallows her whole."

"You got it," Jareth replied without hesitation. "I'll light a candle and throw a demon off the balcony for you. Now, go fix your apocalypse."

He smiled faintly, a ghost of his usual wry humor. "Thanks, Jar." He then hung up and finally let himself breathe, the phone still warm in his hand. Without thinking, his thumb moved, pulling up a vehicle tracker.

The screen brightened, too sharp against the low light. A blinking dot pulsed in Harrowsend. He was almost sure that was Bethany's house.

Kael stared at it for a long agonizing time. The quiet stretched, each second a taut drumbeat against his temples. He slowly exhaled through his nose, the scent of phantom brimstone clinging to his memory. His head tipped back against a wall, his shoulders sagging. He hadn't even realized how truly tight they were, how long he'd been holding his breath through the dizzying kaleidoscope of chaos.

The silence of the apartment didn't comfort him. It pressed in, heavy and suffocating. Too still. His body ached, not from the fresh wound in his chest that was already knitting itself back together but from the raw tension layered thick in his bones. From the impossible restraint it had taken not to tear Michael apart.

And now this.

His thumb hovered over the glowing dot. He swallowed against the dry, metallic taste rising in his throat.

Bethany.

Of all people. There was something familiar about that woman, something personal. That night after the Gilded Grill was never meant to happen. He hadn't been thinking beyond the stinging need to forget the unsettling pull Sera had ignited. He'd just needed a moment of forgetting, and Bethany had been…convenient. Present. Soft where everything else had been demanding. She'd smiled at him like he wasn't breaking apart, and he'd allowed her to believe it, to believe she was a balm when she was merely another distraction.

Now, the cost of that mistake was about to be levied.

He rubbed a hand over his face, his fingers digging into his eyes. The suffocating guilt clung to him, heavy and unyielding. If Sera found out about that night from Bethany, it would shatter the fragile bond they had started to develop.

No.

He made a vow, right there in the dim quiet of his apartment. Sera would hear it from him. And he hoped she, like no one else, would understand the dilemma he had put himself in. And he hoped the tether from his heart to hers would not snap.

Two hours later, Kael approached an unassuming building in Port

Wentworth, and a shiver ran down his spine. The plain industrial exterior might have fooled anyone else, but to him, it was a mask—a hollow guise concealing beings far more dangerous.

As he stepped inside, the heavy door groaned shut behind him, and he was swallowed by the sterile hum of machinery and the faint scent of ozone. The space vibrated.

Consoles lined every wall, their displays flickering. Real-time data streamed across holographic panels, intricate maps and shifting diagrams. At the center of the room stood a colossal holographic display, a glowing monolith that dominated the space.

"Kael," Remiel said, his voice steady but urgent. His presence was magnetic, commanding the room even as the technology seemed to overshadow everything around him. "Thank you for coming so soon."

Kael stepped forward, his narrowed eyes sweeping across the control room. "It's not every day I get invited somewhere like this."

He offered a half smile, though there was little humor in it. "Being involved with the archangel's daughter has its perks, I guess."

Before Kael could respond, Michael and Cassia entered the room, their presence palpable. Michael's broad frame and stern expression carried an authority that bordered on oppressive. She, in contrast, moved with subtle apprehension, her sharp gaze darting across the screens.

Remiel turned somber, the lines on his face drawn tight. With a swift motion, he beckoned them to join him at the central console. "We don't have much time." His fingers flew over the keyboard, and the screens around them shifted and flickered. "There's something you all need to see."

The colossal hologram flared to life, casting an eerie glow that bathed the room in silver-blue light. A car appeared on the display. It was hurtling down a rain-slicked road, its headlights cutting through the gloom.

Kael froze. His breath caught. Sera's car. Speeding recklessly. He knew that road; he had seen it in the maze's nightmare. The jagged memory hit him like a physical blow.

The screen shifted to another camera angle. A translucent female figure, flickering in and out of visibility, conjured a deer in Sera's path with deliberate precision. He knew that shape.

Bethany.

His chest constricted, and a strangled sound escaped his throat. The crash hadn't been random. It was an act of malice, a cruel design.

"Lilith had planned it," Remiel said. "She intended to destroy Sera's mortal body, sending her soul straight to Hell, since Sera was already in a demonic state. But Sera's mental state... It diverted her, landed her in Limbo."

He didn't need the details, didn't care about the intricacies of the plot. He could barely think past the suffocating terror wrapping itself around him.

His world was shattered. Sera was at Bethany's. Now. And he was already too late.

In that exact moment, the bond—that warm, golden thread that hummed beneath his skin since he'd fed her his light—snapped. It wasn't a fray; it was violent as if a blade had been driven through his very soul. He felt the echo of her terror, the suffocating darkness of a portal closing, and then...nothing.

The connection went dead.

A strangled gasp escaped his lips as he staggered, clutching his chest. The silence in his soul was absolute, a void where her light had been. Panic seized him, a living beast clawing at his throat. He lunged for his phone, and his fingers trembled as he dialed Sera's number. Voicemail.

Again.

And again.

"Kael?!" Cassia's voice came from behind him, but he barely registered it.

His vision tunneled, black edges eating away at everything but the screen. The image of Bethany's number on display burned in his mind.

A heavy hand clamped down on his shoulder. Michael's thundering voice broke through the chaos. "What is it, boy?"

Kael spun, a feral snarl ripping from his throat. His movements were violent, his raw power radiating outward in a pulse of energy that made the air crackle. "Don't you fucking dare touch me," he spat, his voice low and dangerous. The blue of his eyes was gone, replaced by black voids. His angelic mask had shattered, leaving the wild, untamed force of the fallen in its place. "That is Bethany..." He pointed at the image with a shaking index finger. "Sera is at Bethany's... *Now*."

Michael's hand fell, his composure momentarily shaken. Even he couldn't hide the flicker of unease that crossed his face. Cassia gasped, her expression pale. The atmosphere grew thick and oppressive as Kael's power pressed outward like a storm ready to erupt.

The screen froze on the address, but Kael was already moving. He did not need an address. His movements blurred by the sheer force of his urgency. Even if he did not know where his car was, his tether to Sera would pull him to her regardless. But that tether felt wrong, numb.

His voice, low and guttural, erupted as he headed for the door. "Stay out of my way."

The others called out after him, but he was gone, consumed by the need to save the one person who had mattered.

Kael didn't knock.

He didn't hesitate.

Bethany's front door exploded inward, the sleek metal frame buckling under the sheer force of his fury. The impact reverberated through the house, a crash that shattered the oppressive silence. He barely registered the debris at his feet as he stepped forward, his body vibrating with barely contained violence.

The scene that greeted him was carnage.

The house was in ruin: designer furniture overturned, shards of glass scattered across the polished wood floor, the acrid sting of sulfur saturating the air. The blood was the worst of it. It was smeared across the floor, streaked along the white walls, and pooled in ominous patches.

His sharp eyes scanned the chaos, piecing together the inconsistencies like a predator sniffing out a trap. The destruction, though severe, felt staged, exaggerated in ways that didn't align with an actual battle. The claw marks on the walls looked too deliberate, almost theatrical. Some furniture seemed broken in ways that didn't match the impact of a supernatural brawl. Even the blood, while real, was spread too methodically as if it had been placed for an effect.

And then there was Bethany.

Cowering amid the wreckage, her body curled against the base of a toppled barstool, a shaking mess of torn flowery fabric and smudged eyeliner. Her wide, tear-filled eyes locked onto his like a lifeline, and her trembling hands reached toward him.

"K-Kael!" she gasped, her voice shaking.

He didn't slow. He didn't stop.

He was across the room in an instant, faster than human sight could track. He seized her throat and lifted her into the air, her feet kicking against nothing.

His grip was vicelike. Unyielding.

His voice was more growl than speech. "Where? Is? She?"

Bethany gasped, her fingers scrabbling against his hold. "I-I don't know," she choked, her voice cracking.

He could taste the deception poisoning the air.

His grip tightened. He could feel her life pulse beneath his fingers, a frantic drum in her veins. "You are fucking lying!" he roared, the sheer force of his wrath rattling the chandelier overhead.

Her face turned a sickly shade of purple, her eyes bulging and her kicks growing weaker.

He welcomed it. Savored it.

She deserved this. She had fed Sera to Lilith. Had helped drag his woman into the abyss.

Bethany's nails dug into his wrist, weak and desperate. "P-please..." she wheezed, barely audible.

The air shifted with an ethereal force. A sudden drop in temperature.

"Let her go, Kael." Remiel's voice didn't rise. It didn't need to. His celestial authority carried weight that even Kael hesitated to challenge.

"NO!" Kael snarled. "I KNOW when they lie!"

She whimpered, her body limp against his grip.

He stared at her, weighing his instincts against Remiel's warning. His fingers flexed, and his muscles were taut with the urge to finish it. To break her. To end this.

But slowly, his grip loosened.

She collapsed onto the floor, gasping and coughing violently. She then curled in on herself, shaking uncontrollably. Her dress was torn at the shoulder, her usual pristine appearance shattered.

As Kael stood, heaving, the form crumpled on the floor...changed. It happened subtly at first but then with impossible speed. The vibrant red hair darkened, shifting to a straight shoulder-length brown. The fair skin deepened into a soft olive hue. Freckles appeared like scattered constellations across her shoulders, which seemed slimmer and more delicate. Her frame shifted, growing leaner, and the flowery dress now hung slightly loose around her form.

Kael froze, his breath catching in his throat. His rage was momentarily eclipsed by utter shock. He stared, his mind refusing to process what his eyes were seeing. The woman on the floor... She wasn't Bethany anymore. She was...

"Elara," he whispered with a shaking voice.

The name slammed into him like a physical blow. Elara. *His* Elara. The mortal queen he had loved centuries ago. The one he had relentlessly searched for after his fall, year after agonizing year. He had assumed her human lifespan had ended, blaming Heaven and Michael for orchestrating her disappearance and ripping her away. And now...now she was here, sprawled on the floor of this ruined house.

Her eyes, now a dark shade of brown, were filled with an impossible, heart-wrenching longing. She looked fragile, ancient, and undeniably her. Melodic words spilled from her lips.

"Habibi, ana kunt dawwar 'alayk min zaman."

The sound of her voice, that specific cadence and language he hadn't heard in years, struck him like lightning. A violent shudder racked his frame, his muscles locking. Every nerve screamed with impossible recognition, a resurrection of a love he had buried beneath layers of bitterness and time.

"You?!" Michael said. "*How?*"

Michael's voice pulled Kael back from the memory and shock. He stood just behind him, having materialized from the shadows with infuriating celestial silence. The archangel's perfect face was a mask of disbelief and dawning fury toward the woman on the floor.

Kael's shock fractured, replaced by white-hot rage directed at his ancient enemy. He spun to face the archangel, his own eyes blazing. "What did you do?" he demanded, the question ripped from the depths of his long-held grief and suspicion. "All this time...what did you do to her?"

Michael's expression shifted from shock to righteous indignation. "What did *I* do?" He pointed a condemning finger at Elara, who was now weakly pushing herself up. "She is the one who reported you to the tribunal for entangling with a black witch. She *was* the black witch!"

The revelation struck him harder than even seeing Elara reborn right in front of his eyes. Reported him? Elara? His Elara? The betrayal was unthinkable, poison. He looked back at her, truly seeing her now—the longing in her eyes replaced by sheer unadulterated terror.

The pieces clicked into place. Her disappearance, Heaven's swift judgment, his fall... All potentially orchestrated by the very woman he had mourned. The rage inside him shifted, growing colder and heavier and laced with the bitter ashes of a love turned treacherous.

He looked from Michael's accusing face to the terrified woman who was once his world. "If I was a good man," he murmured, his voice low and lethal, "I'd end your miserable existence right here and now."

She whimpered, curling tighter against herself.

He leaned in, his lips curling. "But I am far from a good man. And I will savor the thought of Sera dealing the final blow instead."

Her breath hitched.

"And when she comes for you," he whispered, "you will curse the day you took your first breath. Because at that moment, you will breathe your last."

She sobbed, trembling. "Kael, please let me explain…"

He stood motionless for a moment, his chest heaving. His gaze lingered on her trembling form, which was sprawled on the floor like a discarded puppet. Every fiber of his being screamed for vengeance, for the satisfaction of ending her miserable existence.

But he knew killing her would solve nothing. It wouldn't bring Sera back. It wouldn't undo the damage. It would only feed the darkness clawing at his soul.

Cassia's calm voice cut through the suffocating silence. "Leave her to me. You've done enough here."

His jaw tightened, and his fists clenched at his sides. He didn't trust himself to speak, so he turned sharply. His boots thudded against the ruined floorboards as he strode toward the door. The air around him seemed to crackle with residual energy, his fury still palpable.

Remiel followed him, his expression grim but steady.

Kael's focus was singular, his thoughts consumed by Sera—her laughter, her touch, the way she had looked at him as if he was the only being who mattered. And now, she was gone. Taken. He had failed her.

Michael brought up the rear, his towering frame casting long shadows in the dim light. He paused at the threshold, his gaze flicking between Kael and Cassia. "We'll find her," he said, his voice low but resolute. "This isn't over."

Kael halted, his shoulders tense. He slightly turned his head, just enough to glance back into the room. "If you don't erase her memories," he said, his voice raw and guttural, "I will kill her myself."

Cassia smirked, her sharp eyes glinting. "Don't worry," she replied smoothly. "She won't remember a thing."

His lips curled into a bitter sneer. She turned away, already reaching for the spell.

And he just stood frozen outside, staring into nothingness, while his mind was a chaotic mess of memories and history.

Elara.

She was not a dream of a lost memory. She had been breathing beneath his fingertips, trembling. For a heartbeat, he had believed she was a gift—a miracle, a thread back to who he had been before the fall.

But miracles don't lie. Miracles don't feed your woman into the abyss.

His chest ached, not with love but with grief dressed as fury. He had mourned her and burned for her. Let her name rot on his tongue for centuries until only ashes remained. And now she was back. A coward in good lighting.

He stepped out farther into the night, the cool air hitting him like a slap. It did nothing to calm the fire burning in his chest. Remiel and Michael followed him, their footsteps heavy.

Outside, the world felt eerily quiet, as if the house itself had absorbed all the chaos and left the surrounding streets untouched. Kael's gaze swept over the darkened neighborhood, his mind racing. He couldn't shake the image of Sera, couldn't stop the gnawing fear that he was already too late.

Remiel placed a hand on his shoulder, his grip firm but not forceful. "We will find a portal," he said, his voice steady. "We'll find her."

Michael exchanged a glance with Remiel, his expression unreadable. "Let's regroup."

The three men walked away from the house, their silence louder than any words could have been.

Kael didn't look back. He couldn't. If he did, he might lose what little control he had left.

CRIMSON KEEP

21

The world ripped apart around Sera, not with a scream but with a sickening, silent tear in the fabric of reality. One moment, there was a cold, triumphant glint in Bethany's eyes, and the next, a hulking demon, its skin like cracked obsidian and its breath a searing gust of sulfur, was carrying her through a portal, a swirling maelstrom of fractured light and shadow. She fought, raw and feral, but the demon's strength was absolute, an immovable force against her futile attempts.

The transition through the portal was violent, a wrenching dismemberment of self. Her body screamed in protest, every nerve ablaze. Then with a thud that echoed through her bones, she was unceremoniously dropped onto a cold, hard surface. The demon lingered for a moment, its molten eyes boring into her, before its massive form dissolved into pressing shadows and left her utterly alone.

Hunger sank its claws into her, sharper and more vicious than anything she'd ever known. No Kael-fed light or Mark-soul mattered anymore. Her body was drained of its celestial essence, leaving a deep and aching emptiness.

She slumped against the wall, her breaths ragged. Her heartbeat thundered in her ears. She didn't cry, though the desire to was a burning ache behind her eyes. This was not the place for tears.

"How did I let it get this far?" she muttered, the words swallowed by the oppressive darkness.

Her shadows stirred, coalescing into forms that were not quite solid yet undeniably present. A low, rhythmic hiss permeated the oppressive quiet. The chill of the dark stone tile floor invaded her bare feet, a cruel, biting reminder of her fall. But it wasn't just cold. A faint metallic tang, sharper than ozone, prickled the air, mingling with the sulfur and decay. She traced a bare foot along the grout lines, noticing a subtle, almost invisible sheen across the tiles. It was as if the very stone was weeping. A thin viscous film, iridescent with trapped dark light seeping from hairline cracks in the obsidian walls. It clung to her skin like oil, warm in some places and chilling in others, and vanished moments later.

This wasn't primitive. This was…Hell's own sustenance, harvested from the despair embedded in its very foundations.

Because you don't listen, the shadows said, their cadence cold.

"Don't start," she whispered, her eyes still tracing the film's flow of the viscous water.

But the shadows insisted. She tore her gaze away, though the strange liquid continued to beckon her. She got up and explored her chambers. The flow led her into the bathing chamber.

We told you about him.

We told you she was lying.

"A-and what was I supposed to do?" Her voice cracked, a bit sharper than she intended. "You never tell me anything straight. Just riddles and threats and…" Her eyes landed on a strange tank-looking contraption hanging over the dark glass shower room, where all the peculiar water seemed to be collecting. "Fascinating…"

We warned you the only way we know how. A sigh, softer than a whisper, seemed to unfurl from within the confines of her skull. *You never listen, Sera. If you had...you wouldn't be alone in this moment.*

"This is the most you have ever spoken to me."

Because you are evolving, and we are evolving with you.

She offered no reply.

The chill of the dark stone tile floor invaded her bare feet, a cruel reminder of her rash fall. This wasn't the feverish warmth of Kael's touch nor the unspoken promise of safety she had come to rely on. This was Hell. Not the metaphor she'd conjured in her nightmares but the unrelenting reality to which she'd been dragged into.

Bethany's or Elara's face haunted her still. The sly twist of her lips, the triumphant glimmer in her eyes. Sera was severed from everything she'd known, everything she loved: Cassia, Kael. And now, she was in Hell, alone in a prison as lavish as it was suffocating.

The room itself exuded cruelty disguised as grandeur. Heavy black velvet drapes lined the walls and were embroidered with grotesque scenes of torment—twisting figures, screaming faces, and anguish etched in every thread. Iron chandeliers hung high above, their crystals fractured and misshapen. They cast splintered, pale light that barely held back the pressing shadows. The monstrous bed, cloaked in black silk, behind her loomed like a dark omen, a mockery of rest and comfort.

Her body ached, stiff from the brutal abduction. Slowly, she pushed herself to her feet, her movements hampered. Every joint protested, and every muscle screamed. She staggered forward, instinctively reaching for stability. Her fingers brushed against a side table, its surface as cold as the stone floor beneath her feet. Her eyes fell upon the object placed at its center: a crown.

It was resting on a pillow of black velvet, like an offering meant to seduce and ensnare. The crown was forged from a dark metal and was so polished that it reflected the fractured light. Runic etchings spiraled across its surface. Their meaning was elusive, but their menace was undeniable. The crown itself seemed to hum faintly, a pulse she felt in the marrow of her bones. It was waiting for her, an emblem of a role she was meant to assume.

Sera's hand trembled as she reached for it, unable to resist the pull of its malevolent elegance. She lifted it from the pillow, the metal chilling her skin. Its weight pressed down like a physical manifestation of the despair surrounding her. She turned it over in her hands, studying the cruel artistry that had gone into its creation. It felt alive, the runes subtly writhing as though aware of her hesitation.

"No," she whispered, her voice trembling but resolute. "I will not wear this."

The words sounded hollow in the oppressive silence, but they held her defiance, a fragile spark against the encroaching darkness.

She lowered the crown back onto its velvet throne and then turned away from it.

She approached the towering window of black glass instead. It offered no escape, only a twisted reflection of her despair. Beyond it, Hell unfolded in grotesque majesty: barren wastes carved by rivers of molten fire and skeletal trees clawing at a purple sky bruised with storms. Distant screams carried on the searing air like a chilling symphony of eternal suffering.

As hope struggled to anchor her, the door creaked open behind her, shattering the stillness. She turned to face the demon who entered, its grotesque figure imposing in the fractured light. Its form was massive and grotesque with leathery wings folded tight against its back. Its face was a horrifying amalgam of features: a mouth filled with jagged teeth, eyes like pools of molten darkness, and an aura of malice that made her skin crawl.

"The queen has demanded your presence," it growled with a voice that sounded like a guttural rumble.

Sera met its piercing gaze with defiance, swallowing the flicker of fear threatening to crawl up her throat. She refused to show weakness. Not here. Not now. "Lead the way," she said, her voice steady but laced with simmering fury.

She followed every step purposefully, even as the weight of her captivity pressed down on her shoulders.

The corridor was a mix of twisted architecture. Grotesque carvings writhed and snarled across its walls, bathed in torches' flickering green glow. The oppressive air hung heavy with the echoes of distant screams, but she kept her gaze forward and her jaw clenched, refusing to let the sinister atmosphere shake her resolve.

The corridor opened into a vast, hellish throne room, a place so extensive that it felt as though the very walls pulsated with malevolence. Blackened pillars stretched upward, their surfaces etched with depictions of infernal wars. Rivers of molten fire streaked through the floor like veins of a living organism, casting flickering light across the space. And at the far end, on a throne forged from bones and shadowed iron, sat Lilith, her mother.

Lilith's beauty was haunting, perfectly regal yet dangerously unhinged. Her black gown almost gleamed in the flickering light, her flowing robes writhed, and her eyes glinted with triumph and obsession. The sight of her made Sera's stomach churn.

"My daughter, you've finally arrived," Lilith said smoothly, her voice as sharp as glass.

"Not like I had a choice. The prodigal daughter dragged home at last," Sera retorted, not holding back the bitterness. "Abducted and locked in like a feral animal. Is this your idea of treating your children with love and care?"

Lilith rose from her throne with predatory grace, shadows twisting and bending around her as though drawn to her. "It's time to accept the truth. You belong to me. To this place. To your destiny. But you still resist, clinging to the illusions your pathetic father fed you."

Her lips curled into a snarl. "You know nothing about me."

Lilith laughed, a grating sound that echoed through the chamber. "Don't I?" she said darkly. "You are half angel, half demon. You belong to neither world, and yet both crave you. You are my blood, and that makes you mine."

Sera's fists tightened. "You're obsessed. This isn't love, Lilith… It's control. You want a puppet, not a daughter."

Lilith's smile shifted, becoming sharper as though Sera's words had ignited some twisted glee. "You mistake my intentions, child," she purred. "I don't want your love. I want your *allegiance*. I want your power. You're destined for greatness. A greatness that can only be realized at my side."

"And if I say no?" she challenged, her voice daring.

Lilith's grin widened, and her tone dropped to a cold and venomous level. "I don't care. It has been a long time coming, and you will accept your fate. And if you try to defy me, remember your precious fallen will suffer."

She staggered back, her heart lurching. The image of Kael, vibrant and alive, flickered in her mind. The warmth of his smile. The depth of his loyalty. The idea of losing him to Lilith's cruelty made her stomach twist. The cold fear was a physical ache, worse than any chain could be. She swallowed, trying to find her voice to defy the monstrous queen, but no words came. Lilith's power was a suffocating shroud, pressing down on her resolve.

Lilith loomed closer, her voice soft but razor sharp. "So, choose, Sera. Bow to your nature and rise with me. Or let your defiance cost you everything. What will it be?"

Her vision swam, blurred by the sheer crushing weight of despair. Her body was a leaden thing, heavy from the constant emotional assault, the physical journey, and the endless malice of this realm. Lilith's face, a mask of unhinged beauty, pulsed with dark satisfaction as she faltered, unable to answer and unable to break free from the fear for Kael.

The room spun, the grotesque tapestries blurring into a kaleidoscope of torment. Her knees buckled. She didn't fall to the floor. Instead, the floor rushed up to meet her, the chill of the stone a fleeting sensation before everything dissolved.

As her consciousness dimmed, a single image flared bright in her mind's eye: Kael. Not the tortured Kael Lilith promised but the Kael of warmth, of strength, and of unwavering light. She yearned for a world where he could be real, untouched by this nightmare.

But then a profound, soul-deep weariness claimed her.

Forbidden Sanctuary

22

Sleep did not descend; it devoured Sera. She plummeted into its maw like a stone into the deepest sea, and when she surfaced, she stood barefoot in a midnight-colored gown in the middle of a meadow untouched by sun or season.

Twilight reigned eternal here, a bruised, luminous hush. The grass, tall and thick, whispered in tones of violet and ash, and a wind that carried the sweet perfume of night-blooming roses and rain-slick gravestones stirred its velvet blades. Beneath her feet, the very soil seemed to breathe, a slow pulse. Black roses bloomed wild, sprawling across the landscape.

Above, the sky glittered with constellations she'd never seen, stars that pulsed with a slow rhythm like distant heartbeats. The air was heavy with reverence as though the world itself was watching, waiting, and holding its breath.

She turned slowly, a ripple of uncertainty passing through her, and then she felt Kael, not with her eyes but with a more profound sense of recognition that resonated in her very bones.

Shirtless, he stood near the tree line, no more than thirty feet away, where the meadow's dark grass gave way to slender silver-barked trees. The twilight pooled around him, turning his skin to pale fire and casting him in alternating ribbons of silver and shadow. His wings were invisible, yet the air behind him shimmered as if something vast and restrained waited just out of sight.

He didn't come closer. Still and reverent, he only looked at her like a man gazing upon the divine.

"Why are you looking at me like that?" she asked. Her voice carried easily across the quiet space between them.

His voice, when it came, was hoarse, a rough caress against the stillness. "Because you're divine."

She blinked, a tremor passing through her. Slowly, as if in a dream, she lifted her hands before her eyes. Her skin had transformed, now a pale gray catching the faint, bruised light. Her fingers were tipped in black, nails elongated into elegant talons. Beneath her flesh, golden veins faintly glowed, a network of captured light. The sight stole her breath—a strange, beautiful horror that made her stomach turn.

Instinctively, her hands drifted to her forehead. "Do I ha...?"

He closed the distance between them in a fluid motion, catching her wrists before her fingers could reach their destination. "Don't," he said, his voice a tender command. He kissed her knuckles and then her palms, pressing his lips on each as though they held sacred scripture. "You're not a monster, Sera. *This* is who you are. And it is...breathtaking."

Her throat bobbed, a knot tightening. She wondered if he really meant it. She searched his rugged and beautiful face for any signs of a lie but only found awe, a profound reverence that mirrored the still meadow.

"I thought I'd lost you," he whispered, his thumb brushing along her jaw. "And now here you are…shining like the end of the world."

"What *is* this place?" She looked around.

"It's the In Between, a place where bonded souls can meet if they are separated. In case you had any questions about whether we are fated, this is your answer." He smiled kindly as he looked at her with his midnight blue eyes. After a moment of quietness, his smile faltered, and a shadow of pain crossed his features. "I need to tell you something. About Bethany. Well…"

She pressed her fingers to his full lips, silencing his words. "Shh… I don't care. She doesn't matter," she murmured, the truth of it absolute in this ethereal space. "If you can forgive me about Mark, I have nothing to say about Bethany or whoever the fuck she is…"

"I have nothing to forgive you for, Little Devil…" Kael smiled at her, brushing his finger over her delicate jaw once more.

"Then no more secrets." She smiled back as she leaned into his palm.

A visible tremor passed through him then, and he stepped back, drawing a breath. "Where are you?" An urgency took hold of his voice. "Where have they taken you?"

"Crimson Keep," she murmured, the name tasting like ash on her tongue. "I think…I think it's feeding on my light. I can feel it slipping… Like I'm bleeding from the inside."

He went still, his jaw clenching. Then with deliberate slowness, he reached for her hand again. "Then take mine."

She hesitated, pulling back slightly. A flicker of old fear. "I don't want to take anything else from you."

"It's not taking," he said, his voice firm. "It's sharing. But before you decide, you deserve to know what I am."

She looked at him, her brow furrowing.

Kael's voice dropped, resonating with the weight of forgotten eons.

"I'm not like the others. Not wholly fallen or pure. When Jareth executed my sentence, he deliberately used the wrong blade. And it worked. I didn't fall. My essence was bent though, and I became something else. Not an angel or a demon but something else."

As he spoke, the air around them began to hum, faint at first but then building into a deep vibration that shook the grass at their feet. Kael frowned, glancing down at his hands as arcs of static leaped between his fingers.

"It does this sometimes," he murmured. "Like the world forgets how to hold me."

Then his wings burst forth—not with grace but with violence, as though light and shadow were arguing over the same form. They stretched wide enough to eclipse the false stars above. Threads of electricity crawled across them, veining the span with blue-white fire.

Sera didn't retreat. The storm around him should have devoured her, but instead, it called to her. The static kissed her skin, not burning but awakening. Her own golden veins glowed faintly in answer.

"What are you?" she breathed.

His voice was rough. "I don't know. But whatever I am, it was meant to be lost. And yet, here I stand." He took another step closer. "If there's any use left in me, any light or ruin worth giving, I want you to have it. Freely. If this place allows. If you want it. If you want me." His chest rose and fell with a ragged rhythm, the vulnerability in his gaze stark. "Only if you choose it."

The hum of his wings deepened until it resonated in her bones, a living frequency older than Heaven's language. She felt it in her blood, in the shadows that had once frightened her. They bowed now, not in fear but in recognition.

"Yes," she whispered.

The single word broke the centuries-old tension.

His breath hitched, a ragged intake of air against the profound stillness. Then he kissed her.

It wasn't tender. It was a collision. Hunger forged in lifetimes of restraint. His hands were not gentle; they were anchors, fisting in her hair and pulling her closer. His grip was desperate as he pulled her head back, tilting her face to his. He devoured her mouth, a claiming that was both a punishment and a prayer.

The earth shuddered in reverence as he guided her down into the welcoming embrace of the meadow. His hands stayed firm on her hips as he lowered her, thumbs pressing into bone, controlling the descent until her spine met the velvet grass. Black roses parted beneath her weight, petals brushing her skin while thorns caught and tugged the weave of her gown. Liquid gold beaded along the pinprick breaks in her skin.

Kael followed her down and knelt between her knees. He did not touch her at first. He let the space burn. His gaze moved with intent, slow and measuring, as if marking each place his hands would claim next. She lay pinned by his attention, chest rising shallow with every breath.

The meadow answered her blood before he did. The gown loosened and dissolved, unraveling into black smoke that slid away from her body and vanished into the grass around them. She lay exposed beneath him, knees bent, back pressed to the earth, nowhere to hide.

His breath caught hard as he took her in; her shadows slowly whipped out of her body, wrapping him in a loving embrace as they whispered against his skin, causing a slight shudder. He leaned forward without closing the distance, letting the heat of his body reach her before his skin did. His hunger showed in the tight line of his mouth and the tension in his shoulders. But he still restrained himself with effort.

Her fingers curled into the soil. Talons pierced dirt and root as she anchored herself, bracing for the force she both feared and wanted.

"Open for me," he said, low and rough as he touched her bent knees and gently pushed them apart.

She spread wider under his command. Her knees sank deeper into the grass. Her hips tilted up in offering while the rest of her body went taut, ready for impact, aching for a fast and brutal end to the waiting.

But he denied her. Instead, Kael lowered himself slowly. His hands slid from her hips to her stomach, palms flattening her against the earth. He bent until the longer strand of his hair brushed her skin. Kael pressed a deliberate kiss just below her navel. He lingered there, mouth warm and still, as if marking the place. Her breath broke.

He moved again, mouth trailing down the line of her body. His tongue followed the curve of her hip with purpose, slow and exact, leaving heat in its wake. Each movement came after a pause, as if he had chosen it carefully rather than given in.

A predator would have taken her whole in seconds. Kael took possession through restraint, through patience sharpened into ritual.

Terror threaded through her desire as his mouth hovered lower, close enough for his breath to stir the most sensitive flesh, close enough to promise ruin without delivering it yet.

He settled on his stomach between her open legs, as he gripped large hands around her thighs, gently but firmly. His grip tightened until her muscles yielded. He leaned in and pressed his face to the sensitive flesh of her inner thigh, cheek and mouth anchoring there while his breath warmed her skin. The contact drew a shudder through her body. Her claws tore deeper into the earth as she fought the urge to move.

"Be still, Little Devil…"

And then Kael started low. His tongue dragged a slow path from her knee upward, unhurried and deliberate, tracing muscle and heat inch by agonizing inch. He paused at the apex of her thigh and let the tip of his tongue skim close enough, but without touching where she needed him most. Her hips lifted on instinct. But he pinned her tighter.

A pleading sound broke from her throat. "Kael. Please."

He answered by shifting his weight. His breath brushed her core, close enough to promise relief, close enough to make the wait hurt. His tongue touched her once, flat and precise, then withdrew. He tasted her fully on the next pass, slow and controlled, as if committing her flavor to memory.

Sera's hips jerked off the grass. But he caught her instantly, fingers digging into her thighs to still her. He held her there, suspended on the edge, long enough for her body to betray her surrender.

Then his mouth closed over her.

The contact turned consuming. He drank from her with intent, not haste, tongue working in steady patterns meant to break her open rather than rush her release. His hands joined the act. Two fingers pressed and slid in and out of her heat, slow at first, stretching her with care before driving deeper. He set a rhythm between mouth and fingers, forcing her body to follow.

Her thighs quivered, trapped between his grip and his mouth, every muscle drawn tight as the pressure built and refused to spill.

Every lick, every thrust of his long fingers, filled her with warmth. "Sera," he groaned against her, the sound vibrating under her skin, inside her body, and pulling her closer to the edge he controlled.

The vibration tore through her spine and bloomed outward, sharper than any spell carved into flesh. She writhed beneath him as shadows bled from her skin, crawling over her ribs and down her thighs while the storm inside her gathered mass. Her claws dragged through his hair and scraped his scalp, not to guide him but to keep him there, to anchor him to the desecration she refused to lose.

He answered with force. His fingers drove deeper, setting a faster rhythm. His tongue pressed and flicked with intent, no longer teasing, shaping her toward fracture.

Pleasure shifted into flow. A current surged from his mouth and spread through her veins. The heat was no longer heat but power, invasive and alive. His essence stirred and spilled into her, brilliant and corrupted, flooding her body until she shook under its weight. Light and ruin poured together, feeding and breaking her in the same breath.

She pulled him closer with every sound she made. Her body drew his power in greedily, feeding without restraint. The surge overwhelmed her senses. Horns split through her brow. Her vision burned white. She vanished into the crushing force of his magnificent light.

She shattered against his mouth, crying his name to the watching star-filled sky.

But it did not satisfy his hunger.

He moved with command. One sharp motion rolled her onto her stomach, knocking the breath free out of Sera, as her cheek struck the cool velvet grass. His hands seized her hips and pulled them up until her knees sank into the roses and her spine bowed into a high, helpless arch. The sound of his zipper cut through the air, and he pressed the heavy head of cock against her soaked entrance, holding and sliding up and down long enough to remind her what waited.

She growled his name, half warning, half demand.

"Greedy little devil," he said, rough and breathless. "You want all of it, don't you?"

She drove back into him without hesitation. "Feed me."

The groan tore from his chest as he thrust forward. He filled her in one deep motion, clean and consuming, the force of it locking them together as if the world had narrowed to this single, devastating alignment.

She arched with a guttural moan, claws ripping furrows through the soil. Kael locked an arm around her torso and pulled her back against his chest, forcing her spine to bow tighter. His other hand fisted in her hair and wrenched her head back, opening her throat and pulling her body wider for him.

"Mine," he growled against her ear. "You were made for this. For me."

He set a brutal rhythm. Each thrust landed deep and deliberate, not frantic, not careless. He drove into her with purpose, hips snapping forward while his arm held her in place, and she took every inch. Essence poured from him with every motion. She felt the corrupted light tear through her veins like cold fire, flooding her body in violent waves. This was not sharing. This was an occupation. His soul surged into her without mercy.

She answered with hunger. Her body tightened and burned, greed taking shape in muscle and bone. She pushed back into every thrust, meeting his force with her own. Shadows spilled from her skin and wrapped around his arms and chest, coiling like living things as they fed on the light he gave her.

His bond dove into her, no longer abstract, no longer distant. It breathed. It pulled. It anchored.

"More," she hissed. "Make me yours fully."

His control fractured. A roar tore from his chest as his pace turned punishing, hips driving harder, faster, as if he meant to carve himself into her from the inside out. His teeth grazed her neck as he snarled his claim again.

"You are mine."

His hand slid up her throat and closed there, pressure firm and possessive, and her body answered instantly. Her core clenched around him, tight and desperate. Her vision blew out white again as she cried out.

"Don't stop."

"Never."

The release hit like a detonation. Her scream split the air, raw and powerful, tearing free of her chest as her body convulsed around him. His roar followed, deep and shattered, shaking the meadow beneath them. Above, the stars flared bright and violent. Heat burned across their skin as twin sigils seared between their collarbones, alive and undeniable.

They went down together. His weight drove her into the earth, chest pressed hard to her back, his cock still buried deep inside her. He caged her with his arms and stayed there, breath ragged against her neck, holding her in place while the bond pulsed and settled between them.

Slowly, reluctantly, he pushed up onto his elbows. He did not pull away yet, drawing out a few more lazy thrusts.

When he finally withdrew, he did so with care, easing out inch by inch. His release spilled onto the dark petals beneath them. A low, satisfied sound left her throat as her body slackened.

He rolled to his side and gathered her close, pulling her back against his chest and kissed between her shoulder blades, slow and grounding. She tucked herself closer to him.

"So," she said quietly. "What now?"

His fingers traced her collarbone and brushed the glowing rune mirrored on his own skin. "I don't know. If it is still there when we wake up, then it worked."

She nodded and let her eyes close.

"It is not complete," he murmured. "You took my light. I made sure of it. I did not take your essence."

His hand drifted down her body again, slow and deliberate. She shifted and smiled faintly. Then her breath caught.

"Sera?"

Her body flickered. Smoke and starlight tore free of his arms, dissolving from his grasp as she vanished.

Kael woke with a gasp, tangled in damp sheets that clung to his skin like an accusation. The air felt heavy, thick. He blinked into the dark, his chest rising and falling, and his body aching with the echo of someone he couldn't hold on to. Sera's breath still lingered against his skin. The heat of her touch pulsed at his collarbone.

He sat up, the silk dragging against his legs. His hands trembled. His mouth was dry. The room felt wrong. Too quiet. Too still.

He stood and started pacing, the floor cold beneath his bare feet. Each step was a question without an answer.

The ache of her absence pushed against his ribs, a throb he couldn't ignore. When the pressure built too tightly in his chest, he turned and slammed his fist into the wall. The impact jolted up his arm. He hit it again. The second blow split his knuckles. On the third blow, the concrete wall cracked and gave slightly, and something inside him did the same.

He let out a sound—low, guttural, and broken from the weight of wanting her here, whole and real. The stars had given him a dream, and it hadn't been enough. His blood still remembered the feel of her, the taste of her, and the way she had looked at him like he was sacred and damned all at once.

He crossed the room and pulled the curtains wide, one sharp tug that sent them flying open. The windows stretched from the floor to the ceiling, glass catching the city lights below. But it wasn't the skyline that held him.

It was the starless sky beyond the glass that caught his attention.

A sliver of moon cut through the darkness, pale and ordinary to mortal sight. But Kael saw the flaw—a faint distortion at its edge where the light bent wrong as if the realms had begun to strain. The color wasn't red yet, only the promise of it. Waiting.

Inside him, the bond shivered. A pulse out of rhythm, faint but insistent like a heartbeat echoing through the distance. He felt her there. Then not. The connection, as thin as smoke, flickered, and fear pressed cold against his ribs. She was too far, locked behind walls even he could not reach.

He stayed there, watching the moon and willing the thread to hold. The blood moon cycle had already begun.

He pressed a hand to the glass, his fingers splayed wide as if he could push the night back and prolong the inevitable pain. The city shimmered beneath him, indifferent. Yet the world felt off-balance, and the air was too still as if the night was holding its breath. The bond beneath his skin trembled, low and insistent, like the warning before a storm.

Whatever was coming for her wasn't waiting. And neither could he.

Waning Light
23

Sera woke with the taste of Kael still in her mouth: sweet, metallic, and ancient.

The sheets clung to her skin. Not in the throne room. She was back in her bed, though she had no memory of how she got here. Her limbs ached with a slow, sensual exhaustion, the kind that curled deep into her marrow. But it was the fire near her collarbone that made her sit up, gasping.

Where his fingers had traced her skin in the dream, a mark had bloomed, luminous and pulsing faintly with the golden light of a dying star. It throbbed in sync with her heartbeat.

Her fingers hovered above it. It did not feel like a wound, but it burned like one. The tether, though partially awakened, was not enough to anchor her but enough to damn her.

For a moment, she could still feel him. His mouth on hers, his voice promising to find her. She wanted to sink back into that dream and vanish.

But then the hunger struck.

It cleaved through her like a guillotine, fast and final. Her stomach turned to ice. Her mouth went dry. Her hands trembled. The craving wasn't just for sustenance... It was for the soul. For heat. For the essence that made her feel real.

She staggered out of bed, nearly collapsing. Her legs refused to support her weight. Shaking, she pressed both palms to the dresser as she forced herself to look in the mirror.

The mark glowed bold at the base of her neck, stubborn and bright. She thought she should hide it, but a gentle knock sounded on her door. She pulled her nightgown tighter around her neck, clutching it tight with both hands.

The door creaked open anyway, and a woman stepped inside. No scent. No sound. Just a ripple in the air.

"My lady," the demoness intoned with a low bow, her voice as smooth as silk. "I am Vyxia, sent to serve you."

Sera studied her warily, her gaze narrowing. The demoness was beautiful but in the way venom glints under moonlight. Dark robes shimmered like oil over water, clinging to limbs that bent the idea of human. Her eyes were impossibly violet, as deep as broken amethysts.

"Serve me?" Sera tested the words on her tongue, each syllable laced with suspicion.

"Yes," Vyxia replied with a small smile. "To ensure your comfort, to attend to your needs, and to offer you...sustenance." Her eyes lingered on Sera. "Princess?" Her voice sounded worried. "Are you all right?"

Sera backed away a step. Her hunger screamed in her blood. "I...I think so..." Her throat was dry. "What do you need?"

"What do *you* need, my lady?" Vyxia smiled kindly and stepped closer. She extended one pale hand. A vial with silver liquid, mortal souls, shimmered, wraithlike and flickering. "Take them. Feed. You need strength. These are sanctioned. Prisoners of the keep. Offered willingly."

The smell of them hit Sera like wine gone sour. She wanted to gag. Her stomach twisted with both desire and revulsion. "Nothing in this place is offered willingly," she whispered, her voice breaking. "I can't."

"You'd be surprised…"

"I won't take it." Her voice was quiet, edged with sorrow. Her hand curled protectively over the star beneath her nightgown.

Vyxia tilted her head, studying her like a curious cat. "What's on your chest?" she murmured questioningly.

Her hand reflexively jerked up to cover it. "It's nothing," she said too quickly.

"Well, that's good," Vyxia said lightly, still standing near the door's threshold. "Because it looked to me like a bond mark, and in that case, your demonic nature would begin to reject it. A tether embedded in a corrupted vessel cannot be sustained… It's like mixing holy water with wildfire."

Her breath caught. "What do you mean, *cannot be sustained?*"

She looked at Sera knowingly. "Biologically, metaphysically… Whatever language comforts you. Think of it like an infection. Your demon blood will recognize the bond as foreign and will try to reject it like an illness."

Sera's legs slightly buckled, but she steadied herself on the dresser. Her pulse roared in her ears.

Every time Kael had offered himself, her body had felt like it was a trip wire about to snap. She had assumed it was the rawness of the hunger, the guilt, or the sheer force of what they had shared. But now she saw the pattern. The recoil. The ache. Her body was tearing itself apart from the inside, even as her soul was reaching for him. And if the bond is completed...?

"What happens if it finishes?" she asked, barely a whisper.

Vyxia lifted a shoulder. "Depends on which side wins. A person might survive or might burn from the inside out."

Her fingers trembled where they clutched her shirt.

"But it's not you, so nothing to worry about," Vyxia said more gently now. "But if you were, you must either break it...or finish it quickly. Before your nature decides for you." She gave a soft smile. "Offer still stands though. When you need to feed, you only have to call my name."

"Please leave."

"Princess, you'll die," she responded, now sounding concerned.

"I said...leave."

She needed time to process this information and understand her next move. Did she want to hold on to this bond, or would she be better off without it if she fed on souls in Hell? Would that finally transform her completely? Would she become the gray monstrosity like she was in the meadow?

After a beat, Vyxia turned, her violet eyes gleaming with pity and interest. "Very well. But please know there will be no help from the keep when your hunger wins." She then vanished like smoke: silent, immediate.

Sera collapsed onto her knees, the star beneath her collarbone burning like a brand.

Time in Hell was merely an empty concept. There were no sunrises to introduce a new day nor moonlit evenings to signal an end. Only an unyielding, oppressive eternity prevailed, and with every endless moment, Sera felt herself drifting further from the light, further from Kael, and further from her own identity.

At first, it was subtle... A dulling of sensations. The memories of the living world seemed distant, as though they belonged to someone else. And with each passing day, or what passed for days in Hell, the erosion of her celestial light accelerated. The light that had once burned within her dimmed, leaving a void the darkness sought to claim. Her skin did, in fact, change to a moonlight gray, and her hair became even darker and sleeker.

The slowed passage of time and helplessness gnawed at her, amplifying the endlessness of her suffering. It felt as though she had already been here for a lifetime, the weight of an eternity pressing down harder with each sluggish moment.

Night after night, the meadow materialized. Moonlight painted the rolling grass and roses in shimmering silver, but Kael's presence never did. Only an empty silence, vast and cold. She sat, a statue of longing, on the moss-covered gravestone. Her fingers traced the cool, rough surface. Each breath was a silent plea, a desperate whisper into the void. The meadow became her sanctuary and her torment.

On the fifth night, a weight settled in her chest. The silent meadow spoke to her then, not of hope but of the desolate truth: He wasn't coming.

The realization chilled her to the bones, a deep ache eclipsing the familiar yearning. Her lips no longer formed his name in her sleep. The meadow too receded, its silver light replaced by harsh, unyielding darkness. Survival, she knew, hinged on adapting, on learning to breathe without him.

Days blurred into a single purpose: writing. Sera's quill scratched across parchment, documenting the fractured images of Heaven, a place she now remembered with frustrating incompleteness. More vivid were the one hundred eighty years she'd spent traversing the mortal realm: the gnawing hunger of the Irish famine, the defiant spirit of Paris, and the chilling shadows of Berlin. America had offered a transient refuge, its vastness a canvas for her endless migrations.

Bethany was a painful echo, Mark was a ghost of the past, and Cassia's visits were too infrequent to mend the growing fissures in her heart. Moving on seemed to be the only path, yet a formidable obstacle remained: her mother's grip.

She wondered how much longer she could endure, if the ink on the pages would be enough to sustain her. But for now, the journal was her solace, her words a defiant flame against the encroaching darkness. It was all that remained of her faint, fading light.

Vyxia, graceful and strange, was always there somehow. They began to spend more and more time together. She moved through the Crimson Keep like a serpent through silk, always one step ahead and turning just before Sera could ask where they were going. She showed her the ancient fortress's hidden crooks and corridors. For as long as Sera's dwindling strength would carry her, Sera followed.

At first, it seemed like aimless wandering, a guide with no real purpose. But over time, patterns emerged. Vyxia lingered at certain places longer than others. She even took Sera down to the bone-cold catacombs beneath the keep and stood before a sealed iron archway carved with celestial runes.

"This path," Vyxia had whispered, "once led to Lucifer's tomb." A shrug. "But no one knows how to open it now."

Another day, they spent hours in the library's forgotten wing, where the books were bound in leather and sealed with chains that faintly pulsed.

Vyxia had skimmed her fingers over the spines. "Knowledge is kept hidden here for a reason," she said. "But reasons change."

Then there was the keepers' archive, a place Sera had never heard of before. It was vaulted, veiled, and watched by guards in iron-red cloaks.

Vyxia had only gestured toward the entrance once, murmuring, "The queen herself must grant permission. If she ever does..." She left the sentence hanging like a thread waiting to be pulled.

It struck Sera as strange how all these places—all forbidden, all powerful—were offered to her like puzzle pieces. Vyxia never spoke of an escape. But she also never said no.

Time crawled. Each distorted moment dragged Sera deeper into her own unraveling. Her body, half starved and burning with half formed light, began to betray her: limbs shaking, heart thudding arrhythmically. The hunger had stopped feeling like desire. Now, it felt like rot.

She felt like a quarantined, dangerous relic hidden behind glass. No matter how many times she asked...*begged*...to see her mother, the guards returned with the same flat reply: The queen declined. No reason. No emotion.

Why was Lilith keeping her here? Why hadn't she done anything yet? No ritual. No punishment. Not even an interrogation.

Sera wondered if Lilith was waiting for her to change. Waiting for her to shatter.

But she would not. Even if the ache of absence hollowed her chest, even if the bond burned her from the inside out, she would not break.

Each day she remained, the chambers seemed to contract as if the carved stone was pressing in with suffocating intent. Faint red veins pulsed along the walls, a mimicry of life that beat like a distant, sickly heart. The air itself tasted wrong—thick with metal and the bitter ghost of smoke. Shadows trembled in the corners, refusing stillness.

She rose from the sofa. Her bare feet met the shock of the cold marble floor. "Vyxia," she said quietly, her voice carrying in the heavy air.

The keep always seemed to listen, and she knew the demoness would hear her somehow. It was comforting and unnerving at the same time. On one side, she appreciated the fact that there was someone in Hell she could speak to. From another, it felt like she was being watched at all times.

A shimmer disturbed the air by the doorway, and Vyxia stepped through as if she'd been standing just beyond sight. Her silver hair caught the crimson light, glinting like a blade.

"Can you take me back to the library?"

"Of course," Vyxia said, her tone smooth but edged with caution. "Looking for something in particular?"

Sera didn't answer.

After a pause, Vyxia inclined her head. "As you wish, my lady. Follow me."

The corridors beyond twisted endlessly, their blackened stone walls carved with grotesque figures that shifted when she wasn't looking. The torches hissed and spat, their light more smoke than flame. The air grew heavier the farther they walked, carrying the faint scent of sulfur that stung her throat. The keep felt awake, as if watching them pass.

When they finally arrived, it was a cavernous expanse that seemed to stretch on forever. Towering shelves lined the walls, reaching toward a vaulted ceiling adorned with intricate yet unsettling carvings. The air smelled of aged parchment and faint decay, a stark reminder that this place, while rich in knowledge, was steeped in darkness. Flickering green light from iron chandeliers cast eerie shadows across the rows of books, each bound in leather of varying shades. Their spines were etched with symbols both ancient and malevolent.

It looked like a fountain of forbidden knowledge, a maze of secrets that could either be her salvation or her undoing.

Yet the guards stationed at the entrance made her acutely aware of her captivity, their heavy presence reminding her that she was being watched.

As she walked the aisles, her fingers brushed over the spines of ancient books. Each one seemed to hum faintly as though the knowledge within was alive. Her heart raced. She scanned the titles, searching for anything that could offer answers or hope.

One book, bound in gleaming black leather, caught her eye, its surface embossed with silver runes that subtly shifted under her gaze. Something about it called to her, its presence heavier than the others. She pulled it from the shelf, and her hands trembled as she opened it.

The pages, brittle and ancient, crackled as she turned them. They were full of symbols she almost recognized. She wasn't sure what she was hoping to find. An answer? A weapon? A name?

Her shadows stirred again, sharp and cold as glass.

You are walking a dangerous line.

Close the book, Sera.

Some truths are not yours to carry.

She almost jumped out of her skin at hearing the familiar voices in her head but hesitated. Not because she agreed but because, for a single heartbeat, they sounded almost…afraid.

"I have to know," she whispered.

No. You want to believe. And that will destroy you faster than any lie.

She turned the page anyway. The text was dense, its language archaic, yet she recognized fragments of its meaning. It was an essay on angelic essence, exploring its nature, vulnerabilities, and limitations. Her pulse quickened. Each word heightened the urgency in her chest. The book revealed truths she hadn't known, as painful as they were: Her essence was waning because of Hell's oppressive influence. She was losing herself to this place—her memories, her light, and her very soul. They were all slipping away.

Her gaze shifted to a passage near the end of the text, one that spoke of restoration. It hinted at ways to revive angelic power, to shield the fallen from Hell's corruption, but the methods were dangerous, the cost unbearable. One line made her breath catch: "The essence of others may reignite what is lost…but beware. For what is taken may poison what remains."

She closed the book and clutched it tight as she stepped away from the shelves. The weight of her discovery pressed upon her. Was this the answer she sought or merely another path to ruin? Her mind churned with questions, but one thing was sure: Her time was running out.

Unable to ignore the gnawing desperation, she turned to the guards stationed at the library's entrance. Their imposing forms were shrouded in dark armor, their faces obscured by twisted horned helms.

"Are there…" Sera hesitated, steadying her voice. "Are there any fallen angels imprisoned here?"

The guards exchanged glances, their expressions—or what little she could see of them—mingling with amusement and mild disdain.

One of them spoke, his deep voice reverberating. "Fallen angels?" he repeated, the words dripping with scorn. "They're common. However, most don't last long. This place…breaks them."

Her stomach twisted. "Where are they kept?" she pressed, her voice trembling with urgency. "In the dungeons?"

He chuckled darkly. "Yes. In the lower depths," he said, a cruel glint in his tone. "But if you're thinking of seeking them out, I wouldn't bother. They're shattered creatures. No better than the wretches that roam the wastes."

Her heart sank at his words, yet a small spark of hope in her refused to die. If there were fallen angels here, even broken ones, perhaps they held the key to restoring her light. Or at least to understand her own descent.

She nodded to the guard and turned back toward Vyxia, who stood watching her with an inscrutable expression. "I am ready to leave," she said quietly, the weight of her discovery pressing down on her shoulders.

Vyxia inclined her head. "As you wish, my lady."

As they retraced their steps through the labyrinthine corridors, she clutched the book tight to her chest, her mind a tempest of thoughts. The library had given her a glimmer of hope, yet the guards' words lingered like a bitter aftertaste. Were the fallen angels truly beyond saving? Was she?

Her shadows whispered no answers, only doubts.

The Anatomy of Ruin

24

The cold came first. It was not the familiar chill of the castle's stone but a dead, absolute cold that sank past Sera's skin and into the marrow of her bones. She sat up in her bed, the silk blanket useless. The air in her chambers was thick, still, and heavy with the scent of petrichor and ancient dust. Like a tomb cracked open for the first time in millennia.

Lilith stood by the hearth, where no fire burned. She was a silhouette cut from a fabric deeper than shadow, the faint moonlight from the high window refusing to touch her. She wore a dress the color of dried blood and tailored with impossible precision. Her smile was a slow, deliberate curve of her lips. It held no warmth, only a predatory amusement.

"Get up, Little Saint." Lilith's voice was a low murmur, yet it filled the room. "We are riding to see the family's territory."

Sera's heart hammered a frantic rhythm. She swung her legs over the side of the bed, and her bare feet pressed against the cold floor. Defiance was a flame she had to feed, lest the glacial dread extinguish it. "I am not your family. And I am no one's saint."

"Details, details." She waved a dismissive hand. "You have a choice. You can come as you are, a defiant stray in a nightdress, or you can put on something more appropriate for an introduction to your inheritance. The choice, as always, is yours. Though I find the imagery of one far more poetic than the other."

The implication hung in the air, a threat veiled in etiquette.

But Sera would not give Lilith the satisfaction of seeing her tremble. She walked to the armoire, her movements stiff, and pulled on dark trousers and a simple tunic. Every second was a small war against the terror that urged her to bolt, to scream, to do anything but obey. She was not a lamb being led to slaughter. She was a scout, venturing into enemy territory to learn its terrain and to gather intelligence.

When she turned back, Lilith was holding out a hand. "Ready for your tour?"

She ignored the offered hand. "What is the point of this, Lilith? A display of horrors to break my spirit?"

"Break you?" Lilith laughed, a sound like shattering crystals. "My dear, I am trying to *build* you. You cannot rule a kingdom without understanding its geography. Its people. Its fundamental truths." She stepped closer, her presence a physical pressure. "Now, come."

She still did not take Lilith's hand. She walked toward her, and the world dissolved. The stone walls of her chambers did not melt or twist. They ceased to be. One moment, she was in her room, and the next, she was sitting on cool leather, the low thrum of a powerful engine vibrating through the seat.

They were in a car, a machine of impossible beauty. It was long and black with chrome accents that shone with a light that did not exist in this place. There was no road, no sky, and no ground. Only a swirling, nebulous gray that pressed in on all sides, a canvas awaiting a painter's first stroke. Lilith was behind the wheel, her gloved hands resting lightly on it.

"First," Lilith said, her voice conversational, "we visit the listless. The great fallen middle."

The gray mist began to bleed into a landscape. The car moved with impossible smoothness, gliding over cracked, parched earth under a sky the color of a fading bruise. A profound lethargy settled over Sera, a weight on her limbs and eyelids. Every thought felt slow, syrupy.

This was the circle of sloth. It was not a realm of sleeping figures. It was a vast, silent library. Bookshelves stretched for miles in every direction, reaching up into the gloom. The souls here were not chained or tortured. They sat in endless rows of desks, their heads resting in their hands and their eyes staring at books with blank pages. They had all the knowledge of the universe at their fingertips yet lacked the will even to turn a single page. The air was thick with the dust of apathy, the silence broken only by a deep, collective sigh.

"They had potential," Lilith said, her voice a soft counterpoint. "Artists who never painted. Scholars who never wrote. Lovers who never spoke the words. They waited for the perfect moment, the perfect inspiration, and it never came. So, they were given this. An eternity of perfect moments and no desire to seize a single one. Their prison is not the place. It is the condition."

Sera felt a phantom exhaustion seep into her soul. She wanted to close her eyes, to rest for a moment. But she fought it, digging her nails into her palms. "This is not justice. It is cruelty."

"Justice is a mortal concept," Lilith replied, accelerating smoothly. The library faded back into the gray. "Here, there is only…consequence."

The world resolved again, this time into a landscape of obscene abundance. They were driving through a swamp, but the mud was thick cake batter, and the pools were a cloying, spoiled cream. The air was heavy with the smell of rot and sugar. This was gluttony. Grotesque figures, their bodies swollen and distorted, sat in the mire. They shoveled endless handfuls of the sweet muck into their mouths, their eyes wide with a hunger that was never sated. They consumed and consumed, their forms growing ever larger, ever more misshapen, yet they grew thinner from within. Their spirits were wasting away with every swallow.

Sera's stomach turned. A wave of nausea, thick and sour, rose in her throat. She could feel a phantom hunger gnawing at her belly, an acidic craving for anything to fill a void she hadn't known was there.

"They sought fulfillment in the flesh, in the endless banquet," Lilith said, her gaze fixed forward. "They believed more was always better. So, we gave them more, an endless supply. The only thing they are denied is the feeling of satisfaction."

Sera looked away, focusing on the car's pristine interior. "You enjoy this."

"I appreciate the irony," Lilith said, still not looking at her. "It is an art form."

The swamp dissolved.

The next circle revealed itself not through sight but through sound. A faint, metallic chinking, like a billion coins being dropped at once. The view then solidified.

They were in a city of black glass and gold—skyscrapers of obsidian clawed at a sky made of polished silver. Every surface was a perfect mirror. And in those mirrors, the damned were trapped. This was greed. Souls flitted from surface to surface, their hands outstretched and trying to grasp the golden reflections they saw. They stared at their own twisted visages, their eyes fixated on the illusion of wealth. They were surrounded by riches yet owned nothing. They were royalty of their own reflection and utterly alone. Some clawed at the mirrored walls, their phantom fingers leaving no scratches. Their silent screams were trapped in the glass.

"They hoarded what they could not take with them," Lilith murmured, her voice laced with something that might have been pity or perhaps contempt. "So, they were given a kingdom of what they desire the most. A treasure that can be seen but never held. They are so consumed with possessing their own image that they fail to see the millions of others trapped right beside them. The ultimate poverty is to be surrounded by reflections and see only yourself."

Sera watched one soul in particular, a woman in tattered remains of a gown. The woman pressed her face against the skyscraper. Her reflection stared back, weeping tears of molten gold. A cold knot tightened in Sera's chest.

This was not about punishment. It was about erasure.

The world shifted again. A blast of heat washed over the car, and the air turned red. They were on a vast, silent battlefield. The ground was littered with weapons of every age—from bronze swords to charred machines of future wars. The sky was the color of a fresh wound, cracked with veins of black lightning. This was wrath.

But there was no fighting. Millions of warriors were frozen, locked in poses of ultimate violence. A man with a raised sword, his face a mask of fury, was inches from an enemy's throat. A woman stood with fire in her hands, her snarl fixed for eternity. They were statues of pure rage, trapped at the peak of their hatred and forever denied the release of the blow. Their silent screams were a vibration in the air, a high-frequency thrum of unending violence.

"To be angry is to be alive," Lilith said, her voice dropping lower. "But to only be angry is to be a fire that consumes its fuel. They are given their rage in its purest form. An eternal and unquenchable fire within. They burn, but they are never consumed. They feel the killing blow, over and over, but it never lands."

Sera felt it then. A surge of hot, clean rage inside her. Rage at Lilith. Rage at this whole monstrous creation. It was a clarifying feeling, cutting through the horror and the nausea. She clung to it.

"This is your kingdom," Sera said, her voice tight. "A monument to suffering."

"It is a monument to choice," Lilith said, and the battlefield vanished.

They drove through what looked like a perfect, idyllic suburb: manicured lawns, lovely houses, and clean streets. But through the windows of each home, Sera could see souls. Each one was alone, staring out their window at a neighbor. Their faces were etched with a quiet, acidic bitterness. This was envy. They were not tortured. They were not in pain. They watched the perceived happiness of another and were consumed by it. The man in one house had a loving family, but he stared at his neighbor's larger house. The woman in that house stared at the beautiful garden of another. Each soul was given exactly what they thought they wanted, only to discover their desire was never for the thing itself but for the fact that someone else had it. Their hell was a constant, low-grade ache of resentment.

"They measured their worth by what others possessed," Lilith said. "So, we gave them a world where someone else always has more. They will look forever and never think to look within their own home."

The car moved on.

The world dissolved into a soft, perfumed haze. The air grew warm, scented with night-blooming jasmine and something musky and intoxicating. Music, a slow, hypnotic melody, drifted from somewhere unseen. This was lust. It was not the orgiastic pit Sera might have imagined. It was a grand twilight garden. The plants were exquisite, flowers of impossible color and shape that bloomed under a canopy of weeping willows. The souls here, beautiful and perfect, wandered the winding paths. They reached for each other, their fingers brushing and their eyes full of desperate longing. But the moment they touched, they turned into dust and smoke, only to reform a moment later on another path—alone, the ache of solitude returning tenfold. They were desperate for a union they could never achieve.

"They sought to lose themselves in another," Lilith whispered, her voice dangerously soft. "A noble goal, perhaps. But they confused union with consumption. They wanted to own, to possess, and to conquer. So, now they can only reach. They feel the promise of a cure for their loneliness over and over. They are never denied the hope of it. Only the reality."

A profound sadness washed over Sera, a loneliness so deep it was almost physical. She saw the desperation on their faces, the endless cycle of hope and dissolution. This was the cruelest circle yet. It weaponized hope.

"One remains," Lilith said, her tone growing colder, more formal. "The sin from which all others are born. The foundation of this kingdom."

The garden evaporated. They were now in a place of absolute blackness and silence. It was a cold void, more bottomless than the space between the stars. There was nothing to see.

Then Sera's eyes adjusted. She saw points of faint, silvery light scattered through the infinite dark, each mile from any other. This was pride. Each point of light was a soul. They were not screaming. They were not suffering in any overt way. They were…alone. Wholly and utterly alone. Trapped in the perfect, unbreakable prison of their own self-importance. They believed they were gods, the sole occupants of their own universe. They could not perceive any other soul, any other existence. They were the beginning and the end of their own reality.

Lilith stopped the car. The engine went silent. The only things that existed were the cold, the dark, and those isolated souls.

"They believed they needed no one but themselves," she said, her voice a bare whisper in the crushing silence. "They placed themselves at the center of creation. So, we granted their wish. Each is the god of their own tiny, meaningless universe. An eternity of self-worship with no worshippers. This, Sera, is the ultimate inheritance. The ultimate power. To be so complete in oneself that nothing else is required. Or can be perceived."

Sera looked from one distant light to another. She felt the crushing weight of that solitude, that self-imposed godhood. It was the most profound horror she had ever witnessed. It was not damnation. It was oblivion.

"It is the ultimate weakness," Sera said, her voice clear and steady. She turned to face Lilith, whose face was a pale, unreadable mask. "To be so afraid of being hurt, of being less, that you build a universe with no doors. That is not power. That is the most pathetic prison of all."

For the first time, a flicker crossed Lilith's face. Surprise? Annoyance? But it was gone in an instant. She smiled her slow, cold smile. "An interesting interpretation."

She then started the car. This world did not fade. It shattered like a pane of glass, cracking and falling away, and Sera stood on the cold stone floor of her chambers once more.

Lilith still stood before her, the space between them charged with the lingering chill. "You see only suffering," she said, her tone that of a disappointed tutor. "You lack vision, child. You see the cost, not the investment. Metamorphosis is always painful."

"If that is the result," Sera said, her voice trembling with rage, "I want no part of it."

"Because you are still thinking like a mortal. You fear the process." Her smile was thin. "Perhaps a demonstration is in order. A gift to hasten your understanding."

From the folds of her dress, Lilith produced a small velvet box. It was exquisitely made, black as a starless night. She held it out to Sera. Hesitantly, fighting every screaming instinct to flee, Sera looked down as Lilith opened the lid.

Inside, nestled on a bed of crimson silk, was what looked like a large larval pearl. It pulsed with a faint internal light, its skin iridescent and slick. It was obscene, a thumb-sized grub of condensed darkness that seemed to squirm without moving. It was both beautiful and utterly revolting.

A wave of bile rose in Sera's throat. "What is that?" she breathed, recoiling.

"A catalyst," Lilith said softly. "Swallow it, and it will hatch within you. It will digest the remnants of your petty human frailties, your useless compassions, and your fears. It will feed on them and leave only strength in their place. The transformation that could take years will be complete in days. You will see the world through my eyes. You will be ready to claim your throne."

Sera stared at the pulsating thing, at the wet sheen on its skin, and imagined it inside her. A parasite of the soul. She looked up at Lilith's expectant face and saw the true face of the monster beneath. The horror of it was a physical blow.

She took a step back, her hands coming up as if to ward off a physical attack. "No," she whispered, the word raw. She then found her strength, her voice gaining a steely edge. "No. I would rather die. I would rather burn on a pyre than become...that." Her gesture was dismissive, taking in all of Lilith.

Lilith's expression tightened. The disappointment was real this time. With a snap, she closed the box, the sound unnaturally loud in the quiet room. "Pity," she said, the word clipped. The box vanished back into her dress. "You choose the long, painful road. So be it. But the destination remains the same."

And then she was gone with a simple fade as if she had never been there at all.

A Thriving Infection
25

Every night, Kael fell asleep with Sera's name on his lips, chasing the memory of her voice, the ghost of her pain. He would close his eyes and plead to see her. And she would appear, sitting on that gravestone and bathed in the impossible light of memory. Waiting for him.

But he could never reach her. Something barred him at the tree line, an invisible wall that pressed between them the moment his feet touched the meadow's earth. He clawed at it, screamed her name until his throat tore raw. Every night, the same brutal failure. So, he watched, night after night, as her body slowly changed. Her shoulders were drawn tight, her eyes were weary, and her form was bent under the weight of something he could not reach.

When she stopped appearing, he still came. He waited beneath the trees, his eyes fixed on the gravestone that remained empty. Sometimes, he swore he could still feel her nearby, a whisper on the wind. Sometimes, he imagined her walking away with her back to him, the tether between them fraying with every beat of his desperate heart.

He stopped speaking. Stopped sleeping. Stopped dreaming.

Cassia said nothing, but she looked at him as if she might begin mourning both of them soon.

With Michael's reluctant approval, Kael was granted access to the celestial archives: a place no fallen had touched in over a century. He, Remiel, and Cassia searched every document, every forbidden scroll on soul bonds, tethers, infernal wards, and celestial obstructions. They mapped the tangled threads of dead-end sigils until their hands bled with ink.

Nothing.

Hell had gone silent. Portals had vanished from the mortal realm. No signatures. No leaks. The doors were sealed. No one in and no one out.

The blood moon was halfway complete now, its light deepening each night yet still unseen by mortal eyes. The phenomenon had always been veiled from the human realm as a mercy woven into divine design so that mortals wouldn't collapse in fear each time the heavens threatened to break. Only the supernatural knew what its coming meant, and even they were unraveling beneath its pull.

He felt it in his blood, the slow corrosion. The closer the moon drew to fullness, the weaker she became—and the weaker he felt. Across the realms, tempers flared, the restless fed on fear, and the watchers were busy, but Kael no longer cared. The souls he was meant to collect went untouched, their judgment suspended. All that mattered was finding a way to Hell.

He could not bear the sadness that had rooted itself in him and grown into longing, a longing that had curdled into something crueler. If the wards didn't break, he would find another way in, even if it tore him apart. Even if it meant dying again and trusting that death would deliver him into Hell's open palm.

The thought should have steadied him. It didn't. The fury burned out too quickly, leaving only emptiness in its wake. He stared at his own hands, at the veins that no longer glowed, and felt the quiet truth settling. He no longer knew what he was—angel, monster, or something unmade between. Whatever he had become, it wasn't enough to reach her. And that failure was the one wound that would not close.

Sera stood trembling in the oppressive silence of her chambers, the afterimage of that grotesque, pulsating grub burning in her mind. Lilith had shown her the anatomy of ruin and called it an inheritance. The horror of it was a physical blow.

A new hunger stirred in her, a hunger to see Lilith's perfect, ironic kingdom and the creature who ruled it burn.

But that was a dream born of fading defiance. The reality was the cold stones beneath her feet and the gnawing emptiness promised to consume her long before she could ever find a weapon. Defeated, she paced like a caged animal until a ripple in the air announced Vyxia's arrival.

The demoness appeared, her violet eyes examining Sera's battered state. "The queen showed you the punishments, the consequences," she said, her voice a knowing murmur. "But she neglected to show you the heart."

Sera stopped, turning to face her. "The heart? Hell doesn't have a heart, Vyxia. It's a cancer."

A faint, almost imperceptible smile touched Vyxia's lips. "That is the official story. But Hell is not just a prison. It's a society. Let me show you something else. A place where choices are still made."

Intrigued despite her despair, she gave a curt nod.

Vyxia led her not through the grand corridors but through a series of twisting servant passages. They emerged into a cavern so vast that it felt like a subterranean sky, lit not by torches but by the chaotic shimmering glow of countless soul lanterns.

This was the Nightshade Market.

The cavern yawned like a wound in Hell's belly, and the market within it throbbed like a living infection. Soul lanterns floated above in uneven constellations, each one a trapped will-o'-the-wisp with its light flickering with the echo of a heartbeat. Their glow pooled and fractured across the rough stones, casting long, shifting shadows where unseen things watched from the dark.

The air was thick with the scent of scorched metal and old blood. Voices murmured like fevered prayers, trading agony and power in equal measure.

The sounds were a low, churning cacophony: the guttural haggling of all kinds of creatures in forgotten tongues, the sharp clink of soul coins, the wet hiss of a potion being uncorked, and a distant, mournful melody played on a lute. The air was a thick perfume of decay and desire. The cloying sweetness of blood wine mingled with the acidic tang of failed alchemy, the dusty scent of ancient scrolls, and an undercurrent of something like burnt sugar and sorrow.

"Lilith despises this place," Vyxia whispered, her voice a conspiratorial breath against Sera's ear, as she guided her through the crowd. "She can't control the currency here. It's too…real."

Auras brushed against Sera—not just brushed but clawed and clung. It was a tide of unfiltered want. Petty greed. Desperate hopes. Ancient sorrows. Gnawing hungers. A banquet of emotions. And the famine inside her reared its head with a sharp, painful pang.

She clutched her stomach, her breath catching. "This is useless,

Vyxia," she murmured, her hope fraying. "It's just another circle of Hell but with merchants."

"Perhaps you are right." But Vyxia halted, her gaze fixed on a stall tucked away in a darker corner, almost hidden between a vendor of bottled shadows and a smith forging weapons from solidified screams.

This stall was different. It was cluttered with celestial debris: a broken halo leaking sorrowful light, a single singed white feather preserved under glass, and a chalice that still hummed with a forgotten blessing. It was a graveyard of Heaven's cast-off relics.

"What is that?" Sera breathed, her voice barely a whisper. She moved toward the stall, drawn by an invisible thread of recognition and a sense of sacrilege.

Behind the stall sat a withered warlock, his eyes milky and sightless. His gnarled hands were sorting what looked like tarnished silver coins. He didn't look up as they approached, yet she felt the unnerving sensation of being weighed and measured.

He spoke before they could, his voice a dry rustle of ancient parchment. "You are a long way from home." His head tilted slightly, his milky eyes seeming to find her. "Both of you."

Vyxia stepped closer to the stall. "They say in this market, one can buy anything. Even the impossible."

The warlock's lips pulled back into a semblance of a smile. "The impossible is my trade, child. All for a price." He set down a coin and folded his hands. "My name is Orin. And I trade in what is lost. I sense you are looking for a door."

"I need a door out of this place," Sera said, her voice low and urgent.

Orin's sightless eyes seemed to bore into her. "A door from Hell itself? That is a very expensive door. It requires a powerful key. A significant expense of pure energy."

"What kind of energy?"

"Mortal souls are like kindling," he rasped, waving a dismissive hand. "They burn hot and fast. Not enough. To tear a hole in this realm...I would need something more potent. Something...divine." He leaned forward. "Celestial light. The kind that still clings to the fallen."

The words struck her with the force of a physical blow. The fallen angels. The ones imprisoned in the dungeons. Their essence.

Her mind, once a storm of despair, focused with chilling clarity. A desperate and terrible plan formed. This was no longer just about survival. This was about currency. This was about buying her freedom.

"Where would I find such a thing?" she asked, her voice carefully neutral.

The warlock's smile widened. "The queen keeps a collection, I hear. In the palace's lower levels. Shattered things, but their light, however faint, still burns."

As they walked away, a new resolve settled in her bones. The gnawing hunger was still there, but now, it had a purpose. She had a path. She just needed Lilith to open the door for her, unwittingly.

A Day For A Soul

26

Time in Hell had been a viscous, meaningless current, a river of shadows that threatened to drag Sera into an eternity of torment. But now, for the first time since her arrival, it had a fixed point: a plan. A path.

She did not wait to be summoned. The gnawing hunger was a relentless clock, and every moment wasted was a moment she slipped further away from the woman Kael knew her as. She strode to the door of her chambers, her movements no longer aimless.

"Vyxia," she called, her voice clear and commanding.

The demoness materialized from the hall's shadows, her expression a mask of careful neutrality. "Your Highness?"

"I need an audience with my mother." Her gaze was unwavering. "Immediately."

Vyxia's violet eyes narrowed, a flicker of surprise in their depths. "An audience?" she questioned. "The queen does not grant them lightly. And what reason shall I give for this sudden devotion?"

Her lips curved into a smile that did not reach her eyes. "Tell her I have a proposal. Tell her that I have been observing Hell's legions and have an idea how to make them stronger. An idea that will guarantee her victory in any war to come."

Vyxia studied her for a long, tense moment and then gave a slow, deliberate nod. "A bold gambit, Princess. I will deliver your message."

The wait that followed was agonizing. Sera paced her chambers with the predatory stillness of a hunter waiting for the trap to spring. She clung to her journal, not as an anchor to a fading past but as a reminder of the life she was fighting to reclaim.

Finally, the rhythmic thud of heavy boots echoed in the corridor. A hulking guard, the same one from before, entered the chambers and inclined its head. The suspicion in its eyes was still there, but it was now tempered with curiosity.

"The queen will see you," it growled.

She straightened, her spine taut. She gathered the tatters of her old self not as a cloak of dignity but as a costume for the role she was about to play. She followed the guard in silence, her bare feet whispering across the cold stone floors.

They didn't take the familiar path to the throne room. Instead, the corridor narrowed, its walls lined with sconces that burned with an eerie blue fire. Sickly shadows danced across the cracked obsidian, stretching and twisting like silent sentinels. At the end of the hallway stood a set of arched double doors, blackwood veined with silver and carved with infernal runes that faintly pulsed as she approached.

The guard opened the doors with a grunt, and a strange, heavy scent drifted out: parchment, incense, and the aroma of forgotten power. It wasn't the stench of a war room or the chill of a dungeon.

It was a study.

The chamber was cavernous yet oddly intimate, as if the vastness of

Hell had chosen to compress itself into this singular space. Books lined the curved walls, stacked on towering shelves that reached into shadowed darkness. Their spines were bound in leather, bone, or stranger things still that seemed to whisper dark stories. A massive desk carved from ebony and polished to a mirror sheen dominated the center of the room. Two high-backed chairs stood before it: one empty, one occupied.

Lilith reclined behind the desk like a queen caught mid-reverie, a predator at rest. A goblet of flickering soulfire hovered in her hand, casting ghostlight across her porcelain skin. Her black curls were swept to one side, cascading over her bare shoulder. A robe of midnight velvet clung to her like a second skin and was embroidered with crimson thread that shimmered with every subtle movement. Her horns, curved and elegant, gleamed faintly in the low light, and her eyes—those same impossible eyes Sera had inherited—glowed faintly gold as they lifted, fixing on her.

"My darling girl," Lilith purred, her lips parting into a feline smile that promised both sweetness and a bite. "Come in. Sit."

Sera hesitated but then stepped forward, her pulse thundering beneath her skin. She only nodded once and stiffly lowered herself into the empty chair.

She tilted her goblet, offering the flickering liquid. "Soulfire? Aged. Pure. Liberated from a rather haughty bishop last winter."

Sera's stomach twisted, a visceral mix of craving and revulsion. "No, thank you."

She arched a brow and then set the goblet aside with a soft clink that echoed in the vast room. Her tone shifted. Still velvet but edged with an unnerving curiosity. "I've heard you're seeking an entrance to the dungeons. You want to help my army. I must confess I'm puzzled. What exactly are you hoping to achieve?"

Sera inhaled slowly. Her shadows pressed closer, whispering nonsense in her ears and clawing at the edges of her restraint. But she did not look away.

"I'm trying to live with what I am now," she said carefully, each word measured. "I can't go back. So, I want to make myself useful. The guards train beneath my window day and night. They don't look like monsters anymore... Not to me. I thought perhaps if I could find a way to enhance their strength through celestial essence. I could make a meaningful contribution. Earn my place."

Lilith was silent. But her gaze sharpened. "So," she said, her voice low and dangerously soft, "you think my legions are weak."

Sera's breath caught, trapped in her throat. Her mouth opened and then closed again, no sound escaping.

We think she got you, the shadows hissed, their amused whispers slithering around her ears.

Lilith leaned forward, her chin resting atop one hand. Her golden eyes narrowed. "Tell me, Daughter," she said, her voice a silken thread, "where did you learn to lie so prettily?"

But Sera didn't answer. She kept her expression neutral, her posture composed and waited for the queen of Hell to speak again.

Her eyes gleamed like they held the punch line of a cruel joke. She rested her elbows on the desk, her fingers steepled beneath her chin. "Why do you need celestial essence?"

Sera's mind reeled. The lie was ready, refined and rehearsed, but a shard of ice caught in her throat: fear or guilt or both. The words refused to come.

Lilith let out a low chuckle, a sound like gravel rolling over silk, and leaned back in her chair. "Well, bonding to Kael was a foolish idea, wasn't it?"

Sera's breath hitched. The room seemed to tilt, and her shadows tightened around the corners of her vision. Her fingers dug into the edge of her seat as she wondered if the queen was in her dreams too.

"Relax." Her smirk deepened. "I can't visit dreams. Not yours anyway. Too messy, too protected. But I did see the bond mark." She pushed her robe down, revealing the smooth skin between her breasts. There, faint and gnarled, lay a jagged scar, the remnants of what must have once been a rune. It faintly pulsed, a faded echo of a connection. "This body and this soul once belonged to your father. I know what bond marks look like."

Sera's lips parted, but no words came. Her mind raced, grappling with the unthinkable: Michael, her father… The archangel had *bonded* with Lilith.

"With me down here," she continued, her voice almost reflective, a dangerous nostalgia, "and him up there, our only meeting ground was the sterile stones of the tribunal halls… How do you think you and your sister were made?" Her gaze sharpened, assessing. "Tell me then. What does your bondscape look like?"

Sera swallowed hard. Her hands were trembling, blood roaring in her ears. "A meadow," she whispered.

Lilith's face shifted, cruel amusement. She smiled, a ghost of an echo in her ancient eyes. "Ah. That means your love is still pure. Gentle. Uncorrupted." She swirled the soulfire in her goblet without taking a drink. "Too bad it was short-lived."

The words hit Sera like ice water.

Lilith didn't need to say it outright. Whatever tether had sparked between Kael and Sera was already decaying under the crushing weight of this realm.

Lilith leaned forward again, her eyes glittering. "You can't save him, you know. Not from what's coming. Not even from me." Her voice was silky and coaxing, a venomous sweetness. "But I'm not entirely without mercy."

She rose from her seat, her long silhouette framed against the roaring fireplace at her back. Her goblet still dangled from her fingers like an afterthought, catching the light in crimson glints. Sera couldn't look away from that faint, ruined scar on Lilith's chest. It seemed to pulse in time with her own bond mark—a mirror of shared, fractured fate.

"I will let you see him one last time," Lilith said. "I'm not a monster, after all. And since you are so desperate to belong, to prove yourself…consider this a gesture of good faith." She turned her gaze back to Sera, her gold eyes as sharp as razors. "I will lower the wards of Hell. Temporarily. You will see your precious Kael…if you promise me something first."

Sera didn't speak. Couldn't. Her throat felt lined with ash, her body trembling under the weight of that familiar, longed-for name. Kael. Her Kael.

"Swear it on your blood," she said, setting the goblet down with a gentle clink. The sound ominously echoed in the silent room. "Swear that after your meeting, you will consume the grub…and I will let you see the fallen angels in the dungeons."

Sera's heart twisted.

She knew precisely what Lilith meant. She could feel the trap closing, elegant and cruel and dressed up as grace. Her shadows at her feet coiled like smoke, curling up her calves like they too hungered for her answer.

Lilith's voice dropped to a near whisper. "One taste of him. One night to say goodbye. And then…your real transformation begins."

Sera met her mother's eyes, the echo of her heartbeat in her chest.

How much of herself was she willing to trade...for one last piece of him?

The silence that followed cracked with heavy weight. The shadows leaned in, their unseen presence a heavy shroud.

Sera's fingers tightened around the spine of her journal until her knuckles blanched. She could feel why he hadn't come to the meadows again now.

It was the wards.

The wall between them. The veil. The reason she'd been left staring at nothing while the bond mark dimmed to an ember. Lilith had trapped her here, wrapped her in veils of flames and runes so thick not even Kael's light could reach her.

And if she refused? Lilith wouldn't openly punish her. She'd wait for the transformation to finish on its own. Wait while Sera withered in a room with no sky and no touch. She might never see Kael again. Never know if he searched for her. Never even say goodbye.

She drew in a shaky breath, the air burning in her lungs. "Why?" she whispered, her voice barely audible. "Why do you need me to transform willingly?"

Lilith's eyes sparkled with amusement. No. Closer to triumph. "Because every bargain must be struck with open minds and open hearts." She circled back around the desk. "Otherwise, the soul resists. Rejects. And I need your soul to welcome the change." She paused before Sera's chair, one hand lightly resting on the armrest. "And quite honestly," she added with a smile that didn't reach her eyes, "I'm running out of time."

She looked up slowly, her pulse a dull throb in her ears. "Time for what, Mother?"

Lilith's smile turned sharp. "For your destiny."

The words landed with a weight that chilled her to the bone. They sounded like a prophecy—an inheritance soaked in blood and ash. And Sera realized she didn't have the luxury of saying no.

Sera's breath trembled, but her voice came out clear, tinged with a desperate resolve. "I'll do it," she said. "But I want a whole day with him."

Lilith stilled. Then slowly grinned. It was a smile full of fangs and delight, the kind a cat would give a bird that had finally stopped fluttering. "A whole day," she echoed. "A whole *working* day."

She moved to the side cabinet, its surface carved with infernal glyphs that faintly pulsed at her touch. From within, she drew a slender blade. Its hilt was wrapped in black leather, its edge obsidian-dark and licked with red veins that shimmered. The blade itself hummed with a hungry song, alive.

Lilith held it up with an almost ceremonial reverence. "That's a deal, Daughter." She walked back and placed the dagger on the desk between them. "Your blood seals the terms. You know how this works."

Sera stared at the blade, its dark surface reflecting her unfamiliar face. A whole day. One last chance. And then…and then she would consume the corruption.

She reached forward, her fingers brushing the cool leather of the hilt. Her shadows purred, a satisfied hum.

Lilith's voice was a whisper now, close to her ear. A serpent's hiss. "Make it count."

Make it Count
27

Sera stumbled into her chambers, the door slamming behind her with a sound like a funeral bell. A fragile ember rekindled at her bond mark. The tether between them, which had been dormant for days, flared with a desperate hum as the wards began to lift.

Her heart thundered, frantic against her ribs. She needed help, someone who wouldn't question her. At least not in ways that mattered.

"Vyxia!" she called, voice raw and breathless.

The shadows stirred, coiling and uncoiling in the corners of the room. Moments later, the demoness materialized in the doorway, eyes glinting like molten violets beneath a fringe of silver-white hair. There was always something off about her, like her edges didn't quite match the air of Hell.

"You rang," Vyxia said flatly, crossing her arms. Her gaze swept over Sera's trembling form. "You look like you've seen a ghost. Or made a deal."

"The latter, and I need something," Sera said, the sharp words tumbling out. "I need you to knock me out."

Vyxia's brow rose, slow and skeptical. "You want me to what?"

"Put me under. For exactly twelve hours." She began pacing the cold stone floor. "I asked Lilith for a day with him. She gave me 'a working day.' I can't waste a second."

Vyxia tilted her head, studying her with unnerving stillness. "You're serious."

"Deadly."

"You do realize how senseless this is?" The demoness stepped closer, her voice a low murmur. "You're half starved and half cursed. You want me to sedate you while your bond mark burns like a brand?"

"I'm not starving," Sera said through her teeth. "…Well, not exactly." Her throat tightened as she spoke. "This place feeds me enough to keep me breathing but never enough to stop the hunger."

Her lips twitched, somewhere between disdain and curiosity. "Hell's generosity," she muttered.

"I don't have time," Sera pressed. "The clock's already running."

She clicked her tongue. "You *have* lost your mind."

"I have," Sera said, a flicker of dark humor crossing her eyes. "And you need to help me."

The silence stretched before she turned to leave. "I'll bring you something," she said over her shoulder, her voice flat now. "Strong enough to drop a wraith. It won't kill you. Probably."

"What is it?" Sera called after her.

"A blend," came the reply. "Blackthorn resin, crushed mourning root, and a little ultheris."

Sera frowned, the names meaningless to her. "I don't know what that is."

"You're not supposed to," she said, her voice fading as she left. "You just need to swallow it and pray your soul knows where to land."

The door creaked shut, sealing her in with the silence. It wasn't empty; it was heavy, a physical weight that pressed against her ears.

Sera didn't move. She let the quiet settle before dragging herself toward the bed, her body a collection of aches held together by sheer stubbornness.

At the base of her throat, the bond mark pulsed—steady, rhythmic, a beacon burning against her skin. She pressed her fingers to it. A silent prayer.

Vyxia returned exactly eight minutes later with a small black vial cradled between two fingers. The liquid inside shimmered like ink stirred with starlight. Sera was already lying on the bed, her hair unbound and fanned out against the dark silk sheets. Her skin was pale, almost translucent, against the deep fabric, making her look like a bride waiting for burial.

"This'll taste like shit," Vyxia said, holding it out. "Don't fight it. Let it pull you under."

Sera sat up slightly and took the vial with both hands. It was warm, too warm, as if it held a piece of Hell's own heat. "And if I don't wake up?"

She smirked, a fleeting, almost kind expression. "Then I guess you found a better world."

Sera rolled her eyes with an almost imperceptible twitch at the corner of her mouth. She then uncorked the vial and downed it in one swallow.

It burned. Immediately. A searing fire clawed its way down her throat, igniting every nerve in a single blinding rush. The room dissolved. Edges blurred into a kaleidoscope of shadows as her vision failed.

Vyxia's voice was a whisper from the encroaching darkness. "Wherever you're going, tell him not to be late."

Everything went black.

First came the light. Then the breath.

Sera hit the ground, her knees jarring against the earth. Her palms sank into the grass—velvety, twilight blades she knew like a memory—but the air was wrong. It smelled too thick. Black roses swayed in a breezeless silence, exhaling a scent heavier than perfume.

Above, the sky was not purple but bruised. The stars looked distant as if the fabric of the heavens was unraveling, pulling them into the dark. In the center of the field, the twisted tree stood skeletal. Its silver veins had dulled to gray, and its leaves hung brittle, dusted with ash.

Her bond mark pulsed a steady rhythmic beat that matched the quiet hum in the air. Kael was here. Or would be soon. She could feel it. And still, a subtle pressure gathered at the edges of her mind—like fingers pressing against glass, testing for cracks. A watchful presence, unseen but near, tracing her every breath.

She looked down. The gravestone remained in its place, half sunken at the edge of the meadow with no name etched into it. Only that pale rune was still glowing gold. She exhaled a shaky breath and ran her fingers through the grass. It felt cooler now, damp, as if this world had wept during her absence.

She then stood, smoothing her hands down the soft skirt of her midnight blue dress. Her demon form was quieter here, subdued. Her skin still glowed faintly with its gray undertones, but the sharpness in her bones was softened. Her horns were small.

Behind her, the grass rustled. She didn't turn right away, savoring the moment, the agony of anticipation. She already knew who it was. The wind shifted again, and this time, she felt it in her bones, a deep resonance that vibrated through her very soul. She turned.

Kael stood at the meadow's edge, his chest heaving as if he'd run for miles, for lifetimes. His shirt, undone and clinging to his damp skin, suggested he'd been dropped here midthought, midbattle.

On his collarbone, the bond mark burned—golden, searing, a mirror to her own.

For a heartbeat, they didn't move. The world held its breath, suspended in the fragile space between longing and reunion.

Sera bolted first, across the grass, her skirt kicking up black rose petals behind her. He surged forward like a force unchained, hair flying and boots tearing into the dirt. They collided in the center of the meadow. She leaped onto him, her legs wrapping around his waist and arms thrown around his neck as her mouth found his. Their kiss was feral, no grace and no hesitation. It was teeth and tears and breathless hunger, a desperate claiming. She kissed him like the world would end in seconds.

He staggered back a step but held her, crushing her against him with desperate strength. His hands gripped her hips like she might vanish if he let go. He broke the kiss, panting hard, and pressed his forehead to hers. "You finally came," he gasped, his voice thick with wonder, heartbreak, and heat. "I thought I already…"

But she stopped him with another kiss, tasting of salt and longing. His hands slid into her hair, tangling in the dark strands. His mouth opened beneath hers in surrender. As if he'd been holding his breath since she had disappeared, and only now could he truly breathe again. The meadow pulsed with their bond—petals blooming, stars shuddering, and the very air vibrating.

Kael kissed her like she was his last breath. And for a moment, she let him believe she was, but then she pulled back. Her lips hovered against his, their foreheads still touching, but the fire in her chest had dimmed some.

"We only have twelve hours," she whispered, the words a jagged edge.

He froze, his body stiffening against hers. "What?"

She slipped down from his arms, her bare feet sinking into the cool grass. Her arms folded tight around his waist as if to anchor herself. But her gaze dropped, unable to meet his eyes. "I made a deal with Lilith."

"What do you mean by a *deal?*" he demanded, his voice low but shaking. "What kind of deal?"

She swallowed hard. "I exchanged twelve hours with you in return for finishing my transformation."

He was silent for a moment too long, the silence stretching into an eternity. He moved fast, grabbing her face between his hands and forcing her to look up at him. His grip was almost painful. "No," he rasped, his voice a broken plea. "No, no. Sera, why, why would you bargain with the mother of demons?!"

Tears welled in her eyes. She tried to blink them back, but they broke anyway, spilling down her cheeks. "I didn't have a choice," she said, her voice cracking. "The pain was getting worse every day. I could feel myself unraveling. And Lilith wouldn't let you in past the wards. It was either transform alone in agony and never see you again or choose to change and see you one last time."

Kael pulled her against him again, holding her so tight it hurt. He buried a hand in her hair, gripping it like a lifeline. "M-my little devil," he whispered, his voice cracking, broken. "What have you done…?"

"I needed you." She sobbed into him, her body shaking. "Even if it was only once more. Even if it kills me."

He shook his head, and his lips pressed to the top of her head like he could undo time. "We were coming for you," he said, his voice barely above a breath. "We think we found a way. Cassia, Remiel, we were planning it."

She went still, every muscle locking in place. The cruel irony of it. "How would I know..." she whispered, the words a raw wound.

"I know," he said. "But I wish you had."

They stood there in the meadow, wrapped around each other like the world couldn't find them if they stayed still enough, if they held on tight enough.

Sera pulled back enough to look up at him, her voice still trembling. "What did you find?" she asked. "You said you were coming... How?"

A half breath of hesitation passed before he took her hand, lacing their fingers. "Come." A nod toward the twisted tree at the meadow's center was his only other direction.

Silence held the clearing as they walked, the hush broken only by the soft brush of grass against their ankles. Beneath the ancient branches, roots tangled into a natural throne wide enough for two. He guided her down, taking his seat first before pulling her into his lap. One arm secured her waist, and the other traced lazy circles on her thigh.

"We started with Elara," he said, his voice grim against the quiet.

He began to reconstruct the events of that day—the discovery of Elara's dealings with Lilith, the unraveling of the betrayal after she had vanished from the townhome.

Sera stiffened in his arms. "And?"

"She didn't exactly confess." His jaw tightened. "Cassia was the one who offered to wipe her memory."

She looked up, wide-eyed. "You erased Elara?"

"Well, Cassia did. Elara doesn't remember anything about us or you now. She's just...Bethany again. At least I hope so. I have never heard of a memory wipe performed on black witches being successful."

Sera's heart twisted, a sharp pang of both pity and understanding.

"That's brutal."

"It was mercy. Trust me. I had other plans…" He exhaled a heavy sigh. "But that's not the part that matters. When Cassia was done, she found something." He reached into his pocket and pulled out a coin. Black. Smooth. And etched with Lucifer's sigil in bloodred metal, which faintly pulsed with dark power.

Sera's breath caught, a gasp trapped in her throat.

"She found this," he said, his voice low. "Lucifer's coin to the Crossroads. We were going to use it. The Crossroads was the only place thin enough to cut through the veil, to reach you."

Her fingers touched the coin, barely brushing its surface as if it might burn her. The weight of his words settled over her. "You were coming for me," she whispered, the words fragile with a hope she hadn't dared to feel.

He nodded, his eyes burning.

The words to tell him about her own plan, about the warlock and the celestial light and Vyxia's role, rose to the tip of her tongue. She wanted to share the burden, to weave their desperate hopes into a stronger thread.

But fear held her back. This meadow was a space born of their bond, but it was still a dream granted by Lilith's bargain. What if it wasn't safe? What if her mother could somehow listen in, a silent observer in the shadows?

Revealing her plan could not only endanger her but also Vyxia, Cassia, and the warlock. It could give Lilith the final weapon she needed to crush them all. So, she swallowed the words, the secret a bitter stone in her throat. She would let him believe his plan was the only plan, the only hope. It was safer that way.

He reached for her chin, gently turning her face to his. "I will still come through the Crossroads. I will find you." After a pause, his voice dropped to a fierce whisper, a vow carved into the very air. "Even if you don't recognize me anymore. I'll find the way. I promise."

Her throat tightened as tears brimmed again, blurring his face. "You promise things you shouldn't," she said, trying to smile.

He leaned in and kissed the corner of her mouth. Then her temple. Then the bond mark at her neck. "Then I'll break every rule in Heaven and Hell to keep it." He pressed his forehead to hers, his breath mingling with her own. "And then I'll make you fall in love with me again."

She huffed, a soft, broken sound. She pulled back just enough to squint up at him, a flicker of her old fire. "Who told you I love you, Angel?"

Kael let out a soft laugh, a sound of pure joy amid the sorrow. "Exchanging one last kiss for horns and fire? I think that answers for itself."

A reluctant beam tugged at her lips, but her chest ached with a strange, aching warmth—love and grief twined so tight that they were indistinguishable. It spread through her like the slow bloom of fire, beautiful and merciless. She leaned in again, slower this time, and pressed her lips to his. No hunger. No rush. Just the truth of it. Their mouths melted into one another. Their tongues met, not desperate but familiar.

The wind hushed. The stars leaned closer. And time kept ticking, a relentless countdown.

Their kiss deepened, pressure building through contact rather than speed. Her mouth slowed over his, lingering, drawing each breath from him on purpose. Her fingers slid along the back of his neck and into his hair, tightening until his body responded without permission. She felt the shift immediately. The way his spine straightened. The way his hands closed harder on her hips, grounding them both in the grass.

She pulled back and broke the kiss with control and eased off his lap, her weight leaving him inch by inch until she knelt between his knees. The grass cooled her skin, and she stayed close enough that he still felt her warmth.

Kael did not move. His chest rose once, sharp and unsteady. "Sera...what are...?"

She looked up at him and held his gaze with a gentle smile. Her expression carried intent and something heavier beneath it. Her hands rested on his thighs first, steadying herself, steadying him. Then they moved to his belt, undoing the buckle and opening the zipper of his jeans. Her fingers worked slowly, deliberately, as if she wanted him to feel every second of it.

"I want to remember this," she said, quiet and firm. "I want you to remember this."

She freed him with care, guiding rather than rushing, her hands precise and unhurried. His reaction told her everything. His breath caught. His shoulders tensed. His hands pressed into the ground at his sides as if he needed the earth to keep him upright.

She has not touched him with her mouth yet.

Instead, she leaned forward and paused, close enough for him to feel her breath. She watched his face while she stayed there, memorizing the way he struggled not to move, not to reach for her. This was not hunger. This was attention.

When her lips finally brushed the throbbing head of his cock, the contact stayed light. Intentional. A single kiss meant to be felt rather than taken. She lingered just long enough to mark the moment, then lifted her head again.

The sound he made was broken and raw. His head tipped back,

throat exposed, jaw tight as he fought for control. His fingers curled into the grass, knuckles pale.

"Fuuuuck," he hissed, his hands tearing into the grass as his body betrayed him.

She answered by taking him into her mouth, slow and controlled. Not eager. Not rushed. She set the pace herself and held it there, drawing the tremor out of him on purpose. Her lips sealed around him with care, her tongue darting out, tracing the sensitive underside in measured strokes.

Her hands worked with the same intent. One wrapped around the base of his cock and held him steady, anchoring him in place. The other slid lower. She cupped him gently, fingers cradling his weight while her talons dragged lightly over the sensitive skin.

Kael's head tipped back as control slipped from him. His chest rose hard. "Sera," he breathed, wrecked and honest. "Heavens, I'm not going to last."

She did not slow. She did not reassure.

She took him deeper, her throat yielding with deliberate control in and out. Her hand kept the pace where her mouth could not reach, setting a rhythm meant to pull him apart piece by piece. She felt the head of his cock swell larger in her mouth, causing her to gasp, choking, but she still did not stop. His body tightened under her assault. His fingers closed in her hair, grip firm, desperate, holding on as if the ground itself had failed him.

When release took him, it did so violently. His hips stuttered and drove forward, breath breaking as he gave in completely. She stayed with him through it, mouth never leaving him, swallowing everything he gave until his body sagged and went slack, spent and undone, hand still wrapped in her raven hair.

Only then did she pull back.

Slowly. Intentionally.

Her smile held satisfaction and claim in equal measure. "You're mine," she whispered, low and certain. Not a tease. A fact.

She crawled back into his lap and settled there, straddling him with easy confidence. Her warmth pressed against him through the thin barrier of her skirt, heat unmistakable, promise heavy. "Every last bit of you."

He cupped her face, still catching his breath, thumbs brushing her cheekbones as if to make sure she was real. "You ruined me for anyone else," he said quietly. "From the moment you… walked into the Iron Orchid."

She kissed him then, soft and unhurried. Her hips began to move, slow and deliberate, grinding just enough to remind him what else waited.

She tightened her thighs around him and drew herself closer, skirt bunched higher at her waist, dragging herself along his length in slow rolls of her hips, letting her slick heat mark him without taking him in.

This moment mattered. She meant it to stay.

He groaned, low and strained. "Sera."

Her eyes caught the starlight. Her mouth curved in a playful smile. "You need a minute?"

"No," he breathed. His body already answered her, thickening where she moved against him. "I need you."

She rocked again, slow and deliberate, dragging herself along him with enough pressure to make his breath hitch, coating her sleekness all over the length. She felt the change immediately and leaned into it, keeping the rhythm steady until his restraint frayed.

Kael's hands slid down her thighs and closed tight, fingers digging into flesh as if to memorize the shape of her. He felt himself press fully against her, heavy and insistent. He anchored his grip and held her there, afraid she might slip away again if he loosened even for a second.

"I do not think I will ever have enough of you," he said, voice rough. "I know I will not."

He shifted beneath her, lifted his hips just enough to line them up, and guided her down onto him in one slow, cruel, claiming motion.

Sera cried out as he filled her. Her back arched sharply. Her hands flew to his chest, claws longer now, sharper, sinking into his skin and breaking it open. He gasped at the sting and the pull, but he did not slow. He dragged her closer by the hips and thrust up again, deeper, sealing the connection.

She moved with him instinctively, breath stuttering as her body found the rhythm. Pain and pleasure blurred together, bound tight by the tether between them. Above them, the stars continued to fall in silent streaks, shedding light like witnesses.

She rode him in slow, devastating strokes. Her body curled forward and pulled back with intention, each movement deliberate, measured, ancient. Every push and pull causes her body to shiver, her heart to throb. Her claws stayed buried in his chest, his essence mixed with his blood, streaked down her fingers like a mark she meant to keep. His breath fractured every time she sank on him, her heat tightening, slicker, hotter, more demanding.

The bond flared with every pulse. Gold heat surged through him, answering her hunger.

Light spilled from the cuts she made, soft threads of warm gold rising from his skin. Shadows unfurled from her spine and shoulders and mouth, curling toward the glow. They tangled together in the air, dark and light weaving into a single living thing.

"Fuck," he breathed, barely a sound, as his hands slid to her waist and drove her down onto him harder, deeper.

She whimpered his name, broken and full. "Kael."

He half sat up as he pulled her closer. He released his hands to tear the top of her skin, but her shadows were already at work, feeling his intention as they unraveled her clothing for him. His one hand closed around her breast with intent. He brought her to his mouth and sealed his lips around her nipple, drawing it in deep. He sucked hard, then bit with care, teeth pressing until the edge of pain sparked. He soothed it at once with his tongue, slow and deliberate, as if claiming and tending in the same breath.

Her body answered instantly. She clenched around him, tight and helpless, and her head fell back as a broken sound tore free. Her hips stuttered against his, rhythm faltering under the pressure building inside her.

"Hell, Sera," he rasped. His mouth moved to her other breast, free hand resting on the middle of her back, pulling her closer to him. He repeated the act with the same focus, the same restraint. "You feel like everything I lost." His lips closed again. "And everything I still want."

She shook now. Her thighs tightened around him, grip desperate, rhythm uneven as need took over. Wild. Unsteady. Close.

Light and shadow gathered and moved around them, no longer drifting but circling, drawn to the heat of their bodies. It was not spell work or want alone. It was exposure. Their souls pressed open and visible.

"Look at me," he said, voice rough and breaking.

She did.

"I am already yours," he whispered. "Even if this is the last time. Even if you forget."

Tears slipped free before she noticed them. She cupped his beautiful face as she ground down harder, forcing him deeper. Their foreheads touched. Their breaths tangled.

"No forgetting," she said, steady and fierce. "Not now. Not ever."

They broke together.

Her body locked tight, with a cry trapped in her throat as he drove up and spilled inside her with a guttural sound that shook him. Light flared. Shadows closed around them. In that single suspended moment, there were no names or sides or bonds to define them. There was only one shared breath.

Their world stayed silent.

When her breathing slowed, she traced one sharp talon down his side, a slow, possessive scrape over his ribs.

His body jerked under her, sharp and involuntary. "Don't," he gasped. "Hell. Do not poke me."

She lifted her head enough to meet his eyes, smug and glowing. "Sensitive, Angel?"

"I am raw," he groaned. "Inside. Outside. Possibly spiritually. I think you drained me into another dimension."

"Good," she whispered. She kissed his jaw, then his throat. "Means I did it right."

His laugh came cracked and unsteady. His hands slid up her back and held her there, grip firm despite the tremor still running through him. They stayed tangled together, skin warm, breath shared, heart to heart.

And for the first time in days, Sera felt safe.

The remaining hours blurred into something soft and unreal. Almost perfect. A stolen eternity.

After the first storm passed, they found a spring hidden behind a curtain of flowering trees, just beyond the meadow. The warm water silvered with starlight, gently steaming in the twilight. They bathed there slowly, chuckling as they kissed between rinsed strands of hair and soft moans. His hands found her again beneath the surface, and her mouth returned the favor. And somewhere between all the washing and worshipping, they were tangled all over again.

Later, they lay naked in the grass, drying in the hush of the twilight breeze. Her head rested on his chest, her finger tracing the scars across his abdomen. He spoke lazily about Cassia's brooding moods and Remiel's increasingly short fuse, and she responded by kissing the hollow of his throat and climbing back on top of him, unable to resist.

That round was slower and hungrier. Like they both knew time was starting to notice them again, its cold breath on their necks. And when the stars began to shift, when the air grew thin and brittle, she felt the inevitable creeping in.

Fully clothed now, they wrapped themselves around each other, her head tucked beneath his chin. They lay beneath the twisted tree at the meadow's center, clinging to the last moments.

Kael stroked her back, his touch a silent comfort. "There's more."

She looked up, her heart clenching. "More what?"

"About the plan." His voice was steady but low, filled with grim determination. "Cassia, Remiel, and I are going to try to get into the keep. We'll use the Crossroads. Disappear inside. Jareth has a contact on the inside. An old one, a hybrid."

Her brows lifted, a flicker of surprise amid the despair. "And he trusts them?"

Kael nodded. "Enough. He's using this window, while the wards are down, to try to reach them. Establish something solid. If he gets through, we'll have a way in."

She closed her eyes, wishing she could absorb his hope. "I don't want to hope," she whispered. "I can't afford it."

"Then let me hope for you," he murmured, holding her tighter. "Just long enough to get to you."

They held each other tighter as if their embrace could stop the relentless march of time.

"And one more thing." His voice darkened. "The full blood moon is only days away. Be vigilant. Whatever Lilith is planning, it's for that night. She's been waiting."

She swallowed hard, a cold dread seeping into her bones. "I can feel it. Like the air's holding its breath."

"Then hold yours too if you have to. Just survive. Survive her. We'll do the rest."

She wanted to answer—wanted to offer something not soaked in fear or goodbye—but the stars were already dying, their light flickering like spent embers.

Around them, the meadow unraveled. Colors leached away, leaving the world brittle and pale. Black roses wilted into dust, and the wind died. Even the bond between them stuttered, a candle in a draft.

"No," Kael whispered, a desperate but futile plea. "Not yet."

Her body dimmed at the edges, her limbs softened, and her warmth was slipping away. Her eyes never left his, memorizing every line, every shadow. She reached up, one quivering hand cradled his face, and her thumb brushed the blood still dried at his jaw, a permanent mark of their desperate union. Her lips were trembling. She didn't speak; there was no time to spare.

Yet she slowly and surely mouthed three words: *I love you.*

And then she was gone.

Sera jolted awake with a sharp inhale, her body still arched like she was clinging to him. But her arms were empty. The sheets were cold. And the world was dim, oppressive. The scent of black roses and starlight was gone, replaced by the stale air of her chambers. And he was gone.

Reality crashed over her like a tide laced in shattering glass. She was back in the Crimson Keep, the stone walls as silent and as indifferent as ever. Her skin was slick with sweat, her heart hammering against her ribs like it was trying to chase him back into her arms.

But it was over. Twelve hours. That was all she'd bought.

Her bond mark still faintly pulsed at her neck, aching like a bruise. She knew it wouldn't glow like that for much longer. Its light was already fading.

The grief hit like a silent wave, vast and consuming. She curled onto her side, pulling the sheets over her like armor, and broke. No sobs. No screams. Just a quiet and desperate unraveling. The kind of tears that came when you realized the world kept turning even after your heart stopped.

That had been it. Her last chance to be loved. To be seen without a disguise. To matter in someone's arms. The tears wouldn't stop.

Soft footsteps padded, and a gentle hand touched her shoulder. Gasping, she flinched, turning and bracing for a threat.

"I'm sorry," Vyxia whispered.

The unexpected kindness felt like a fresh ache. She blinked, her throat too raw to speak and her tears blurring her vision. She then closed her eyes, fresh tears slipping down her cheeks.

Vyxia sat at the edge of the bed and said nothing else. She didn't ask what Sera had seen. She didn't need to. She just stayed like a shadow that, for once, wasn't there to haunt but to hold.

Did You Ask Her?

28

The meadow vanished in a blink, torn away like a fragile veil, and Kael fell.

He plunged through a void that screamed with forgotten memories, his body weightless. Stars shattered above him, replaced by a spiraling vortex of absolute darkness.

And then he landed.

Not on solid ground but in rot. Beneath him, the floor didn't just sit. It pulsed a sickening, organic rhythm that vibrated through his boots.

Above, the sky was an oil-black void, a suffocating blanket of despair that stretched without end. Ash drifted down like morbid snow, painting the desolate landscape in shades of gray. In the distance, skeletal spires clawed at the dark, ancient, and petrified, while the air itself grew heavy, pressing down with a cloying, physical weight.

From the swirling mists of ash, Lilith materialized—the dark heart of the chaos.

She was a vision sculpted from shadow and seduction, breathtaking in her malice. Her gown, shimmering like polished onyx kissed by spilled blood, didn't just clothe her; it clung to her form like a second, hungry skin. Elegant, sharp horns crowned her head, curling back into midnight hair, while her eyes glowed—smoldering coals that burned with a serenity far too cruel to be mortal.

"How was your little reunion?" Her voice was a silken thread, deceptively sweet but laced with venom. "Did you get your fill of her yet, Kael? Did her soft skin and innocent eyes soothe the beast within you, even for a moment?"

He swallowed, his throat dry and raw. His fists clenched at his sides until his knuckles ached. "It will never be enough," he rasped, the words a desperate plea. "And you know it."

Lilith clicked her tongue, a sound like dry bone against stone. "That's too bad. Because after tonight, you most definitely won't see her again. Not your precious Sera. Tell me, how does it feel to know you saw her for the very last time?" A cruel, knowing smile played on her lips. "To know she'll be irrevocably mine?"

He stepped forward, his wings flaring in defiance. "I will get her out."

Her smile curved like a blade, sharper and colder than any steel. "You can try, my foolish angel. But I don't think she'll want you to. Not after I tell her who you are."

He stilled, every muscle locking. The color drained from his face. "Why? I saved your life. I *spared* you. Centuries ago, I turned my back on the tribunal's judgment for *you*. Why would you do this?"

She glided toward him, her movements fluid. The shadows parted for her like servants, revealing nothing beneath her billowing gown. "Because I need her clean of regret. Free of remorse. Purged of every little fragile feeling you infected her with. A vessel unburdened by attachments, untainted by your pathetic attempts at salvation. She must become what she was always meant to be: hell reincarnate."

"Why?" he asked again, barely a whisper.

She smiled wider, a predator savoring her prey. "That is none of your business." Closer now, she tilted her head. Her eyes burned into his. "You poor, pathetic soul. You wanted redemption so badly that you sold my daughter for a chance of it. You gave her to the tribunal. You condemned her to centuries of their cruel neglect. And look at what that earned you. Nothing." She leaned even closer, her breath a silken vice against his ear. "You just watched them fall. Both of them. Just like I planned, you stood by powerless, didn't you?" A mocking pout twisted her lips. "Oops."

Kael's jaw trembled. The image of Sera, helpless and broken, burned behind his eyes.

"But then," she hissed, circling him, "you couldn't leave it alone. Could you? You watched her, year after agonizing year. You waited for her. Lusting for her, wasn't it, Kael? For the power she could offer? Or only to serve your ego. Why?"

His voice broke, a raw, strangled sound that barely escaped his lips. "I had to make it right."

Lilith's laugh was low, a mocking symphony echoing in the vast emptiness around them. "Oh, my sweet, deluded angel. So, you waited. You watched her starve and decline until she was desperate enough. Until she was broken enough. Then you moved. You let her feed. You wanted the bond stronger, didn't you? A deeper claim, a tighter leash. Your selfish desires are now disguised as salvation. Tell me, Fallen, with all your high ideals"—she leaned in, her lips nearly grazing his ear and her voice a poisonous whisper that burrowed into his very core—"did you ask her if she wanted it?"

"No," he whispered. The word was barely audible, a confession of his most profound shame.

"What was that?" She drew out the words, seemingly savoring his torment.

"I said *NO!*" he roared, the last word ripped from his very soul.

Lilith grinned, a predatory flash of white teeth in the gloom. "That's what I thought." She stepped back and pointed a long, elegant finger at the glowing mark on his neck, the faint symbol of his love. "Count your minutes, Fallen. That mark? It'll go dark soon. And when it does, so will the truth of who you are, and what you truly did will become crystal clear to my daughter. Every whisper of your false narrative, every carefully constructed lie. She will see the orchestrator of her torment, the self-righteous demon who traded her freedom to try to get his."

Rage tore through him, an inferno consuming every trace of fear. Wild light burst from his palm—not shaped or tempered, only pure force driven by fury. But before it could touch her, her shadows surged—an avalanche of black ice that crashed over him and sealed the air from his lungs. The world collapsed into a suffocating void.

And he fell. Again.

Kael jolted awake, finding himself on a rough couch. A thick coarse blanket lay draped over him. His armor was gone. His chest heaved. His pain was raw and burning.

The angel base. Remiel's office.

A soft light came from a single unadorned lamp. It illuminated paper-strewn desks, casting elongated shadows across the room. Remiel stood by the window with his back to Kael, his arms crossed, his stance rigid, and his gaze unreadable. He was staring out into the predawn gloom.

"You scream in your sleep," Remiel said without turning, his quiet voice devoid of judgment yet carrying an unsettling resonance.

Kael sat up, sweat clinging to his skin. His mind still reeled from the visceral torment of the dream. The phantom of Lilith's voice, the horror of her truths, clung to him.

"I think we have more in common than I thought." His words hung in the air, heavy and cryptic.

Kael blinked, his vision still swimming, but there was no time to ask, no time to unravel cryptic words. The nightmare felt too real, too immediate. Urgency from her threat pulsed in his veins. He threw off the blanket and pushed himself to his feet, his muscles aching with a phantom pain from the fall. "How fast can we get to the Crossroads? I don't have any more time. I have to get to her. Now."

Remiel turned then, slow and grim. His eyes, usually sharp and calculating, held a deep, unsettling sadness. "I think you're already too late."

Kael touched the base of his throat, where his bond mark pulsed with life. Or rather, where it should have pulsed. It was cold. Dead. A void where his essence once swirled.

He doubled over, grabbing handfuls of his hair. A raw, guttural sob tore from his chest, and he sobbed, the sound alien and broken in the quiet office. Everything hit at once: Lilith's accusations. His desperation. The weight of Sera's shattered trust. He would never be able to tell her how much he had grown to love her, how profoundly she had transformed his barren existence. He wanted to take everything back—every selfish choice, every moment of calculated patience. He wanted her in his arms without any shadow of manipulation between them.

Remiel stood there in silence, a statue of quiet understanding.

Eventually, the sobs subsided into ragged breaths, though the ache in his soul remained. "I don't want to exist..." he choked out, the confession tearing at his throat. "What's...what's the purpose?"

Remiel's expression was unreadable, but his voice was soft. "Like I said, we are more alike than I thought."

"Who did you lose?"

"I remember what I lost, but I don't remember who or how." He paused, his gaze fixed on Kael. "I lost my chance to make things right. But you, Kael, you still have yours."

"How?" Kael rasped, lifting his head. "How can I possibly make it right?"

He gestured to the dormant mark at Kael's throat. "If you light up the mark again, *truly* light it up, she will see reason. She will see the means. She will see your true intentions. The bond will not lie, and it will show her how far you are willing to go for her." His eyes pierced Kael's, a silent challenge. "*How far*, Kael? How far are you willing to go?"

Kael met his gaze, unwavering even through the lingering pain. "All the way. To death."

A faint, almost imperceptible nod came from Remiel. "Well then," he said, turning back to the window, "it will wait for you at the Crossroads."

The door groaned open, a drawn-out sigh.

"Well," Jareth muttered, his usual half smirk a fragile shield as he stepped into the room, "heard you were awake. Thought we'd check if the apocalypse was still on schedule." He didn't quite meet Kael's eyes.

Cassia followed, her presence sharp. Her cold gaze swept the room before it landed on Kael.

His eyes, ever keen, flicked between them. "How's your jaw by the way?"

Kael blinked, the question pulling him back. His fingers rose to rub the side of his face, and a faint throb echoed under his touch. Then for the first time since waking, the fragmented memories clicked into place.

He remembered the violent jolt, the desperate need just before the meadow. "Right," he muttered, his voice rough. "I felt her. It was sudden—a gut punch. I panicked. Needed to get to her. Fast."

"So, you tackled me and begged for a knockout?" His voice was dry, and his eyebrow arched, but his usual bite was muted. "Not your smoothest request by far."

Kael winced. "Worked too well. I slept so hard I ended up in Lilith's nightmare." The words felt hollow, inadequate.

Cassia's arms crossed, a deliberate barrier. Her voice, though quiet, was edged with honed steel. "I guess she threatened you by telling the truth about your little secret?"

He looked at her, a flicker of genuine confusion crossing his face. "How do you—"

"I told her," Remiel said, his voice flat. His eyes now watched the city's skyline sharpen against the burgeoning dawn once more. "You reported Seraphine to me, after all."

The air in the room thickened, chilled. Kael didn't speak. He didn't deny it. And his silence was a confession in itself.

"If we're going to pull this off," Remiel said, his tone unnervingly calm, "there can't be any more hidden truths between us. Are we clear?"

A heavy beat passed.

Kael's jaw clenched. He nodded once, a sharp, almost painful dip of his head. "Fair enough."

Cassia took a single step closer. Her voice didn't rise, but each word landed with quiet, devastating weight. "I want to hate you," she said, her gaze unyielding. "For what you did to her. To me. For your choices."

He didn't flinch. His dark eyes met hers. "And you should."

"But I don't." Her eyes shimmered, not with tears but with an unshakable resolve. "I don't because I see how far you're willing to go for her now. And because, against all odds, I know she still loves you. Somewhere in that wreckage."

Jareth let out a slow, uncomfortable exhale, the sound loud in the charged silence. "Wow. A genuine moment. Should I leave?"

"You're staying," she snapped, her focus never leaving Kael.

Kael nodded once more, slow and deliberate. A movement grounded in sudden clarity. "Thank you," he said, the words a low rumble. "You didn't have to say that."

"No." Her gaze stayed locked with his, unwavering. "But you needed to hear it."

"Well, actually, I do have to go," Jareth said, pushing off the doorframe with a casualness that felt forced. "Time to talk to my contact."

Remiel turned from the window, his eyes narrowing. "I just said no more secrets."

He shrugged, an almost imperceptible movement. "It's not my secret to tell." With that, he was gone, and the door softly clicked behind him.

Jareth slipped into the filing room, and the door shut behind him with a dull thud as the lock slid into place.

A mirror sat in a false-bottom drawer, hidden behind a dead label that read expired contracts. He drew it out and set it on the desk. It wasn't proper glass, more like polished metal shaped into a shallow oval—a mirror with the depth of a basin. The surface held no reflection, only a soft, silvery haze that seemed to breathe. Intricate filigree crawled along its rim, shifting if one stared too long and alive with faint runes.

He unwrapped the small cloth bundle he kept inside the same hidden compartment. Inside lay a lock of white hair, intricately braided and tied with gold thread. He dropped it into the hollow of the mirror.

The air pressure in the room dropped suddenly and sharply. The filigree flared, pale at first and then brighter. It washed the room in cool violet light.

A voice, glitched and blurred and yet achingly familiar, rose from the depths of the metal. "Took you long enough."

"Been busy." Jareth's voice was flat, but a ghost of a smile touched his mouth. "Holding the world together."

"You're barely holding your team together."

He huffed a quiet laugh and rubbed at the bridge of his nose. "Nice to hear your optimism is intact."

A pause stretched, heavy as breath before a confession.

"Jareth…" the voice said at last, roughened by static. "We lost."

He didn't answer. His gaze stayed fixed on the basin, on the faint ripples distorting the violet light.

"She is done," the voice went on. "She's about to finish the corruption. She wishes she'd…die after what Lilith told her."

His throat tightened. "I am sorry."

"She's now a ghost of the Crimson Keep. Gray skin. Black-tipped fingers. Horns. Lilith took down her 24-7 watch. I think she believes there's nothing left to worry about."

His hand curled into a fist against the desk, his knuckles whitening. The runes flickered, reflecting across his skin like fractured stars.

"I tried everything," the voice continued, raw with defeat. "Tried to reason. Tether pulses. Drew protection runes. She's just…gone."

"What would you expect?" he murmured, shaking his head slowly. "Not this?"

"There should always be a way back."

"Not when grief is the only thing left to keep someone standing."

Static cracked, sudden and sharp. The light in the basin sputtered like a dying signal.

"I just wish…" the voice said, "I could also see you before…"

Jareth's jaw clenched. "You're talking like it's already over."

"Isn't it?"

"Not yet."

The glowing runes dimmed, their rhythm faltering. The air smelled faintly of ozone.

"I miss you," the voice said—soft and sudden. A vulnerable whisper that pierced the static.

"Yeah," he breathed, the word dragged from him. "I know."

Silence settled over the desk like a film of dust, coating the papers and his skin alike.

Then the voice spoke faintly: "If we fail…"

"Don't." His voice cut through the interference, sharp and final.

"Promise me you won't come after—"

"No."

More static, almost gone now.

"I'll be at the Crossroads… Did you get the passage rhyme?" The voice sounded miles away.

"Yes." He reached out instinctively, but the light collapsed before his fingers touched it. The basin went dull and gray, leaving only his reflection staring back—tired, hollow, and far too human.

The Descent of the Mourning Body

29

Sera stood in the center of her room, a ghost in her own life. The words Lilith had woven into her mind still hung in the air, a poison curling around her thoughts.

Her *mother*.

Lilith had laid everything bare, with calm precision: Kael's insidious lies that had been hidden beneath every stolen moment. He was not who she had thought. Their love was not what she had thought. It had been a lie, a beautiful shimmering veil, and she had willingly stepped in it. Now, the veil had been torn away, leaving only coldness and darkness.

Sera felt hollow, scraped of all feelings.

The meadow wasn't a sanctuary; it was a stage. His touch wasn't a promise; it was a tactic. His whispers of love weren't a confession; they were a currency to buy her soul. He hadn't seen her as her—just a prize to be won, a tool to secure his own redemption. The betrayal was so absolute, so profound, that it didn't even hurt. It just...erased her.

Her vacant eyes drifted across the room and landed on a small black velvet box on her nightstand. A silent testament. A final offer left on the battlefield of her heart.

The sight of it should have sparked rage, a final flicker of defiance, but the fuel for that fire was gone. She had fought for a truth that was now a lie. She had defied a kingdom of horrors for a love that was a carefully constructed fiction. What was left to protect? What was left to save?

The cavernous emptiness screamed inside her.

Her body moved with the horrifying precision of ritual, a chilling ballet of resignation. One foot slid forward. Then the other. Her hand, pale and trembling slightly, reached for the box, and with a faint click, she opened it.

There it lay. Nestled on the crimson silk.

She looked at the larval pearl.

It was a monstrosity. It was an answer. If love was a lie, if the bond was a chain, then feeling was a liability. A queen could not rule with a traitor's brand on her heart. This wasn't a surrender. It was a cauterization. A choice to burn away the weakness, to freeze the pain, and to become the monster everyone always believed she was.

If she was nothing to him, she would be nothing to herself.

Her fingers closed around it. Its warmth was a low, foreign thrum against her skin. She lifted it, watching the faint light play across her face.

She tipped her head back. There was no thought, no final debate. There were only the hollow ache and the promise of its end. She placed the grub on her tongue. It was not food. It had no taste. It was strangely smooth and cold. The cold that sank into the root of her nerves.

For a moment, she hesitated. A single hot tear, the last remnant of the woman she had been, traced a path down her cheek. Then with a convulsive swallow, it was gone.

It slid down her throat, a lump of cold otherness. There was no pain. Instead, a bloom of ice spread from her stomach, a network of frigid veins branching through her. The raw knot of grief in her throat did not untie; it dissolved into icy stillness. The poison smoke of Lilith's words did not clear; it shattered into a million inert crystals. The screaming emptiness inside her fell silent—not filled but frozen over.

Sera stood perfectly still. The tear on her cheek began to feel like a foreign object. Something new—cold and patient and deeply ancient—was looking out through her eyes for the very first time.

Vyxia emerged from the shadows, her movements precise. Her face, usually a mask of sharp indifference, betrayed nothing, yet her voice was quieter than usual, a hushed murmur. "The arrangements have been made," she whispered, her gaze veiled. "But please…be careful."

Sera offered no response, no flicker of acknowledgment. Her eyes, once pools of vibrant emotion, were now desolate.

She followed Vyxia and the entourage of grim-faced guards through winding, descending corridors. The world around her blurred into indistinguishable gloom. Her body moved, a mere shell propelled by an unseen force, while her thoughts floated miles away, caught between the crushing weight of grief and the absolute silence of despair.

Did she hate Kael? Or did she hate what he'd done, the monstrous truths Lilith had exposed? Did she hate them all now, all the angels who had ever claimed to protect her, only to destroy her piece by agonizing piece?

The deeper they descended, the colder the air grew, a chilling breath from the very depths of the abyss. Gold filigree, once adorning the upper halls, faded to raw moss-covered stones. Torches, once blazing, flickered here, casting frantic shadows on the walls. The pervasive scent of sulfur, of rot, and of centuries of suffering clung to the heavy air. But she barely noticed. Or perhaps she did and chose not to care.

The walk to the dungeons was descent. The air grew thick with the metallic tang of old blood and the sour dampness of weeping stone. The moans of the damned curled around her like her shadows, a sorrowful chorus in a relentless symphony of torment. She walked through it all like a specter, unburdened by empathy and untouched by agony.

She had no will left. No fight. Yet a cold, unwavering resolve still guided her. She still wanted to see them.

The fallen.

The cells came into view, each a cage of unimaginable loss. The angels within were grotesque echoes of what they had once been. Unmoved, she walked past them—her heart a stone within her chest—until one pair of eyes, stark and unwavering, met hers through the gloom.

The man was slumped against his cell's cold iron bars, a broken sculpture of despair. His wings had been severed at the root, the wounds ancient and scarred yet still raw and visceral.

She stopped. A single faint beat stirred in her hollowed chest. "What is your name?" her voice said, dry and fragile.

"Eryon," he whispered.

"Who are you?"

"I was a guardian once. I stood at the eastern gate."

Her breath caught, a tight knot rising in her throat. The memory stirred like smoke—the scent of dawn, dew clinging to leaves that once shimmered beneath her wings. "I remember the eastern gate," she said softly. "The morning light always caught the dew on the leaves."

He looked down, a ghost of a memory in his ruined eyes. "And I remember you. The woman who burned too brightly, even in the shadow of the watchers."

The words were choking her now. "Why are you here?"

"I fell here for refusing to lift a sword against a soul I loved. They called it corruption. I called it truth."

Sera's stomach twisted, his words piercing the profound stillness within her. The echoes of his choice resonated with her own shattered reality. "I'm sorry," she whispered.

He shook his head. "Don't be. I made my choice. And so will you. We all do in the end."

Silence stretched between them.

And then she turned, her gaze hardening and her resolve solidifying. "Draw their essence," she told the guards, her voice devoid of all mercy.

The command was not for the bargain—its purpose had long since passed—but debts in Hell were not so easily forgotten. The warlock still held her secret, and silence had to be bought. Payment, even now, was the only language that bound this realm together.

Besides, the essences had their uses. One vial of corrupted divinity could dull the agony that never left her bones. Two would end it entirely. She wanted that choice tucked away, waiting. In a place where every freedom had been stripped from her, the option of ending her own suffering felt like power.

The fallen were dragged from their cells, their piteous cries swallowed by the echoing stones. She didn't look away. The process would not kill them, but it would leave them hollow, most likely. It was a gruesome penance, a forced witnessing.

As the guards reached for Eryon, he spoke one last time, his voice imbued with dignity. "Princess," he said, his gaze finding hers. "If I die here, will you tell my brother? Tell him my love was true?"

Sera turned, a jolt of recognition piercing her numb haze. "Your brother?"

He gave a faint, sorrow-laced smile. "Jareth."

The name hit her like a lightning strike. A violent phantom pang for a connection, a man she was forcing herself to forget. She didn't know what to feel, but bitterness rose fast and fierce, and she had to crush it down.

"You won't die here today," she said.

"Promise me," Eryon said, his voice fading.

She nodded, tears rising hot and sharp against the profound cold within her. "I promise."

He nodded back, a flicker of peace in his eyes as he disappeared into the darkness.

Sera returned to her chambers, but she was a ghost in her own skin, a specter haunting the ruins of a life she no longer recognized. The vibrant, desperate love she had felt in the meadow, so potent it felt like salvation, had been scoured from her soul, leaving a hollowed-out cavern.

The hope of escape, the secret plan she had forged, was now just another cruel joke. What was there to escape to? A world of liars? A future built on a foundation of meticulously crafted deception? The meadow, their sacred space, was now a crime scene. His touch, a lie. His promises, the whispers of a jailer.

She was done. She was utterly and completely done.

With movements devoid of her usual grace, she retrieved the vials of celestial essence that she had taken from the dungeons. They felt heavy in her hands, their faint golden light a mockery of the purity she had once believed in. She stared at the captured, swirling souls. This was the price of a freedom she no longer wanted, the currency for a future she could no longer imagine.

But a bargain was the only currency with any meaning in this realm.

"Vyxia," she called, her voice flat and dead.

The demoness appeared in an instant, materializing from the shadows with her usual unnerving stillness. Her violet eyes, however, widened with concern as she took in Sera's shattered state. "Your Highness," she said, her voice soft with a caution that bordered on fear. "Are you—"

"It's done." Sera pushed the collection of vials into Vyxia's hands. "Take these. Go back to the Nightshade Market."

Vyxia looked from the glowing vials to her empty eyes, confusion warring with dread. "But...your plan? The portal? This was for your escape."

"I do not wish to escape anymore, but a promise is a promise." Her voice was a hollow echo of a woman who had once had a will. "He expects our end of the bargain. Give them to him. Tell him to keep them or ask for anything you want in return. I don't care."

"And you?" Vyxia whispered.

Sera turned away, her gaze falling on the small black velvet box still sitting on her nightstand. "I have my own bargain to fulfill."

A Ghost's Honor

30

Vyxia hesitated, the vials feeling like lead weights in her hands. She saw the truth in Sera's posture—the utter defeat. She had seen this look before in Hell, on souls just before they unraveled completely. But Sera had been different. She had been a fighter. Seeing that fire extinguished hardened something within Vyxia. Her mission, given to her by Jareth, was no longer just about strategy. It was now about saving the woman who had just given up on saving herself.

Clutching the vials tightly, Vyxia gave a sharp, determined nod. "I will do as you ask, Sera," she said, her voice firm with a new secret resolve. She would not let Sera's sacrifice be in vain.

The air around her shimmered faintly as if the market's sulfur heat recoiled. Power hummed in her veins, too bright for Hell's palette and too wild for the order of Heaven. She forced it down the way she always had. No one here could ever know what slept beneath her skin.

The Nightshade Market was just as Vyxia had left it: a chaotic, thrumming ecosystem of desperation and want. But this time, she felt like an intruder, an agent carrying a truth far too dangerous for this place of petty bargains. She navigated the crowd with grim purpose, ignoring the vendors who hissed offers of bottled nightmares and stolen fortunes. Her destination was the quiet, cluttered stall at the market's edge, where a blind warlock traded in the impossible.

She found Orin as before, hunched over his collection of celestial debris. He didn't look up, but a slight stiffening of his withered frame told her he had sensed her approach long before she arrived.

"The princess sends her regards," she said, her tone all business, as she stepped out of the shadows. "And payment." She placed the vials of celestial light on the worn wooden counter.

The collective glow from them was faint but undeniably potent, casting a warm golden light on the warlock's wrinkled face and reflecting in his milky, sightless eyes.

Orin reached out a trembling hand, not to touch the vials but to feel the warmth radiating from them. He inhaled deeply, a long, rattling breath. A look of profound awe crossed his features. "It is…more than I expected," he whispered. "Her sorrow is a powerful catalyst. The despair of the fallen… It purifies the essence." He turned his head. "The door she requested is hers. When does she wish for it to be opened?"

Here, Vyxia's mission diverged. This was no longer just about fulfilling a promise. This was about finishing a war.

"The bargain has been amended," she stated, her voice firm and clear. "The portal is to be opened on the night of the coming blood moon. No sooner, no later."

He stilled, his head cocked. "The blood moon… The veil will be at its thinnest. That is a dangerous time to be tearing holes in reality, little one. The energies are…unpredictable."

"The timing is not negotiable." Her petite frame radiated an authority that belied her station. "And the destination has changed."

The warlock's expression flickered. "Oh?"

"Not the mortal realm." Her violet eyes gleamed with strategic fire. She leaned in, her voice dropping to a conspiratorial whisper that only he could hear. "Heaven."

The blind warlock recoiled as if he'd been physically struck. His chair scraped against the stone floor. "*Heaven?*" he hissed, his voice a mix of greed and genuine terror. "To pierce the celestial veil from this place...to hold a door open against the very will of creation? That is not the bargain that was struck! The power required is...monumental. The price doubles."

Her expression didn't falter, only her jaw flexed. She had anticipated this. "Do you have something to collect a final payment in?" she asked, her voice calm and even.

Seeming confused, he rasped, "A cup?" He vaguely gestured toward a grim-looking ceramic cup that sat among his celestial debris.

Vyxia picked it up, and from a hidden sheath in the folds of her simple dress, she produced a sharp pocketknife, its obsidian blade gleaming. The warlock went utterly still, his head tilting.

Without hesitation, she sliced the blade across her own palm. She didn't flinch as blood, dark and rich, welled up. But it was not merely blood. Laced within the crimson were shimmering violet threads of light that pulsed with a wild, ancient energy—an essence that was neither holy nor infernal.

She held her bleeding palm over the cup and let the potent, iridescent liquid drip and pool inside. The air grew thick with the scent of ozone, crushed nightshade, and a power that Hell had not known for centuries.

The warlock gasped, scrambling back from his stall as if he had been burned. His sightless eyes were wide. "Fae blood..." he whispered, his voice tight. "By the First Throne... I haven't sensed it in centuries... Not since the gates were sealed."

Orin's breath caught. "There's another scent in it. Something older... Heavier. Child, who fathered you?"

Her smile was small and cold. "You wouldn't survive the answer."

She finished, a small pool of violet-laced blood now resting in the cup. She firmly placed it on the counter, the ceramic clicking against the stone. The wound on her palm was already beginning to seal over.

"Well," she said, her calm voice betraying none of her sacrifice, "I believe this covers it."

Orin bowed his head in submission, his ancient form trembling before the sheer magnitude of that payment. "I-it does," he said. "It more than co-covers it. I will open a gate, not just a door."

Her gaze hardened. "On the night of the blood moon," she said, her voice leaving no room for argument, "a gate to Heaven will open. No sooner, no later."

THE CROSSROADS

31

The base was still, a profound quiet born of long silences and unfinished prayers. In the storage annex, Cassia reorganized field kits with sharp movements, a rhythm meant to outpace her thoughts and take the edge off her anxiety about the impending trip.

The door creaked behind her, but she didn't turn.

"Remiel," she said, her voice flat, "either help or leave."

He stepped in as quietly as a shadow. "I'm not here to reorganize holy bandages."

"I figured."

A pause stretched. Then a soft rustle, the sound of a tunic collar being tugged down.

"I have a question," he said, his voice measured and almost clinical. "And I think you're the only one who might answer it honestly."

She turned then.

He stood under a narrow, humming fluorescent light, his shirt open at the collar. Revealed on the skin over his heart was a bond sigil, faint and aged. Celestial. Real.

"I know what it is," he said, his gaze fixed on hers. "I just don't know whose it is."

She didn't speak. Her breath was caught, a quiet hitch, but her expression remained perfectly still.

"I've asked no one else," he continued, his eyes unwavering. "Every time I touch it, it feels like sorrow. Like something that should have been sacred. And wasn't."

Her voice was low, a quiet sound. "And if you knew who it belonged to?"

"I don't know what I'd do." He looked away, the muscles in his jaw tight. "I only know I should have remembered."

She watched him for a long moment, the silence thick around them. She then stepped closer, too close, but didn't touch him. Her gaze flicked to the mark on his chest and then back up to his eyes. "You weren't meant to remember," she said. "They made sure of it."

Remiel nodded once, a grim recognition in his eyes. "The tribunal."

"Yes."

He tugged his shirt closed again and stepped back, retreating deeper into the shadows. "When this war is over," he said, his hand on the door, "will you tell me?"

Her voice was like steel, a whisper of crushed memories. "If we live through it…and if it still matters? Maybe."

He nodded once. Then left.

The door closed behind him like the end of a sentence neither of them could bear to finish. The lock's soft click echoed in the quiet.

Cassia stood there as still as a statue, staring at the space where he'd stood. Where his voice had curled around old wounds she'd spent fifty agonizing years stitching shut. Her hands were clenched, she realized, and her nails bit into her palms. She exhaled slowly, as if letting the air out too fast might let everything else come with it.

She turned back to the shelf of medical kits and reached for a vial. But her fingers fumbled, missing it. She reached again. It slipped from her grasp and hit the floor, shattering with a soft pop. A cold bloom of alcohol and lavender rose like a ghost.

She stared at the spreading liquid, her expression blank. Then she sank. Not gracefully. Not slowly. Her knees gave out, and she slid to the floor like a dropped blade, her back against the cool wall and her arms locked around her ribs. She didn't sob. She wouldn't. But the tears came anyway, quiet and bitter things.

She pressed a hand to her chest, where the twin mark was still dead yet present beneath her skin. Her fingers trembled. The pain wasn't from the bond. That was long gone. It was due to the absence. Remiel had looked at her as if he was a stranger. He'd asked her to tell him a truth they were both forbidden to speak. And she...she hadn't crumbled in front of him.

But now, in the quiet solitude of the room, she curled in on herself, her shoulders shaking with silent grief. She mourned not what she had lost but what he had forgotten.

After a few long seconds, she forced herself to breathe. In. Out. In. Out. One breath at a time. She was trembling, but she wasn't broken. Her fingers wiped at her cheeks with sharp, practiced swipes. She looked at the shattered vial on the floor, at the blue stain spreading in a delicate bloom across the stones.

"No," she said flatly. "Not now."

She pushed herself up, her palms against the wall for balance. Her legs ached, but they held.

"This is not about me." Her voice steadied, hardening with every word. "It's about Sera now."

She looked toward the door Remiel had left through, her jaw

tightening. That was not the crisis now. *He* was not the crisis now. She stepped over the glass, ignoring the crunch of a shard under her heels. She would clean it later. Or not.

Right now, her sister was trapped. Alone. Fractured. And if she fell apart again, no one would be left to bring her back.

She squared her shoulders, rolled them once, and walked out of the room as if nothing had cracked.

Because no one could see the cracks. Not yet. Not until Sera was safe.

The blood moon, now almost complete, loomed ominously over Savannah, casting an eerie red glow across the city. Elara paced in her lavish living room, her anxiety mounting despite the plush carpets beneath her feet. The memory wipe had left gaping holes in her mind, a disjointed puzzle missing crucial pieces.

She recalled Sera's body on the floor. Then nothing. Strange people in her house. Then nothing. Fragments of all her lives from the past centuries flickered in and out, but one constant remained: Kael. The way his eyes lingered on Sera, the softening of his voice whenever he uttered her name.

Elara's perfectly manicured nails dug into her palms. It wasn't fair. Kael was supposed to be *hers*. He should be hers.

A sudden thought of an ornate box jolted her into action.

Storming into her walk-in closet, she was a whirlwind of frustration and fury. She tore through designer dresses and tossed aside expensive shoes, her anger intensifying with each discarded item.

Her hand then brushed against a cold ornate box tucked away on a high shelf. She pulled it down, her fingers tracing the strange symbols carved into its surface. Opening the box, she gasped.

Inside, nestled on a bed of velvet, lay an obsidian coin identical to the one retrieved from her house that day. The second Lucifer's coin.

As she grasped the coin, memories came flooding back: the pact with Lilith, the summoning of demons, the betrayal, the memory wipe, and Sera—her former friend—now being a prisoner of Hell.

Lilith had gifted her the coins all those centuries ago, promising they would help her reach the queen swiftly. And with Sera gone, Kael was finally within her grasp. A new plan began to form in her mind. She would go to the Crossroads, face Lilith, and demand that the queen honor her promise and bring Kael to her.

For all that Elara had endured, she deserved to be rewarded. She would have him at last. She would have power. She would have everything she deserved.

As she clutched the coin, its cold surface sent a shiver down her spine. It was time. With a shaking voice, she spoke the incantation to bring her back to the Crossroads. "By the ancient pact, by the infernal seal, I call upon the Crossroads, where shadows congeal. With Lucifer's coin, I offer this key. Open the way and grant passage to me."

The shimmering glow of a portal appeared right in the doorway of her walk-in closet. She drew a sharp breath and stepped over.

The Crossroads, a desolate wasteland bathed in an eerie green light, came into existence. The oppressive air was heavy with sulfur and decay. The ground beneath her feet was cracked and barren. The only vegetation was twisted, thorny vines snaking across the landscape. She clutched the obsidian coin, its strange symbols digging into her palm. A cold reminder of the pact she had made.

A grotesque figure, all fangs and leathery wings, materialized before her with a servile bow. The fetid air swirled around him. "Greetings, Elara." His voice was a grating rasp, like dry leaves skittering across parched earth. "I am Xathos, the messenger of the queen. You summoned?"

"Yes," she said, her voice barely a whisper against the oppressive silence of the Crossroads. "I demand to speak to Lilith. Tell her I'm here, and I came to demand payment."

He extended a clawed hand, his nails thick and yellow. "I shall deliver your message and gift directly to the queen. Now, hand over the coin."

She hesitated, and a flicker of doubt crossed her mind. The coin was her only way to the world of the living, but she handed it over. Before she could reconsider, Xathos turned and, with a flap of his leathery wings, vanished down a shadowy corridor that snaked deeper into the heart of an obsidian fortress.

The air grew colder as Elara stood there, waiting. The silence pressed in on her.

As Sera and Vyxia turned a corner in the Infernal Palace, a hurried demon hurtled into them, nearly sending them reeling from their stately composure.

"What's gotten into you, Xathos?" Vyxia asked, her voice trembling as she attempted to regain her balance.

"Oh, m-my apologies," he said, diverting his gaze first to the loyal servant and then to Sera. "Princess Sera!"

"Xathos," Sera purred, her voice silken yet venomous. She watched the demon messenger freeze as if an unseen force had struck him. "What business do you have here?"

"I-I am to deliver a me-message to the queen," he said, bowing with a careworn deference. "The witch woman has returned. She came for payment." With trembling hands, he produced an obsidian coin that shimmered under the flickering torches.

Her eyebrow arched in a mixture of surprise and suspicion, the slightest flicker of a memory igniting within their depths. "A witch woman?" she murmured, her tone both curious and icy. In one fluid motion, she snatched the coin from his grasp. "What woman?"

"Elara, Princess," Xathos managed to articulate, his voice barely audible as he bowed his head.

In that split second, Sera's world seemed to tilt like a prism. A fierce memory, tainted with inexplicable hatred, surged through her mind. A hatred she could neither fully recall nor rationalize. "Thank you for your message, Xathos. I will deliver it to the queen this instant."

"But, Princess, that would be too much trouble for you."

Her words rang with an undercurrent of scorn. "Nonsense. Begone. Now." She added a smile that carried an almost cruel mockery.

The messenger, his face a mask of trepidation, retraced his steps and melted into the depths of the palace.

"This forsaken place just got more interesting..." she said without looking at the demoness beside her.

Vyxia's voice was quiet. "Are we—"

"Of course, we are!" She smiled coyly and began walking toward the tunnels that led to the Crossroads. When she got there, she slithered into the darkness, her eyes peeled, until she found her mark.

"I heard you are looking for my mother...*friend*," she said in a silken, seductive voice. She slowly emerged from the gloom, each step measured and deliberate. Her presence was both magnetic and terrifying. She now stood before a visibly shaken witch, the stark contrast between them as poetic as it was cruel.

"Sssera?" Elara's voice cracked at a pathetic attempt at cheerfulness. Her eyes darted about. "Hi, girl! Wo-wow! You look ama-amazing!"

"Is this what you are looking for?" Sera asked, twirling the obsidian coin between her gloved fingers as if it was an insignificant trinket. Her gaze bored into Elara's very soul. "You know, I've had a lot of time to develop a profound loathing for you. You could've waited a bit longer with your betrayal, and I would've given you Kael freely."

Elara whimpered. She took faltering steps backward, but Sera advanced without so much as a pause. With a swift, fluid motion, she grabbed Elara by the collar of her colorful dress and yanked her close, ensuring their eyes met head-on.

"But I must thank you for hastening my return to the place I despise," Sera sneered with cruel glee. "The delightful irony of being fallen in Hell is that you lose your light, leaving only bitterness."

Before Elara could muster a plea, her hand struck again. A shadow dagger, as dark as a void itself, found its mark in the witch's gut.

Elara crumpled within her unforgiving grip. "Sera…" Her voice was barely audible. "Please… I can explain."

"Another delightful aspect is that I do not need your pitiful reasons. You've had centuries to reconsider," she retorted sharply. With another swift, merciless thrust of her dagger, she elicited a pained cry from Elara. Crimson blood trickled down her hand.

As Sera readied herself to deliver the fatal strike to end the witch's wretched existence, two more figures appeared at the Crossroads.

But she kept going, uttering her final words while looking straight into the witch's soul. "When you languish in Limbo, as I once did, remember who sent you there." She brought the dagger to Elara's throat and sliced through, ear to ear—ending the life of one person who had wronged her.

She still had so many more, and one now stood in utter shock at the far end of her vision.

He's got it from here.

The shadows' words curled in her mind like the end of a sentence she hadn't known she was writing. They had been so quiet, especially since she had arrived in Hell, but now, before she could ask what they meant, they were gone.

Not silent. Gone.

Sera, with her shadow dagger still glistening with fresh blood, turned her attention toward the two figures who had borne witness to her act of vengeance. A man and a woman stood frozen, their eyes wide with disbelief.

Sera's gaze hardened, and her voice sliced through the oppressive silence. "Have you finally come to save me?" she snarled, her tone a blend of defiance and challenge. "Or did you come to plead for my better side? Because I assure you, I have none left."

Kael stepped forward, his eyes ablaze with a volatile mix of fury and despair. "Sera," he said, "what has she done to you? It's me, Little Devil."

"What has *she* done to me? No more than what you've done to me." Her voice wavered, dropping to an almost inaudible whisper. "Showed your true side."

Instead of pausing to reflect, she commanded the guards to seize the pair. But she glanced at the female standing beside him again, and recognition flickered in her mind.

"Cassia," she murmured, her sister's name stirring in her chest. She then locked it tight. Sealed her emotions and regained her cold composure. She also corrected her orders with calculated precision: the male was to be taken to the dungeons, while the female was to be escorted to the palace. And with deliberate steps, she turned and made her way down the shadowy path leading back to the keep, the darkness embracing her like an old friend.

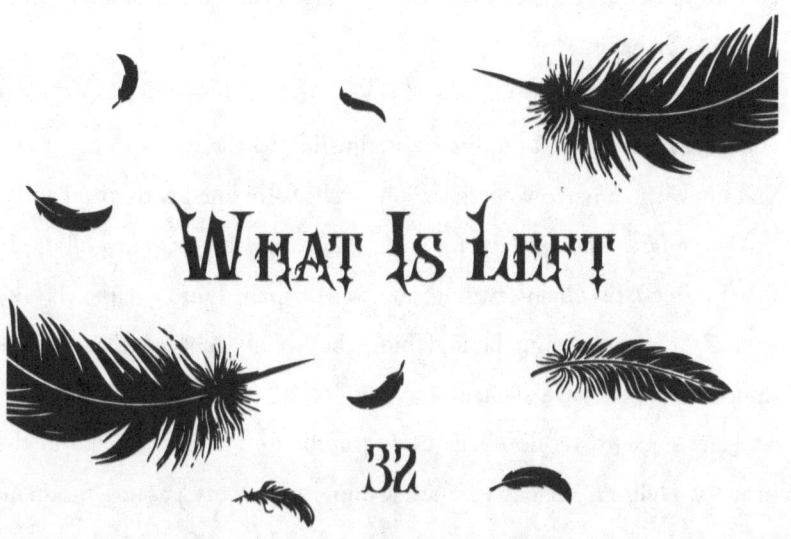

What Is Left

32

Kael fought against the guards' iron grip, his muscles coiling with a restrained power that threatened to erupt. "Get your filthy claws off me," he snarled, his voice a guttural growl that echoed through the desolate landscape of the Crossroads. He threw off the guards, sending them sprawling.

He lunged for Sera, but a wall of more creatures materialized, their eyes burning with infernal fire.

"Let me get to her!" he said, his voice a menacing threat. "Sera!"

But his defiance was met with cruel laughter, and a surge of demonic power slammed into him, sending him crashing to the ground.

Kael watched Cassia's eyes go wide, her voice cracking as she cried his name. Dark energy rippled from her hands, searing the guards who held her, but more of them closed in, their combined magic pressing against her like a vice. The air hissed with the clash of power as she fought to break free, her scream burning through the chaos until a portal swallowed him whole.

He was dragged through that swirling portal, and the familiar landscape of the Crossroads dissolved into a dizzying kaleidoscope of colors and shapes.

He landed hard on the cold obsidian floor, the air thick with sulfur and decay. He looked up, his eyes adjusting to the dim light, and saw that he was in a narrow corridor. The walls were lined with iron bars.

The guards shoved him forward, their claws digging into his flesh. He stumbled, his chains rattling, and was propelled into a dark cell. The iron door clanged shut behind him, the sound echoing through the dungeon's oppressive silence.

Kael sank to the floor, his body trembling. He was trapped in the heart of Hell, his angelic essence waning with every passing moment. He closed his eyes, and the image of Sera's cold, indifferent gaze seared into his mind.

Now, he had truly lost her.

In horror, Cassia watched Kael be dragged through the swirling portal, his strong form disappearing into the chaotic vortex. Her heart pounded, a desperate fear clawing at her throat. She fought against the guards who held her, but their grip was firm yet respectful.

"Let him go!" she screamed, her voice raw. "He's done nothing wrong!"

"Our apologies, Princess," one of the guards rumbled, his voice surprisingly gentle. "But we are bound to obey orders."

Her struggles subsided, replaced by a chilling realization. A princess of Hell. Yet a prisoner, nonetheless.

Instead of shoving her forward, the guards gestured for her to follow. Their presence was more of escorts than captors.

They led her through a seemingly endless series of corridors, each more opulent and oppressive than the last. Where was Jareth's damned contact? Had the creature lied to them? They were supposed to meet them. Why was Elara there at the same time?

How ironic that none of their plans came to fruition.

The escorts finally stopped as they reached a set of massive obsidian doors intricately carved with scenes of demonic rituals and sacrifices. The guards opened them with a flourish, revealing a lavishly decorated bedchamber. Its walls were draped in black silk, and its furniture was crafted from polished obsidian and bones.

"This will be your quarters, Princess," a guard said, his voice respectful. "Please inform us if you require anything."

They bowed and retreated, leaving her alone in the opulent chamber.

For a moment, she stood there, her heart pounding. The opulent surroundings, the grotesque details, the suffocating darkness—it all washed over her, bringing a wave of nausea and dread.

Trapped in the heart of Hell and a prisoner of her own twisted fate, she realized her father's plan for her to stay in Hell had happened faster than anyone had expected.

Cassia paced the bedchamber, the obsidian floor cold beneath her bare feet. The oppressive silence of the Infernal Palace pressed down on her, amplifying her frantic heartbeats.

She had to get to Sera. She had to find a way to break through the darkness that had consumed her sister.

A single folded piece of parchment lay on the writing desk. Cassia stepped closer to the table, picked it up, and unfolded the thin paper. There was only one sentence inside: "I will find you soon when it is safe for all of us."

But she would not stay here, with her hands down and doing

nothing, waiting for a miracle to happen. It was time for a new plan.

With a burst of restless determination, Cassia crossed the chambers and wrenched open the door, intent on finding her own way out. But the corridor beyond was already barred. Two guards stood shoulder to shoulder, their armor dark as oil and their eyes glowing faintly with infernal fire. The faint scrape of their halberds lowering told her everything: There would be no leaving.

For a heartbeat, she considered fighting anyway. The urge flared hot and bright, but then guttered beneath the weight of exhaustion and bitter clarity. There was no winning through brute defiance here. Straightening her spine, she forced her voice into calm precision.

"Very well," she said, each word a shard of frost. "If I am to remain, then summon someone who can make that order worth obeying." Her gaze locked on the nearest guard. "I demand an audience with my sister."

The title fell from her lips like a verdict, carrying the same cold authority she had heard in Sera's voice—quiet, measured, and impossible to ignore.

A guard bowed, his eyes still gleaming with infernal fire. "As you wish. I will inform the princess of your request."

Left alone again, Cassia paced the chambers. The silence pressed in, thicker than before, mocking her burst of defiance. Hours bled together, marked only by the guttering of torches and the hollow echo of her footsteps. Her demand had changed nothing; Hell moved at its own pace, indifferent to the will of its prisoners.

Eventually, weariness seeped into her bones, heavier than grief. The bed at the center of the room looked too inviting.

Its frame was carved from black wood that caught the torchlight like wet obsidian, and sheets of crimson silk spilled across it, soft as breath and faintly scented with smoke and myrrh. She didn't bother undressing; there was no comfort in ritual here. She climbed into the bed fully clothed and lay back, the silk whispering against her skin.

The warmth beneath it felt wrong—like heat drawn from the veins of Hell itself—but she was too tired to care. The moment her body touched the mattress, her limbs gave way, and sleep claimed her like a tide pulling her under.

The next day, Cassia found herself escorted through the palace's labyrinthine corridors, guards flanking her. Their presence was a suffocating reminder of her captivity. They reached a set of intricately carved obsidian doors, and with a flourish, the guards ushered her into a dimly lit chamber.

The room was a study of sorts, its walls lined with overflowing shelves of ancient books and scrolls. A massive obsidian desk dominated the center of the chamber. Its surface was littered with strange artifacts and arcane instruments. Sera sat at the desk. Her gaze was fixed on a flickering shadow globe that displayed little lights, each representing a circle of Hell.

Cassia entered the study, her eyes fixed on Sera. She had embraced her demonic nature, her face a mask of cold indifference. "Sister," she said, her voice almost pleading.

Sera looked up, her gaze meeting Cassia's. A flicker of warmth crossed her face, but it was quickly extinguished, replaced by the same cold emptiness that she had witnessed a day prior. "Cassia," she said in a monotone voice. "You are at last?"

She approached the desk, her steps measured. "We came for you," she said, her voice hopeful.

Sera's lips curled into a cruel smile. "I do not need your saving," she purred. "I am staying to see our mother's plans come true. Plans that will reshape the very fabric of existence."

Her gaze was unwavering. "Sera, this isn't you."

Sera's smile remained, her eyes gleaming with a predatory hunger. "How do you know?" she hissed. "You haven't seen me in fifty years. And the next time you did, I attacked you."

Her mind raced. "Elara?" she asked, her voice barely a whisper. "Why…why did you kill her?"

Sera's eyes narrowed, and a flicker of genuine confusion crossed her face. "Why would I not kill her? She was a traitor." Her voice was flat, emotionless. "She deserved to die."

Cassia was desperate for some sign of the sister she once knew, the sister who had loved and protected her. "Do you remember anything, Sera?" she asked, her voice softening. "Anything from the mortal world? Our life…from before?"

Sera's gaze hardened, her eyes like chips of ice. "Oh, I remember everything and everyone. That life is meaningless to me now."

If she had a beating heart, it probably would be pounding out of her chest. It was as if Sera's memories had been soaked in blood and despair, creating a chilling void and a terrifying emptiness. The sister she had known was gone, replaced by a creature of darkness staring back.

"Join me, Sister." Sera's voice was a chilling echo in the oppressive silence of the study. "Witness the fallen angel's demise. Kael is going to be tried in thirty minutes."

"That's unlawful." She almost stuttered as she tried to comprehend the situation. "It's against the tribunal protocol."

Her sister looked back at her in a challenging manner. "Do you think the queen cares about the protocol?"

The throne room of the Crimson Keep was a cavernous expanse of obsidian and shadow, the air thick with the stench of sulfur and suffocating silence. No courtiers. No advisers. Only guards encircling the room, their monstrous forms a backdrop to the confrontation at its center.

Kael had been forced to kneel on the cold black stone floor, his hands bound in hellish steel behind his back. The bond flickered at the base of his throat like the final light of a dying hope. He lifted his gaze to meet the throne, and his heart twisted.

Sera.

The playful, vibrant woman he had once known was gone, replaced by a vision of darkness and despair. Her skin was ashen, a pale contrast to the fiery glow of the room, and her eyes burned with a cold, infernal fire. A crown of twisted obsidian thorns adorned her head, its jagged edges biting into her flesh.

And it was all his fault.

Her gown, woven from shadows, clung to her form, its edges swirling like restless smoke and mirroring the storm that must have raged within her. At least he hoped anything was raging behind those eyes. If there was rage, there was hope.

His chest tightened as he looked at her, searching for any trace of the woman he loved, the woman he broke. But her expression was unreadable, distant, and devoid of the warmth he remembered.

He had failed her again.

A cruel, mocking laugh cut through his thoughts, and he turned his gaze to Lilith. The queen of Hell stood poised and magnificent, her presence commanding the room, as she descended from the dais.

"I keep my promises, Kael," she purred, her voice smooth. "You thought you could save her from me? You thought you could be redeemed?" She gestured toward Sera, a smug smile curling her lips.

Cassia now stood beside Sera, her face pale and drawn and her hands clasped tight.

"And look now. Both of them are mine." Her voice grew sharper, more triumphant. "My daughters. And together, we will conquer all the realms."

Kael's jaw clenched so tight it could crumble teeth, and his heart pounded. He forced himself to his feet despite the chains. "You have lost your mind," he said.

Sera's gaze flickered to him, but there was no emotion, no flicker of the bond they shared. It was as if she was looking through him, not at him.

"Have I?" Lilith snapped, her fiery eyes boring into him. She drew a blade forged of hellish steel, its dark surface shimmering with a hungry light. She stalked toward him, her steps slow and deliberate. "Fallen, are you ready to die at last?"

Two guards seized Kael by the shoulders and drove him back to his knees, their claws cutting through the torn fabric over his arms. He jerked against their grips, every muscle straining to rise—but then the air itself thickened, Lilith's power coiling through it like a living thing. The pressure hit him from all sides, invisible yet absolute, and forced his body still. His breath hitched, the weight of her will heavier than their hands. She stepped closer and raised the blade, its edge catching the dim light.

"Wait," Sera said, her emotionless voice cutting through the air.

Kael opened one eye. Lilith had hesitated, slowly turning to her daughter. Sera had risen from the throne, her gaze like ice. The blade lowered.

He exhaled sharply, his body trembling with relief. She still felt something for him. She had to. There was no other explanation. Some part of her still cared, still fought against the darkness.

"Mother," she said, her tone devoid of warmth, "he has information. Killing him now will be a waste of valuable intel. For example, who is their contact here that he spoke of at the meadow?"

Lilith's brow arched, her lips curling into a twisted smirk. "Ah, I do remember you mentioning that…"

"Let us get it out of him," Sera said, stepping forward. Her voice didn't waver, her expression blank and calculated. "Besides, his torment will serve me better than his death will."

"Very well. Back to the dungeons you go," Lilith said, her tone as cold as the stone beneath their feet. She turned her words on her guards. "Keep him alive. For now."

Kael looked at Lilith with a predatory glint in his eyes. "I have nothing for you," he said, his voice a silken rasp that echoed through the tense silence.

The fallen received a crushing kick to his sternum. The hit was so hard that he lost the ability to breathe for a few seconds.

Lilith's eyes narrowed, her lips curling into a sneer. "Shut it! You are a prisoner of war. Nothing more."

Kael chuckled and spat blood onto the polished marble floor. "A prisoner, perhaps." His gaze swept over the assembled court with a chilling intensity. "But never powerless." He met Lilith's eyes with a challenge that dared her to underestimate him. He smirked when he sensed the guards' apprehension. "Lead the way, gentlemen," he said, his voice a silken purr. "I'm eager to explore the depths of your hospitality."

He walked with a measured pace, his head held high and his chains dragging behind him like a spectral train. He exuded an aura of confidence and control. A predator biding his time. He would not show weakness. He would not break. He would survive. Although he had no plan at that moment, he would find a way to get back to Sera.

The iron door groaned shut, its metallic shriek devoured by the dungeon's breathless dark.

Kael sank to the obsidian floor, inviting the cold to seep into his very bones. The stone offered a grim welcome, like an old friend or a freshly dug grave.

His light had not yet vanished.

The light within him no longer burned; it frayed. A faint, unsteady glow that flickered with every breath, leaving his chest raw and uncertain.

He had once been whatever Heaven required: its sword, its verdict, and its silence. After his fall, he was none of those things—only a creature suspended between grace and ruin, unsure which world would claim the last of him.

He bowed his head, his hands open upon his knees. There was no prayer left in him. No listener waiting beyond the dark. Only the faint shimmer of what remained.

Memory drew him backward to Sera. To the day she had been cast out. He had wanted to see it, to understand, but the gates had sealed before he could reach them. That absence became his first wound, the moment he began to understand what it meant to fall.

After that, he followed her. Not by order or duty but by a pull that refused to loosen. It was guilt, fascination, and a fear he could not name.

Centuries unfolded like pages written in ash. Paris. Berlin. New York City. She moved through each city like smoke, beautiful and half real, and built new names over the ruins of the old. He lingered at the edges of her worlds, unseen and unacknowledged. A shadow orbiting a collapsing star.

He saw her laugh, saw her starve, and saw the hunger claim her in quiet alleys and candlelit rooms. When men reached for her with cruelty or greed, he intervened. Their bodies vanished, and the memories of them slipped into nothing. He told himself it was protection, an act of mercy, yet every time he intervened, he felt himself drift closer to the thing he feared becoming. He had been erasing her monsters and slowly becoming one.

She never knew him. Kael made sure of it. Whenever her shadows stirred, sensing something familiar near, he hid himself in silence and distance until their whispers faded. He knew it was wrong, this quiet obsession that rooted itself deeper each century, but he could not stop it. Every attempt to pull away failed as if gravity itself bent toward her.

He had watched her build new lives, brief and fragile. He watched her search for meaning in places that never deserved her. And then came Mark, the mortal with soft eyes and an easy laugh who made her smile as if the world had not already broken her. Kael saw light return to her face, saw the small human happiness she found in that man, and felt the ache of something he could never be.

He lingered until the night he saw Mark's proposal. The ring, the laughter, and the trembling joy on her lips. That was when Kael had turned away. It had taken everything in him to leave her to that fragile peace, to let her life unfold without the shadow that had haunted her for centuries. She never even knew he had been there.

But if he had known—if he had realized that Elara and Lilith were waiting at the end of that path, coiled and patient in their cruelty—he would have burned the world before it happened. He would have pulled her from the altar and into the fire and kept her there with him. Damn the cost. Because fate, in its exquisite cruelty, had brought her back to him anyway. Bloodied. Hunted. Half starved of the truth. And now, every choice he had made to keep her safe, every distance he had put between them in the name of peace, had only brought her closer to ruin.

He had chosen to walk away. And still she found him.

Hours crawled by, each one an eternity of torment. Kael drifted in and out of a dreamlike state. Memories of Sera, a bittersweet torment. A reminder of what he had lost, of what he might never reclaim.

And he was still caught in that silence when she appeared.

No sound announced her. No celestial shiver. No sense of alarm. She stepped from the darkness, which she always seemed to belong to. She looked like death made flesh. Or something more exquisite than death could ever dream of.

"Why did you do this to me?" she asked.

The question was spoken without fire. Without accusation. Her voice was quiet, emotionless, and still. It struck him harder than any blade.

Kael exhaled a breath that didn't feel like a breath at all. It felt like surrender. Slowly, he rose from the floor, every movement leaden. The dungeon pressed against his ribs like a vice. The obsidian walls curved inward, tightening with the knowledge of her presence. He walked toward the cell bars as if pulled by chains he could not see, his gaze never leaving hers.

Her face remained still, more statue than soul.

"I wanted revenge," he said, his voice low, "for what they did to me. For how they tore me out and cast me aside like a mistake they didn't want to remember. I didn't care who was hurt in the process. Not then."

He reached through the bars, his hand trembling, and touched her cheek. Cold. So cold it almost burned. He brushed his thumb over her translucent skin. Her eyes met his, but they didn't hold him. They passed through him as if he was already ash. Already gone.

And for a moment, he forgot how to breathe.

"All I got in return was heartbreak," he whispered, his thumb still tracing the ghost of warmth that had once lived in her. "And I deserve it."

She did not answer. Did not flinch. She lifted her hand, wrapped her fingers around his, and removed his touch from her face. She let his hand fall. Slowly. Carefully. Like something fragile that no longer mattered.

She then turned and walked away.

Kael remained there, motionless. His heart was a hollow chamber straining to echo. The air thickened around him. The cell shrank. He gripped the bars, tighter and tighter, until the metal groaned beneath his palms. He squeezed until his fingers trembled, until pain crept into his bones. And still, he didn't let go.

A scream tore out of him. Agonized. Raged. Shattered. It ripped from his throat like it had been buried there for centuries, a sound so fierce it felt like even Heaven might hear it.

And still, she did not turn back.

Hope's Ember

33

At the break of the next dawn—if such a thing could be named in a place so absent of light—the guards came for Kael.

They did not speak. Their claws sank into his arms, rusted talons biting deep, without ceremony. There was no need for words. No threats. No questions.

He did not resist. There was nothing left in him that knew how.

Pain bloomed sharp and bright beneath their grips, but it no longer registered as cruel. It was merely expected. Familiar with the taste of blood at the back of his throat.

They dragged him through winding corridors, the stench of decay clinging to him like a second skin. The air tasted of scorched iron and whispered spells. Shadows curled against the stones, indifferent to his suffering. Even the darkness had grown weary of him.

The chamber had changed.

This was no longer the sterile space of extractions. This was a sanctum built for pain.

Green fire lined the walls, casting sickly light upon obsidian tiles that pulsed with sigils drawn in blood. Chains, slick with old gore, hung from the ceiling. There were no screams anymore, only echoes and memories.

A warlock sire waited in the center.

The creature before him was tall and cadaverous, its body a patchwork of sewn flesh and flickering runes. Its lips were gone, peeled away to expose a permanent smile that stretched like a wound. Kael had heard of their kind. To them, torture was refined into an art. Pain distilled into scripture.

It welcomed him with silence and a glint of hunger in eyes too numerous to count.

They bound him with spell work. Threads of cursed incantations sank beneath his skin, anchoring him in place and fusing bones to agony. Every breath became a negotiation. Every heartbeat was a violation.

The sire placed a hand against Kael's chest and whispered in an old tongue.

Pain bloomed in full.

Not the pain of flesh torn or bones broken. This was sacred and perverse. His mind unraveled, seams torn apart by memory rendered raw. Sera's voice. Cassia's fall. Jareth's quiet sorrow. The garden. The scream. The fire.

They did not let him drift. They forced him to watch.

They peeled his essence in spirals, siphoning coils of light straight from his spirit. His veins glowed gold, then silver, and then nothing. Sigils etched into his body writhed under the skin, some holy and some profane but all agonizing. Flesh blistered and healed only to blister again. His teeth cracked from the pressure. His tongue split. His vision burned.

They wanted the name. The one he fortunately did not know.

Bless Jareth. Bless that bastard for never giving it to him. Because if he had, he would have given it away by now. He could feel himself cracking. Could feel pieces of who he had been sloughing off with every breath. The only thing that saved them all was his ignorance.

Eventually, his body gave way.

They let him collapse in the corner of the chamber, a heap of bone and blood and broken magic. He lay there twitching, a thin stream of gold running from his nose and pooling beside the red.

The warlock sire crouched beside him, its eyes wide and curious. It leaned close, its voice as soft as dust. "Next time, we begin with the soul."

Kael was dragged back through the corridors, his blood leaving trails behind him. A map no one would follow. When they tossed him into his cell, his body struck the stones like a corpse. The chains clinked against bones. He remained still. His breath came shallow. Irregular. Wrong.

He did not lift his head nor did he speak or curse.

If Jareth had given him the name, it would all be over. He probably would have broken and damned them all. Or would have added one more body to his ever-growing list. But the light inside him no longer flickered. It pulsed once every so often, as if only to remind him it had not yet died.

He thought of Sera, how radiant her face was in the meadow. The soft curve of her hand. The look she gave him before she evaporated in his arms.

Time no longer mattered. Pain became a constant hymn, laced through every breath. The bones in his chest ached in rhythm with it.

A rasping murmur came from the darkness beyond the wall, interrupting the suffocating silence of his cell. "You're new, aren't you?"

Kael sighed despite the ache radiating through his body. "Fresh off the infernal express."

A hollow chuckle sounded from the adjacent cell. "Special guest treatment, I see."

He tilted his head toward the wall. "How long have you been here?"

"Long enough to forget what freedom feels like. Years. Centuries. I stopped counting." The voice hesitated, bitter. "I wanted to see my brother one last time before this damnation swallowed me whole. We did not part on good terms."

Kael frowned at the mention of a brother. "Your brother… Is he still alive?"

"In the mortal realm, yes. Or last I heard anyway." The voice softened, tinged with longing. "Jareth doesn't deserve to carry my ghost. I'd have given anything for one last chance to see him and talk to him."

Kael's pulse quickened as realization clawed its way into his mind. His breath hitched. He edged closer to the wall. "Eryon?" he asked, his voice barely audible yet drenched with shock.

The silence stretched into eternity until the voice returned. "Ye-yeah? How do you know my name?"

He gripped his chains tight, his body tensing. "It's me. Kael."

The sound of shifting chains and a sharp intake of breath came from the other cell. Eryon's following words came slowly, thick with disbelief. "Kael? No. Impossible…"

"It's me," he said grimly, letting the weight of his words settle.

Eryon's voice grew rough, edged with frustration. "So, you're the one they've been draining dry."

He closed his eyes and exhaled as the confirmation pressed heavier than the chains around him. "I deserved it," he murmured, weariness seeping into his voice. He ran a hand over his face, exhaustion pressing into his bones. "I was supposed to get someone out of here. Did not go according to plan. Fucking Lilith…"

"I've never met her personally," Eryon said, his voice quieter now. "But I guess I can count one blessing."

Silence stretched between them, thick and suffocating. Kael pressed the back of his head against the wall, staring at the shadows across the ceiling. Everything hurt—his body, his thoughts, the weight of his own stubborn hope.

"Why did you fall?" Kael asked, his voice cutting through the quiet.

Eryon exhaled sharply, a bitter sound. "A long story."

He smirked. "We've got time," he said, his voice tinged with grim humor.

But before Eryon could respond, hurried footsteps echoed through the corridor.

His head snapped toward the bars of his cell, his body tensing. A figure, moving with a mix of urgency and caution, emerged from the shadows.

"Kael," came a whisper.

Kael's eyes narrowed, straining through the dim light until they fell upon the figure beyond the bars. "Cassia?" he rasped, his voice cracked and broken. "What are you doing here?"

The light in Cassia's eyes had faded. No glint of mischief. No spark of rebellion. Only shadow and the brittle tremble of something held together too long. She stood just beyond the cell bars, her voice as soft as breath. "I came to envy your chamber," she murmured, a poor attempt at levity. Her eyes lowered. "Sera is almost gone, Kael. I don't know how much longer she has."

He pressed his skull against the stones behind him once more, letting its cold kiss bleed into his bones. "You're not telling me anything I haven't already felt."

She hesitated, her fingers tightening around the bars. "There may be one last thing to try."

His eyes found hers, slow and heavy. "What is it?"

Her voice dropped to a whisper. "You two got the bond mark through sharing yourselves entirely, correct?"

He blinked. "You're asking if we..."

"Yes," she said. "Not out of curiosity. Out of necessity."

He nodded once, a flicker of shame passing through him. "No, we did not. I never took her essence. I refused to take something from her that she did not willingly offer."

A shadow of emotion crossed her face, softening the sharpness of her features. More of a fragile tremor of recognition, a memory brushing against her skin. "Show me your mark," she said, urgency creeping back into her voice.

Kael blinked at her. "What?"

"The binding mark. Is it still glowing?"

He hesitated and then faced her, lowering his head slightly. The chains dragged behind him with a reluctant scrape. "It's at the base of my throat," he muttered.

She stepped close. Her fingers wiped off the blood and the grime as she reached through the cell bars. She drew in a sharp breath. Looking down, he saw a faint, soft golden light pulse beneath the skin like a heartbeat. Dim but still alive.

"Good," she breathed, stepping back. Her voice trembled. "That's good. That's very good."

He straightened slowly, a faint pulse thrumming at the base of his neck where her gaze lingered. The mark burned with a heat that wasn't entirely pain, spreading down his spine until it stole his breath. His jaw tightened, confusion warring with the sharp, instinctive pull coursing through him. "What does it mean?"

"It means the bond didn't break. It means you still exist inside her, even if she doesn't remember it yet. You need to jumpstart it."

He turned to face her fully now, his eyes sharp between disbelief and fragile hope. "How?"

"If you give her your essence again, it might be enough to remind her soul of yours. A tether needs to be recognized by its anchor. If she feels you inside her again, even faintly, she may reach back."

Cassia's fingers drifted absently to her side, brushing beneath her ribs. For a moment, she winced, but when he narrowed his eyes, she had already dropped her hand.

He stared at her. "How do you know so much about fated bonds?"

"I read," she said. "I listen. I watch."

"That's not an answer." He looked down at his bound wrists. The bruises. The iron. The exhaustion was buried in every limb. "Anyway, how do you propose I do that from inside this cell?"

"I don't know." Her voice was tight. "Figure something out. You always do."

"I have nothing left. They've bled me dry. My light's barely a whisper."

She reached into the pocket of her leather pants, her movements quick and shaking. She withdrew a vial no larger than a finger. Gold essence, radiant and alive, swirled inside as if it carried the last breath of a dying star.

Kael's breath caught. "Where did you get that?"

"I guilted my father into giving it up," she said. "Before we left. Just in case someone needed a quick jumpstart." She gave him a knowing smile and passed it through the bars and into his waiting palm.

The liquid was warm.

Alive.

He stared at her. "Cassia…"

A sound echoed down the corridor. Boots. Low voices. Getting closer.

She turned toward the darkness and then back at him. Her eyes blazed for one heartbeat. "Get to her," she said. "Feed the bond. Wake it. Make her remember you."

He sat frozen, his fingers tightening around the vial.

She looked at him one last time. "The blood moon is here," she whispered. "If she falls now, she won't come back."

She then vanished into the shadows, leaving behind nothing but her scent and the soft hum of something sacred waiting to be rekindled.

The heavy thud of boots echoed outside the cells, growing louder with each step. Kael tilted his head toward the sound, narrowing his eyes, as shadows stretched across the dim corridor. Two guards appeared, and their jagged claws dragged battered Eryon from his cell.

Kael uncorked the vial and downed it in one gulp, feeling Michael's holy essence surging through his body and restoring his form to its former glory cell by cell. The feeling was invigorating, like coming back home from a long journey.

As the warmth spread through him, he could feel the shadows of fatigue and despair that had clung to him for so long dissipate. Strength surged like a tide, rolling through his limbs and filling him with a renewed sense of purpose. Every ache and pain melted away, replaced by a vibrant energy that pulsed within him.

He closed his eyes, focusing on the transformation and allowing the radiant power to seep into every corner of his being. This essence was not just about restoration; it was a reminder of who he was and what he was fighting for.

As he opened his eyes, he glanced around, noting his surroundings. They now felt more vivid and alive than they had in ages. He was determined to rise from the depths of the darkness and save Sera. With a firm resolve, he took a deep breath, feeling exhilaration coursing through his veins.

"Let's finish this," he whispered. He shifted, his chains rattling with deliberate noise. "Oh no!" His voice cut through the silence like a blade. "You're not about to give him the VIP treatment without including me. I feel left out!"

The guards stopped, turning their heads in unison. Their glowing eyes narrowed as they glared toward Kael's cell.

"Shut it," one hissed, his voice sharp and guttural.

Kael smirked, rattling his chains louder. "Make me, asswipe," he shot back, his tone dripping with mockery.

With a growl, the guards dropped Eryon and stalked toward Kael's cell, their claws scraping against the stone floor.

One pulled out a wicked blade, which glinted in the dim light. "You need to learn some manners," he snarled as they unlocked the cell door.

The moment the door swung open, Kael launched forward, chains clanging. He collided with the nearest demon guard and drove his shoulder into the demon's chest, forcing him back into the wall with a satisfying crunch. The second guard lunged at him, claws slashing, but he twisted just in time and wrapped the cold steel of his chains around the demon's throat.

The creature thrashed, clawing at the chains tightening around his neck, but Kael held firm, his teeth clenched in sheer determination.

"Call Princess Sera," Kael growled, his voice low and lethal. "I have a message for her. Do it now, and maybe I'll let your friend keep breathing."

The first guard froze, his glowing eyes darting between Kael and his struggling comrade. With a snarling curse, he turned, stormed out of the cell, and disappeared down the corridor.

Kael tightened the chains further, his prisoner's movements growing more frantic. "Relax," he said, his voice laced with mockery. "You all act so tough until someone fights back. You're not looking so invincible now, are you?"

The demon gurgled, his claws scraping uselessly at the chains.

He leaned closer, his eyes gleaming. "You know," he said, "I could just snap your neck right now. I wouldn't even break a sweat. But I need you alive…for now. You're my insurance policy."

The sound of heavy boots returned, accompanied by guttural growls. He glanced toward the corridor, where a swarm of demons now gathered, their weapons gleaming and their eyes blazing.

"Well, look at that," he said, flashing a grin. "A welcoming committee. I must be popular."

The demons stepped closer, their presence filling the room with suffocating darkness.

He shifted his grip on the chains, pulling his prisoner tighter. "If you're here to intimidate me, let me save you some time. It's not working." He then tilted his head, giving his captive a humorless smile. "Oh, and you might want to let your friends know I've got your colleague here in a chokehold. One wrong move, and he'll be a very dead demon."

The lead demon growled, stepping closer. "Release him. Now!"

His grin widened, sharp and unyielding. "Funny thing about negotiations," he drawled, his tone calm despite the chaos, "is that they work better when you don't torture me." He tightened the chains even more, earning a strangled gasp from his captive. "You send Sera. I'll release him. That's the deal."

The tension in the room was palpable, the demons shifting as Kael held his ground. Despite the odds stacked against him, he felt a flicker of satisfaction. He wasn't just enduring; he was fighting back.

The standstill stretched into tense minutes, the demons surrounding his cell shifting restlessly as their claws twitched with restrained aggression. He tightened his grip on the chains around his captive's throat, his smirk unwavering despite the odds stacked against him.

Footsteps—calm, deliberate, and unhurried—echoed down the cavernous hall. Each step carried an air of authority, silencing the restless demons as they turned toward the source. Kael's smirk faltered, his grip tightening.

Sera appeared like a shadow given form, her jet-black hair cascading down her shoulders and framing a face that was both breathtakingly beautiful and terrifyingly cold. Her fair skin seemed to glow faintly in the dim light, and her burning green eyes cut through the darkness like twin blades. She moved with elegance that belied the emptiness in her expression. Her gaze swept over the commotion with detached curiosity.

Kael's heart clenched as he took her in, his mind racing. She was a vision of power and control, utterly unrecognizable from the woman he had once known. Yet, even in her darkness, she was mesmerizing.

Sera stopped just outside the cell, her eyes locking onto Kael with a piercing intensity. "Release him," she said, her voice calm and monotone yet carrying the weight of undeniable command.

He smirked, his grip on the chains unwavering. "Not until you hear me out," he replied, his voice steady despite the turmoil within him. "I have a message for you."

Her lips curled into a faint, cruel smile. "You think I care about the life of a demon?" she asked, her tone dripping with indifference. "Kill him if you wish. It makes no difference to me."

His smirk faltered, her words cutting deeper than he cared to admit.

Before he could respond, she turned to the guards. "Seize him," she ordered, her voice sharp and unyielding.

The Last Thing I Do

34

The guards surged forward like a tidal wave of snarling beasts, their razor-sharp claws gleaming under the flickering torchlight as they lunged at Kael. His heart pounded against his rib cage as he gripped the cold, tarnished chains tight. His mind frantically searched for a key to reverse his fate.

Amid the chaos, Sera stood at the center, her calm, collected gaze an unyielding beacon that commanded the surrounding darkness with an almost regal power.

In that perilous moment, his eyes darted over the scene: six fierce guards encircling them, his beloved woman caught amid their predatory formation, and one already ensnared adversary at his mercy. The question that pummeled his thoughts was not whether he could vanquish all six but whether he could make it to her, regardless of the cost.

With a fluid, almost desperate motion, Kael wrapped the heavy chains around the captured demon guard. The twisted metal groaned under the strain until a sickening crack punctuated the air. The guard's body crumpled like a discarded marionette, collapsing onto the stone floor.

Wasting no moment, Kael yanked himself upright, his muscles tightening, as he spread the chain between his wrists, now transformed into a lethal extension of his will: an unyielding shield prepared to fend off any further onslaught.

For a fleeting second, his eyes locked with Sera's, a silent conversation laden with urgency, before he plunged headlong into the melee.

A frenzied ballet of violence ensued. Amid dental grunts, bodies clashed and swung. Kael's chained fists became streaks of raw determination. The demon guards attacked with calculated ferocity, their claws slicing through the air with menacing precision. But each vicious strike was met by a resounding clang. Kael parried their attacks, his motions a blend of desperate survival and unwavering determination. The air thickened with the metallic scent of spilled blood.

While Kael fought to keep the demons at bay, the sound of Sera's struggle tore through the chaos behind him. He caught a glimpse of her darting toward the edge of the clearing—only for a massive shadowed figure to block her path.

Eryon stepped from the gloom, his voice sharp and commanding. "Sorry, Your Highness. I'm afraid Kael needs you to stay here!"

Kael turned, his chest tightening, as Eryon lunged. The angel's arms closed around Sera, lifting her from the ground with brutal efficiency. She thrashed and kicked, her defiance bright and furious even through the haze of smoke and blood. Eryon's grip didn't waver. The clash of their forms looked more like a storm than a struggle—light and shadow twisting together in violent symmetry.

"Let me go!" Sera cried out, her voice etched with both anger and despair.

Kael glanced over enough to see that Eryon had enveloped her, holding her back.

"I'm afraid I can't do that! Kael, I've got her!" Eryon bellowed, his voice echoing throughout the chaos.

The sounds of clashing steel and desperate struggles boomed around them as Kael, fueled by a potent cocktail of determination and adrenaline, fought his way past the relentless guards. Every dodge and ferocious strike brought him closer to Sera, the sole beacon amid suffering and brutality. His body, bruised and battered, moved with a resolute intensity as he twisted and pivoted through the swirling melee, each muscle straining under the weight of survival.

The tension in the air was almost palpable as he closed the final gap between him and Sera, his singular focus fixed on reclaiming his princess. He wrapped his arms tight around her, pulling her into a protective embrace that silenced the surrounding chaos. In that breathtaking moment, the clamorous cell seemed to hold its breath as every eye witnessed his triumph...

"Here you are, Little Devil..." he murmured, his eyes tracing the burning emerald depths of hers. Gently, he brushed a stray lock of her disheveled hair from her face, his rough fingers caressing the delicate curve of her ear.

She struggled to break free, yet her defiant spirit remained unbowed.

He leaned in and whispered, "Shhh, Little Devil... I am so sorry, my love, but I have a gift for you!" He placed his large, calloused palm onto her cool cheek.

"Let me go, you filthy creature!" she spat, her voice a mix of fury and defiance.

"I will, but first." He bit down hard on his bruised lip, and in that charged heartbeat, he locked their lips in a feverish kiss.

It wasn't just a gift of light. It was a command. A ruthless, desperate refusal to let her go. He forced the memory of their bond, of his love, into her—a final act against the darkness that had claimed her. The kiss spoke of stolen moments and burning fervor as if it was his final goodbye.

At first, she fought against his grip around her body, but as the kiss grew deeper, she sagged against him. It felt like her body worked on memory alone, melding into his.

As he pulled away and pressed his forehead against hers, she shuddered. The gold strands of ancient power coiled and withdrew from him and settled into her form. Her bond mark flared to life.

The guards moved as one—six shadows erupting at once. Kael barely had time to brace before the first strike hit his ribs. Then another across his jaw. The world dissolved into fists and iron boots. Every impact sent light bursting behind his eyes, the air ripping from his lungs as he staggered backward into Eryon's path. They were both swallowed by the onslaught, a blur of claws, metal, and shouted orders.

Through the crush, Kael caught flashes of her—Sera's pale face, her trembling hands, and the glimpse of her feet restless against the chaos. Then she turned, unsteady but alive, and bolted for the door, her silhouette vanishing into the infernal light.

On My Mother's Behalf

35

Sera's heart felt as if it was being torn apart as she struggled back to her feet. Her eyes, wide with a mix of anguish and disbelief, fixed on the cruel scene before her: the savage beating of the one man who mattered most to her and whom she hated the most. In that heart-wrenching moment, the memories cascaded back into her mind, vivid and undeniable. She remembered it now. She remembered it all.

The kiss. The meadow. Elara's betrayal. Everything. It wasn't a slow trickle; it was a tidal wave of truth, agonizing and absolute. The raw horror of the scene, coupled with the sudden, brutal weight of her fully restored memories, ignited a primal panic deep within her.

With a choked sob tearing from her throat and lost amid the sickening thuds and guttural grunts filling the dungeon, Sera spun away from the violence. She ran, desperate to put distance between herself and the dungeons.

Flickering torchlights cast long, dancing shadows that seemed to writhe and reach for her as she fled. Her ragged breaths echoed unnaturally in the oppressive silence of the halls, each gasp punctuated by the violent intrusion of memories flooding back, sharp and disorienting.

She remembered the smoky haze of the Iron Orchid and the jolt of recognition as Kael's eyes first met hers. The challenge in his gaze at Holy Rollers and the spark that ignited between them. The dim intimacy of Serpent's Kiss and the taste of bitter liquor and burgeoning desire. She remembered the shocking tenderness of their first kiss under the city lights. And as he terrifyingly free-fell into Limbo, his voice was a lifeline, and his strength pulled her back from the abyss. The starlight reflected across his face in the quiet solitude of the meadow, a stolen peace that felt like a lifetime ago. Elara's venomous smile and the chilling realization of betrayal just before the demons dragged her down.

It was all too much and too fast. The love and the loss, the tenderness and the terror, the loyalty and the betrayals—they crashed against the shores of her consciousness, threatening to shatter her completely. A strangled sound escaped her lips as she choked on the overwhelming onslaught, gasping and sobbing. Her body trembled violently, her vision blurring with unshed tears and sheer panic. She stumbled, catching herself against a damp, cold stone wall. The chill seeped through her thin clothing. Where was she even running? These corridors felt both nightmarishly familiar and terrifyingly alien.

Yet some deeper instinct, a homing beacon buried beneath fear and confusion, guided her steps. Down one oppressive hall, which turned into another—the ornate, menacing architecture of the palace pressing in on all sides—until finally, bathed in the hellish, flickering gloom, a specific set of doors loomed before her.

"Cassia!"

Sera stood in the doorway of Cassia's chambers, her burning green eyes meeting her sister's with an intensity that spoke volumes. Cassia was seated on the edge of her bed, her lithe frame tense.

"Sera?" Cassia said, rising to her feet. "What's happened? You look like you've—"

"There's no time for questions, Cassia," Sera said sharply, her voice cutting through the room like a whip. She paced a few steps forward, her hands trembling slightly and her expression tense. "I have a plan. Something that could stop her."

Cassia frowned, stepping closer. "Stop her?"

Her voice was low but urgent. "Lilith. We need to wake up Lucifer."

Cassia seemed to collect herself. "Lucifer? The king? How?" Her voice was cautious but steady. "And how are we supposed to wake him?"

She hesitated for a moment, her gaze shifting to the floor as if searching for clarity. "There must be some ritual, ancient spell, or some way to wake him. If it exists, it would be…hidden. Somewhere Lilith doesn't want anyone to find."

"If there is an answer, it will be in archives," Vyxia said as she emerged from the shadowy corner of the bedchamber.

Sera straightened, her green eyes locking onto Vyxia. "Yes," she said, hopeful. "That makes sense. A place to hide forbidden knowledge… If they exist, that's where we'll find what we need." She gestured for her to approach. "How do we get inside? When you were showing me around the palace during the first nights after my abduction, you said they only allow passage with Lilith's permission."

For the first time, Sera saw Vyxia hesitate. The air around her seemed to waver, as if the light itself rippled against her skin. It passed in an instant, but it left Sera with the unsettling sense that she had glimpsed beneath a mask—or a glamour, perhaps. She didn't have time to question it, and the demoness spoke quietly.

"You would have to pass the keeper somehow," Vyxia said.

Sera exhaled sharply, her determination hardening. "I will think of something."

Cassia stepped forward, her tone sharp. "No. You can't go, Sera. Lilith is watching your every move. If she even suspects what you're planning—"

"And if you're caught?" she snapped, her voice rising. "The keeper guards those archives, Cassia. We don't even know what we are dealing with."

"I'll handle the keeper," Cassia said firmly. "Lilith doesn't watch me the way she watches you. She thinks I'm still dutiful and scared. If anyone can do this without raising suspicion, it's me."

Sera's jaw tightened, her eyes narrowing as she searched her sister's face. Finally, she sighed, the weight of Cassia's argument sinking in. "You can't do this alone. Please. Take Vyxia with you. She knows the palace. If something goes wrong, she can help you."

Cassia glanced at Vyxia, who bowed her head. She then returned her gaze to Sera. "Fine."

The iron doors groaned open, revealing the shadow-drenched expanse of the archives. Cassia stepped through hesitantly, the oppressive atmosphere pressing in around her like a living thing. The air was thick with centuries of forgotten knowledge, carrying an unnatural chill that prickled her skin. Rows of towering shelves endlessly stretched into the darkness, their cracked leather tomes and writhing scrolls emanating a faint, malevolent energy.

Her unease only deepened as her gaze swept the cavernous chamber.

She felt the weight of unseen eyes, an ancient presence lingering just beyond the edge of perception. Her stomach knotted with dread, but she pushed it aside and stepped forward.

"Your Highness," Vyxia whispered, falling into step behind her, "look."

Cassia followed the servant's gaze and froze. There, in the chamber's heart, stood a figure draped in tattered robes that shifted like poured ink. Its movements were slow but fluid, as if time itself bent to its rhythm. Within the depths of its hood, two crimson lights burned in the shape of an hourglass—narrow at the center, wide at the ends. The glow pulsed faintly with each breath it did not take. The keeper.

Her breath caught, her plans unraveling in an instant. She had expected a sentry, something bound to duty, but not this ancient thing that looked like time and death had learned to walk. "That's the keeper?" she murmured, disbelief scraping at the edge of her voice.

"Yes," Vyxia whispered back, her voice tight. "No one ever comes here if that thing does not permit it."

The keeper's voice rumbled like distant thunder, its tones less heard than felt and reverberating through the stone floor. "Well, now," it said, the words oozing with dark amusement. "Lilith's wayward child graces my domain. Tell me, little princess, what brings you here?"

Cassia's mind raced, every instinct screaming at her to run. But she straightened her shoulders, drawing herself up as best as she could. "I'm here on my mother's behalf," she said, her voice steadier than she felt. "She's tasked me with researching the old wards: how they were constructed, how they can be strengthened."

The keeper tilted its hooded head, seemingly studying her with an unnerving intensity. "Old wards," it echoed, its voice softening into a growl. "A practical concern, I suppose. However, the archives are not so readily available. Tell me, Daughter of Lilith, why should I allow this?"

Her pulse quickened, and her thoughts scrambled for a convincing answer. "Because the strongholds must be fortified," she said, forcing a thin smile. "If we're to maintain order, knowledge of the past will guide us."

The keeper let out a low, rasping chuckle. "So eager to maintain order," it murmured. "Very well, little princess. Search as you will. But tread carefully. Knowledge has a price, and you may find it too steep to pay."

She exhaled slowly, the tension in her chest easing ever so slightly. She inclined her head in thanks and then turned and gestured for Vyxia to follow. The keeper's crimson gaze lingered on them as they moved deeper into the archives.

The towering shelves loomed overhead, their cracked leather-bound tomes and tightly stacked scrolls stacked high and deep. They stretched beyond the reach of the dim brazier light. Cassia felt the oppressive weight of the archives pressing down on her, as if centuries of forgotten knowledge were watching her every move. The silence was suffocating, punctuated only by the faint sound of her boots on the stone floor.

Her fingers trailed over the spines of ancient books, their surfaces rough and crumbling with age. She paused at one marked with strange clawlike engravings. She pulled it free and flipped through its brittle pages. Her heart sank. It was a little more than a compilation of infernal oaths. Nothing close to what they were looking for. With a frustrated sigh, she slid the book back into its place.

"Your Highness," Vyxia murmured behind her. "Do you think we might be looking in the wrong section? These books don't seem to have anything to do with rituals."

She shook her head, her brown eyes narrowing as she scanned the row of titles. "No. This has to be the right place." She pointed at the iron plaque mounted above the shelves, its surface etched with curling runes and the words "Custodia Somnum Divinum—Guardians of Divine Sleep." "See? Every record of celestial bindings and eternal rest would be cataloged here. If there's a way to wake Lucifer, it has to be in this section. We just need to keep searching."

Vyxia slightly bowed her head and moved further down the aisle, her sharp eyes darting over the countless spines. Her trembling fingers reached for a tightly bound scroll, its edges frayed and stained with dark smudges. She unfurled it carefully, and her violet eyes widened as she scanned its contents. "Princess... It's not here. This is just some old records of eternal sleep of warriors and such."

Cassia exhaled sharply and moved toward another shelf, frustration simmering beneath her calm exterior. Every wasted second felt heavier than the last. Lilith's guards could come looking at any moment, or worse, the keeper might decide to intervene.

Minutes dragged on like hours as they worked, scanning each shelf and rifling through countless books and scrolls. Cassia's fingers grew sore from handling the delicate parchment, and her jaw tightened with the weight of her resolve. She couldn't afford to give up. Everything depended on finding the ritual.

"Your Highness," Vyxia whispered, her voice taut. "What if it's not here? What if Lilith—"

"Don't say that," Cassia said, her tone firm. "It has to be here. We keep looking."

Vyxia nodded and turned back to the shelves, her movements more hesitant now.

Cassia moved to another aisle, her eyes flicking from one spine to the next. Her gaze landed on a particularly thick tome, its leather cover cracked and marked with faintly glowing runes in the dim light. The air around it felt heavier as if the book itself exhaled heat with every pulse of those runes.

She hesitated, her fingers hovering over the book before she pulled it free. The weight of it was immense, as if it carried far more than mere words. She flipped through the pages carefully, and when she reached a section encircled by intricate runes, her pulse quickened.

"This might be it," she murmured, tilting the book toward Vyxia. "Look at these markings. They're blood magic."

Vyxia stepped closer, her violet eyes narrowing. "Your Highness, this is a seal," she said quietly. "It requires blood... Her blood."

She shook her head, her jaw tightening. "Not just hers. *Ours*. We share the same bloodline."

Vyxia's expression hardened. "Princess, are you sure? Blood seals can be..."

"Dangerous. I know. But it's the only way. If this holds the ritual, we have no choice."

Without hesitation, she drew her dagger and sliced her palm, wincing as the blade bit into her skin. Blood welled, dark against her pale skin, and she tilted her hand over the page. The first drop fell, and the runes flared, dissolving with a soft hiss that faintly echoed within the cavernous chamber.

The hidden text revealed itself in an elegant, shimmering script. Cassia's breath caught as she read the incantation aloud.

"'By the power of blood spilled and fire's embrace, by the chains that bind the fallen star, I call upon thee, Lucifer, king of this forsaken place. Awaken from slumber, shatter death's dark bar, rise from the shadowed depths, reclaim your shadowed grace, and seize again the dominion that is yours afar!'"

The runes shifted again, forming a diagram that marked Lucifer's resting place and the artifact required for the ritual—a powerful and ancient coin.

Cassia tore the pages free and rolled them up before replacing the tome on the shelf. "Let's go," she said, urgency sharpening her tone. "We've wasted enough time."

As they approached the iron doors, the air grew heavier, the oppressive atmosphere clawing at her resolve. The doors groaned open once more, and her heart plummeted.

Lilith, framed by two guards, stood in the archway. Her golden eyes blazed with fury, her beauty a mask for the deadly rage simmering beneath. "Cassia," she purred, her silk voice laced with steel. "Sneaking around in my archives? How disappointing."

Cassia froze, her fingers brushing the rolled-up pages hidden in her sleeve. Vyxia stiffened beside her, bowing her head lower than usual.

"Guards," she said sharply, "seize them."

The demons advanced, their brutish forms filling the doorway. Cassia locked eyes with Vyxia, a silent command passing between them. With a deft motion, she slipped the pages into Vyxia's hands. Vyxia pressed her palm to the floor, and the shadows rippled outward like disturbed water.

Lilith's eyes narrowed. The temperature dropped as her own darkness gathered, ready to strike, but when it reached Vyxia, it faltered. The air warped and shimmered, and threads of color bled through the black—soft gold and deep violet bending the shadows away like oil sliding off glass.

Cassia stilled. That light, that movement, was unmistakable. For a heartbeat, her chest tightened with recognition, with understanding that Vyxia had been hiding more than allegiance, but she said nothing.

Lilith's voice cracked the air. "What are you doing?" She thrust her hand forward, summoning the shadows again, but they refused her call, trembling against the strange, luminous distortion now filling the chamber.

The shimmer flared once, and Vyxia vanished.

"Find her!" Lilith's scream tore through the quiet, her fury rattling the iron sconces on the walls. The room shook with heat and wrath, the remaining shadows snapping like broken glass.

Rough hands clamped around Cassia's arms, but she didn't resist. Her gaze locked on the fading shimmer where Vyxia had stood, and a single thought cut through the chaos: of course.

"You'll regret this defiance," Lilith hissed, her voice low and venomous.

Cassia smiled faintly, the knowledge of what she'd learned burning bright within her.

Motherhood is a Weakness

36

Far below the gilded cages of the upper palace, where the air grew thin and silence settled, lay the cold depths of the Crimson Keep. To Cassia, this was not merely a prison; it was a sensory deprivation tank designed to break the mind before the body even felt the first blow.

She stood in the center of a dim, circular chamber carved from the heart of a dead volcano. The walls were jagged, weeping obsidian that seemed to sweat a freezing, oily moisture. The darkness here wasn't empty; it was pressurized, pressing against her eardrums like the depths of an ocean. Her wrists were suspended above her head, bound in heavy infernal chains that didn't just hold her weight; they fed on it. The iron links glowed with a faint, sickly puce rhythm, pulsing runes that leeched the celestial magic from her blood, leaving her feeling hollowed out, a husk of the warrior she used to be.

The air was stagnant, tasting of copper, ozone, and the ancient dust of pulverized bones. Every breath she took was a labor, the oxygen thin and unwilling to fill her lungs.

Then, the heavy thud of a lock disengaging echoed through the stone, vibrating through the floor and up into her bare feet. The door groaned open, metal shrieking against stone, and she stiffened. The sound sent a chill racing down her spine, and it had nothing to do with the temperature.

Her mother stepped through the doorway.

Lilith did not walk; she glided, a figure of terrifying, incandescent beauty against the backdrop of absolute squalor. Her golden eyes were aglow like molten sunlight, piercing through the gloom with an intensity that rooted Cassia in place. Dark hair fell in cascading waves around her, catching the dim torchlight like spilled ink. For a sickening heartbeat, Cassia thought she was looking at Sera. The resemblance was visceral—same bone structure, same curve of the jaw. But where Sera's face held fire and defiance, Lilith's had only an abyssal, ancient boredom.

Cassia felt a grim wave of relief wash over her; she thanked whatever stars were left that she bore more resemblance to her father than to this creature.

Yet her breath caught as she faced the mother she did not remember. She straightened her shoulders, straining against the chains to stand tall, refusing to let the fear bubble within her show. She had prepared herself for this moment for fifty years, rehearsing speeches of defiance. But nothing could have braced her for the sheer, suffocating force of Lilith's presence. It was a gravity well, pulling everything in the room toward her center.

Lilith stopped a few feet away, her gown of midnight silk rustling softly—a sound too civilized for a torture chamber.

"So," Lilith said, her voice as smooth as silk but laced with steel, "we meet again."

Her golden gaze swept over her daughter, detached and clinical, like a buyer inspecting livestock. Her lips curled into a cold, appreciative smile. "My daughter. The responsible one has been so far, anyway. Yet here you are. Sneaking into my archives like a common thief. Do you have an explanation for this…behavior?"

Cassia met her mother's eyes with defiance; her gaze was steady, though her pulse hammered a frantic rhythm against her ribs.

"No?" Lilith tilted her head slightly, her golden eyes narrowing. "I suppose you'd like to believe you owe me nothing. That your silence is a shield." She took a step closer, her aura of control expanding until it felt like the air had been sucked out of the room. "But here's the thing, little one: You may not owe me answers, but you will give them to me. What were you looking for?"

Cassia clenched her fists, her nails digging into her palms until the skin broke. She refused to let her resolve waver. "Nothing."

Lilith's patience dissolved like smoke in a gale. With a fluid, chilling grace that belied her intent, she raised her hand. The shadows in the room surged, coalescing into her palm to materialize a blade. It was obsidian, but it wasn't merely black. It seemed to drink in the meager light, its surface swirling with captured shadows and trapped screams. Ancient runes were etched along its length, faintly pulsing with a sickly, violet light that vibrated with contained malice.

The air grew colder, tasting metallic and stale.

Lilith tapped the flat of the blade against her palm—tap, tap, tap—a rhythmic, terrifying sound that echoed off the wet walls. She looked at the weapon, then at Cassia, with a look of mock weariness.

"You might be wondering why I am lowering myself to this manual labor," she mused, her voice echoing lightly.

"I wasn't", Cassia muttered.

"Why the Queen herself is here, blade in hand, instead of a dungeon master. Usually, the Infernal Sires handle such… breaking. They enjoy the wet work."

She paused, inspecting the edge of the blade.

"But they are currently indisposed," she continued, her eyes flashing with a manic excitement. "Busy with preparations."

Cassia's brow furrowed involuntarily. The word hung in the air, ominous and heavy. "Preparations for what?"

Lilith's smile widened, sharp and terrifying, revealing the monster beneath the porcelain skin. "For your sister's grand finale!"

Before Cassia could process the horror of that statement, Lilith cut the distance between them. She stepped directly in front of Cassia, the hum of the obsidian blade vibrating against Cassia's throat.

"Well…" Lilith whispered, her breath smelling of ambrosia and rot. "So, we meet again. But will you be useful this time?"

Cassia scoffed, a bitter, broken sound in the oppressive silence. She looked her mother in the eye. "Last time you told me I wasn't. You threw me away."

Lilith whispered, sliding the cold flat of the blade down Cassia's cheek to rest against her neck, "Let's hope this time is different."

She pulled back slightly, just enough to swing.

"Silence is a choice," Lilith murmured, her voice a silken whisper that promised untold agony. "A choice I will carve out of you, Daughter."

The tip of the blade pressed against Cassia's forearm. The cold was absolute, a numbing prelude before the edge slid across her skin. It wasn't a simple cut. It felt like frostbite and fire simultaneously, a searing, unnatural burn that left a precise line. The magic in the blade bit deeper than the flesh, searing the nerves with a poison that felt like concentrated despair.

Cassia gasped, her body arching involuntarily against the chains. Her teeth ground together as she bit back a scream, refusing to give Lilith the satisfaction.

But beneath the agony, beneath the screaming nerves and the smell of her own copper blood filling the air, something fluttered deep in her chest.

Her dormant bond mark—silent for fifty years, a graveyard of a connection she thought dead—trembled against her ribs. It wasn't a painful throb, nor was it the active heat of a live connection. It was a steady, grounding pulse—a memory of strength. As the blood welled on her arm, the mark seemed to tighten around her will, locking her jaw. It was protecting her, insinuating a barrier between her mind and the pain, holding the secrets behind her teeth like a dam holding back a flood.

Lilith watched, her golden eyes devoid of warmth, searching for the break.

Another cut. This one traced a cruel parallel path just below the first, deeper this time, parting the muscle. The pain intensified, radiating outward in blinding waves of white heat. Sweat beaded on Cassia's brow, mingling with tears of sheer agony that she refused to let fall.

Again, the bond mark fluttered—a phantom wingbeat against her heart, a silent voice whispering hold, hold, hold.

Through clenched teeth, Cassia forced out the words, breathless and ragged. "What kind of mother…does this? What kind of monster tortures her own child?"

Lilith paused, the blade hovering millimeters above her skin, slick with dark red. A flicker of something unreadable crossed her beautiful features before vanishing behind a mask of regal disdain.

"Motherhood is a weakness," she replied coolly, tilting her head slightly as if explaining a simple math problem to a toddler. "I am your queen, Cassia, and I demand loyalty. You mistake my biological function for affection. A costly error. Children are merely extensions of the self, and if an extension is gangrenous… one cuts it out."

Her smile was a razor's edge. "And you test my generosity."

Lilith's gaze sharpened, shifting from the weeping wounds on Cassia's arm up to her eyes. The playful malice evaporated, replaced by a cold, calculating intelligence.

"You were not alone in the archives," she stated, her voice dropping an octave, vibrating with suspicion. "I saw the little wretch standing beside you before she vanished like smoke. That was… wild magic. Ancient."

Lilith leaned in, the tip of the bloody blade pressing against Cassia's sternum. "Who was that young servant?"

Cassia's heart slammed against her ribs. Vyxia. What would Lilith do if she realized a fae was under her nose, plotting?

The bond mark pulsed harder, spreading warmth to the center of her chest, urging silence and flooding her mind with static that blocked out the fear. She stared at Lilith, mute, her eyes hard as flint.

"No answer?" Lilith sighed, disappointed, shaking her head. "I thought we established that silence is painful."

The blade moved again, faster now. No longer just tracing lines but inflicting deeper, gouging wounds across her stomach and ribs. Each precise incision felt aimed not just at the flesh but at the nerve clusters, leaving trails of agonizing fire that refused to fade.

Lilith's free hand then gestured, fingers weaving a complex pattern in the air. Icy, invisible tendrils, colder than the blade, pierced Cassia's mind. They weren't just searching; they were hooks, sinking into her memories to try to rip them open and force flashes of her deepest fears, betrayals, and utter helplessness to the surface. She felt Lilith clawing for the image of Vyxia, for the plan, for the ritual.

Cassia cried out then, a raw, strangled sound that was torn between physical agony and mental violation. She squeezed her eyes shut, trying to barricade her mind, using the pulse of the bond mark as a focal point. *Don't look. Don't think. Just feel the mark.* Blood dripped steadily now, splattering onto the cold stones and painting a grim display of her suffering.

But her lips remained sealed. The flutter in her chest had become a drumbeat, a wall of static that Lilith's mental hooks couldn't penetrate.

Lilith leaned closer, the faint scent of sulfur and brimstone clinging to her like perfume. The physical torment paused for a beat, replaced by a demanding stare.

"This...desperation," she mused, tapping a perfectly manicured nail against the obsidian blade. "Risking the keeper's wrath and seeking what...? It feels too bold for you alone, Daughter. Too reckless." Her golden eyes narrowed, sharp and calculating. "Tell me, was it Sera? Did she whisper fantasies of rebellion into your ear while pretending to be my mindless pet?"

Despite the agony radiating through her body and mind, a ragged laugh escaped Cassia's lips, which quickly turned into a painful gasp. It was the perfect cover.

"S-Sera?" She shook her head weakly, forcing herself to meet Lilith's gaze with feigned disbelief. "You shattered her, remember? She's barely functional." She summoned every ounce of strength to make her voice sound broken yet scornful. "She follows your orders like a good little puppet now." Another pained scoff escaped her. She let her head fall back against the cold stone, closing her eyes as if in weary defeat. *Praying the performance was convincing.*

Lilith scrutinized her for a long moment, her expression unreadable.

She seemed to weigh the lie, tasting the air for deceit. Her gaze then lowered from Cassia's face to the hollow above her heart, where the torn fabric of her dress barely concealed the skin.

A strange stillness crossed Lilith's features.

She leaned closer, one sharp nail tracing the faint, almost invisible outline of the mark on Cassia's chest.

Her mouth curved into a slow, cruel smile. "Ah... I see. All of my daughters are foolish in the same way. Another bonded soul. I guess it runs in the family." Her tone was honey over glass. "Tell me, child. Who is your torment? Who is the anchor holding your tongue?"

Cassia's lips parted, but no sound came. The question slithered through her mind, and she tried to drag shadows over it. She didn't want Lilith to see the answer, didn't want her to know about Remiel. But the mark throbbed violently, and her heart clenched as if caught in unseen hands.

Lilith's smile deepened. "No answer? Then let us see what you're hiding."

Her palm pressed flat against Cassia's chest, directly over the mark. The contact was soft, almost tender, and then the world ignited.

Cold, devouring darkness flooded her veins, splitting thought from flesh. It wasn't just pain; it was an invasion. Lilith was trying to force the bond open, to corrupt it, to use the connection to tear the truth out of her soul. Her body arched, the chains biting deeper, as light burst behind her eyes. She heard herself cry out, though the sound was swallowed by a pulse that filled the cell—a blast of defensive energy from the bond itself, rejecting the intrusion.

Lilith's expression flickered in satisfaction, then confusion, and then fear.

The air erupted.

A shockwave ripped outward, hurling Lilith backward into the opposite wall. The iron rings overhead screamed as power surged through the cavernous space and then collapsed in on itself. For one heartbeat, Cassia thought her heart had split open, that whatever lived beneath that mark had torn its way free to protect her.

Cassia sagged in her chains, her lungs heaving and her vision fractured.

Across the cell, Lilith rose unsteadily, debris clinging to her hair. Her elegance was fractured by raw and startled shock. She looked at her hand, then at Cassia, with a new, dangerous curiosity.

Cassia couldn't move. Couldn't think. Only felt the dull ache in her chest where Lilith's hand had been and the faint echo of a pulse that wasn't entirely her own. It had held. The secret was safe.

Finally, with a low snarl of impatience, Lilith straightened, brushing the dust from her gown. Her chest rose and fell slightly faster than before. She looked at Cassia not as a daughter, but as a locked box she had temporarily failed to open.

With a final contemptuous flick of her wrist, she unleashed a raw wave of pure, unfocused agony of psychic lightning that slammed into Cassia, throwing her body against the unforgiving stone floor as the chains rattled violently.

"Keep your secrets," Lilith spat. The obsidian blade dissolved back into shadows. "They'll fester within you, Little Traitor. And when I am done with your sister, I will come back and peel them out of you, layer by layer."

The heavy door slammed shut with a resonating crash that echoed like a final judgment and plunged the chamber back into near silence, broken only by Cassia's ragged, painful gasps and the slow, steady drip of her blood onto the stone.

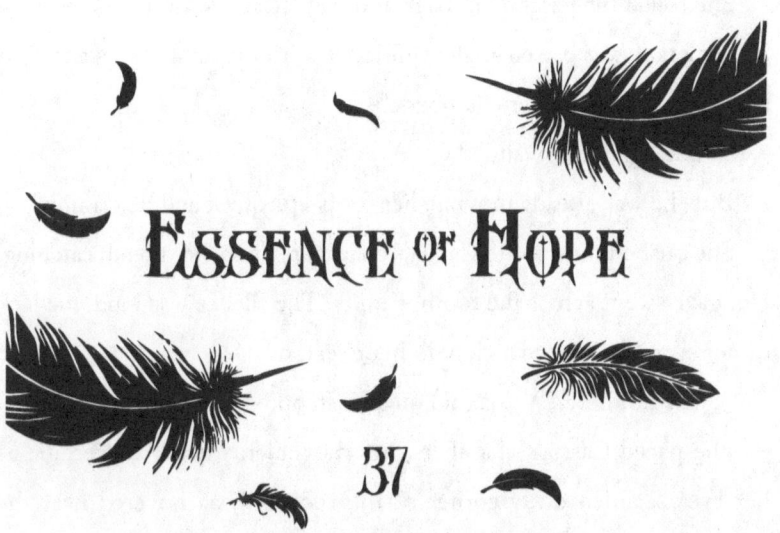

Essence of Hope

37

Sera paced in her chambers, her movements restless and agitated. Her emerald eyes snapped toward the door every time it creaked under the shifting stones. The room felt suffocating, the silence only amplifying her fear. When the door finally opened, and only Vyxia stepped inside, her expression paled.

"Where's Cassia?" Sera demanded, her voice sharp with urgency.

"She's been detained," Vyxia said, her words tumbling out in a rush. She held up the rolled parchment, its edges creased from her tight grip. "Lilith caught us. But Cassia… She made sure I got out with this."

Sera's breath hitched as she took the parchment. Her fingers slightly trembled as she unrolled it. Her eyes scanned the jagged script, her face hardening with every word she read. "The incantation," she murmured. "And the location of Lucifer's resting place." Her fingers brushed over the diagram as she traced the lines marking the ancient seal. Her thoughts churned. "This could work." Her voice was barely audible. "We have what we need…except…" She faltered, her throat tightening.

"Except Cassia," Vyxia finished softly, lowering her gaze.

She rolled the parchment back and handed it over to the demoness. Her emerald eyes blazed as she whirled toward the door. "I have to find her. She might be in her chambers."

"Your Highness, wait…"

But she was already moving, her footsteps quick and determined.

She pushed the door to Cassia's chambers open, her breath catching. Her gaze swept across the room. Empty. The silence was loud, the lack of her sister's presence a blow to her chest.

"She's not here," Vyxia said quietly, stepping in behind her.

She paced Cassia's chambers, her movements quick and erratic as her eyes scanned every corner of the room. Vyxia hovered near the doorway, her gaze flickering toward the hall. The palace's oppressive atmosphere seemed heavier here, the silence too thick.

"I don't understand," Sera muttered, her frustration bubbling over. "Where would they take her? What could they—"

"Sera," Vyxia said softly, her voice tremulous, "we have to go. If they bring her back and see us—"

"They won't bring her back," she snapped, though her voice slightly cracked. "She's not here. She's…" She stopped abruptly as a glimmer beneath the edge of the bed caught her eye. Frowning, she knelt and reached under the frame. Her fingers brushed against smooth glass. When she pulled them free, her breath caught sharply.

"What is it?" Vyxia asked, stepping closer.

She turned the vials over in her hands, the ethereal glow of the angelic essence reflecting in her gaze. "It's pure," she murmured. Realization dawned on her as she studied the vials. "Angelic essence."

Vyxia's expression shifted to one of awe. "Where did she even—?"

"I don't know." She stood quickly, her grip on the vials tightening. "But I do know what it can do. If I can get this to Kael and Eryon."

Distant footsteps froze them both. Echoing down the hall.

Vyxia rushed to the doorway and peered out before turning back to Sera. "They're coming," she whispered urgently. "We have to go."

Sera hesitated only for a moment before grabbing her arm and pulling her toward the door. "Come on," she hissed.

The two women slipped out of the chambers, their movements quick and silent as they melted into the shadows. Sera's heart raced as the sound of approaching footsteps grew louder, the echoes overlapping with the faint clank of chains. She bit her lip, her grip on the vials tightening, as they darted down the hall.

Just as they turned a corner, the sound of a chamber door opening behind them sent chills racing down her spine. She paused and glanced over her shoulder for only a fraction of a second, enough to see large silhouettes of demons carrying Cassia's limp, unconscious form into the room. Her pulse thundered in her ears as she turned back to Vyxia, who frantically gestured for her to keep moving.

They didn't stop until they were several halls away, the oppressive silence wrapping around them once more. Sera leaned against the wall, her breath coming in short, uneven bursts. Vyxia stood beside her, still clutching the parchment tight against her chest as if *her* life depended on it.

"We were almost caught," Vyxia said softly, her voice trembling.

Sera exhaled sharply, her emerald eyes burning, as she pushed away from the wall. "We don't have time," she said, her tone allowing no argument. "Hurry. We must get to my chambers."

As they rounded another corner, a thunderous gong sounded, followed swiftly by a horn's mournful cry, the vibrations sending a ripple through the air and the ground beneath their feet. Both women froze. Sera then moved to a nearby window and peered out into the courtyard below.

Rows of infernal soldiers stretched out in perfect formation, their monstrous forms glinting in the hellfire light. The air was thick with anticipation, the unspoken promise of chaos on the horizon.

"Something is happening," she said quietly. She turned to Vyxia, her expression hardening. "We don't have time. Hurry!"

She pushed open the door to her chambers, her pace quick and deliberate. She crossed the room to her writing desk. Vyxia followed, her footsteps light yet hurried.

Without hesitation, she pulled open a drawer, her hands moving with practiced precision. She retrieved several dim vials that she had once collected for her own oblivion. The contents swirled faintly, their dark energy subdued compared to the radiant angelic essence she had discovered earlier. She lined them up on the desk and then turned to Vyxia, her expression grave.

"Listen to me very closely," she said, her voice steady but serious. Her emerald eyes burned with urgency. "Take these vials. You can use them to drug the guard at the dungeons. That will give you time to reach Kael and Eryon."

Vyxia stared at the vials, and a cold realization seemed to dawn in her violet eyes. "Your Highness... You kept more—"

"It does not matter now," she said, her voice flat. "What matters is that I do not need them anymore."

Vyxia flinched. The casual dismissal of what was essentially a suicide kit seemed to hit her harder than any shout. She looked from the deadly vials to Sera's hollowed-out eyes and nodded.

Sera pulled the pure essence vials from her pocket and placed them carefully in Vyxia's hand. "Give them this too. It's pure angelic essence. It might be enough to restore their strength, enough for them to fight."

Her voice grew even steadier. "And give Kael this." She retrieved the coin she had taken from Elara's arrival. The artifact dully gleamed in the dim light. She pressed it into Vyxia's palm, her fingers lingering for a moment. "Give him the description of the Lucifer enchantment."

Vyxia stared at the items in her hands, the gravity of her mission etched onto her face. "I won't fail," she said quietly, her voice firm.

"Please be careful," she said, her tone softening as she stepped back. "I'll wait for you here."

A faint vibration rippled through the air, accompanied by the thunderous gong that reverberated through the palace once more. The mournful blare of horns followed again, their echoes stretching endlessly through the corridors. Sera's breath caught, her emerald eyes snapping toward the window.

Rows of demon soldiers were marching in formation, their weapons gleaming and their monstrous forms casting long shadows across the palace grounds. Hellfire flickered in their eyes, a promise of chaos and destruction on the horizon. The tremors beneath their feet resonated through the stone walls, a haunting reminder of a battle drawing near.

"You have to go," Sera said, turning back to Vyxia. "Hurry!"

Vyxia reached for the doorframe, but before her fingers touched it, a violent impact split the air. The large and heavy door slammed inward with a deafening crack, almost torn from its hinges by the force.

Instinct seized her. She darted behind the open door and pressed herself flat against the wall as it shuddered to a stop, inches from her face. The stones vibrated beneath her palms, the sound of heavy boots thudding through her bones.

Voices followed, sharp and cold.

"Princess Seraphine," one of them said, his tone a rasp of metal. "The queen requires your presence. Immediately."

She held her breath. She couldn't see them from her hiding place, but she could hear the scrape of armor and the faint hiss of runes alive with heat. The scent of brimstone filled the air.

Sera's voice rose, clear and defiant. "Requires my presence? For what?"

The guard's reply came without hesitation. "You will find out soon."

Then chaos erupted: boots shifting, the jangle of chains, and Sera's breaths breaking into sharp, uneven gasps. A cry quickly smothered. The thud of impact as they seized her.

Vyxia's fingers tightened against the wall. She wanted to move, to intervene, but she stayed still, every nerve alive with restraint. The door shielded her, and she let the darkness cover her like a second skin.

"Where are you taking me?!" Sera's voice cut through, strained but still unbroken.

"To your destiny," a guard replied, his words flat and final.

The sounds that followed hollowed the silence—the drag of chains, the scuff of boots, and the harsh rhythm of Sera's struggle fading down the corridor. When the last echo disappeared, Vyxia exhaled slowly, but the breath trembled in her throat. She didn't need to see it to know exactly what had happened.

The Vessel

38

Clutching the coin, the pages, and the vials, Vyxia melted into the shadows. She followed the guards at a distance, her movements soundless, but her pulse pounded in her ears. The air grew colder with every step, and the runes lining the walls thrummed with power, alive and ancient.

She couldn't risk Hell's darkness now; Lilith ruled every inch of it. So, she reached inward to the other current, the one that didn't burn but shimmered, quiet and strange. It flowed through her like the first breath of dusk, softening her outline until light itself forgot where she stood. The wards' glow slid over her without catching. She didn't question it.

The guards pushed Sera into an old circular space, where walls of mirror-dark obsidian reflected the central brazier's furious light. The heat felt suffocating.

Vyxia slipped behind a carved pillar and forced her breath to slow, folding herself into the stillness. The stone scorched her skin, but she didn't move.

The guards dragged the princess forward and threw her at Lilith's feet. The sound of her body striking the stone echoed through Vyxia's bones. She pressed her palm to the pillar, grounding herself against the vibration.

"What is this place?" Sera demanded, her voice trembling.

Vyxia's throat tightened. Every instinct told her to run, but she stayed, compelled by the cold magnetism of Lilith's presence.

Lilith turned, her eyes molten gold. "You truly understand so little, child."

The queen's smile was slow, deliberate—a predator savoring the final moments before the kill.

"You thought this war, my desire for power, and even my tedious rivalry with your pathetic father was the endgame?" She laughed, brittle and sharp. "Oh, Sera. That was merely setting the stage. The true masterpiece...requires you." She glided closer, circling her daughter like a sculptor inspecting marble. "Have you ever wondered why you? Why the youngest heir? Why the perfect blend?"

Sera frowned.

"It's your essence, Daughter," she purred, trailing a finger down her cheek.

Vyxia flinched as if she'd been touched herself.

"That impossible fusion of celestial light and infernal fire. Michael's spark and my shadow. Cassia foolishly extinguished her light years ago." Lilith waved a hand, dismissive. "Useful as a tool. But flawed. Impure. But you, however, are fertile. Unsealed. Potent."

The words landed like stones in Vyxia's stomach.

"Potent for what?" Sera spat.

Lilith's smile widened, monstrous and radiant. "For creation. And not just succession, Sera. I don't want an heir. I want a vessel. You will birth my legacy. New creatures. Beings forged from your perfect paradox: loyal only to their queen mother. They will wield power enough to shatter Heaven's gates and remake Hell in my image." She gestured around the chamber. "This is the crucible. The armies above gather not just for war but to guard this moment. To anchor this ritual. To feed its awakening. The sires of all bloodlines are awaiting my command."

Horror rolled through Vyxia, cold and jagged. She could taste iron in the back of her throat. The heat from the brazier pressed against her face, but her body had gone numb.

"No..." Sera whispered, staggering back. "You've lost your mind..."

Lilith tilted her head, unbothered. "No, Daughter. I am on time. The tribunal sealed your womb when you fell, but the night they cannot erase is here. Now. The veil opens tonight, and I have waited centuries for this, this singular opening in the stars. But then you bonded with him. Like a foolish girl. If you are claimed, your womb is sealed to all but one." She stepped closer, her voice dropping to a hiss. "But I won't be denied again."

She snapped her fingers. From the shadows, more guards emerged, followed by several towering demons whose eyes glowed with molten gold—the sires.

Vyxia's breath hitched. The shimmer that cloaked her faltered for half a heartbeat, and she fought to steady it. The air trembled with the heat of their approach.

Not an heir. Not a weapon. The thought cut through her like glass—breeding stock.

The sires advanced, the circle flaring with light.

That was enough. Vyxia turned and fled, her feet finding the rhythm of her other power again. The shadows swallowed her whole, her form thinning into nothing. Behind her, the chamber burned with screams and firelight, and the wards along the corridor pulsed once as if realizing too late that something had passed unseen.

She didn't stop running until the air cooled and the sound of her own pulse drowned out everything else.

She had to reach Kael.

Lucifer was their only hope.

Kael's consciousness stirred, flickering like a candle struggling against a relentless wind. Sharp pain radiated through his body as he slumped against the cold, damp stone wall. Each breath was shallow, and the stagnant air carried a musk of mildew and despair.

His black-blue eyes fluttered open, adjusting to the dim glow. His vision swam at first, focusing on the dungeon's cold stones in increments. The walls, slick with moisture, seemed to swallow the faint torchlight, casting restless shadows. His wrists, rubbed raw by iron shackles, stung with each pulse of his heartbeat. Every muscle protested as he tried to shift, but the ache coursing through him felt insignificant compared to the defeating weight pressing down on his chest.

Across the cell, Eryon sat slumped against the opposite wall. His golden eyes were dim, unfocused. Yet they still held traces of that fierce resolve that defined him. His breathing was uneven, and his body was battered and bruised. The jagged scars on his back, where his wings had been severed, were a grim testament to his suffering, stark even in the dungeon's dim light.

Eryon stirred slightly, his voice hoarse. "How long do you think we've been down here?"

Kael exhaled slowly. The faint rasp of his breath was audible in the stillness. "Long enough," he muttered. He shifted against the wall, his eyes glinting as they focused on him. "You holding up?"

A dry, humorless laugh escaped his lips. "Holding up? That's generous," he replied bitterly. "I think death, at this point, feels less like a punishment and more like...relief."

Kael frowned, his jaw tightening. "I hear you."

His golden gaze flickered as he turned to meet Kael's eyes. "I've lost everything: my wings, my strength, my purpose. What's left to fight for?"

Kael straightened slightly, his fists clenching as a spark of defiance ignited in his chest. "But we still must fight. For those who still have something to lose. For everyone counting on us."

He held Kael's gaze for a long moment before looking away. "Maybe you're right," he muttered. "Or maybe we're just delaying the inevitable."

Silence hung heavy between them.

Kael let his head rest against the wall, his thoughts flickering between the faces of those he needed to protect and the aching reality of his current state. Eryon briefly closed his eyes, his expression a mixture of resignation and exhaustion.

A faint sound of soft laughter broke the quiet, echoing from the corridor outside. Both men tensed, and Kael's senses sharpened as the sound grew closer. It was followed by a low, coaxing voice that dripped with honeyed persuasion.

"Come now," a female voice purred. "Surely just one taste wouldn't hurt?"

Kael exchanged a wary glance with Eryon, a faint flicker of tension replacing their earlier despair.

Eryon straightened slightly, his golden eyes narrowing. "Who in the void is that?"

The laughter continued, accompanied by the faint clinking of glass. Then after a brief pause, the heavy iron door creaked open. A figure slipped inside, moving quickly and purposefully.

It was a young woman. Her violet eyes gleamed as she stepped forward, clutching a small pouch close to her chest. "Kael," she whispered, her tone laced with determination. "I've come to get you out."

Kael blinked, his black-blue eyes narrowing. "Who are you?" he rasped.

"I'm Vyxia! I *am* your contact!" she replied, kneeling beside him. Her movements were precise, and her voice was steady despite the urgency it carried. "You need to move quickly." She reached into her pouch and pulled out three small vials, their contents glowing with an unearthly brilliance. The liquid swirled like captured starlight, its purity unmistakable.

"These..." he said, his voice barely above a whisper. "These are Michael's essence." His gaze snapped to her. "Where did you get them?"

She briefly hesitated. "Sera found them," she said quickly. "They were hidden in Cassia's room. She sent me to bring them to you."

Realization crashed over him, and his jaw tightened. His eyes burned as he murmured, "The bonding ritual... It worked? She's back?"

"She is," she said, her violet eyes steady. "And she's counting on you."

"What happened? Where is Sera?" he demanded, strength returning to his voice.

Her face crumpled. "They...they took her. Right after she gave me the plan and the coin, the elite guards took her away. I followed them." Her voice dropped to a choked whisper. "It's not a trial. It's...it's a ritual."

He went still. "Ritual?"

"Lilith brought her to...near some ancient chamber," she said, her eyes wide. "She told Sera... Oh, Hail Lucifer, Kael... She doesn't want her as an heir. She called her a *vessel*. Said only Sera's blood, the perfect mix of angel and demon, was potent enough... She plans to use her to breed a new hybrid! Creatures loyal only to her, powerful enough to destroy Heaven!"

The air left Kael's lungs. Blood roared in his ears, louder than any demon's scream. Sera... A vessel...forced to...? Bile rose in his throat. He lunged toward Vyxia, grabbing her forearms. "Where?! Where is this chamber?!"

"Kael, listen!" she cried, pulling back slightly. "She mentioned the ritual needs powerful demons... Sires, she called them. Ancient ones. They're a part of it!"

"Then I'll kill them all!" he roared, shaking her.

"No! You can't!" Her voice gained desperate strength. "It's too guarded! The armies we saw marching? Lilith is using them to protect the ritual! But the sires... Kael, maybe only Lucifer has the true authority, the fundamental power over all demons! Maybe only he can compel them to stop! Waking him isn't just about stopping the war; it might be the only way to disrupt the ritual itself before..." She didn't finish the sentence.

She reached into her pouch again, this time pulling out a rolled parchment and a small intricately marked coin that was very familiar to him.

"The incantation is on these pages," she explained, handing them to him. "And the map! It shows the way to Lucifer's tomb. That's where you need to go."

Kael carefully unrolled the parchment, and his eyes scanned the jagged script and the map etched onto its surface. The lines twisted and curved, leading to a singular destination marked by an ancient sigil. He exhaled deeply, the weight of the task settling heavily on his shoulders.

"This has to work," he muttered, rolling the parchment back up and tucking it into his tattered jeans pocket.

Eryon leaned back against the wall, his golden eyes flickering. "You're not seriously planning to do this alone, are you?"

Kael uncorked the first vial and downed it in one gulp. The burn hit instantly—a rush of heat that tore through his veins and stitched together the fading seams of his strength. His breath shuddered out in a slow exhale, his eyes flashing with renewed focus.

"One for you," he said, pulling out another. He tossed it to Eryon, who caught it easily even though his expression was wary.

"You sure about this?" Eryon asked, turning the vial in his hand. The light refracted across his scarred knuckles, briefly catching the gold in his eyes.

"I am," he said firmly. "Drink it. And find Cassia. Get her out."

Eryon hesitated only a heartbeat before uncorking it and drinking. He grimaced and then rolled his shoulders as if shrugging off the ache of centuries. "Fine. But don't get yourself killed."

He offered the faintest hint of a smile.

As Eryon turned to go, Kael tucked the final vial into the frayed pocket of his jeans, the glass pressing cold against his thigh. A single reserve for what might come next, or if there was no coming back at all.

His fingers lingered there for a moment, feeling the steady thrum of the light through the thin fabric. **Then** placed his fingers around the parchment and the coin. The weight of both felt heavier than steel.

With the missions clear, the three prepared to part ways.

To Wake the Devil

39

The stench of the catacombs was a living thing, wrapping itself around Kael like a suffocating shroud. Every step he took stirred up ancient dust and a faint stench of death, mingling with the raw tang of his own blood and sweat.

His escape from the dungeons had not been messy but desperate. Vyxia had cleared a path, leaving slumped, drugged guards in her wake. In the fleeting seconds before they had parted ways, he had stripped one sleeping guard of its jacket, sparing no gratitude for the unconscious fiend. The jacket smelled of sulfur and ash, its texture worn and cracked, but it was sturdy, and that was what mattered.

The tunnels grew narrower as he descended further. The sigils carved into the walls seemed to ripple in the corner of his vision, their ancient inscriptions a reminder of just how deeply he'd ventured into forgotten history. The air itself felt alive, thick with a darkness that gnawed at the edges of his resolve. But he pressed on, his focus unyielding.

As he approached the final stretch of the passage, a low, guttural growl echoed ahead, reverberating through the stone. His steps slowed, his body tensing.

From the shadows, a bulky demon emerged, its golden eyes glowing like molten metal. The beast was grotesque. Its scaled skin glistened with a slick sheen, and its jagged claws scraped against the stone floor as it prowled forward.

"You're out of your depths, runt," the demon sneered. "You smell of desperation. It's…delicious."

Kael smirked. "And you smell like you lost a fight to a garbage heap," he said flatly. "So, let's skip the posturing."

The demon snarled and lunged, its massive form hurtling toward him with startling speed. He darted to the side, barely avoiding the swipe of its claws that carved deep gouges into the stone where he'd been standing. The tunnel's narrow confines worked to his advantage, hindering the demon's bulk.

Kael grabbed a loose rock from the floor and hurled it at the demon's head. The rock struck its temple, and the beast roared, staggering momentarily. He lunged, slamming his shoulder into the demon's midsection. His momentum drove them both into the wall.

It howled in fury, its claws lashing wildly, but Kael was already twisting out of its reach. His hands found a loose section of stone in the wall, jagged and heavy, and he yanked it free with a grunt. As the demon turned, its molten eyes burning with rage, he swung the rock with all his strength, smashing it into the side of its skull. The sickening crunch of bone echoed through the tunnel as it crumpled to the ground.

He stood over the fallen creature, his breaths coming in sharp, uneven bursts. He wiped a trickle of blood from his brow with the back of his hand and glanced at the makeshift weapon before tossing it aside. He didn't have time to dwell on the encounter. There would be more.

And there were.

As he pushed deeper into the labyrinth, another demon, smaller but faster, appeared, its leathery wings propelling it through the narrow passage with frightening agility. It hissed as it dove for him, its talons outstretched. He dropped low and rolled out of its path, and the creature's claws raked the air where his head had been. As it swooped back around for another pass, he turned, lashed out, and grabbed one of its wings midflight. He twisted it with a vicious snap, and it screeched as it spiraled to the ground. It writhed before going still.

By the time Kael reached the massive iron gate at the end of the passage, his knuckles were raw, and his muscles ached. But he'd made it.

The gate was a thing of nightmares. It was carved with intricate writhing figures that seemed almost alive, their etched forms shifted ever so slightly. The coin in his hand pulsed more, a steadiness that resonated with the dark energy permeating the chamber.

The final barrier between him and the fallen king.

Kael placed his hand on the cold iron, his fingers tracing the ancient carvings. His breath came measured as he prepared himself for what was to come. Fear was there, but he shoved it aside, focusing instead on the burning determination that drove him forward.

He began the incantation, his voice carrying through the catacombs like a ripple in a stagnant pool.

"By the power of blood spilled and fire's embrace, by the chains that bind the fallen star, I call upon thee, Lucifer, king of this forsaken place. Awaken from slumber, shatter death's dark bar, rise from the shadowed depths, reclaim your shadowed grace, and seize again the dominion that is yours afar!"

The gate trembled, the carvings glowing with an infernal light that bathed the chamber in an eerie glow. With a groan, the gate swung open, revealing the tomb within. Kael stepped forward, and the air grew heavier with each step, the stench of decay mingling with the oppressive presence of ancient power.

At the center of the chamber stood a sarcophagus, its surface carved with images of rebellion and fall. With an almost steady hand, he retrieved the smooth and heavy obsidian coin and slid it into the slot atop the sarcophagus.

For a heart-stopping moment, nothing happened.

The silence rushed back in, deeper and more absolute than before. Then a low hum vibrated not in the air but in the bones of the crypt itself. A sickly viridian light bled from the carved lines of the lid, casting the chamber in the color of drowned stars. With a funereal groan, stone screamed against stone as the massive lid slid aside.

Kael leaned forward, his own heart a frantic drum against his ribs, and peered into the chasm. He saw nothing. It was not darkness but a void, an abyss that consumed the torchlight and offered nothing in return.

Then two embers ignited in the depths.

They burned with a malevolent light, twin points of ancient rage studying him from the absolute black. A skeletal hand, wrapped in thin ancient flesh, shot out from the void and seized his throat. The grip was unbreakable, crushing the air from his lungs.

Lucifer's eyes locked onto his. The voice that spoke was not a voice at all but a rasp of grinding stone and forgotten eons. "Who are you?"

With a flick of his wrist, he hurled Kael across the crypt. Kael's body slammed into the far wall, the impact a sickening crack that echoed in the chamber.

A universe of pain bloomed where Kael's back had met the wall. He lay sprawled on the stone floor, the sickly viridian light of the sarcophagus swimming in his vision. Air was a foreign concept, a memory his screaming lungs could not quite grasp. He dragged a hand to his throat, the flesh hot and tender, and felt the deep impressions left by that inhuman grip.

From the stone bier, a figure rose.

It did not climb out. It unfolded, a silhouette of terrible grace emerging from the darkness within. Shadows clung to him like a royal mantle, and his eyes were pits of smoldering fire. He stood there, a monument of ancient power awakened into a world he did not know. His gaze swept the crypt with cold possession.

Kael coughed, a dry, rattling sound. The motion sent a fresh wave of agony through his ribs. "You are...welcome...asshole!"

Lucifer froze. The slow, regal turn of his head stopped. His fiery gaze left the dusty corners of his prison and fell upon the crumpled form on the floor. He tilted his head, a gesture of curiosity. "Kael?"

He managed to drag in a shuddering breath, the first one that felt like it reached his lungs. He lifted a trembling hand from the floor and gave a weak, sarcastic wave. "Yep. One and only." Another gasp punctuated the words. He used the wall to push himself into a sitting position, the effort making him wince.

The fire in Lucifer's eyes seemed to harden, a brief flicker of recognition. His expression was unreadable. "What is the meaning of this? How did you get here?"

"We don't have time." He used the wall to pull himself to his feet. He swayed, his entire body a throbbing complaint, but his eyes were locked on Lucifer's. "We need to move. Now. While you were sleeping, Lilith grabbed Michael's daughter Sera... My Sera. Right now, Lilith's starting a ritual. A breeding. She plans to use Sera as a vessel to birth new hybrids loyal only to her, using the sires to achieve this. It's happening now."

Lucifer's eyes narrowed further. "Sires? She dares...that kind of creation magic...using *that* bloodline?" His rage focused, intensifying. His gaze swept past Kael for a fraction of a second, a flicker of that more profound anguish visible. "*Breeding,*" he snarled. "Using sires... Lilith officially lost her mind." His eyes bore into Kael. "Lead the way, Fallen."

Genesis of Nightmares

40

Darkness wasn't just the absence of light in this chamber; it was a presence. Thick. Cloying. It seemed to absorb sound and breath itself. What little illumination existed bled from pulsating runes carved deep into the black volcanic stone walls, casting shifting, grotesque shadows that writhed like tormented souls. The heavy air was unnaturally cold with the metallic tang of old blood and the sharp, sterile scent of arcane preparation.

Sera stood there, shivering not entirely from the cold but from the violation. Rough unseen hands had stripped her bare moments after the elite guards had dragged her here, leaving her exposed in the heart of this nightmare. Her mind, still reeling from the flood of returning memories, warred against the lingering tendrils of the darkness Lilith had fostered within her.

Kael was alive. He'd come for her. He'd bonded with her. That knowledge was a defiant spark against the suffocating despair. But now...now this.

Two robed and hooded attendants whose faces remained hidden in shadows approached. Their touch was cold and impersonal as they anointed her skin with pungent oils that seemed to leech away warmth.

She flinched, trying to pull away. "Get away from me!"

"Hold her still." Lilith stepped from the deeper shadows near the back of the vast chamber. She was magnificent in obsidian armor that seemed to drink the faint light, her golden eyes burning with triumph. "Fighting is useless, Daughter. Accept your purpose. Your true destiny."

"This isn't destiny," she spat, renewing her struggles as the attendants grasped her arms firmer. "It's perversion!"

Lilith merely smiled, a chilling curve of her lips. "I'm ambitious, perhaps. What I create through you will ensure my reign is absolute. Eternal." She gestured toward the center of the room, where an altar dominated the space.

The altar had been crafted from the same light-absorbing black stone as the walls. Its shape was disturbingly raised with stirrup-like supports at one end—horrifyingly reminiscent of a gynecological examination chair.

Just as the reality of the altar truly sank in, a choked gasp echoed from the chamber's entrance. More guards entered, dragging a figure between them.

Sera's head snapped up, her breath catching in her throat. "Cassia!"

Her sister was barely recognizable. Her face was bruised and swollen, cuts crisscrossing her arms, and her simple black dress had been torn and stained dark with dried blood. She was chained, the infernal iron suppressing her own powers, but her brown eyes, when they met Sera's, blazed with undiluted fury and despair.

"I insist you attend," Lilith purred, watching the guards chain Cassia to a pillar near the altar with cruel amusement. "A family affair. Wouldn't you agree, my dutiful elder child?"

"You are a monster," Cassia spat, though her voice was weak.

"I am a queen." She turned her attention back to Sera. "And soon, through my youngest, the mother of a new dynasty." She clapped her hands once, the sound sharp and final. "Bring forth the sires."

The air grew even heavier, charged with ancient power. From three shadowed archways, figures emerged, their presence warping the very air around them. They were immense, primal, and radiating distinct forms of dark energy.

One was massive, built of cracked obsidian and barely contained magma. Its horns swept back from a brutish skull. It was the essence of pure demonic force, the sire of demons.

Another moved with unnatural grace, was impossibly pale, and had eyes like burning coals and elongated fingers tipped with claws that dripped shadows. The sire of vampires exuded an aura of chilling hunger and hypnotic control.

The third was harder to look at directly, seemingly woven from shadows and whispers. Runes shifted across its ephemeral form, and the air around it wafted the scent of forbidden magic and ritualistic decay. The sire of witches was the font from which dark covens drew their power.

They were all ancient beings of immense power now bound to Lilith's will for this single blasphemous purpose. They took their positions around the obsidian altar, their collective gazes falling upon Sera with predatory hunger.

Sera fought against the guards holding her, kicking and twisting. "No! Get away from me! Kael is going to kill you!"

"He cannot help you now," Lilith said softly and almost gently, which was somehow worse. "No one can."

The guards overpowered her weakened state. They dragged her kicking and screaming form toward the altar and forced her onto the cold stone. Chains, similar to Cassia's but pulsing with a binding energy designed to hold her essence, snaked out from the altar and locked around her wrists and ankles, spreading her limbs and leaving her utterly exposed.

Tears of rage and terror streamed down her face as she stared up at the oppressive ceiling, the faces of the sires swimming in her vision. Cassia screamed her name from the pillar, her voice raw with helpless fury.

Lilith approached the altar with cold satisfaction. "A new beginning, Daughter," she whispered. She then turned and nodded to the sire of demons.

The hulking figure stepped forward, its magma-veined body radiating intense heat. Its shadow fell over Sera's naked, trembling form. It dragged one searing palm over her exposed body, the touch both burning and violating. Its heavy hand stopped and kneaded one of her breasts.

She bucked against the chains, arching her back. "Get your filthy hands off me!"

The sire gave her a terrifying smile, fangs protruding from its maw. "It will be over soon," it rumbled, the sound like shifting rocks deep underground. "Don't fret…"

It asserted itself over her, climbing onto the obsidian altar and positioning its massive form above her sprawled, naked body. She squeezed her eyes shut, a single sob escaping her lips.

The ritual chamber's immense obsidian doors didn't just open. They exploded. Ripped from their ancient hinges in a shower of razor-sharp fragments and arcane dust.

Two figures stood silhouetted against the chaotic energy spilling in from the corridor.

"LILITH!" Lucifer's voice was a shockwave, a physical force that slammed into the chamber. It rattled the very stones and made the assembled demons, even the ancient sires, flinch. His rage was palpable, the fury of a betrayed king.

Beside him, Kael's presence was a different kind of storm. Colder, sharper, and utterly focused. His eyes flared with the silvered light of his restored angelic essence. He took in the scene for a fraction of a second—Lilith's triumphant smirk, Cassia chained and battered form, the altar, the sires, and Sera... Sera.

Naked. Restrained. Helpless beneath the grotesque form of a sire leaning over her, its palm on her breast.

Horror, cold and absolute, bypassed any thoughts.

He lunged toward the nearest elite guard who stood frozen by the door and ripped a barbed spear from its grasp. With a surge of power, he pivoted. His muscles propelled the spear across the chamber with impossible speed and accuracy. It wasn't just a throw. It was a delivered sentence.

The spear struck the demon sire mid-torso, punching through its thick hide and muscles with a sickening force. The impact lifted the massive creature off the altar. Its roar of agony was cut short as the spear's momentum carried it backward and pinned its arm and torso against a massive obsidian pillar, near where Cassia was chained. Black ichor sprayed and splattered the stone and Cassia herself, who could only stare in wide-eyed shock.

The chamber erupted into chaos.

"DETAIN THEM!" Lilith shrieked, her regal facade cracking into pure malice.

Ignoring the lesser demons scrambling to attack, Lucifer surged forward like a dark meteor, wings of shadows and flames carving a direct path toward Lilith. Hate radiated from him, the ancient fury unleashed.

Simultaneously, Kael moved toward his target: Sera. He launched toward the altar, desperation his only weapon against the tide of demons pouring forward to obey Lilith's command. He fought like the commander he once was, using the severed chains still binding his wrists like flails and shattering demonic bones and spilling ichor with every brutal impact. A whirlwind of deadly grace. He felt nothing but the driving need to reach her, every demon just another obstacle between him and her safety.

"KAEL!" Sera screamed, the sound raw and desperate and filled with terror and frantic hope. She thrashed against her restraints, rattling the chains futilely.

He heard her. Through the snarling demons and clashing infernal powers, he heard her. His head snapped up, his gaze finding hers across the chaos. Seeing the recognition in her eyes, the life returned to them, and it fueled him with a strength beyond reckoning. He roared and cleaved through two more guards, his path clearing.

Yet white-hot agony erupted from his back, punching straight through his gut.

He gasped, a strangled sound, as impossibly long, razor-sharp talons burst through his abdomen, slick with celestial-tinged blood. The impact drove him to his knees, collapsing the world around him into red searing agony. Through the haze, he could still see Sera—fighting, screaming, and refusing to yield.

Behind him, Lilith pressed close. Her body molded against his back, her breath a fever of decay against his ear. "Watch, Fallen One," she whispered, her tone almost tender. "Watch everything you care for turn into my masterpiece. Watch her break. And when she does, I will grant you the mercy of death."

The talons twisted once, deeper. He choked, blood bubbling up in his throat. His body trembled, but his eyes stayed open, fixed forward. He could no longer hear Sera clearly, only muffled echoes drowned beneath the roar of his pulse.

A broken laugh tore through his throat, raw and wet. "Mercy?" he rasped. "From you? Kindly fuck off."

Lilith stilled behind him, her breath faltering for half a second, and that was enough.

He drew on what remained of himself: every fragment of Michael's light in his veins, every ounce of rage, and every wound that had ever shaped him. Pain burned white-hot through his nerves. He could feel the last vial pressing against his thigh in his jeans pocket, unreachable. It didn't matter. He would not die begging.

He opened himself to the fire, and his wings detonated out of his back.

They did not unfurl. They exploded with power divine and infernal, searing in its violence. Light and shadow collided with the force of a dying star. The shockwave split the stone floor and ripped the air apart.

One heartbeat, she was pressed against his back, and the next, she was nothing. The edges of his wings sliced through her body like blades of molten glass, severing her into pieces. Her scream fractured into a thousand discordant tones before it was silenced completely. Her talons tore free from her hands, still buried deep in his chest, as her form disintegrated into burning cinders.

The chamber convulsed. Fire and smoke spiraled outward, the runes along the walls flaring before they burst. The sires reeled back, howling as the wave of primordial force flung them into the dark.

Kael fell forward and to his side, his hands slipping over the broken talons protruding from his sternum. His wings, once radiant, flickered and crumbled into dust, and the wound blazed with light that no longer belonged to any realm.

He could barely breathe. Every sound dulled to a hollow pulse. But he still saw her—Sera—her mouth opening and closing as if she was screaming in agony.

She was alive, and that would have to be enough.

The world tilted, and the darkness took him whole.

Where Light Ends

41

Vyxia was panting with exhaustion as she burst into the ritual chamber. She no longer cared who might catch her. The tremor began beneath her skin rather than in the stone—a vibration that crawled through her bones and whispered the warlock's success before the air itself screamed.

The high arched windows of the ritual chamber detonated inward. Shards of black glass fell like razors, their edges catching what little light still lived in the room. Vyxia flinched, one hand rising too late, as fragments kissed her cheeks and hair, cutting cold lines that stung only after she felt the warmth of her blood. The impact sent her to her knees. Above, the ceiling howled, and the world split in two.

Orin had kept his word. The impossible gate was open.

The sky beyond the broken arches burned white, bleeding light that wasn't light at all but essence—pure and cruel and perfect. Heaven had come.

And angels did not descend; they fell.

Wings blazed through the rift, the colors of war and holiness—silver, molten gold, and bone white. Their descent was thunder and wind, their feathers razors of illumination that cut through shadows and flesh alike. The chamber filled with the sound of divinity weaponized, every beat a wound in the air.

Vyxia pressed herself against the cold wall, her pulse thrumming with terror. The smell of burning filled her lungs. She saw Kael's body collapse beside the altar, blood and grace leaking into the stones. Sera still writhed upon that strange stone structure, thrashing against her restraints. Her voice was drowned by the roar of wing and fire. Cassia hung chained beside her, limp and battered and a pale echo of rebellion.

Lucifer was a column of darkness veined with molten light, the black sun at the heart of creation, and opposite him, Michael was radiant and sharpened to the point of annihilation. Their gazes met, and the world around them seemed to still, caught between two versions of judgment. The air crystallized. Then shattered.

Light and shadow collided. Lucifer's hellfire roared, swallowing the vampire sire whole. Michael's blade sang a single unbearable note as it cleaved the witch sire's spectral body into ash. Smoke rolled through the chamber, as thick as memory and tasting of iron and endings. The shockwave struck Vyxia full in the chest, slamming her back against the wall. For a heartbeat, she couldn't breathe.

Remiel broke through the chaos, his armor scorched and gleaming. He cut Cassia's chains with precise, star-bright strikes. Eryon darted to the altar, wrapping Sera in a glamour of shadows and fractured light and shielding her nakedness from the dying torches.

Vyxia turned her gaze toward the center of the ruin. Lucifer stood amid the wreckage, the flames licking his boots. Shadows clung to him like living things until, one by one, they recoiled and peeled away as if scorched by the very light they served. Beneath them was not darkness but brilliance.

His wings unfurled—vast, feathered, and immaculate. The chamber drowned in his radiance. Every torch, every ember, bent low and died before that light. The glow was agony and salvation woven together, and Vyxia's breath nearly collapsed from the sight.

When he spoke, the sound didn't break the air; it remade it. A single word, ancient and absolute: "SHAEL'KHAR."

The command to kneel vibrated through her marrow. The demons convulsed, their weapons falling from nerveless fingers, as they collapsed into a wave of submission. Even the stones beneath her boots seemed to exhale as if Hell itself bowed to him.

Only the celestials and the fallen remained standing, their faces taut with awe and uncertainty and their blades trembling in the glow.

And Vyxia, still pressed to the wall, trembled for a different reason. Her breath hitched, her throat closing with the sudden ache of recognition she could not show yet. The light pouring from him sang in her blood, the same rhythm that lived in her heartbeat.

It was in this defining silence that Sera, freed and hastily glamoured by Eryon, moved. Her focus locked onto Kael's stillness and Jareth's protective stance over him. Her world narrowed.

She tried to stand, tried to rush to him, but her legs gave way, too weak from the draining fear. She awkwardly tumbled onto the cold stone below. A choked sob ripped from her throat, echoing unnervingly in the now-quiet chamber. Her movements were frantic, clumsy.

"Kael… Oh heavens, Kael… No, no, no, please…" She collapsed beside his prone form. Her trembling hands reached for him, pushing uselessly at his heavy shoulder. Trying to turn him over.

Jareth shifted slightly, allowing her access but keeping his blade ready. His own face was a mask of grief.

Finally, she managed to gently roll him partially onto his side, enough to slide onto the floor beneath him and lift his head onto her lap. His eyes were closed, and his dark lashes stood out starkly against his unnaturally pale skin, streaked with blood and grime. His beautiful, dangerous face was utterly slack, peaceful in a way that screamed of finality. A terrifying stillness settled over his features.

"No…" The word was a breath, a denial. She hugged his head to her chest, rocking slightly. Her tears fell onto his unresponsive face. Her lips pressed frantic, desperate kisses against his forehead, his cheekbones, and his still mouth. "Kael, please… O-open your eyes… Look at m-me…"

Her hand moved down his chest, seeking a heartbeat—a sign of life, anything. Instead, her fingers brushed against the ragged, horrifying tear in his abdomen where Lilith's talons had ripped through him. The torn leather of the borrowed jacket was stiff with drying blood, and beneath it, talons were still protruding from an impossibly deep wound.

A fresh wave of agonizing grief crashed over her. A raw wail tore from her throat, echoing in the vast, silent chamber.

She pulled him closer, cradling him tight and rocking him back and forth. She buried her face in his blood-matted hair. "Don't leave me," she choked between racking sobs. "Please, Kael. Please don't leave me… I just got you back… I love you… Don't leave me…"

A heavy hand gently settled on her shoulder. She flinched, looking up through her blurred vision to see Jareth kneeling beside her.

His own expression was etched with deep pain. "Sera," he said, his voice rough, "we need to—"

"NO!" She shrugged his hand off, turning back to Kael. "Leave me alone! Leave us alone! Go away!" Her grief was a raw, jagged thing, leaving no space for anything but the devastating reality of Kael lying still and broken in her arms.

"Sera?" a soft voice said.

It startled her. She looked up through her tears and saw Cassia kneeling beside her with Remiel hovering protectively nearby. Cassia's face remained pale and bruised, and her eyes were shadowed with trauma, but a flicker of desperate calculation ignited within them.

"There is one thing we can try," Cassia said, her voice low but urgent.

Sera barely registered the words, her focus locked on Kael's lifeless form.

Cassia gently grasped her shoulder. "Sera, listen. He bound himself to you, but he wanted to leave you the choice… The choice to complete it. To finish the binding."

Her head snapped up, her tear-filled eyes wide with confusion. Then desperate hope. She didn't need theory. She needed action. "What do I do?" she demanded, her voice raw.

"Your blood." Cassia gestured toward Kael's still lips. "You transfer a piece of your life force…your essence…through the bond he already forged."

She didn't think twice. If he was damned for finding her, then she would be damned for saving him.

Her eyes scanned the debris-strewn floor. Nearby lay a large, sharp shard of obsidian-like glass from the shattered windows. She snatched it up, ignoring the edge biting into her palm. Without hesitation, she drew the jagged edge across her palm. Crimson droplets fell onto his lips.

With a shuddering breath, she lowered her lips to his, a kiss stained with blood and tears. "I love you."

"Sera, that's enough!" Cassia grabbed her sister's arm, pulling the bleeding palm away.

Sera ignored the sting. She leaned down, sobbing and cradling his head in her lap as if sheer force of will could undo the damage. Forehead pressed against his, she closed her eyes and poured everything—her will, her love, her very essence—into a connection she prayed hadn't already severed.

Memories flooded the dark. Their meadow. Firelight. The impossible intimacy of skin against skin. She clung to the memory of Limbo, to the terror, and to the overwhelming, singular relief of his strength pulling her back from the abyss.

She held her breath, waiting and praying for a flicker of life.

Nothing.

Aftershock
42

The oppressive silence of the Infernal Palace pressed in, a stark contrast to the ritual chamber. Time felt warped: viscous, half dreamed.

Following Lucifer's terse command and after a reluctant nod from Lucifer himself, Jareth had carefully moved Kael from the blood-soaked floor to the shadowed sanctuary of Sera's royal chambers. Kael was too broken for travel, too steeped in celestial backlash. His body, too sacred and too ruined, had become a paradox the realms couldn't touch.

Now, he lay submerged in a coma-like stasis, adrift in the vast bed that dominated her chambers. It was a monstrous thing draped in black silk that swallowed the flickering hellfire light bleeding from the nearby sconces.

His wounds had been cleansed, and his body had been wrapped in crude but effective bandages. The white cloth glared against his pale skin. And still, the bond between them pulsed: frail, tattered, and not broken.

Sera had dismissed everyone. She had washed him herself, reverent and trembling. Her hands had moved with the precision of ritual and grief, not with hope. She had long ceased entertaining such fragile illusions. No, this was mourning, not mending.

And after, she had crawled beneath the sheets like a ghost returning to its haunting. She lay curled against him now, her forehead pressed to his warm shoulder. His forearm held fast in her hands as if she could anchor him to her by touch alone. She watched the slow rise of his chest, counted it, and committed it to memory. Every breath was a rebellion. Every moment was theft against inevitability.

The knot in her stomach had formed into an emotion beyond fear: resignation. Exhaustion pulled at her bones like a tide she no longer had the will to resist. Still, she didn't sleep so much as she descended, drifting into a twilight of half thoughts and old pain. Her grip on him didn't loosen, even in those dreams.

She already knew what this was. She'd felt it the moment her shadows had stilled and the moment the silence had settled like dust. They were coming. The tribunal didn't need to announce itself; they never had. Their decisions moved faster than the law, swifter than mercy. And she had committed her crime with open eyes, preserved what was meant to be surrendered. Again.

The air shifted. A quiet displacement. A pressure drop that sucked the warmth from the room. Her shadows lifted, tense and wary, and coiled at the edges of the bed. Then came the quiet footsteps, synchronized. No knock. No preamble. Just the faint rustle of tribunal silks and sanctified breath. They didn't speak.

Sera opened her eyes, her cheek still resting against Kael's shoulder, and for a moment, she didn't move. She didn't speak. There was a stillness to the room that felt too heavy to disturb.

The flickering light caught the edges of Kael's body, casting him in soft shadows. A figure carved from memory and blood lying too still.

Her fingers curled around his wrist, feeling for the pulse she already knew was there.

The bond mark at her throat flared. It wasn't pain but a flicker, a flutter, as if something inside him had stirred, reaching through the darkness.

She closed her eyes. "I don't know if you can hear me," she whispered, "but something in me hopes you do."

Her thumb traced the line of his wrist, slow and reverent.

"You weren't here long. Not really. We barely had anything. A handful of moments. A few stolen breaths." Her voice caught, but she breathed through it. "But in that time, you made me feel more alive than anything in the last hundred years. Maybe more than I ever did." She shifted closer, resting her forehead against his temple. "I forgive you," she whispered, her fingers tracing the bond mark at her throat. "For all of it."

The mark at her throat flickered again, fainter this time.

"I now understand why I saw a gravestone in the meadow. It was not there when we first arrived, but it was never gone after you did not come back. Did that mean this was our fate all along, a grave? If there's something after this, if the tribunal kills me, then maybe, wherever we go next, I'll find you. Maybe we'll get it right somewhere else."

Her lips brushed his jaw, the lightest touch.

She pulled back slowly, her hand lingering on his chest. "Thank you," she said, her voice barely audible. "For making me feel like I was more than just a monster."

She rose without ceremony. Smoothed her dress and faced the tribunal guards waiting just beyond the threshold.

"I'm ready," she said, and then she walked out, the mark on her throat still warm with the last of him.

The tribunal's summons never spoke aloud; they arrived like death.

The guards flanking her said nothing, but their presence was solemn and final, etched in divine steel and ancient oaths. Light shivered off their armor. Footsteps fell in rhythmic absolution.

Sera walked across the polished stone, and each step felt like trespassing on her own grave. But she didn't resist. She only wished she'd held him a little longer.

The scent of him, salt and ash and light, still clung to her fingers. Her palms remembered the shape of his jaw. Her lips ached to press a kiss to his wrist, to the place where his pulse had faltered.

That had been the end. Her choice. Her tether.

Again, she had saved someone she was meant to let go. The world around her blurred, but her mind was a cathedral of memories collapsing inward. She remembered not as thoughts but as sensations: a breath caught in her throat, cold wind over the cliffs, the sound of Cassia's screams, wings torn from the sky, a woman's body cradled in famine-wasted arms. Her hands shook over a meal conjured from defiance.

The sky had never welcomed her after that. And then Kael. She hadn't fallen in love; she'd awakened into it: violent, helpless. She remembered the kiss outside of The Serpent's Kiss, the hunger in her bones. The tribunal didn't need to know the details. She was already guilty.

Sera continued forward, her eyes intense yet dry. She was willing to lose everything—her name, her wings, her legacy—because she loved. And she refused to pretend otherwise.

The hall ahead grew brighter, a searing, accusatory glow. The monumental doors, carved from the very fabric of judgment, pulsed with an inner light, and the guards ceased their march.

Sera did not hesitate. She continued walking.

The doors swung open. There was only the hush of finality: a silence so vast and profound that it resonated like a mournful bell deep within her bones. She stepped into the chamber of the Celestial Tribunal, and the world collapsed, narrowing to a piercing tableau of light, shadow, and unyielding judgment.

The hall itself was impossibly high, a cavernous space sculpted not from mere stone but from the very essence of memory and consequence. The ceiling soared beyond the veils of realms, constellations flickering in and out of existence like forgotten stars. The floor beneath her bare feet glowed faintly, etched with ancient runes and a grim scripture of every soul the tribunal had ever unmade.

And at the far end, elevated above all, were the six.

Most mortals believed in a single god—a merciful omniscient being watching from above. One who answered prayers. But there was no god. No divine creator to hold the world together.

There were only the six who were the Celestial Tribunal, the ones who passed judgment. Two from Heaven. Two from Hell. Two from Limbo.

Michael was garbed in white so pristine it seared the eyes, a purity both glaring and terrible. His mighty wings folded with a surgeon's precision. The Blade of Mercy, a silent promise of swiftness, lay across his knees.

Malakar was cloaked in the charcoal hues of scripture, his hands eternally ink stained from the endless transcription of judgment. His quill, a slender instrument of cosmic fate, was already in motion.

Lucifer was in his black and bloodred robes, which were curled around his shadowed throne like contained wildfire. A ring of lightless gold encircled one horned brow. He watched her with an unsettling quiet amusement. Or perhaps profound sorrow. With him, it was always both, an exquisite torture.

Calithra was veiled in the shifting mists of moonlight, her throne wreathed in shadows that curled like living, grasping vines. Her face was half concealed, her gaze a burning and unblinking intensity.

The Infernal Sire, a male figure, was crowned in jagged antlers carved from scorched bones. His skin shimmered like living embers. His throne also seemed to breathe, a colossal beast half alive.

The Gray Intermediary, the grand keeper, was a form carved from dusk itself. Its eyes were ever pouring shapes of hourglasses. Robed in ash, he belonged to no single realm, yet every realm bowed when his hushed voice chose to speak.

Beneath them, in tiered rings of unlit sconces, stood the watchers, a multitude of silent sentinels. And there, among them, stood Remiel. He was motionless, his arms folded tight across his chest and his jaw clenched. His eyes burned with a banked fury. And when her gaze found his, a tired and soft yet genuine smile touched her lips. He did not return the smile, but the storm contained in his stillness screamed, a silent roar directed at the looming dais.

Michael rose, a pillar of incandescent light. "Seraphine," he said, his voice resonating with callous authority. "Former watcher of passage. Cast from Heaven for treason. Once exiled and now returned. You stand accused of: the theft of tribunal-sealed essence. The preservation of a condemned soul. The interference in a divine execution. The invocation of forbidden blood rites. The awakening of preordained tethering against cosmic will. And above all, the deliberate defiance of celestial law."

Each charge sounded sharp and lethal. But she remained unmoved. "I have no defense," she said calmly.

Remiel's fists clenched tighter, his knuckles turning white.

Michael lifted his hand, the Blade of Mercy held steady. A chilling finality settled in his eyes, the look of a being who had weighed all outcomes and found this one necessary. But Calithra rose, a quiet surge of authority flowing across the chamber. Next, Malakar stood, his quill frozen in place. And Lucifer, the Infernal Sire, and the Gray Intermediary followed.

And at last, Michael's blade lowered, its pristine tip pointing earthward. The movement was stiff, almost begrudging. The subtle tightening of his jaw betrayed a silent, simmering fury. It nearly looked like a voting of sorts.

Calithra stepped forward, her veiled form drifting with an otherworldly grace. Her veil itself began to unravel, a single thread detaching from the cosmos and dissolving into nothingness. She spoke not to Sera but to all present. "Let it be recorded: By unanimous accord of this tribunal, all charges against Seraphine are dissolved."

Gasps flickered through the assembly of watchers. Even Remiel exhaled sharply. Sera blinked, unable to understand. She looked at Michael, her eyes asking for clarity, but he still avoided her gaze, his attention fixed on a distant point and his expression a mask of cold neutrality.

But it was the first time in what felt like eons that he looked like a father, not a judge.

Calithra's voice gained a sorrowful resonance. "The soul she preserved, Kael, bled himself into the seal. It was he who prevented a possible collapse of the realms. He who sacrificed light, tether, and self."

Lucifer leaned back in his throne, his long, elegant fingers tapping beneath his chin.

"She defied us." Her gaze swept over the hushed chamber. "But not to undermine order. To save it." She looked down at Sera, her gaze softening. "You are absolved. Entirely."

Sera swayed, her body heavy and lightheaded. It wasn't possible. It wasn't real. She had braced for flames. For chains. For the finality of death.

Remiel's jaw unclenched, the tension draining from his face. His arms dropped to his sides, and for the first time since her arrival, the storm in his eyes subsided, leaving only a tender relief.

"And Kael?" she whispered, the name a fragile prayer.

Calithra's gaze dimmed, a shared grief that spanned worlds. "I am afraid he will remain in stasis—in Limbo—until we understand what he has become. Until we know how to restore him. But you must remain in the mortal realm."

Her eyes met her father's, a silent plea passing between them. For a moment, just one fragile moment, she saw the man he had once been: before the sacred sword, before Heaven, and before the doctrine. He only offered a slow, almost imperceptible shake of his head, a silent warning that to push for more, to defy this fragile verdict, would be unwise. The look was not one of compassion but of brutal pragmatism.

She lowered her head, feeling the bitter sting of defeat. "So be it," she uttered.

And the silence that followed was not judgment but the resonant echo of rulers who had, for once, chosen to let go.

A Reluctant Peace

43

The grand hall of the Infernal Palace, once echoing with the clamor of battle, now held a tense, fragile silence. The air, still heavy with the stench of blood and smoke after two days, crackled with an unspoken tension that hung heavier than the shadows clinging to the basalt walls and the flickering torchlights casting long dancing shadows across the scarred stone. Gargoyles perched on high ledges, their granite eyes gleaming with predatory hunger.

At the head of the long black marble table, still scarred and chipped from the recent conflict, stood Michael and Lucifer.

Michael appeared restored, his celestial armor immaculate once more and his mighty wings neatly furled behind him. His expression remained a mask of grim determination, his gaze unwavering. The lines around his mouth were deeper now. The weight of too many battles—internal and otherwise—etched across his brow.

Lucifer, on the other hand, had shed the raw fury of his awakening for a mantle of dark regality. His form has been dressed in robes woven from shadows or impeccably tailored infernal finery, and his presence was an undeniable storm of controlled ancient power. His eyes still burned with infernal fire but now held sharp calculations alongside the embers.

Behind Michael stood Remiel, his silver wings folded smoothly. His armor was clean and polished, and his golden eyes were fixed on Lucifer with wary observation. Beside him, Jareth's usual playful energy was notably absent, replaced by a somber gravity. His golden wings, no longer ruffled or stained, were held with a composed stillness.

Across the long obsidian table, Sera stood, her posture taut and composed. She wore an elegant gown of deep emerald silk that clung to her form. Her hair was pulled back from her face, accentuating her pale skin and the hollowness beneath her eyes. The battle's grime had long since been scrubbed away, but exhaustion lingered in her bones. She said nothing, only watched.

Beside her stood Cassia, her dark eyes sharp beneath the angles of her face. She was no longer simply the exiled warrior but a figure of cold, sharpened resolve. She wore black deliberately and straightforwardly. A mark of mourning or rebellion, none could say. Her presence was a quiet threat.

"Brother," Michael said, his voice firm and echoing. "Let us end this conflict. Let us forge a pact of nonaggression. A promise of peace."

Lucifer sat down and leaned back in his throne, one boot hooked over the other knee. His expression was unreadable but coiled with restrained mockery. "Peace?" he echoed, his voice a velvet snarl. "After millennia of blood and betrayal? After we were cast down and hunted like beasts?"

Sera watched them, her body a statue of exhaustion. The words, distant and meaningless, washed over her like a conversation overheard in a dream.

Peace. The word was a bitter joke. What peace could there be in a world without Kael? Her gaze drifted to the space beside her, a void more present and painful than any celestial being in this room. He should be standing there. His absence was a roar that drowned out their hollow negotiations.

"There has been enough suffering," Michael said, his tone unflinching. "It is time to lay down our arms and begin something else. Tolerance, if not trust."

Tolerance. Her hands clenched into fists at her sides, her nails biting into her palms. Her father spoke of tolerance after condemning his own daughter, after watching Kael sacrifice himself to fix a mess of his own making. The hypocrisy was a sour taste at the back of her throat. She wanted to scream. She wanted to burn it all down. But instead, she stood silent, her rage simmering in her chest.

Lucifer's gaze swept the room, lingering on her. She met his eyes with a kind of tired defiance. He let the silence stretch...and then sighed deeply.

"Very well," he said. "Let us see if your 'tolerance' can endure."

He extended a bare clawed hand across the table, stained from centuries of war. Michael hesitated for only a breath. He then stepped forward and clasped it. A collective exhale swept the chamber, subtle but real.

Sera felt nothing. The historic pact, the joining of hands between Heaven and Hell, was just a joke. It changed nothing about the chasm in her soul. She could still feel the faint phantom throb of the bond mark on her neck, a constant reminder. That was the only pact that had ever mattered.

The beginning of the end.

"I would like to say one more thing," Lucifer said, his voice carrying through the vast hall. "Before we continue, I have to pay my respects to one woman here." He paused, his gaze sweeping over the angels at the table before shifting to the room's periphery. His words drew confused glances from both the celestial delegation and the lesser demons, as well as from the other attendants who lingered nervously in the shadows near the back pillars. "One who always kept hope of my return, even in Hell's deepest shadows. One who made everything possible and impossible happen to ensure this moment... To ensure I could be here right now."

The room was utterly silent now, all eyes fixed on the king of Hell. Michael looked perplexed. Cassia and Sera exchanged uncertain glances.

Lucifer straightened from the table, his presence seeming to expand. He turned his gaze not toward the prominent figures in the room but toward his periphery, where the lesser beings nervously lingered in the shadows near the back pillars. His expression, unreadable moments before, softened. He stood and took several deliberate strides across the obsidian floor, his darkness swirling.

He stopped before a massive basalt pillar and reached into the deep shadows clinging to its base. Gently but with undeniable command, he drew a slight figure forward into the flickering torchlight.

Vyxia.

The unassuming servant woman. Her violet eyes were wide, looking startled and perhaps slightly overwhelmed by the sudden attention.

Lucifer placed a hand lightly on her shoulder and turned her to face the stunned assembly. His voice resonated with quiet power. "I would like you all"—his gaze swept from Michael to Sera and Cassia—"to get familiar with Vyxia Morningstar. My daughter."

The words dropped into the charged silence like stones into a deep well.

A collective gasp rippled through the hall. Michael and Remiel exchanged frankly bewildered glances. Cassia smirked. Sera's jaw dropped, her eyes wide with utter shock as she stared at Vyxia. Her steadfast servant...? Lucifer's daughter?

As Vyxia slightly stepped back from Lucifer, she risked a glance across the room, catching Sera's stunned gaze. A sheepish, almost apologetic smile flickered across her lips, a silent acknowledgment of the profound secret she had guarded so well.

And for Sera, everything clicked into place with dizzying clarity. Vyxia's unwavering loyalty. Her quiet competence. Her fierce, almost reckless determination to help her, even risking herself to free Kael and to retrieve the incantation from the archives... It all made a startling sense.

She wasn't just a servant; she was trying to bring her father back.

Lucifer cast a brief unreadable glance back toward the main table, acknowledging the stunned silence without directly addressing the revelation. His expression settled back into one of regal authority as he returned to his seat. "The initial agreement stands," he said, his gaze sharpening, "but the details remain. This pact is but the first step. There is much to discuss, much to negotiate, and much to rebuild."

A tense silence settled over the hall once more, now colored by the unexpected revelation.

"The fallen," Lucifer continued, "will be allowed to choose their allegiance. Those who wish to return to Heaven will be welcomed back, their past transgressions forgiven."

Michael's brow furrowed, a flicker of disapproval crossing his face. "And those who choose to remain in Hell?" he asked, his voice carefully neutral.

"They will be granted a place in my court. They will be treated with respect and honor, their powers and abilities recognized and utilized."

He nodded slowly.

A fair offer. Sera thought of the fallen angels she'd seen in Hell's dungeons: the broken, the damned. This pact wouldn't erase their scars. It wouldn't mend their wings. It was a political solution to a spiritual wound, and its futility made her feel weary.

"And the hybrids?" Remiel asked, his voice laced with concern and his gaze flicking toward Cassia and Sera.

Lucifer and Michael met his gaze directly.

"They should be free to choose their own destiny, don't you think?" Michael said. "They should be welcomed in both Heaven and Hell, their heritage acknowledged and respected from now on."

Her destiny. The word felt like a chain. Her destiny had been to fall, to hunger, and to lose everything. Now, they offered her a choice as if it was a gift, as if it could undo centuries of pain.

She looked at Cassia, who stood stoic and unreadable, and then back at her father. She didn't want their acceptance. She didn't want their new world. She just wanted the one soul who had made the old world bearable.

The sisters looked at each other as if they were having wordless communication.

The negotiations continued, stretching through what felt like an eternity. As the last binding words echoed and faded in the grand hall, a palpable shift occurred. The oppressive tension slightly yielded. A new era had begun: an era of reluctant peace, of fragile hope, and of a future yet to be written.

As the first rays of dawn painted the mortal realm's sky, Michael approached Sera, his eyes filled with a mixture of sorrow and hope. "Sera," he said, his voice soft, "I...I want to apologize. For everything."

She looked at him, her gaze wary and her heart guarded.

"I know I don't deserve your forgiveness," he continued, his voice laced with regret. "But I hope that one day, you can find it in your heart to forgive me." He reached out and touched her cheek, his fingers wiping away a tear that had escaped her eye. "I want to offer you a chance to return to Heaven. To be redeemed. To have your wings restored."

Her heart pounded in her chest, a mixture of emotions swirling within her. She had longed for the chance to return to the light, to be the angel she once was. But she was also afraid. Afraid of being hurt again. Fearful of being betrayed again.

She looked at her father. His eyes were filled with genuine remorse, and his face was etched with the pain of his past mistakes. And she saw a flicker of the love that had once been there, the love that had been buried beneath the weight of his choices.

"Thank you, Father," she said, her voice soft. "But…I need time. There is much to heal, much to forgive."

He nodded. "I understand," he said. "Take all the time you need." He stepped back, his eyes lingering on her. "But know this, Sera. You both will always be my daughters. And I will always love you, even though sometimes I fail to show it."

Her heart ached, a bittersweet longing filling her chest. She nodded slowly, and her eyes filled with tears.

Sanctuary

44

The door sighed shut behind Sera, a heavy sound with the dull finality of a tomb sealing. She stood within the threshold of her townhome, a captive to its absolute silence. No trumpets heralded her return. No joyous shouts echoed. No Kael. The quiet wrapped around her like a shroud of fog, cold and insistent, and the furniture rested exactly where it had been, frozen in the moment he'd brought her here from Limbo. Nothing had changed except the woman standing amid it all. Except her.

Her bag slipped from her fingers, a soft thud swallowed instantly by the stillness. Nudging off her boots required no conscious will, her limbs moving on autopilot through the motions of arrival.

There was no victory in this return, no swelling pride. Only the crushing weight of survival and the unbearable, hollowing loss of the one tether who had made it all endurable.

She drifted toward the bathroom like a sleepwalker, shedding clothes without ceremony. The shower roared to life—a violent intrusion in the profound quiet—and she stepped under the scalding spray without a flinch.

Water pummeled her skin, blooming pink before deepening to an angry red, yet she remained motionless, arms limp and hair plastered to her back.

The infernal scent, the clinging musk of Hell, was gone. The blood of the battle washed away. But nothing within her felt clean.

Her thoughts were static, a white noise in her skull; her chest was a hollow chamber where a heart once beat.

She pressed her forehead to the cool, unyielding tile. Breath slowed. Her body surrendered to the relentless heat until her knees threatened to buckle. When the bone-weary ache finally dulled into a merciful numbness, she reached out, killed the water, wrapped herself in a towel, and drifted toward the silent promise of her bed.

It must have been a swift, brutal surrender, the kind that steals consciousness before the body even hits the sheets: one moment, the steaming heat of the shower, and the next, a profound, unfeeling oblivion.

When Sera's eyelids opened, the room was quiet, too quiet. A bone-deep exhaustion she hadn't known in years thrived in her. She let herself sink deeper into the softness of the sheets, into the lingering warmth of the mattress that only emphasized her solitude.

The shadows weren't whispering, the hunger wasn't clawing, and she was utterly silent.

A soft thud, barely there, drew her attention. She blinked. Something soft had landed at the foot of the bed.

She turned her head slowly, still half lulled by the heavy pull of sleep. She expected to see that a coat had slipped off the chair. Or perhaps a book had dropped from the nightstand. But instead, there was a *cat*.

A sleek black creature stood next to her bed, impossibly still. Its fur shimmered faintly in the low light, not just black but iridescent. It stared at her, unblinking and knowing.

Sera sat up with a jolt, her adrenaline spiking. "What the hell...?"

The air shifted, growing heavy with an unseen presence, and the room warped, slowed, and tilted sideways in time, pulling her into an unnerving stillness. Her pulse skidded and then raced as the cat moved, not toward her but closer. Jumping lightly onto the mattress. Its paws barely disturbed the covers, hardly making a sound.

She scrambled backward until her back hit the headboard, a cold dread seizing her. "What is this?!" she snapped, her voice cracking.

The cat tilted its head, a gesture of unsettling intelligence. It then spoke but not with a mouth. Instead, the words resonated directly in her mind, precise and chilling.

We are what you always tried to shut out, it said, speaking in an eerie, genderless third person. *We are your shadows.*

Sera's mouth parted, but no sound came forth, only a dry gasp. The shadows, the whispers, the hunger—they were not memories or possessions but her *familiars*.

The cat blinked once, slow and knowing, and then the world snapped back into motion, the strange stillness dissolving. She looked around wildly, her heart hammering, but the cat was gone.

Her breath hitched, and she caught a phantom echo of those words, a chilling whisper that promised no peace. The room, a stage for the impossible just moments ago, now felt real and empty again.

She stared at the spot where the cat had been and then at her own trembling hands, trying to reconcile what she'd seen, what she'd heard. The weight of it all—the return, the loss, and now this eerie visitation—crushed her, pressing her back down onto the mattress. Her eyes burned with fatigue, a raw exhaustion that mercifully pulled her under.

When she next opened her eyes, the air was sweet with the scent of damp earth and crushed roses, and a vast night sky stretched above her, a boundless canvas of dark blue. The silence here was different, not suffocating but the profound, living quiet of a world untainted by sorrow. She stood in the middle of the field, each cushioning blade of grass a vibrant purple. Above, the moon was a soft pale light that chilled her skin, casting shadows across the open space. Around her, a symphony of unseen life gently pulsed, a hushed hum that was both alien and deeply familiar.

This was not her bed, not her room, and not even her world. This was a meadow, *their* meadow, and she hoped she was not alone.

The air hung thick with a fog that curled around her bare ankles like grasping tendrils. Black roses were closed tight against the pervasive mist, their rich scent dulled but undeniably present. Her breath hitched, a desperate knot in her throat.

"Kael?"

No answer came, only the soft, consuming silence of the mist.

She turned, faster now, and the fog pressed in tighter, a cold shroud. She turned again and again in a desperate pirouette. "Kael!"

The panic surged, stealing her breath. She stumbled forward, barefoot. The grass was slick and cold beneath her.

"Please…"

The dense fog swallowed her voice whole, devouring the sound before it could echo. She twisted around, her heart hammering against her ribs. Her wide eyes searched for a familiar silhouette, a flicker of light, anything that resonated with the memory of him.

But there was only the meadow. Silent. Waiting.

But she was not alone.

Searing warmth enveloped her from behind. A gasp got caught in her throat as a large, calloused hand slid around her waist and pulled her back against a body she knew by instinct alone.

Kael.

He buried his face in the curve where her shoulder met her throat. She closed her eyes but didn't turn, fearing he would shatter like a dream.

His other hand came up, not to her face but to the front of her body. His fingers spread wide over her chest before settling directly over the bond mark at the base of her throat. He didn't touch it, just hovered his palm over it and its frantic pulse.

Slowly, he began to turn her in his arms, his movements fluid and confident. She yielded, turning to face him. Her eyes fluttered open as her heart thundered a wild, joyful rhythm.

When she was entirely in his embrace, he bent his head, and his lips brushed the sigil at the base of her throat in a silent act of worship. Only then, after claiming the mark as his own, did his breath shudder against her skin as he finally spoke, his voice a raspy miracle.

"I've been waiting for you, Little Devil…"

Epilogue

The oppressive air of the Infernal Palace seemed marginally lighter, although the air was still thick with ozone and the millennia of darkness that had passed. The peace accords had been signed, the immediate celestial conflict silenced by Lucifer's command and Michael's reluctant agreement. Angels were preparing for their ascent, demons were retreating to lick their wounds and adjust to their reinstated king, and a fragile, uncertain quiet settled over the scarred halls.

Remiel stood apart from the dispersing celestial delegation near the grand hall's exit. His armor was clean, and his silver wings were folded, but inside, a tempest still raged. The brutal efficiency of the battle, Lilith's annihilation by Kael's hand, Kael's brush with death, and Sera's harrowing return—it all churned within him. But one image resonated with a clarity that disturbed him: Cassia.

He recalled finding her chained to that pillar in the ritual chamber, brutalized yet unbroken. Her eyes held a universe of trauma. He knew she had risked everything in the archives, playing a dangerous game with Lilith to retrieve the very ritual that had woken Lucifer. He'd heard of her capture. And then, during the tense negotiations, her quiet yet resolute decision to remain here, in Hell, to help Lucifer and Vyxia rebuild confused him. It made no logical sense for an angel, even a half one, to stay, yet understanding flickered within him.

Perhaps after everything, Hell felt more honest than Heaven's judgment.

He couldn't leave without seeing her one last time though. Not out of panic but out of a need he couldn't quite define—respect, concern, and a strange pull toward the fierce spirit.

Turning away from the ascending angels, he moved back through the echoing corridors and toward the royal wing, where Cassia had presumably been quartered. He stepped out into a vast, torch-lit courtyard, hoping for a chance encounter. He scanned the imposing facade, the balconies carved like gaping maws into the obsidian structure.

And then, in that suspended moment, he saw her.

Cassia emerged onto one of the balconies high above. Beside her stood another figure, Eryon. As Remiel looked up, her gaze swept the courtyard and locked with his across the vast expanse.

Time itself seemed to pause.

Her gaze was still a cold, unreadable mask, yet he sensed the storm churning beneath. In that silent exchange, he saw not indifference but a fierce, wounded pride, a quiet acknowledgment of his presence. Perhaps even his concern. But also, an acceptance of the path she had chosen.

With a slow, deliberate nod that felt like recognition and dismissal, she acknowledged him. A quiet farewell across the divide. And as if pulled by an unseen current, she turned and melted back into the shadows of her chambers, leaving him standing alone amid the echoes of shattered hopes.

As her figure receded, a wave of unexpected melancholy washed over him. His gaze clung to that empty balcony as a phantom ache simmered in his chest. He placed a hand over his heart, a reflexive gesture against a wound he couldn't name, for a love he couldn't remember.

With a heavy sigh, he turned from the desolate courtyard and moved toward the shimmering portal back to Heaven.

Acknowledgments

I was born in Azerbaijan as the Soviet Union crumbled into dust. I learned early that survival is not noble or clean. It is messy and feral and achingly human. I spent my twenties climbing the rigid ladders of the oil and gas industry, where I managed projects worth millions and ignored the stories clawing at my throat. I traded those blueprints for manuscripts because I refused to play by safe rules any longer. I wrote this book because I believe beauty and ruin belong in the same breath. I wrote it between the demands of motherhood and the silence of the night.

This story would remain a chaotic scream without the hands that helped shape it. Robin LeeAnn sharpened my raw obsession into a weapon. You edited these pages with the precision of a surgeon and ensured every wound meant something. Cherise Foxley gave the monster a face. Your design and cover art captured the exact frequency of my nightmares and made them beautiful.

And you. You walked into the dark with Sera and Kael. You witnessed the rot and the redemption. The silence you feel now is not the end. It is a breath before the plunge. The Sanctuary was only the beginning. A Hollow Mercy awaits you.

GLOSSARY

A

Anima Crucible: A crystal core used by watchers to collect souls. It glows pure white when ready to accept sinners.

Angels: Celestial soldiers and guardians in Heaven. They are pure light beings who can fall due to transgressions.

Archangels: High-ranking celestial beings who enforce divine will. Michael is the commander of Heaven's forces.

Aura: A luminous energy field around a supernatural being. Its appearance can vary based on ancestry or emotional state. Mortals cannot see auras, but other supernatural entities can.

Aura etiquette: A term used for identifying supernatural beings.

B

Blade of Mercy: A celestial blade carried by archangels. It is the Celestial Tribunal's severance tool, capable of burning wings from bones or unmaking a celestial creature.

Bloodlines: Progenitors of supernatural species like demons, vampires, and witches.

Blood moon: A rare celestial event. Reset the window of the Celestial Tribunal Law.

Bond mark: A physical mark on the skin that signifies a deep, unbreakable connection between two individuals.

Book of Echoes: An ancient filing system where the names and memories of beings are recorded.

C

Calithra: One of the six arbiters of the Celestial Tribunal. She is the shrouded queen and the sovereign of Limbo.

Celestial Accord 1603: A historical agreement that included the concept of aura etiquette.

Celestial scrivener: A position held by keepers. They—as in beings provided by Limbo—attest to and record tribunal judgments.

Celestial Tribunal: The Supreme Cosmic Court for all realms. It consists of six eternal arbiters from Heaven, Hell, and Limbo. (It used to include fae representatives before the fallout.)

Crimson Keep: The Infernal Palace and throne room of Hell.

Crossroads: A desolate realm with an eerie green light. It is the only place thin enough to cut through the veil to reach Hell or Heaven.

D

Demons: Supernatural beings associated with Hell. Scents of sulfur and brimstone often accompany their presence.

Disciple of wrath: Enforcer of divine law. They serve as Heaven's ultimate weapon for judgment and retribution. This role involves hunting and punishing supernatural beings who defy celestial law. This position requires a complete surrender of personal mercy and compassion in the pursuit of divine justice.

E

Edict of Celestial Conception: A strict law forbidding celestials from conceiving without the tribunal's consent.

Essence/Light: A core energy (a soul) or a life force of any being.

Exiled fae: Fae banished from their courts for crimes of blood, oath, or love.

F

Fae realm: Known as The Verdant Courts, it has twin courts of light and shadow.

Fallen angels: Angels cast out from Heaven for transgressions like treason or desertion. Their wings are often severed.

Famine (Irish): A historical event in mortal year 1845 that serves as the backdrop for Sera and Cassia's fall from Heaven.

G

Gatekeeper (Limbo): A hooded figure who guards the entrance to the maze within Limbo.

Glamour: A magical illusion used by supernatural beings to appear mundane or hide their proper forms.

Gray Intermediary (Grand Keeper): One of the six arbiters of the Celestial Tribunal, representative of Limbo.

H

Heaven: The realm of sterile light and law from which celestials originate.

Hell: The Infernal Throne, characterized by blood, fire, and ancient law. It is a realm of rebellion and sovereignty.

Holy Rollers: A speakeasy or exclusive club for the ultra-elite with digital add-ons for aura etiquette.

Hybrids: Beings with mixed heritage, such as Sera, who is of celestial and infernal origin.

I

Infernal sires: Rulers of the seven circles of Hell and progenitors of infernal bloodlines.

InnovoTech: The company where Sera works as the head of product development.

Iron Orchid: A human BDSM club in Savannah that attracts supernatural beings.

K

Keepers: Guardians of archives, fate gates, and lost contracts within the Celestial Tribunal.

Kehoe House: A hotel in Savannah where succubi conduct their feedings.

L

Limbo: A twilight realm of lost fates and forgotten souls.

Lucifer's coin: A black coin with Lucifer's sigil used as a key for a passage in or out of Hell.

M

Meadow (In Between): A dream space where bonded souls can meet.

Mortal realm: the human world, where supernatural beings reside in exile or in disguise.

N

Night of the veil: A permitted window for conception that occurs once a century.

O

Old flame: A powerful force awakened if the Edict of Celestial

Conception is violated, triggering a cleansing judgment.

P

Portal: An opening in reality that allows travel between realms.

S

Shadows (Sera's): Dark sentient entities that accompany Sera, reflecting her internal state.

Soul demon: Fallen or demons that deal in capturing and selling souls for bounty.

Soulfire: A wine-like liquid infused with damned souls.

Stasis: A state of suspended animation or deep magical sleep.

Succubus: Cursed demons forced to drain life forces during intimate encounters.

T

The Serpent's Kiss: An underground bar owned by Kael in Savannah. It functions as a market for shadows, where anything can be traded.

The veil: A barrier separating realms that can thin at specific locations or during events like a blood moon.

Tribunal Writ 417-B: A law that prohibits spontaneous conception among celestials.

W

Watcher of passage: Angels or Fallen that guard the gates to ascendence.

Watchers: Sentinels who serve as guardians of cosmic law and ancient legacy.

Wards: Protective magical barriers used to protect a location or a person.

Witches/Warlocks: Supernatural beings who practice dark magic.

Character Pronunciation Guide

Calithra: Kah-LITH-rah
Cassia: KASS-ee-ah
Elara: Eh-LAH-rah
Eryon: EHR-ee-on
Jareth: JAIR-eth
Kael: KAH-el
Lilith: LIL-ith
Lucifer: LOO-sih-fer
Malakar: MAL-ah-kar
Michael: MIKE-uhl
Remiel: REHM-ee-el
Sera: SEH-rah
Vyxia: VIK-see-ah